'Karina Lickorish Quinn has rendered on the page a person and a place in all their conflicted histories so convincingly and dizzyingly and singularly that the very ink haunts. It leaves a shadow text on the reader's psyche. *The Dust Never Settles* is a marvelous, vertiginous work that mercilessly conveys the post-colonial state.'

Caoilinn Hughes, author of *The Wild Laughter*

'Rarely has a haunting been so eloquent and arresting, so painterly and polyphonic, demanding urgently to be read.'

Chloe Aridjis, author of *Sea Monsters*

THE DUST NEVER SETTLES

KARINA LICKORISH QUINN

ONEWORLD

A Oneworld Book

First published in Great Britain, Ireland and Australia by Oneworld Publications, 2021

ISBN 978-0-86154-044-0 (hardback)
ISBN 978-0-86154-185-0 (trade paperback)
eISBN 978-0-86154-045-7

Typeset by Tetragon, London
Printed and bound in Great Britain by Clays Ltd, Elcograf S.p.A.

This is a work of fiction. Names, characters, places, and incidents are either the product of the author's imagination or are used fictitiously, and any resemblance to actual persons, living or dead, businesses, companies, events or locales is entirely coincidental.

Oneworld Publications
10 Bloomsbury Street
London WC1B 3SR
England

FSC
www.fsc.org

MIX
Paper from
responsible sources
FSC® C018072

For Tom.
And for Athena.

It was the custom of the dead to visit one another, and they hosted great dances and revelries. Sometimes the dead came to the houses of the living, and sometimes the living went to the houses of the dead.

PEDRO PIZARRO, 1571

CONTENTS

PART I

3

PART II

189

APPENDICES

They say that there was a mountain. Its name was Tampu T'uqu because it had three windows. Some say inside it and some say on top of it there was a Paqariq Tampu. It was a cave or maybe a house, a kind of lodge in which things came to life.

In this birthplace, out of the three windows, three peoples were born. From the window named Maras T'uqu, the Maras people were born. From the window of Sut'i T'uqu, the Tampus people were born. But out of the middle window, the one called Qhapaq T'uqu, came eight siblings: the four Ayar brothers and their four sisters.

The Ayar brothers and their sisters were not like any other people who lived in the world. They emerged from the mountain wearing fine clothes, woven with gold given by Father Sun. Around their necks they carried bags inside which were catapults, and sister Huaco and brother Ayar Manco (whom the sun also named Manco Cápac) brought with them golden staffs.

The eight siblings left the mountain and set out in search of land to cultivate. Ayar Manco and Mama Ocllo would throw their golden staffs and see if they would penetrate the soil, but time and again the golden staffs could not sink into the earth because the ground was too hard. Then Ayar Cachi, who was the strongest of the brothers, became frustrated and, from a very high peak, cast four pebbles into the distance with his catapult. He was so strong that his pebbles levelled mountains, crumbling them utterly and leaving valleys in their place.

I

Then the other Ayar brothers became afraid of Ayar Cachi because he was so strong, and they plotted to get rid of him. They told him they had forgotten some golden vases back at Paqariq Tampu and sent him back to fetch them. Ayar Cachi did not know that his other siblings had followed him and, when he re-entered the mountain, they rolled huge stones over the windows so that he could not get out again. They waited until they heard him hammering on the insides of the mountain, screaming out for help, and then they knew that Ayar Cachi could not escape and they left him there.

The siblings believed Ayar Cachi had died and, with time, they felt guilty about what they had done, but by then they had forgotten where the Tampu T'uqu was and could not find their way back. So they journeyed on and founded Cusco and the Inka Empire with its Four Realms, the Tawantinsuyu.

When generations to come told the story of the siblings, some would say that Tampu T'uqu was near the shores of Lake Titicaca. Others said it was further north, deep in the Cordillera or even as far inland as the jungle. But there was one who knew the exact location of Tampu T'uqu because she had seen it during her time ascended into janaj pacha, where she sojourned with the saints and the stars. There she had also seen that Ayar Cachi had not died but had simply been interred inside the mountain, waiting to be released.

PART I

ONE

Last night the ice-cream pedlars haunted me. They came to my hotel room and danced around my bed. I knew them from my childhood, when I had stood in the window of Mama and Abue's house and watched them sell their wares to the children from the houses at the bottom of the hill. They never made the strenuous journey up to la Casa Echeverría to sell anything to us. Even when Abue tried to appease me by buying a hand-cranked ice-cream maker and when Carmen made the empleadas churn milk in the kitchen all day, my cravings could not be satisfied. No matter how much ice cream they made, no matter how many hours they worked, turning over the milk, folding in home-grown lúcuma or Mama's manjar blanco, what I wanted more than anything was to be like the children who I watched from the upstairs windows, playing barefoot games of football down in the Avenida or laying out glass bottles as skittles in the sand of Los Polvos and eating their neon-coloured ice pops.

My primos and I were not allowed to go out and play with those children. It was not only because the armed conflict that had begun in the highlands had by then reached the city, though the adults did worry that there might be Reds out there among the shacks of Los Polvos – 'resentidos' who would seek to evict us. I did not understand the conflict then, did not understand the meaning of land or how history piles and piles upon itself until it cannot bear its own weight, but I overheard some of the younger staff say the war was a pachacuti, that space and time were turning over and the world would be left upside down and inside out. The high would be made low, they said, and the low lifted high. Others said this was nonsense and that they had better watch their tongues.

But it was not only because of the war that we were not allowed to go down to Los Polvos. It was also because, Reds or not, they were not our kind of people. That is what the adults said. Not our kind. Then the adults would try to distract us with new toys and pretty songs or, when we became petulant and said that we would run away to live in the other town at the bottom of the hill, the aunts and uncles would scoff and say, *Really? You want to live without food or clean water? Without a pretty house and a garden or a roof over your head?* Still, what I wanted was to befriend those other children whose games I watched in secret but never joined. And I longed for the men in the canary-yellow outfits to pedal their carts up the hill and sell us their cellophane-wrapped, half-melted, branded ice-cream sandwiches. But they never did.

And so, after the many years in which I had forgotten all about them, last night the ice-cream vendors came to me. I sat awake for hours while they pedalled their yellow cart-bikes around my room, blaring their kazoos and peddling their goods to illusory customers. They sold rancour-flavoured cones and bittersweet neon ice pops. They pelted me with ice cubes that melted around me until my sheets were soaked and my body was clammy and shivering. They filled my dreams with painful memories and screamed in my face with gaping mouths and hollow eyes in which I saw only a gaping darkness.

Around my hotel bed they rioted, tearing through the cushions with their teeth and swinging from the curtains like demented monkeys. They were furious with me, and I cannot blame them, because today I will hand over the keys for Mama and Abue's house to the developers who will begin tearing it down tomorrow. For my treachery, for betraying Mamabue's house, the ice-cream men

6

came to punish me with havoc, breaking into every last one of my suitcases and strewing my belongings across the floor.

I left them to their insanity and wandered the halls of the sleeping hotel – the empty corridors, the desolate lobby, the dining hall plunged into darkness. To know one Hotel Vivaldi is to know them all. This one, El Hotel Vivaldi Miraflores, is identical to all its brothers scattered across the world, with its ceilings glittering like hammered gold and its neoclassical statues in white resin or bronze plate that stand sentry along the hallways and around the circular lobby. It was at the Hotel Vivaldi Park Lane that Rupert asked me to marry him in the gilded dining room where mirrors upon mirrors replicated us a thousand times over until I had seen myself from every angle and wasn't sure whether the trembling in my fingers was from the enormity of being proposed to or from the fear of not knowing which me was flesh and which reflection. I was everywhere, refracted – in the glass windows, in the polished marble floors, in the lacquered furniture: nowhere could I escape myself.

It was the same last night. Even with the hotel unlighted and unpeopled, the slivers of light found me and cast my shape on the mirrored walls. She fascinated me, the woman in the glass, this midnight fugitive, a racing figure draped in a white robe, borrowed and far too large, hurrying from a carnival of tiny ice-cream men disembowelling her luggage. As she ran, the Vivaldi statuary seemed to come to life. The semi-naked women draped in falling linens gathered into gossiping huddles, the muscular soldiers turned their heads in judgement, while the horses and cloven-footed creatures flared their nostrils in disdain. Under these watchful eyes, she did strange things in the night-time – kissed the open mouths of the clean white orchids in the stairwell and stuffed her pockets with the silver-wrapped candies in the lobby. In the empty dining hall, where the pianola played on alone and the tables were all set identically, row on row, waiting for diners who were now all sleeping, she

7

climbed onto the bar, spread her arms, and began to spin, slowly at first, then faster and faster until the reflections all blurred together into a haze of white.

'¿Señorita Gest?'

I did not remember immediately who she was – Miss Gest – in this place where I had booked a room under my father's surname to avoid the inquisitive looks, the enquiries about my health from people who knew someone who knew someone who knew my Titi's ex-husband's best friend's grandfather's psychologist's parrot… In Lima, the Echeverría name is known to everyone, but Gest has, except in academic circles, retained some anonymity. For archae-ologists, historians, anthropologists, Professor Leonard Gest has some middling consequence; to the rest of the world, as to me, he is an unknown. So I used my father's name here to render myself invisible.

'¿Señorita Gest?'

I came to an abrupt stop and waited for the dizziness to subside and the three misty and floating valets to merge into one with his feet pressed firmly, shoulder width apart, on the marble floor.

'Are you all right, señorita? Is there something you need?'

'Nothing, thank you. I am quite well.'

'Breakfast is not served until six…'

'Yes, I know. I was just taking some air.'

Finding my way back to my suite, drawing my robe closer around me against the night's chill as I crept along corridor after identical corridor, I realised I had forgotten my way. On which floor was I staying? And on which side of the hotel – north or south? Facing the sea or inland? Into the pockets of my robe I stuffed my hands, rifling anxiously with my fingers, but there was no door key, only hoards of Hotel Vivaldi candies whose wrappers seemed to rustle and hiss at me as I searched.

Back at the front desk, the gold-suited concierge stood rigidly, like a tin soldier, eyes wide but glazed, staring far off into the distance, or into the past. I waited for him to acknowledge me, my hands folded on the desk in an attempt to convey calm and self-assurance. If I touched my surroundings – the desk, the tiled floor, the backs of the black velvet-covered chairs – I could anchor myself here, make myself familiar, seem as though I belonged. But as I waited, touching things, running my fingers over the lacquered desktop, fiddling with the pen, smoothing the pages of the visitor book, the concierge continued immobile and distant, his eyes unseeing behind the cataracts of sleep.

I thought of waking him – of rousing him by his name, *Javier*, embroidered in gold on his jacket. What would he say if I explained myself, if I told him how I was locked out of my room in the middle of the night, lost and wandering the empty, darkened corridors in my bedclothes like a restless spirit? No, I couldn't wake him for that. The alternative, though, was to wait until the morning for the elegant guests to descend and find me curled up in one of the high-backed armchairs of the lobby hugging my nightdress around my knees like an insomniac child.

The tremors in my fingers returned – tremors I have endured since childhood, which descend suddenly and often, for no apparent reason, taking possession of my hands as if they were not mine but a stranger's, clumsily grafted onto my wrists without sympathy for my instructions or wishes. To still their trembling, or at least to hide them from my sight, I plunged my hands into my pockets again and with such force that I sliced my right forefinger on something thin and sharp – the door key, which had been in my pocket the whole time. I had not found it because my hands had been searching for metal, not a plastic magnetised oblong, without character or feeling. I had forgotten: humanity is phasing out the old. The metal key, the written letter, the landline telephone. Already in Rupert's London apartment block the metal key is obsolete: every resident has a sleek black electronic key card to unlock their home.

With a thin stream of blood trickling down my finger, I held the key card up to my eyes and examined it closely. On one of its corners a tiny nick in the plastic had created a sort of sharp little mouth with fangs, now stained red.

I have trouble with new things. I injure myself with them – or they attack me. Gadgets give me electric shocks and the appliances I use always break. *It's your energy*, the Tías used to tell me. *Tu energía* – it interferes with the current. Rupert has tried to train me into carrying a mobile phone so he doesn't have to worry when I leave for my walks. He made me promise to switch it on and contact him as soon as I arrived in Lima. Where is that telephone now, I wonder. Buried, I imagine, somewhere in my luggage.

Returning to my room, I found the ice-cream vendors had melted away leaving only one man behind, faded now and shrunken, reduced to the size of a doll, slumped, exhausted, on my suitcase in the corner of the room. Only his eyes were lively, sticking to me wherever I moved.

I know what you think of me. There is nothing to be done.

If you wanted it enough, you would find a way.

I grabbed the vendor around the waist and shook him violently. He did not resist but hung limply in my hands, his limbs flailing loosely, neck folding backwards and jerking precariously as if, at any moment, his head might snap off and roll away. I wanted to shake him to pieces, to dust, and sweep him out of the window and away towards the sea, but he would not disintegrate, so I threw him inside my suitcase and shut the case quickly, snapping closed the padlock.

Now, here on the floor in the dark, sucking on my bleeding finger, surrounded by my dispersed clothes and the disorder of the devastated room, the eviscerated pillows, the scattered papers, I cannot ignore that the tiny vendor is right – I will have to face the ghosts. I thought that I would face them yesterday at the Iglesia Santa María Reina during the Mass for the repose of the Echeverría dead: all day I waited for them as the priest read name after name of departed relatives, with the living Echeverrías gathered around me muttering interminable prayers, but the familiar dead did not attend.

It is a necessary pain of having a large family that someone is always dying. It is a merciful relief of having a large family across the waters that it is impossible to attend all of their funerals. For years I have been losing Titis and Tíos almost every month and, every time, my mother would call to inform me of their passing and, every time, I ignored the phone, listening from across the room to her voice reciting a message. I never called her back. What was there to say? Another relative had retired from life but between her and me nothing had changed.

Each time she called, I marvelled that it was not to announce the funeral of my Tía Consuelo, the great-aunt who has been dying for fifty years, confined all this time to her room at the rear of la Casa Echeverría by countless ailments – or, perhaps, by just one all-encompassing and devastating disease no doctor could ever name – accompanied constantly by her ancient doll, Conchita la Freak, with the mismatched body parts. But it appears that, though everyone else has succumbed at their allotted hour to the inevitable; though her brother, Ignacio Segundo, shot himself in the face while polishing his revolver; though her nephew, Tío Lucho, plummeted from the peak of Huayna Picchu; though her cousin, Almendra la Amarga, yielded at last, at the age of ninety-six, to a particularly strong dose of ayawasca that stopped her heart in the village of Tamshiyacu to which she had travelled to discover what the purpose of her life had been, Tía Consuelo lives on.

Yesterday, during Mass, while the priest took a rest break from the punishing labours of reading through the list of the countless Echeverría dead, with my aunts and uncles embracing and kissing and pulling me this way and that, laying their hands on my stomach in prayer, laying their palms on my forehead in concern – *You look pale, hija, are you ill? – Of course the girl is ill: she's pregnant!* – I asked them if they knew what had become of la Tía Consuelo.

But nobody knew. Childless and unmarried, Tía Consuelo has for decades been nobody's concern. *But I assumed she had died ya*, Tía Mimi said. *Oye, Pulpo, do you know anything of la Tía Consuelo?* And that was the message that was passed from person to person through the church as we waited for the priest to return: *What has happened to Tía Consuelo? Does anyone know anything about Tía Consuelo?*

As the priest droned on, I listened for Consuelo's name but did not hear it, perhaps because it was not read or perhaps because I was distracted by the little pink fish that torments me. It is with me still, bobbing irritatingly against my right cornea, refusing to be ignored since the day three months ago when I sat in a toilet cubicle in my graduation cap and gown, knickers round my ankles, a pregnancy test between my fingers, waiting for pink lines to materialise, which they did – both of them. And with those two pink lines appeared the little pink fish, only a speck then, a minuscule spot on my vision, a particle of dust, I thought, easily blinked away.

But the little fish has not faded: it has grown and become more insistent for my attention – attention divided evenly between it and the incessant waves of nausea that radiate from my guts. It hovers on the waterline of my right eye, tiny but resolute, eyeballing me with a gaping mouth in which I can see my past stretched out and mapped like a star chart. It can only be the size of a poppy seed, no bigger, but when it opens its mouth, it seems to have swallowed the whole universe.

Before I began my journey back to Lima for the first time after all these years, I stayed with the Napiers, Rupert's family, at their country home. We were celebrating our engagement – mine and Rupert's (though I had not yet said yes). There, I prayed a novena regarding this torturous little fish. It was not easy explaining to the Napiers why I had insisted on locating the nearest Catholic church nor why I traipsed there through the countryside every morning after breakfast for nine consecutive days in order to pray. Seven years they have known me and been my surrogate family, ever since I appeared on my father's doorstep, soaking from the rain, fleeing Perú and the ghosts and too many memories and he, unable or unwilling to father me, thrust me upon them. In all that time, I have not often gone to Mass, not once gone to confession. In truth, it was not easy explaining to myself, a lapsed Catholic, why I felt so compelled towards divine supplication. Perhaps the little pink fish made me feel my need for God. Or perhaps it was the Bible verse Titi María Dolores embroidered on the handkerchief she sent me from Lima two weeks ago:

> *Herencia de Jehová son los hijos;*
> *cosa de estima el fruto del vientre.*

The fruit of the womb is an inheritance from the Lord, and every child is a blessing, the Tías wrote in the card that they had all signed and enclosed in the box along with the handkerchief, a gold medallion engraved with the icon of Saint Gerard Majella (patron saint of expectant mothers), a litre bottle of orange-flower water (distilled by Tía Gring's own hands), and a book of prayers for pregnancy. I don't know how they knew I was pregnant: I suppose Titis always know.

On the ninth and final day of my prayers, with an early transatlantic flight and an intense bout of morning sickness, I lifted my petitions to God and completed my novena in the multi-faith prayer room at Terminal 5 of Heathrow Airport. I knelt at the front of the room, without a cushion, on the grey-blue standard-issue geometric airport carpet, underneath the rotating carousel of religious icons, all of them chained down to safeguard against theft. Inserting a pound into the slot, I turned the wheel through the options (a stainless-steel menorah; a resin Buddha; a flaking painted statuette of Pushan, the Hindu god of marriages, journeys and the feeding of cattle), found the figure of the Blessed Virgin, and made her face me.

Hail Mary, llena de gracia, the little pink fish is with me still, getting entangled in my eyelashes and making my eyes water.

13

Dios te salve, María, perhaps you remember the business with the spirits. I have evaded them, now, for many years and have no desire to return to the days of the visions and conversations with those that others cannot see.

I leave it in your hands, this trouble with the little pink fish. Si es la voluntad de Dios, I ask you to make it leave me.

As I clicked my rosary beads clumsily between my fingers, out of practice, the Virgin Mary looked down at me with benevolent eyes of azure blue, her alabaster palms held out, robes quivering slightly in the flickering light of the fluorescent tube above us.

Santa María, Mother of God, I asked you yesterday – I am sure you remember – about my pregnancy. The nausea is espantoso. I ask you to take it away or give me the patience to bear it. The nausea, that is. And the pregnancy. Because you know – of course you know, Holy Mary, madre de Dios – that I don't really want this baby. Blessed art thou amongst women, and blessed is the fruit of your womb.

And again, I lift Rupert up to you – he has asked me to marry him, and I have not said yes, nor have I said no. I have said to wait. So we are waiting, he for my answer and I for no sé qué. A sign, I suppose. From you or from God...

In my pocket, the Napier engagement ring pulsed against my hip bone. Rupert wanted me to wear it, despite my lack of conviction. He said he knew, just knew, that we were destined for each other, as if the future were written, as if nothing was left to the vagaries of choice in this world. To save on awkwardness, and to save hurting his mother, his sisters, I wore it in the Napier house. How could I tell them that I felt suffocated by it? That I felt they were trying to absorb me, dissolve me, swallow me into their clan when they already thought of me as daughter, sister? But when I left their house I always removed it and put it somewhere out of sight. And even then, through the thick fabric of my jacket, it bothered me – the weight of the gold, the sharp angles of the diamond, the bulk of its presence.

Kneeling in the airport chapel, as I reflected on my potential engagement, on the imminent sale of my childhood home, and on my own demons, la Vírgen María contemplated me sorrow-fully from her place on the pay-as-you-go carousel of divinities. A single tear of blood seeped from the caruncle of her right eye and trickled, painting a track of red, down her cheek to her chin, where the drop hung tenuously.

Behind me a family of worshippers had gathered to watch and wait for their turn at the altar. I did not want them to notice that I had made the mother of God cry. As I reached up with Titi María's handkerchief to wipe away the scarlet tear from the Virgin Mary's face, staining the white cotton with a crimson bloom, the Holy Mother reached down to me and pulled me by the wrist with a cold, stiff alabaster hand. With my head next to hers, she whispered:

Aunque vengas disfraza'o, te conozco, bacalao.

Even when you come in costume, codfish, I will always know you.

Reflected from behind me in the telescreens of flight informa-tion, I could see the waiting family, absorbed in their chaos: the woman – the mother, I supposed – weighed down by bags and surrounded by restless, impatient children, looked weary and des-perately in need of her deity.

Holy Mary, Mother of God, ruega por nosotros, sinners, ahora and at the hour of our death. Amén.

Hurriedly, breaking free from the Virgin's grip, I let the young family take my place. The mother inserted a pound coin into the slot and turned the wheel to the resin statue of Buddha.

As I wandered the terminal and waited, I turned the Virgin's words over and over: *Aunque vengas disfraza'o, te conozco, bacalao. Te conozco, bacalao, aunque vengas disfraza'o.*

These are the words that Mami always used when Leandro and I tried to blame the ants for breaking the pottery or the ghost of Francisco Pizarro for drawing on the walls. *Aunque vengas disfraza'o, te conozco, bacalao*, she would say: *Even if you come in disguise, I know you, codfish*, and she would wag her finger and shake her head with a knowing smile. It made me laugh and imagine a codfish in a trench coat and fedora, shuffling around on its tail fin, trying to fit in, going about its daily business, driving a car, buying groceries, trying to conceal its fishy smell.

After she came to work for us, Q'orianka learned the phrase too, but over the years she shortened it, first to *te conozco, bacalao* and then, at last, to *bacalao*, so that when we lied she would cry *Codfish! Codfish!* and chase us around the house until we confessed, collapsing in a giggling heap, sweaty and breathless.

Leandro, my brother, namesake of our father, should be with me on this journey, but he is too busy. He posted me his signed documents, appointing me as his legal agent, in an envelope with an EC1A postmark and a scribbled note on headed paper from the bank where he works:

Soz can't come. Work MANIC. Waiting to exchange on Pan Peninsula apt. Bad timing.

Then his signature and, squashed into a corner, an afterthought, *Besos a todos.*

So Leandro has not come. And Rupert, too, has more important things to do. If he knew about the two pink lines he might have found time. But I have travelled to Lima alone. No, not alone: I have the little fish. Though perhaps the little fish will not join me today when I go to meet the developers at la Casa Echeverría – when I go to sign the papers for the sale of Mamabue's house. Perhaps little fish do not like to witness ancestral casas being sold and razed.

Aunque vengas disfraza'o, te conozco, bacalao, said the mother of God.

These same words were on the lips of my relatives at la Iglesia Santa María Reina yesterday as they took in my appearance. *Strange transformation she has made, this girl,* they seemed to say. *But still the same, underneath. Still an Echeverría inside.* Although not quite. I never was completely one of them either. Here or there, London or Lima, it doesn't matter. Even with my mother no longer living to tell me, I cannot escape those words reminding me that wherever I go, I have always been a codfish in disguise.

My homecoming journey took me into the past. Everything was just as I remembered. On the flight from New York there was the same atmosphere of jubilant homecoming among the passengers that I remember from childhood. A few rows behind me there was a family of four generations – from bisabuelita to newborn – returning to Perú for the first time in decades after making their American fortune. The padre of the family, whom they called el gordo, was a fat señor with laughing eyes and a gold chain bracelet on his fleshy wrist; he kept standing on his seat to rouse the entire plane into enthusiastic renditions of the Peruvian national anthem:

¡Somos libres!
¡Seámoslo siempre! ¡Seámoslo siempre!

Beside me, a young backpacker with blond dreadlocks asked me to translate the words for him.

'We're free,' I told him. 'We're free. Let us always be.'

But when the enthusiastic gordo began to sing traditional huaynos, the backpacker could not understand how I was able to sing along but not to translate the words.

'This is in Quechua,' I explained. 'I don't speak Quechua.'

'You don't speak Quechua, but you can sing it?'

'Yes,' I said. 'Our maid taught me. But she didn't teach me what it means.'

He looked at me with puzzled amusement, as if I were a quaint curio in a glass cabinet. After that I closed my eyes and pretended to sleep to avoid having to speak with the backpacker again.

Disembarking the plane at Jorge Chávez airport, I was immediately bathed in the Limenian humidity. The air is close here. And tactile. Not aloof and tasteless. It demands to be felt and to feel, like the insistent affection of tías abuelas after years of absence. And with the humidity came the briny, algal smell of sea that stirred in my guts a feeling I had forgotten – a feeling galvanised by years of self-protective distraction from remembering. It was a species of longing and, at the same time, of recuperating – of losing and of finding what was lost. It was a feeling that made me, suddenly, quite seasick and I stumbled, had to reach out my hand to steady myself. My hand fell on the arm of el gordo, the singing padre de familia from the plane. He placed his enormous hand over mine and said, 'Returning home is felt in the intestines, no es así mija?'

It felt warm to be called *mija*: it had been a long time since a stranger had called me their daughter.

'Es así,' I told him, because he was right – homecoming is felt in the viscera.

As we walked across the tarmac towards the terminal, already I could see the arrivals concourse was teeming with families clutching bouquets of helium balloons, giant stuffed animals and cardboard signs, all pressing urgently against the steel barricades and craning their necks to catch a first glimpse of their loved ones. I walked behind the maletero I had hired, who pushed a trolley heavily laden with the five pieces of luggage in which – unsure how long it would take to sell Mamabue's house – I had packed enough of my clothes to see me through at least a year in Lima. I would not learn until later, until after the Mass for the repose of the Echeverría dead, that the buyers were already lined up, that the papers had been prepared, that the signing and completion of the sale would take place the next day.

Just in front of me, as we headed to the arrivals hall, triumphantly leading his clan, was el gordo, who, when he emerged from the sliding glass doors, was greeted by a rapturous cheer from an enormous crowd of relatives all wearing identical lime-green T-shirts emblazoned with his face and the words *¡Los García Siempre Regresan!* – The Garcías Always Return!

Wailing cries of joy, a stout lady with the same thick wrists and black eyes as el gordo threw herself against the barricade with such force that it collapsed with a crash, and the García relatives surged forward, clambering over the metal, tumbling over each other, weeping and laughing, until el gordo, his wife and their children were swallowed by the crowd. Taking advantage of the breach in the barrier, other families poured out, falling upon the arrivals – not always the ones for whom they were waiting – with kisses and songs, while European tourists looked on with ashen faces, dodging unsolicited affection, calculating the quickest route out of the amorous chaos.

In the confusion, as the guards tried to contain the crowd, I was separated from my luggage while people whom I will never know filled my hands with candies and flowers and coins. Pushing against the current of bodies, I searched desperately for a face I recognised.

Then, his head protruding above the horde, I saw him – Tío Pulpo, my mother's brother, Mamabue's eldest and the last survivor of his siblings. According to tradition, it should have been Tío Pulpo living in the casona all these years but, after he returned from college in the United States, he had no interest in Mamabue's house.

'Anaïs!' Tío called above the roar of the crowd, waving as if from a great distance. He was there with his wife, my Tía Mimi, who wrapped her arms like a straitjacket around me and led me hurriedly from the mayhem out into the twilight morning where my maletero was waiting in the car park with my bags.

'¡Loco, loco, loco!' Mimi cried, gripping my arms with her hands and surveying me intently as if to check for injuries. Or shortcomings. 'Certainly these things never happen in England. ¿Estás bien?'

Without waiting for a response, she kissed me absently on both cheeks and held me in a tight embrace. On her hair I could smell perfume and coffee. Over her shoulder I watched my Tío questioning the maletero. *Are the bags all there? Sí, señor. Are they untampered with? Sí, señor. Yes? Sí, señor. Here's a tip for your honesty. Gracias, señor. My car is this way. Sí, señor.*

It made me anxious, the frankness with which Tío Pulpo distrusted, and the resignation with which the maletero responded to the inquisition. How often was he accused in this way? How had he developed the forbearance with which to accept it? What made him yield so coolly to the presumptions of criminality imposed upon him?

As Tío led the porter to the car, Mimi walked with me, one arm around my waist, the other planted on my belly, chattering to me about los primos – *all the cousins* – and what impressive things they were doing and how much they wanted to see me. In the corner of the car park a family were conducting a party of bienvenida out of the boot of their car, blaring tropical love songs from a transistor radio and drinking pisco sours from white plastic cups, the security guards trying, and failing, to move them on.

While we waited for the maletero to cram my suitcases into Tío's car, Mimi looked on with pursed lips. We had to hurry, she told me, to get to the church on time.

'For what, Tía?'

'For the Mass!'

I had not known before now about the Mass planned in my honour to compensate me for being unable to attend the scores of family funerals I had missed over my years of absence. The Mass to allow me to join my petitions to those of my relatives for the Echeverría departed. I was not appropriately dressed for a funeral, I told her, but there was no time – *no time, querida* – for me to change. Padre Alfonso had been booked and he was very clear that we must start punctually because the Mass would certainly take all day: there were a lot of dead to get through.

*

As we drove from the airport along el Circuito de Playas towards Miraflores and the church, I watched the city passing by, and it was just as I remembered. It was early, but the esplanade was already full of people: painters touching up the murals on the dusty walls of El Callao, runners beating the pavement, dog walkers tripping over leashes along el Malecón, lovers trysting under the amorous clay bodies of the lovers of *El Beso* and along the undulating mosaic walls of el Parque del Amor. Salsas, cumbias, bachatas played out of apartments and car windows and on the beach below.

Above all, my focus was on the sea where, far from the shore, blocking the horizon, my old friends, the islands of San Lorenzo and El Frontón, had always created the familiar shape of a whale. As a child, sleepy after a day at the beach, salt in my hair and sand between my toes, wedged into the back seat of Abue's Cadillac between Mami and Leandro and too many of the cousins, I would watch the whale through the window and tell it about my day. It would give me an idle smile and sing me to sleep. But yesterday, I saw no whale – just two large rocks in the water, one now reserved for the exclusive use of the Peruvian navy, the other a graveyard for anti-colonial pirates and inmates of El Frontón penitentiary.

Now, standing on the balcony of my hotel suite, the drastic curve of the Limenian coastline and the lights of the city stretching out below me, the salt wind playing with my hair and tugging at my robe, I wait for the sunrise. With the sun will come the wake-up call. The valet will inform me that my taxi is booked. I will wash and dress and, after breakfast, let myself be driven to the yellow house on the hill, where I will be expected to sign it away.

But the little pink fish will not let me rest. In these tiny hours of the morning, before the light has returned, it has been speaking to me, asking me again and again: What happens to the past? Does it fade and fall like leaves in autumn? Does it nest in the highest nooks of our mind, out of sight, like a condor, waiting to swoop? Does it rot like a body underground?

21

I cannot answer the little fish because I do not know. I remember what the nuns of Santo Domingo told me – that the dead will not return until the Resurrection. I remember what the psychiatrists told me – that the subconscious mind is artful in wish fulfilment. I remember what my mother screamed at me in desperation – *Enough with this obsessive mourning!* But the things I have been told have never resonated with my experience of reality.

'Whale!' I whisper into the night sky. 'Whale!'

Out in the sea, she appears, grumbling, and half-opens a big blue eye.

'Were you sleeping?' I ask.

Yes.

'I'm sorry.'

What's wrong with you?

'I can't sleep.'

So you wake me?

I shrug.

Pretty inconsiderate.

'I know.'

Why can't you sleep?

'I was wondering.'

Wondering what?

'What happens to the past?'

The whale groans and rolls over. The seawater rushes over her back like a landslide.

'What happens to the past?' I insist.

The whale opens her eye again and fixes it on me.

It passes, the whale replies.

'It passes?'

It passes through. It passes on. And, sometimes, it passes by.

DOS

For decades Mamabue's house was the grandest of the baroque casonas of Miraflores, a testament to the taste and good fortune of the Echeverría family. It was imagined into being by Tatarabuelo Ignacio – whose father had made his wealth in bird shit – as he took his siesta one sweltering December afternoon in 1893 and, as soon as construction began in the new year, the house became the envy of fashionable Limenian families who decimated their fortunes in trying, and failing, to equal Ignacio's masterpiece. Across the barren dust plain that then dominated the district, mansions sprang up. Each was more ostentatious than the last, with a rococo stucco here, a Moorish balcony there, until the district was a farrago of opulence, with houses of mismatched styles standing shoulder to shoulder, sprouting colonial balconies, baroque pediments, neoclassical columns. But none came close to the glory of la Casa Echeverría, which glittered like a crown on the brow of the hill known as the Mound of Defeat, though no one by then remembered how the Mound had gained that name.

The mansion was cool in summer, warm in winter and by some sorcery seemed to repel the stifling Limenian humidity. Even when the darkest fogs rolled in over the city from the Pacific, la Casa Echeverría glowed like a beacon in the gloom with its electric lighting and facade of lúcuma yellow. This colour was the only feature that had not resulted from the meticulous imaginings of

Tatarabuelo Ignacio or the assiduous designs of his wife, Ari-ari-mamie Colombe Fantonbleu de Echeverría, the fiercely practical Frenchwoman who had saved her husband's money from his careless spending by taking control of it and investing it, first in the railroads and later in the rubber boom. Still, she allowed herself one aesthetic indulgence in planning the house her husband had dreamed into being: she had ordered that it be painted primrose yellow, the same shade as her grandparents' Alsace cottage. But with her halting Spanish she could not communicate with the painters and the house ended up the colour of the lúcuma instead, a shade she quickly realised so far better suited the vibrancy of the New World in which she now lived that neither she nor any of her descendants would countenance painting the house any other shade except, briefly, during a period that became known as the Olive Years. After Bisabuelo Eugenio was killed in an automobile accident on the Avenida Abancay when his Ford convertible coupé collided with a milk cart (killing a donkey, four men and a woman), his wife, Bisabuela Elena, went mad from the heartbreak and the house was turned a shameful and garish green and the shutters painted red. The reputation of the house plunged into ignominy on account of both its olive hue and the drunken lover Elena took to distract herself from mourning. Once Elena had composed herself again, the house was returned to its true colour and, because of the way it glimmered, it was referred to fancifully as Paititi, lost city of the Inkas. Later it became known simply as the yellow house on the hill.

The doorway of the mansion, modelled on the doors of the cathedral of Cajamarca, was intricately carved by a talented young cajamarquino, so homesick that his melancholy permeated deep into the stone. Forever after, that doorway afflicted all who passed there with a feeling of nostalgia that so gripped the throat they would succumb to bouts of severe retching that could only be cured with spoonfuls of orange-flower water. Many years later, Ignacio Echeverría's great-great-granddaughter, Anaïs Rose Echeverría

Gest, would stand on the threshold of that very doorway and vomit profusely, overpowered by her own gut-wrenching homesickness and the inexorable nausea inflicted by the child in her belly.

Suspended on the front facade at the west of the house were Moorish balconies of mahogany carved to resemble confessionals with scenes of the martyrdom of the saints – a collection of beheadings, Catherine wheels and crucifixions. When the balcony of Titi Toto's bedroom fell during the earthquake of 1974, she refused an exact replica because she found the carved executions morbid and instead commissioned a replacement in the shape of a masquerade mask. She was not aware that her builders were admirers of the work of Antoni Gaudí and they drew for inspiration not, as she intended, on the Venetian carnivals of spring, but on Gaudí's House of Bones. The moment the balcony was unveiled to the family, it was also revealed to a throng of journalists, architecture aficionados and busybodies. As the tarpaulin was pulled away, the crowd gasped in horror because the new installation had the appearance of a skull staring out from the house, keeping sinister watch over passers-by in the street below.

Occupying the entire eastern stretch of the house was the ballroom, where Ignacio had wanted to install a marble floor of pure white until Colombe had made him see sense, on account of the constant washing that would be needed, and changed his mind to parquet de Versailles instead, which would also be much kinder on the bare feet of the marinera dancers who performed every month at the renowned Echeverría dinner parties. The enormous chandelier, shipped from London, had five tiers of crystal icicles and holders for one hundred candles, despite being wired to the mains, so that the light it cast could be matched to the occasion – electric light for dancing, candlelight for dining. The entire ceiling was painted with a quadratura mural of the animals entering the ark of Noah, although alongside the identifiable species were several creatures produced entirely by the painter's overenthusiasm for Peruvian cocaine, so that when one looked up the ballroom seemed to extend far into a landscape filled with turtle-skunks and lion-toads marching towards the ark, while in the distance, frolicking on blue hills that sprouted hands and feet, decadent masses engaged in orgies with swarms of scorpions and crabs, limbs mingling until leg was indistinguishable from pincer was indistinguishable from penis. While the mural's whimsy enchanted Tatarabuelo Ignacio, Ari-ari-mamie Colombe was appalled, not by its obscenity but by its lack of realism, and, many years later, upon finding God, their granddaughter María Dolores would take a decade-long fast from looking upwards indoors so as to protect her eyes from the hellish vulgarity depicted on the ballroom ceiling. But there was never a question of painting over the mural: the ballroom was in constant use and the Echeverría family could not do without it for long enough to allow a new piece to be completed.

The library, however, was mostly idle. Ari-ari-mamie Colombe had been entirely against building it. She had no patience for reading fiction: she had had quite enough of the high-flung ideals of the Romantics and saw little point in realism either – what use had she for the mimetics of quotidian life when she could simply step out of bed and live it for herself? She explained to her husband that a copy of the tenth edition of the *Encyclopaedia Britannica* and subscriptions to the main newspapers from each of the world's major cities would be sufficient to keep the family educated and could all be housed in a small study. Ignacio did not read fiction either, but he found the idea of reading romantic and his vision of a grand house was incomplete without a library, so it was built on the south-western corner of the house. The library was used for storing an enormous collection of books, for playing card games and hosting cocktail parties, but not for reading, except by Colombe's elder brother Gustave, an aspiring historian, sent to Lima by his parents to learn from his sister how to be a man of action, a man with sense, instead of burying his head all the time in his books.

He arrived by transatlantic liner in the winter of 1907, dropped his bags at the door and headed straight to the History section of the library, from which no one ever saw him emerge. Colombe's children, grandchildren and even some guests claimed to have seen him there in the shadows, slipping in and out among the rolling stacks of periodicals, but Colombe dismissed these claims as fantasy and always maintained that her brother must have slipped away unnoticed and returned to France.

Upstairs were bedrooms upon bedrooms, enough for every family member for generations to be housed comfortably, connected to one another through internal doors that never seemed to open onto the same room twice, so that one day Anaïs's bedroom might open onto the nursery and the next onto Tío Ernesto's study until she could no longer be sure whether the bedrooms were undertaking a perpetual waltz or if she had forgotten her way. All of the bedrooms opened onto the Sevillian patio and cast kaleidoscopic shadows onto the waters of the central fountain around which, standing guard, were twelve legendary marble creatures – many-headed, long-tailed, sharp-toothed beasts – from whose mouths a stream of water gushed every hour on the hour so that the waters of the font were, whatever the weather, always turbulent. The patio had been modelled, according to Tatarabuelo Ignacio's precise instructions, on the courtyard of the lions at the Alhambra palace, because it was in that very place that he had been struck by the conviction that he would one day make himself a great man. And he was not mistaken, because ten years later to the day he was arranging for the importation of seven hundred and fifty thousand Andalusian azulejo tiles while Ari-ari-mamie Colombe discussed with her architect how to direct the flow of water from the fountain through subterranean channels to irrigate the seventy orange trees that were being planted in the garden, which was to be constructed in tiers, like a wedding cake, in imitation of the gardens of the Palazzo Borromeo.

At the rear of the house, the garden terraces had been intended to descend all the way down the hill, but when the inheritance from the guano fund ran dry and the rubber boom deflated because of the rubber trees the British had planted across their Empire from stolen South American seeds, Tatarabuelo Ignacio could no longer afford to extend the garden to the bottom of the hill. Instead a border wall was built and the stretch of desert behind the mansion, still technically Echeverría property, was left empty. This empty plain was Los Polvos de Nadie y Nunca. And though Ari-ari-mamie Colombe had a fence constructed around it to keep out the land-grabbers, and though Bisabuela Elena wanted to turn it into a cemetery so that her husband could be buried nearby, and though Ignacio Segundo warned his brother Julio time and again that, unless they used the land, the Reds in the government would take it and give it to the undeserving, Los Polvos remained empty.

Until one winter in 1969, after General Velasco had completed his coup and issued Decree Law 17716 declaring land would be given to the tiller, Peruvian soil would be for the Peruvian... Then the people came. The people who would later be known as the Polvorinos. They came with their corrugated metal and straw matting and plywood boards and staked their claim over the dust. Among them would be a baby. A girl. A child with a mark on her cheek in the shape of a lopsided egg. And one day, not very many years later, this child would come to the door of the yellow house on the hill in search of employment and, at that house, from a window on the second floor, she would fall and die and her blood would stain the azulejo tiles. In her death she would become a ray of hope to the Polvorinos and she would return lost souls to their rightful places.

But that is not yet.

In the heyday of the Echeverría family at the start of the twentieth century, when Tatarabuelo Ignacio and Ari-ari-mamie Colombe slept in the master bedroom and their children were small, when the grouting between the tiles was still pristine and the majolica was uncracked and unstained by the blood of falling women, the house was immaculate and full of space. The bedrooms upon bedrooms were kept uninhabited but exquisitely furnished and ready for an army of guests, because foreign dignitaries and world-renowned artists had the habit of dropping in on the Echeverría household from across the oceans. During that era the only time the house had felt crowded was during three weeks in 1905 when the entire cast of *Lakmé*, along with all the orchestral musicians, sojourned at the mansion because – since the municipal theatre had burned down during the Chilean occupation of the city two decades earlier – the most suitable venue for their performance was the Echeverría ballroom and there was evidently nowhere more comfortable for such distinguished performers to rest their heads than the Echeverría bedrooms. Decades later, many of the singers and musicians would return to the casona, drifting disoriented through the bedrooms in search of a place of more permanent rest, drawn back to the house where they had been most comfortable, and their music would be heard faintly, as if from a great distance, by the Echeverría descendants.

But by the time Anaïs was first laid in her Moses basket in the shade of the orange trees, the house was rather more crowded and unruly. The cats were partly to blame. In Mamabue's house one was never more than a few feet away from a cat, although most of the time one would not notice it. The cats looked down from the top of cabinets, peered up from under sofas and peeked out from inside cupboards with doors open just a crack. Outside, cats lounged on walls or crawled into bushes. The cat proliferation began with the second generation of Echeverrías, once Bisabuelo Eugenio had taken over the family business with all the practicality and iron will of his mother and then, with all the romanticism and whimsy of his father, had married a touring musical actress with a heart-rending sympathy for stray kittens. Colombe was scandalised: it would have been one thing for her son to marry a singer of the highbrow zarzuelas composed in the nineteenth century, but for him to choose a mere revue actress seemed an affront to good taste and family values. And Colombe would not hear it, though her son told her a thousand times, that the play in which he had watched his beloved perform had been hailed by critics as a return to the glory days of the zarzuela. But Eugenio married the girl – Elena, the soprano from Málaga – and hung above the doorway in the entrance hall the fan he had caught when she threw it into the audience at the end of her flamenco. It still hung there ninety years later when his great-granddaughter returned from Europe, reluctantly pregnant and fearful of the future.

Bisabuela Elena had a great compassion for strays and brought home all the orphaned kittens she found in the streets of Lima, a habit which to Colombe's mind simply confirmed the girl's lack of good judgement. Over the years, Elena's sympathy grew and she returned with strays of all kinds: three-legged dogs and one-legged pigeons; guinea pigs sold at the market for food and chinchillas as pets; an Amazonian caiman discovered, emaciated and afraid, crouched behind packing crates in a consignment of rubber from Iquitos; and Salvador Dalí, an eight-limbed black-chinned emperor tamarin that had lost his way home, so named on account of his upturned white moustache. When the fad for wild pets reached Perú, Elena took in the misfits: a tigress blinded in transit from India, a koala suffering from alopecia, and a giraffe with vertigo. Bisabuelo Eugenio had a wing added to the rear of the casona to house Elena's orphans. Once Elena died, the Echeverrías took scant care of the misfit menagerie so, by the end of the twentieth century, all that remained were a few geriatric creatures and generations upon generations of cats – cats that had bred so prolifically no one was sure exactly how many there were. But the cats were unobtrusive, languid and content to coexist with the family at a distance, rarely intervening in human affairs as long as they were fed.

Even more numerous than the cats were the ants. Unlike the cats, the ants were stubbornly intrusive. No one could say when the epoch of the ants had begun, but everyone agreed that the invasion had been prolonged and insidious. When the new millennium arrived, the occupation of the ants was complete and they were everywhere: they scuttled in and out of cracks in the tiling; they swarmed upon any food left uncovered and carried it entirely away, piece by tiny piece; they huddled around plugholes like witches around a cauldron. The one mercy was that they did not often bite. Still, every successive empleada waged an interminable war on the ants with potions, powders and boiling water, but the ants were persistent and not even Q'orianka, the longest-serving of the maids, had ever conquered them.

Had it been just for the cats and the ants, Mamabue's house might not have felt so full, but as well as these rapidly multiplying guests were the multitudes of possessions accumulated by the Echeverrías, of which there were many because, to Ari-ari-mamie Colombe's horror, her Málagan daughter-in-law proved to be voraciously fertile and gave birth to no fewer than nine living children, each with a penchant for accumulation. For Tía-abuela Consuelo – so named because her birth was a consolation for the tragedy of the stillborn first child – the vice was dolls: German bisque dolls with enormous eyes; English babies in christening gowns of silk and lace; wooden children with articulated limbs; infants that called out 'mama' and cried real tears that she would wipe away as she held them tightly so they would not fear the solitude found in the depths of the night. For Tío-abuelo Ignacio Segundo, it was weapons: wooden swords and BB guns, fencing rapiers, poisoned arrows and medieval daggers, miniature cannons that exploded with packets of black powder, firecrackers to simulate the sound of gunfire, and crossbows that shot suction darts so strong they took hours to dislodge. When Ignacio Segundo chose to wage war on a sibling, he was stealthy and unrelenting. He slid up trees to snipe a brother from above. He hung upside down from chandeliers to lasso his sisters, hoist them up and leave the girls swinging from the ceiling. He kidnapped Consuelo's dolls and positioned them at the mercy of loaded cannons that were packed with gunpowder and rigged up to elaborate mechanisms designed to fire if a careless cat or hobbling pigeon touched a tripwire. Consuelo would sit on the terrace weeping into the ransom note which had arrived with snippets of the doll's clothing or strands of its hair until one of the servants – all of whom would be rushing about the house – had found the doll and rescued her from slaughter.

When members of the Echeverría clan died or moved away, their possessions were left in place, lovingly positioned and carefully dusted and polished – the dolls in their cots, the BB gun on its wall stand, flamenco fan above the door, freshly picked oranges, pearl necklace on its velvet pillow, the English china, the peacock feathers, the tablecloths of Spanish lace folded neatly, and the gramophone in the ballroom with the chest of vinyl records lying by ready for a party – everything waiting for its owner to return. Yes, the Echeverría siblings were demanding and expected their rooms to be maintained for visits, which they would inflict upon Mamabue at will, without warning and with much pomp and revelry, bringing their children and, many years later, their grandchildren also.

As for the dead, they made the overcrowding worse still, for they refused to leave, and though the family could not see the dead, they could sense them as a heaviness in the air. The living moved around beneath an immovable weight thinking it was just grief for the loss of the past, for the days when the casona was filled with operas, elegant balls and stately dinners with outlandish performers. For the days when parents were alive and dancers would waltz across the ballroom. For a time of earlier innocence, before loss – before this sister had died of encephalitis or that uncle had been crushed inside an overturned automobile or, above all, before a daughter had taken her own life, overwhelmed by the hallucinations that tormented her.

But the heaviness felt by the family was not grief alone. It was Time that crowded into the casona, rising from the mound of earth below its foundations, rolling in from the sea, pressing down from the neblina that shrouded the sky above. Time accumulated, thick and insistent as the Limenian dust, from all directions. The very house seemed to breathe it in, to squeeze moments, lived and not yet lived, into its walls, its floors, into its empty spaces, until the day when it could not withstand the crowding any more and a pachacuti had to come.

THREE

Standing on the threshold of Mamabue's house, where for seven years I have both longed to be and resisted being, I am suddenly overcome by a terror of crossing over. From outside the gates they are all watching me with narrowed eyes, thinking I will lose my nerve. They stand at the foot of the hill – Tío Pulpo, Tía Mimi, the notary, the foreman sent by the Edificios Pacífico construction company – in the middle of the Avenida del Guanero around the architect's car where the drawings, plans and contracts of sale are spread across the bonnet under the shadow of the haulage trucks that will be filled with Echeverría furnishings for distribution to auction houses, orphanages or scrapyards. They expect me to return to them, to take up the pen and sign my name. In truth, I expect the same – that I will sheepishly, resignedly, placing my feet carefully lest I stumble and fall, pick my way back down the stone steps that wind around the hill from Mamabue's house to the street. That I will rejoin them, apologise – blaming a sudden attack of nostalgia, a resurgence of the childish need for the familiar, an unresolved trauma – and sign the papers. That I will ignore the pull I feel towards the past, tug against it the same way I have tugged against it these past seven years, plodding resolutely onwards, letting a film of numbness wrap around my heart like plaque around a tooth.

But the past draws me. It is – it pretends to be – a familiar friend with long arms welcoming me back. I can feel it reaching for me, stroking me with the tips of its fingers, its hand poised to snatch at me if I get too close, to drag me backwards, down, and under.

I had convinced myself I should behave stoically. Rationally. On the way here, as the taxi carried me from the hotel and the driver told me his stories of woe, I persuaded myself of the needfulness to move forward. It's all about being flexible, the taxista told me. It's all about being willing to evolve. That is what life asks of us. He, for example, was a qualified doctor, señorita, but there was no work in his field. What else was there to do, señorita? Bills to be paid; money to be earned; adaptations to be made. That is how it is in this country, he said. *¿Me entiendes?*

As he slowed to stop at a crossroads, I was almost soothed into acquiescence by the pretty song on the radio about photographs of old lovers and by the swinging to and fro of a pendant of San Fiacre that moved just out of time with the tick-tick of the car's indicator – until a klaxon blared out from behind, making us jump, and my driver, uncertain as to who exactly had been the aggressor, wound down his window and cursed at no one in particular.

'Eat shit, son of a whore! May you and all of your vermin children eat shit forever!'

The car behind us shot past and screeched away.

'Impatience,' the driver said, shaking his head as he wound up the window. 'It's the reason this country never goes anywhere. Impatience! Imprudence! No one cares about experience any more. Just speed and youth. No place for maturity in this godforsaken city. No place for the lessons of the past.'

I fixed my eyes on the road ahead to soothe my motion sickness.

With the little fish undulating in my vision, every movement I make induces a nausea so potent it is as though all the fluids of my body have escaped their sacs. My skeleton has disappeared and I am a bubbling pouch of liquids – a cyst waiting to erupt. Waiting here on the step of the casona, as my head continues to swill, all I can do is double over and hope that the maelstrom will subside.

This morning there is no orange-flower water to still my gut. No one has prepared for me. In the past, when guests were expected for a party or a wake, crystal flutes of agua de azahar – the Echeverría anti-emetic distilled from the blossoms of the naranjos – were left on silver trays all along the stone pathway up to the casona. On this hill, under the shade of the orange trees, the Tías would sit together and sift through basket after basket of orange blossoms, flicking away the bugs and the debris and the browning flowers, keeping only the cleanest and creamiest of the petals. Those evenings the air would be filled with the bittersweet scent of neroli that ascended through the house in a white vapour, curling and winding seductively all night long, lacing our dreams.

But now, no one is left to prepare for me. The house is desolate.

No, that is not right. Inside, Q'orianka waits. Of all the staff, only she and Uriel remained when the family vacated the house – Q'orianka to maintain the interior, Uriel to preserve the exterior. What will happen to them if the house is sold? Who will employ them? I did not even think to ask Pulpo and Mimi about this. I was only thinking about myself, my own attachment to the place. But what is their stake in all of this? And what must their lives have been all this time since my mother died, with no other living souls for company, circulating an empty three-floored mansion, sweeping away the dust of absent friends, endlessly cleaning up after no one? What alterations has Q'orianka made inside? Has she removed Mama's knick-knacks, her cachivaches, and wrapped them in cellophane to make her dusting easier? Has she closed up the twenty-seven bedrooms now that there is no one to sleep in the beds? Has she stopped feeding the cats and let them find new homes elsewhere? And is she bothered much by the sounds of invisible dice games and weeping phantoms in the night?

What I expected, I do not know. I suppose I thought that the city would wait for me as if it had all been an elaborate piece of performance art for my sole benefit and that it could, the moment

I left, be dismantled, the actors dismissed, and all the props – the casonas, the plazas, the roving stray dogs – stored in labelled boxes in the wings, ready for the spectacle's revival when I returned. *Unpack the Plaza de Armas! Re-assemble El Callao! La señorita Anaïs is returning!*

An hour ago, in the taxi, I searched greedily through the window for places I once knew. On La Mar the old cevichería was heaving with diners. Outside the Farmacia San Juan, the same street vendor sold the same candies: fried plantain chifles and strawberry suckers, Frunas chews and Sublime bars. At the gates of the carpenter's yard on Calle Manuel Tovar, the same leathery old men of my adolescence – reeking of varnish, white spirit and hot wood – leaned against piles of antique furniture and bared their teeth at me.

But when we turned the corner onto Mamabue's street, the flame trees were gone. This is what I noticed first: where there were once rows of pichkari trees bursting with orange blossoms like Pentecostal tongues of fire, there are now only patches of dried earth littered with cigarette butts flicked aside by labourers. *The flame trees are gone.*

'La Avenida del Guanero, señorita,' the driver said. 'You should have seen it in its glory. But this, they tell me, is progress.'

He drove slowly, gesturing with an open palm out of the window. The vibrant Limenian mansions of my childhood were also no more. No longer the lines of fruit-coloured houses with black wrought-iron balconies and terracotta pots of geraniums and the lily of the Inkas. No longer the insectan buzz of hummingbirds' wings as they dart and glint in the sun. There was only building ground after dusty, abandoned building ground.

'It will be clean and modern when it is finished,' Tía Mimi explained as she helped me from the taxi and Tío Pulpo paid the driver. *Ocho soles, you say? Sí, señor. Come, man, that's not the usual rate. Not for a flag-me-down cab, señor – but for a pre-ordered taxi, yes. Listen here, I will give you seven.*

Mimi drew me away from the car, wrapping her arm around my shoulders and turning my back to Mamabue's house. 'There will be dozens of new apartment buildings just like that one,' she told me and pointed towards the one building that is almost complete and stands where La Vieja used to live in a mock-Tudor, thatched, half-timbered house known throughout Lima as La Casa Inglesa. She must be dead now, La Vieja, and gone is her fairy-tale cottage, replaced by a silvery glass-paned cuboid with a concierge's desk, underground parking and a waterfall in the entrance hall.

'We have bought a three-bedroom apartment in a new complex on Generál Córdova,' she went on. 'Off-plan, of course, but it will be ready before Easter. It will have a terrace and integrated air conditioning.'

'Qué bien, Tía,' I said.

From up here on the doorstep, I can hear her bracelets jangle as she lifts a hand to shield her eyes from the sun. She is assessing my resolve. How long will it take me to abandon these sentimental notions? She has never had patience for my quirks. Without a doubt she expected me to give up some time ago, perhaps as she watched me kicking and furiously shaking the gates, which had grown rusty and stiff, lashed together by vines thick as ropes and interlacing thorny branches at which I tore wildly, cutting my palms and releasing blood under my fingernails. I was aware – painfully aware – of how I must have looked: I was at once within, compelled by emotions I did not care to stem, and without, observing, judging, devising treatments. *A clear case of histrionic personality disorder – seeking attention through excessive displays of emotion. Deprive her of the emotional response she craves. She will wear herself out – like a child in a tantrum.* That is what they might have said – the white coats – if they were here. In a way, they are always here. Always hovering or, perhaps, inside.

And so, as I lashed at the brambles and thumped my body against the iron bars, the others did not intervene, neither to help nor to hold me. They just watched.

'That Uriel hasn't been doing his job,' Tío Pulpo remarked.

'Have we been paying him?'

'Yes, we've been paying him.'

'And with no one to supervise him?
Of course he's been shirking!'

They were wrong. As at last I squeezed between the gates that I barely managed to wrench apart, writhing through the dense greenery away from the condescending gaze of the notary, the foreman, the haulage truck drivers, I could see that, far from shirking his duties, Uriel had been doing his job: quietly, diligently, unseen and without praise or gratitude, nurturing the garden into a resplendence far beyond any it had possessed in my time at the casona. The gallito trees had blossomed riotously, their crimson wattle-shaped blossoms so arrogantly swollen that they seemed to have been plucked from roosters the size of elephants; the naranjos groaned under the weight of their bloated fruit, though Uriel had harvested several kilos and stacked them in crates along the side of the house; the alstroemeria and cantutas that bordered the steps, still bearing trembling drops on their petals from being watered only hours before, were almost blinding in their pigments, their colours unnaturally bright, as if they had been painted, each one, by hand.

Uriel must be here, somewhere on the grounds, around the corner of the house or just over my shoulder. Uriel, who never insisted that I speak, who accepted my silence as I followed him about the gardens. He spoke to me about pacha and the plants, taught me that space-time was expressed through nature's fractals – how patterns repeated themselves in the leaves of the fern, in the spirals of the succulent, in the branches of trees and the formations of river deltas. He said time, too, was made of fractals: that all of history was just moments spawning identical moments until infinity.

In my memories Uriel is always easy to find, for he moves within a cloud of noise – singing, whistling, the assertive thump of work boots on stone or the roar of a mower in the distance. But today he moves in silence, hidden among the trees, hose in hand, a trowel in his tool belt – watching me too, perhaps? Or asking himself, *Who is this stranger, landed from overseas, encroaching on my garden?* Would he still know me?

As I climbed the stone stairs towards the casona, it seemed that I clambered for hours, that on either side of my path the earth fell away in steep precipices and the air became thinner as if the house were at the peak of a mountain and I was ascending into the sky, though I know this could not be the case. There is no mountain on the Avenida del Guanero – just a minor hill, not even high enough to be called a cerro – little more than a mound by Peruvian standards.

Though each step left my spectators further behind and below, I was conscious of their eyes upon me, *ojeándome*. What would Tía Consuelo say? *Beware the mal de ojo, niña!* And she would make me strip down to my underwear and rub an egg over my skin – *to absorb the evil, niña* – and then crack it into a saucer and leave it under my bed. To distract myself from their ojeo, and to give myself an air of confidence, I raised my face towards the house, lifting my chin in defiance, and surveyed the facade.

It was as if the house had been preserved behind glass, shielded from the salt winds, the winter damp and the desiccating glare of the sun. The yolk-yellow paint was unpeeled, unmarked; the mahogany balconies had been sanded and polished until they gleamed; the lintels and ledges of windows were pure white, unstained by the purple-grey shits of the desert pigeons that plague the city; even the grout between the azulejo tiles had been scrubbed and bleached.

'Leave her.' Through the wall of vines and weeds, Mimi's voice penetrates: 'Just leave her.'

'But querida, how can we leave her? Remember Paloma.'

There it is. I had forgotten after these seven years about the equation of me with Tía Paloma, my mother's sister. Poor Paloma. Wretched Paloma. Paloma, in whose tragic footsteps I was doomed to follow. There was an incident when I was an infant, an incident I do not remember, but it terrified the family, made them think that I would follow her path. That I too would become just a memory, alluded to in maudlin tones, spoken of slantwise and cryptically, wept for a little when someone walked past a photograph on the wall or on a side table. So they enlisted doctors to save me.

'Ay, Pulpo. This one is nothing like Paloma. She is just dramatic. And she is like all the Echeverría women – she can't take a little discomfort. The pipes aren't working; the electrics are down. We can return tomorrow. And then she will beg to sign the papers.'

Mimi speaks as much for my benefit as theirs. She means to shake my resolve – and she is succeeding. Now, caught inside the gates, outside the house, I stand in-between, on the step, breathing in quivering gulps, one hand leaning against the door for support, unable to lift the key in my hand to the lock, wavering between two intolerable movements – backwards towards the street or forwards into the casona.

I have lived this moment already, I am sure of it, but was it just now or perhaps twenty years before? I see myself from outside myself, from behind and also from above – the curve of my jaw, the slouch of my shoulders, which the Tías always bemoaned, and the inward roll of my feet so that my knees are almost touching.

Yes, I have lived this moment before – one Sunday in July when, after an argument with my mother, I ran away from home. *I'll show her: she will miss me when I'm gone.* For three hours I roamed the Avenida del Guanero, anointing my wrists with tears, falling into the dirt and lying bedraggled, digging my hands into the dust and weeping like María Magdalena. When I returned, my cheeks inflamed and my passions spent, I found the house locked up and everyone gone out for un cafesito at El Haití, so I stood on the front step and knocked relentlessly, fully aware of the futility: the staff were all away.

I see myself standing at the door washed in light, colours faded as if in a photograph, overexposed, because this is – is it not? – how memories look. Diaphanous scenes with faces misted and outlines dissolving. Squint to see them more clearly, as if looking into the sun, because the colours blur together and tend towards bright whiteness. No, not whiteness: transparency. Memories tend towards pellucidity and then they disappear.

Any moment she will round the corner, this girl with wild hair and dirt under her fingernails. She will circle the house, pressing her palms against the walls, peering up against the sun at the windows (all shuttered and barred), testing, with desperation, the doors (all locked and bolted), calculating whether it might be possible to break in via Tía Toto's balcony. Her mind will be full of melodramatic reflection, which the narcissism of her adolescence will mistake for an epiphany, about the poignancy of being excluded from her own home by the measures intended to be impenetrable to thieves and trespassers. She is here now, I am sure of it, and will stumble upon me and take me for an intruder. How will we negotiate our dilemma? She, desiring to enter but unable: I, holding the key but afraid. She, assured of her entitlement; I – how shall I put it? – doubting. But doubting what? Myself, certainly, and what now awaits me beyond the door.

If I can enter *with* her – if she should invite me in – I could find the courage. There is safety in numbers. I will gather others to me, others like the one I now feel watching me from up in the boughs of the naranjos with black feral eyes. She is the wild little chupacabra hiding from María Dolores and the ragged branch and holy water. And there is another, the one Julia called Ojitos Negros, squatting in the geranium bushes at my feet, clutching in her fist the ancho-veta thrown from Julia's hand as she plummeted from the second floor and landed with a crunch, terracotta shattering inside a sack, a clattering of bones thwacking against the patio with a rolling of eyes, rasping of air and an explosion of red on the lawn. Moments before, Uriel had been singing and raking leaves. Moments later, I saw a pale silvery liquid shivering down the hill and understood that a human soul is like mercury.

Oh, Julia! Too terrible a death for too kind a person. I am sorry. So very sorry. I cannot bear to see it again, but I do. You are still falling and the girl you called Little Black Eyes sees you falling as she squats down there in the bushes eternally, but Ojitos Negros will never tell anyone what she saw and I have never stopped wondering since that day if it was my fault.

You came back to us, Julia. I saw you – thought I saw you – and you drew the population of Lima to our door. But now your devotees seem to have forgotten you. I did not notice any offerings at the gates, and the shrine they kept below the second-floor window from which you fell is no longer there. Even saints, it seems, are abandoned with the passing of time.

But what is the good in ruminating? The past cannot be changed. It will only replay again and again, the same, which is why Ojitos Negros is down there still, watching the never-ending plummet of the one she possibly loved the most. Is that right? Or is that sentimentality? I am not sure.

There is also – how could I forget her? – she who stands behind the door, inside but facing out, luggage in hand; not two hours have passed since Abue's burial and she is already leaving. She will open the door and peer into the day. We will be face to face and then we will trade places. She will pass through me to leave and I will arrive, wandering the empty rooms of the casona while she boards a plane and flies to England and meets Rupert and lives my past, lives these last few years, before slowly winding her way back to this spot to plant her feet where mine are planted and to hesitate at the door, where the cycle will continue.

A riot of wings behind me, a squabble of branches, and Tía Consuelo's macaw, Delibes, climbs the violet sky. They emerge from their hiding places – the chupacabra, the black-eyed imp within the geraniums, the dishevelled Magdalene with dusty hands – and join me on the step. We will pass over the threshold together, attached by wrists and ankles like a string of paper dolls. But no: this way we will not fit through the door. We will have to fold back together, each iteration of myself concertinaed on top of another but liable, at any moment, to fan back out, be unravelled and keep unspooling, copy after copy falling away from the chain, spilling like a deck of cards from the hand.

A car door slams and they are gone, scurrying into the bushes and up into the trees. I hear them leave, the copies of my former selves and also my adversaries way down in the street: the notary rustling papers in agitation, muttering grievances under his breath; the Pacífico foreman yelling at the drivers, slamming the doors of his pickup, revving his engine, driving away; Mimi, with her jangling bracelets, and Pulpo, grumbling, and their car starting up, its wheels grinding into the dirt as they make a turn in the road, the purr of its motor receding. The truckers remain the longest, eyeing me with interest, like pumas, through gaps in the greenery. They came expecting loot – Italianate dining suites and English crystal and Parisian pieces of art nouveau – and they are reluctant to depart with the bowels of their lorries unfed. At last, though, their vehicles groan to life, crawling resentfully, hissing and grunting, into the distance.

Now, silence. No traffic on the Avenida, though it is midday and there should be klaxons and shouting. No labourers on the building grounds. The diggers and bulldozers all slumbering, gathering dust. Hard hats and steel-toed boots thrown aside among cigarette butts and empty Inca Kola bottles. Where are they, these pioneers of the future, constructing the New Lima with steel and chrome and panes of glass?

A tickle in my palm reminds me there is blood on my hands. Yes, my palms – both slashed by the thorns and vines during my fit of frenzy at the gates – are stained pink where the blood has mingled with sweat from clenching my hands into fists. I wipe them on my trousers and examine the wounds, a criss-cross of scratches – not deep but, now that I have noticed them, I realise they smart.

You need a doctor, querida.

Nonsense! What doctor?

The child needs nothing more than a poultice.

What garbage! Fetch a physician!

A poultice of shredded potato and some aloe.

A doctor! A doctor!

I have a dread of doctors. I saw too many for too long. Doctors for the stomach – *she has a nervous bowel* – and doctors for the mind – *she has a nervous mind*. Doctors for the throat and doctors for the ears. Optometrists and speech therapists and neurologists and shrinks. They came to the house in their droves ever since I can remember with battered leather bags embossed with the staff of Asclepius, arriving in dark cars with tinted windows. They prodded my bowels and stuck tubes into my gullet. They tried to startle me with loud noises – *to see if the child might be deaf* – and shone sharp lights into my eyes. They poked me and jabbed me and poured tinctures into my mouth and spoke over my head as if I could not understand. For many years I sat below them, complying with their requests – *Open wide. Look into the light. Push back as hard as you can* – wondering whether it might be time to speak at last and let them know there was nothing wrong with me. But by the time I found my voice, I wasn't so sure.

Once I began to speak, they sent me to a psychotherapist – my first psychotherapist. He was a specialist in 'disordered minds' and he said inside my head was like a messy playroom with everything thrown all about, but he would help me pick up all the bits and pieces and tidy them back into their places, and wouldn't it be more fun to play that way, ah, with a neat and ordered space?

I sat opposite him on his verandah in a wicker armchair so large it seemed to swallow me into its maw. On a small table next to him was a statuette of a saintess that he touched occasionally, absent-mindedly, with the tips of his fingers. Where we sat, we overlooked his garden, where hummingbirds were fretting among the cantuta flowers, and down there, standing under an avocado tree, was an old woman singing, vehement and shrill. She screeched so loudly that I struggled to hear what the therapist was saying and I asked him, at last, if the old woman could sing somewhere else. *What old woman?* he asked me. The old woman by the tree. What song was she singing? He wanted to know, which seemed strange to me – surely he could hear her himself. Still, I told him: it was a song I knew well, familiar from Tía Consuelo's gramophone. The 'Air des clochettes' from Delibes's *Lakmé*.

He threw me out, shooing me urgently towards the car where my mother was waiting. He could not help me, he told her, thrusting the statuette of the saintess into my hands. She was Christina the Astonishing, patron saint of millers and the mentally disordered, Tía Consuelo told me later, turning the resin woman over in her hands.

The psychotherapist said he could not help me and I was not to come back. It was his mother I had seen, long dead, singing on his lawn. This is what he claimed. He said what afflicted me could not be explained by his science because how could I have known, *diablos?* How could I possibly have known the song she most liked to sing or the tree that she, with her own hands, had planted? Many times since, I have reflected on these questions. There are so many explanations – perhaps I saw a photograph on his wall, perhaps a copy of *Lakmé* lay on a shelf somewhere as I was led through his house, perhaps it was just the coincidence of my childish thoughts triggering his own griefs and fears.

At the rumble of tyres on rubble, a car driving up the Avenida, the little pink fish jolts. Someone is coming. Someone Mimi and Pulpo have sent for me, most likely. A taxista, perhaps? Sent to collect me and take me back to the hotel. They have had pity on me. *Send a man to fetch her, Pulpo. She's only a child. A silly, silly child.* Yes, they have sent me a driver, and I can't say I'm disappointed. The decision has been made for me, whether to cross over or turn back. I will go back to my hotel and sign the papers, relieved of the burden of choice.

Or perhaps they have not sent me a taxi. Perhaps they have sent a Tía. To reason with me – or scold me. Yes, they have sent me a Tía to put me in my place. Tía María Dolores, most likely. She with the sharpened tongue. *Child! Basta with the stupidities and get in the car!* I will not go with her. I will not be dictated to as if I were still four years old without the faculty of reason. I will send her away and do as I wish.

From the steps of the house, with the advantage of height, I see the car still some way along the Avenida; it is a dark saloon with tinted windows, and I know then whom they have sent.

The doctor is here, querida.

  Come down and greet him.

        'I have no need whatsoever of a doctor.'
A small, inconsequential examination.

  It won't hurt a bit, querida.

Any moment he will arrive and climb up the steps towards me, leather bag in hand, stethoscope curling around his neck like a serpent. He will want to prise open my eyelids and inspect my tonsils, measure my temperature and probe my nodes. I will not let him examine me. I am well. There is nothing – absolutely nothing – wrong with me.

If I find Tía Consuelo, she will defend me, hide me in her closet among the body parts of broken dolls, just as she always did when they brought me a new physician.

Have you seen the girl?

                          Not all morning.

But the doctor is here for her.

                Perhaps he can examine you instead.
In my rush to unlock the front door, my hands tremble and I drop the key into the geraniums. On my hands and knees, fumbling

among the flowers, I catch the odour of anchoveta piercing through the cacophonous green fragrance of the leaves and my stomach convulses, a wave of nausea surging from my bowels. I vomit violently, my body shuddering from the effort, my breath clawing in pitiful gasps.

Below, outside the gates, the car is slowing to a stop and I hear the engine cut out. A door opens. Shoes scrape on gravel.

My hands scramble through the vomit-splattered foliage as I hold my breath against the fragrance of flower and leaf, the stench of rotting fish, the sour smell of stomach. My fingers close around the shaft of the key and, without a moment to wipe it clean, I thrust it into the lock, throw myself against the door as it opens, and stumble across the threshold into the silent house, slamming the door behind me.

The cry of the door crashing shut reverberates through the house a thousand times, repeated again and again from room to room like rumours whispered by eager tías. In the darkness, where my eyes are momentarily redundant, I can hear the ants' metallic scuttling on majolica and the screams of Inti-Killa, the two-headed cat that we expected would die many years ago. There are no other noises.

The house smells the same – of warmed wood, azahar and mothballs – sweet and resinous and bitter all at once. The spiciness of star anise and cinnamon and cedar wood from Abue's cologne stirs the air as if he had this instant walked by, just as the punchiness of insect poisons stings the skin inside my nostrils.

In the dark, I can make out only shadows – incoherent colourless silhouettes separated by chasms of blackness so they communicate no familiarity, bear no relation to anything I know. Without light to see, the shapes seem to move further apart and then encroach again on one another and me, as if in a languid, suffocating dance. Without walls or floors to contain them, I cannot tell how high or how far the shadows extend, whether Mamabue's house is here at all, or if I have stepped across the threshold into an abyss of floating forms.

But as my eyes adjust, the shapes gain mass and location: they anchor to floor, press against wall, hang from ceiling. They have the familiar bulks and heights and angles of Mamabue's furniture but are draped under dust sheets which begin to glow through the murk, as if from their own light. There is no breeze, but the white sheets billow as if breathing, and, where they skim the floor, the edges seem to ripple.

'¿Consuelo?' I whisper.

The house is desolate; the walls are still. There is no one waiting for me in the gloom. I cannot hear the clattering of dice against a tabletop or the incantation of a nursery rhyme to soothe a phantom child.

CUATRO

On the morning of Wednesday the eighteenth of June in the year 1986, Julia Álvarez Yupanqui, long-suffering maid to the Echeverrías, fell from the second-floor window of the home of her employers and, when she reached the bottom, died in an explosion of red and white on the majolica. As she fell, life flashed before her eyes. Not her own life, however. At only seventeen, Julia had not amassed enough memories to fill the time between stumbling from the window and exploding onto the azulejo tiles below, but the spirits of the air intervened, opening to her the recollections of those who had come before so that she was distracted from the terror of a swiftly approaching death by observing the lives of others.

The first vision she had, as the heels of her hands slipped from the window ledge and her body teetered forwards, was through the eyes, four hundred years dead, of Sayani Cahua, the peasant from Huamanga who had volunteered to take the place of his ailing nephew in the mita. Sickly since birth, the boy would have been exempt from the Inka's work laws but was not spared by the labour tribute demanded by Viceroy Andrés Hurtado de Mendoza to extract toil from the people in the colony as a mark of their gratitude to the Crown for lifting them out of pagan savagery. Sayani Cahua would now, for thirty years and a day, in his nephew's place, be the slave of Hernando Echeverría y de Vargas, working in his mines, scratching at the earth's bowels in search of precious metals. But it was not the glimmers of gold in the darkness that Julia saw, nor the bleeding of the sun rising behind the mountains as the mitayos marched mineward at dawn. What Julia saw through the eyes of Sayani Cahua was the back of another mitayo's head – the lice teeming in his hair, the crusting of blood in patches where skin had been torn away, the oozing sores on the neck where the necklace of iron had rubbed the flesh raw. This was the view of Sayani Cahua each morning and each night as, yoked together by the neck with his fellow mitayos, he shuffled to and from the mines through the cornfields always under the watch of Don Juan Uybua, whose father had been a kuraka, magistrate to the last Sapa Inka, and who now was the chosen of Hernando Echeverría to oversee the workers.

Born in the year 1536, three years after the death of Atahualpa, Cahua's mother had named him on the insistence of her gut: *He should be named 'I remain standing'*. Twenty years later, marching in Uybua's chain gang, he would chant his name to himself, one syllable to each step. *Sa-ya-ni. Sa-ya-ni.* Other men were not so fortunately named. Their mothers' wishes had been too lofty. They had wished for their sons to fly, naming them after birds: Cuntur and Guaman and Quinti. These were the men who struggled the most against the manacles. They tried to stand too erect, refusing to bow to the weight of the chains on their shoulders. And so the necklaces cut deeper into their skin. Their hearts and bones grew weary under the shackling of their bodies. Unable to soar, they began to stumble. Their toes caught on pebbles in the dust and they toppled, dragging others down with them. Uybua had no patience for clumsy walkers. He would abuse them in Spanish with words they did not understand, placing his hand on the hilt of his sword.

Up, you filthy desert rat! Up!

But one day the fallen desert rat did not rise. Guayasamin Quispe lay in the dust, his breathing coming in rasps and retches.

He needs water, kuraka! He is dying!

In falling to the dust, Guayasamin Quispe had dragged the men before him and behind him to their knees. One of these was Sayani Cahua who, for the first time, examined carefully the face of the man the rear of whose skull he had come to know so well. He learned, as he watched Quispe writhing in the dirt, how his own face might have come to look, the copper of the cheekbones faded by a patina of yellow ash ground deep into the pores, the regal high arch of the nose crumpled and crushed under the blows of Uybua's fist, proud black eyes dimmed, fixed on the sky but all the time losing light.

Kuraka, release him! Let him rest, Don Kuraka, please!

Hearing the pleas of the mitayos under his care, Don Juan Uybua, the kuraka for that Spaniard Echeverría, did see fit to release Quispe from the iron shackles that bound him. The condors screamed and circled as the men, dragging their feet through dust, staining their toes with blood, shuffled with desperate care so as not to stumble over any stone or branch or – the gods forbid it – the head of Guayasamin Quispe, which rolled, wide-eyed and yellow, emptying of its juices, severed from the body by three clumsy hacks of Uybua's blade. In their workmate's absence, the other desert rats would have to work harder, mine deeper, make up for his loss, and Uybua whipped them to let them know it was time to move on: too much time had been lost over the fallen man.

Through the eyes of Sayani Cahua, Julia Álvarez Yupanqui saw, in her fall from the balcony, the empty, bloodied iron neck brace swinging to the beat of the chain gang's march, and she felt on her cheek the tickle of a piece of Guayasamin's meat which Sayani dared not lift his hand to flick away, lest he draw the attention of the kuraka whose hand still sat on the hilt of his sword.

Sa-ya-ni. Sa-ya-ni. Sa-ya-ni.

All of this Julia saw in the flicker of an instant. A tiny speck of time past scratching at the cornea, which is no sooner felt than is blinked away and replaced by another. Fragments of time, irritations to the eye, the substance of the universe, fractured and ground to powder, whipped up by the winds to blind us like a sandstorm in the desert. Yes, the whole world is a desert, and we drag our feet through dusts of time elapsed but lingering.

Inflamed by the scratch of Sayani's vision on her eye, Julia blinked, and the dusty chain gang left her. An afternoon this time. Bright, cloudless. Lilac Andean sky. This is what she saw between the fluttering of her lashes as her knees left the window ledge and her fingers spread into the open air. The creamy smell of naranjos in the Echeverría orchard below folded into the onion odour of sweat rising from a teeming crowd of spectators gathered many years before. She was among them, looking through the eyes of Catalina Álvarez Cahua, who huddled in the nervous mass surrounding the black-draped scaffold, darkly dressed, hood pulled down over her furrowed brows, feeling in every follicle the vibrations of impend- ing gore. Soon the ground will rumble with the sound of shattered bones shuddering against cobblestones as the prisoners, tied by the ankles and wrists, are dragged behind horses with flaming eyes and foaming muzzles, but Catalina will not watch as the bodies leave tracks of skin and blood on the streets. She will not watch as the tongues of prisoners are sliced from their throats and tossed into a frothing pile. She will not watch the beatings or garrottings or quarterings. She will keep her eyes fixed on the face of the Visitor General, that José Antonio de Areche sent from across the seas by a foreign king whom Catalina had seen only in her dreams as an enormous mouth on legs, all the time feasting, belching, gobbling gold and silver and human flesh because if he ever stopped eating he would die. As the cries of the tormented rang out through the square, Catalina searched the face of the Visitor General, far above the crowd, watching the executions from a velvet-draped balcony, flanked by armed guards. Not once did he flinch. Not when Túpac Amaru II's body was thrown into the air by the bolting apart of four horses. Not when his wife was clamped by the garrotte or later when, after her slender swan's neck saved her from strangulation, she was bludgeoned to death. Not when the screams of their son, Fernandito Condorcanqui Bastidas, tore through the sky, unleashing the ferocious storm that would beat down upon the city for three days and nights. The face of the Visitor General, powdered and pale, set like marble, revealed nothing to Catalina other than confirming her suspicions that these white-faced rulers had come from another world where human pain bore no meaning.

One month and two hundred and five years later, the descendant of Catalina Álvarez Cahua will sprawl in mid-air, suspended in the Limenian humidity, the ties of her white apron stretching like tentacles, and she will hear the shriek of Túpac Amaru II's son as audibly as if it came from the garden below, while the battle cries of the inmates revolting at El Frontón will sound distant, as if a thousand years away, swilling and whirling with the susurrations of waves beating on the Chorrillos shore. At the exact same moment when Julia will turn a somersault, at the exact level of the lintel of the window of Doña Consuelo's first-floor bedroom, the cabinet of President Alan García will meet in the Pizarro Room of the presidential palace, gathering under the painting of Túpac Amaru II to discuss the quelling of Maoist uprisings breaking out in prisons across the nation. Julia will not know this: seconds later, she will erupt across the Echeverría patio in a flare of red and white – a blaze of blood and bones – and leap, in an instant, from the confines of her pale blue maid's uniform into the bosom of the sisterhood of Santa Rosa, Mother Teresa and Sarita Colonia.

But first, before she lands, she has more memories to witness. Hanging like an upturned beetle, belly to the sky, she contemplates the clouds – not the mournful glaucous clouds of Limenian winter but the wispy, dappled clouds above Pampamarca which she sees now through the cataracts of Josefa Puyucahua. Josefa's world has been melding into haze for years, veiled by the film of milky grey creeping across her irises that has turned her black eyes white and earned her the reputation of a prophet, gifted in old age with the ability to see beyond sight and commune with the world of the spirits. Now, as she stands on the edge of the village, the cataracts protect her, shielding her from the details of a vision she must now confront. Hanging from the branches of a queuña tree in bloom, secured at the elbow by a length of frayed and bloodied rope, her daughter's arm, with blackened fingers, swings. Beside it hangs the leg of her son, Antonio Bastidas Puyucahua, and the tongue of her son-in-law, Túpac Amaru II, sent under the command of that pale-faced ghoul Areche as a warning to any other natives who might conspire to resurrect the glory of the Inkas. The torsos were burned at Picchu – so she heard – and the heads impaled at Tinta. As Josefa stands, leaning on the trunk of the queuña tree, squinting to no avail through the clouds that float before her eyes, she wonders what it is about these Spanish that makes them so eager to separate head from neck and limb from socket, what it is that makes them need to reduce their enemies to morsels. Overcome, Josefa Puyucahua closes her eyes and the visions are gone. For a moment Julia sees the world as it is: sky rushing away from her, yellow walls of la Casa Echeverría speeding past, her limbs stretched out and fingers reaching, releasing the anchoveta that had been in her grip, fingers scrabbling to grasp, but there is nothing substantial to hold...

Except the pickaxe, grazing at the palm. The pickaxe, weighing in the arms. The pickaxe that must be swung ten times each minute from dawn until dusk, twelve hours each day for the eight years of indenture on this island of bird shit to which Leung Huang promised himself while still twelve thousand miles away at the marina in Macau by his signature on paper. That was the first time he had ever signed anything in his life, and he now belonged to a man named Echeverría. This much he knew, and he understood little else from the incomprehensible Spanish that was roared at him daily. But he understood the language of whip and chain, and he had learned to interpret the mannerisms of foremen who towered above him, abusing the indentured in foreign tongues, urging them to imitate the shrieks of seabirds and howls of guard dogs or, on pain of refusal, be tied to a post and flogged. He understood that here he was seen as less than animal. A mere beetle in the dung. Scrabbling in the shit heap. He will die before the eight years are up, as will all of his comrades, and Leung Huang from Guangdong Province understands well that he will leave no trace in this world. Through his eyes Julia sees the island's grey-capped peaks, almost like snow, but pestilent and rank. From a distance, crowded on the tug from Callao with the other new arrivals, Leung had marvelled at the sight – what type of frost was this that could withstand the heat of American sun? But as the boat drew closer, drawing them into the fetid vapours that enveloped the island, and when he saw the crowds of seabirds – the green-grey tinge of the glistening stalagmites, the splatter patterns on the boulders and the drip stains on the cliffs where dust-encrusted chinos scurried up and down like ants – then Leung Huang understood very well that he had been brought to mine on a floating pile of avian turds.

Watching Leung Huang as he thrust his pick into the muck was Domingo Julio Tercero, so named by his master for being the third male slave on the Echeverría plantation to be born on a Sunday in July. Domingo Julio heard it said that the trade in African slavery had ended but, if that was true, the news had not, as of December 1852, reached the ears of the owner of La Hacienda Echeverría in Pisco. But the news that *had* reached Echeverría's ears in early 1849 was that there had been another slave uprising in the Chicama Valley, and it threw him under a dense cloud that did not pass for days. He sequestered himself in his study with his mastiffs and sat hunched at his desk, his low, dark eyebrows knitted in consternation over his eyes as black and sharp as a falcon's. Day and night he remained there, surrounded by his hounds, thinking, massaging with his long reedlike fingers the angles of his jawline and his prodigious chin. He was locked away for so long that the foremen suspected he had died and each, unwilling on account of the master's notorious temper, drew straws to determine who should knock on his door and enquire as to the state of his health. The task fell to Héctor Álvarez Uybua, the youngest, most newly hired of the foremen and the one who could least afford to lose his position, a father to five with another little mouth on the way. He approached the master's quarters with halting step and trembling fingers, all at once hoping the man would be dead, imploring God to forgive his murderous wish, dreading what might ensue should the master be alive behind that door, and rehearsing the delicate words with which he would strive to appease the great man's temper.

He need not have worried: before he could raise a fist to rap on the door, Enrique Echeverría burst out from his isolation uplifted by the cunning of his plan. The era of African slavery was – he saw so clearly now – doomed. The slaves were revolting up and down the nation. There was talk of emancipation in the halls of power. It was inevitable. And imminent.

You will be freeing the Africans, Don Enrique?

Freeing the Africans? Don't be absurd!

The master had devised a plan – a plan most assiduously designed to safeguard, above all, his business interests. The slaves could not be suppressed by threats of violence any longer – within days the news would reach them of the Chicama uprising. They would get braver. They might, *¡carajo!*, invade the house and murder them all in their beds. The situation needed deft handling, yes, it needed foresight and cunning. The slaves must be given hope.

Hope, Don Enrique?

Yes, yes, carajo, hope!

The Africans must be given hope – of respectability, of freedom: this is what the master of La Hacienda Echeverría instructed his foremen. No more beatings. No more humiliations. There would now be smooth words and enticing promises. Promises that, for the men who worked the hardest, who complied and caused no ruckus, there would be promotions.

Promotions, señor?

Yes, I said it, carajo, promotions!

And so, punishments exhausted, they would be rewarded – not the elderly, who in their weakness and infirmity no longer posed any threat, and not the women, who concerned themselves too much with their children to think of revolt or retaliation, but the young men, the ones who, despite the beatings and indignities and unceasing demands of the labour, retained the flash of steel in the eye. Those young men would be rewarded with the opportunity to leave the plantation, to be elevated away from the fields of Quebranta grapes and become foremen of the Echeverría workers out on the Chincha Islands.

The Chincha Islands? We have workers on the Chincha Islands?

The master, in spite of himself, laughed, for this was the best part of his plan. For some time now, he had been watching from afar the guano bonanza, calculating ways in which he could profit. He had, for almost a decade, held a state concession to sell the produce from his hacienda on the guano islands, but this was insufficient. The bird shit was making a killing in Europe and he could not sit by and watch the profits float away from him. He had taken note of the talk of 'labour problems'. The bird muck was there for the taking, but finding the workers to do the taking was another matter entirely. The plebs in Europe would not come: they had heard of the stinking hell that awaited them in Perú. And the Africans, those rebellious masses, carajo, would not quietly accept any further indignities: within a decade the Africans would be free, that was undeniable. And indenturing the natives was, well, how shall we say, problematic with that mestizo Castilla in office, carajo! No, there was no question of indenturing the natives, Goddammit. Besides, they were needed inland to help resurrect the nation's agriculture, which, during the war of independence, had been allowed to go to mierda.

So, yes, there were labour problems. But Enrique Echeverría had found a solution. He had heard from a sea captain – a rough-tongued

Englishman with whom he communicated in tangled franglais –
that there was, across the Pacific, a new source of labour emerging:
multitudes upon multitudes of workers flocking, lo juro, simply
flocking, to come to the New World.

The Chinese would be his new investment.

And so, during his dark days sequestered in his study, he had
drafted a law that provided for the payment, by Congress, of thirty
pesos per head for any imported labourers arriving in groups of
fifty or more. Payment, of course, being to the importer: it was
only fair, *¡carajo!*, for the man who had paid the labourers' passage
to receive the boon!

Yes, he was resolved: he would import, carajo, chinos.

Echeverría's law was passed by his friends in government in
November 1849, and within twelve months he had imported three
hundred and fifty-four Chinese men and, with the profits, purchased
a neighbouring plantation owned by an ailing elderly merchant who
was rapidly losing his sense and wished to set sail at the earliest
opportunity to Cádiz and be buried in the soil of his motherland.
The old man was lucky – sí, señor, very fortunate – to have found
in his neighbour not only a willing purchaser but a most obliging
friend who could arrange for him the transatlantic passage by
pulling some strings with the kindly English sea captains he knew.

But none of this was seen by Julia Álvarez Yupanqui as she fell,
back first, towards the patio, sky racing away from her, salt breeze
from the sea blowing dust into her eyes. What she did see was
through the eyes of Domingo Julio Tercero, a towering, muscular
man – the one who, in Echeverría's nightmares, overpowered the
mastiffs and rent the locks and burst through his bedroom door to
gut him like a fish but who in reality, despite his height and size,
was an anxious man, given to cracking his knuckles and ripping
with his teeth the skin from his cuticles until they bled. Through
Domingo's eyes, she saw the seventy-five Chinese men he had been
installed to oversee when he was induced to come to the islands

of Chincha with promises of freedom for his children, freedom
for his woman, freedom for himself, if he served his master well.
Freedom and (moderately) good wages.

Domingo Julio Tercero did not know that the freedom with
which Echeverría had tempted him to the green-grey hell of the
islands of shit was a freedom which, in less than two years, would
be signed into law without the need for him to consign himself to
the pestilential dung mounds. Nor did he know that in 1855 Enrique
Echeverría would receive three hundred dollars as compensation
for releasing him – and a further three hundred dollars apiece for
the release of every other man, woman and child on the hacienda.
It will not be until 1856, when Domingo returns for his yearly rest
from the guano islands, that he will learn of his emancipation. He
will not see a cent of the emancipation compensation. Sitting in
Echeverría's study, he will be given the choice: immediate release
from his contract to oversee the guano workers – so that he and
his woman and his four children can leave the hacienda and be on
their way – or his continued service on the guano isles for the same
pay. Of course now, as a free man, he will have to pay rent – board
and lodgings – for his woman, his children. It's only right, carajo!
It's only proper. That, Domingo, is the plight of the free man for
being free, nothing comes free. No such thing as a free lunch, carajo!
Or, of course, you're welcome to leave the Echeverría service – to
find yourself a home, an employer, elsewhere in the Ica region…

He was reflecting on this conundrum when, on the morning of
Sunday the eighteenth of June 1856, he saw a pillar of flame emerging from the mists on the horizon and he half-expected to see the
ocean parting and Moses himself walking towards him on dry land,
staff aloft, followed by a crowd of Israelites, pursued by the cavalry
of Pharaoh. The same floating tower of fire was seen by Leung
Huang and his fellow labourers, who lowered their pickaxes and, for
the first time, were not chastised in doing so, for the foremen had
become distracted for the same reason. The Chincha Islands were,

for once, still. No scurrying back and forth across the shit peaks, no squeal of the whip slicing through air. All watched the floating inferno approaching – not a divine manifestation, but the *María Ugarteburu* set aflame by the prisoners held below deck, crammed into the hold, festering in their own juices ever since Macau with only scraps of food passed down to them through the holes in the lattice hatch, not allowed up onto the deck since the captain, a John T. Smith from Liverpool, had heard of the ruthlessness with which the Chinese strove to escape their contracts: he had heard of the mutinies and the cutting of throats and the setting aflame of ships.

But Captain Smith had underestimated the determination of his consignment: for weeks they had been building themselves a pyre below deck and, when they heard the cries that Peruvian land was on the horizon, they beat their fists against the hatches, shrieking and wailing, until the captain commanded that shots be fired through the lattice, and it was a matter of minutes before that gunfire had set the pyre alight and eaten through the partition wall to the gunpowder store and the *María Ugarteburu* went off like a fire-work before Captain Smith had time to load his crew into lifeboats.

The winds changed and blew the blazing ship off course, away from the port of Callao and towards the islands of hell where Leung Huang, his lungs burning with pneumonia from which he would die before the month was out, and Domingo Julio Tercero, his pride still smarting from the humiliation of having chosen to remain under the servitude of Echeverría, watched it floating shoreward, hot ashes blowing towards them, burning their faces, the black smoke curling and coiling, lacing the sky with ebony fili-gree, reaching out with gnarled fingers and then spreading thick and fast like a pall across the sun. This is what Julia sees stretched across the sky like a storm cloud, but there are no storm clouds in Lima – only shrouds of smoke billowing from burning slave ships centuries before. She feels the hot ashes on her skin and the aura of heat on her face and smells the burning of fat and hair and skin and wonders what strange treats Carmen la cocinera is preparing for lunch way down in the Echeverría kitchen. Meanwhile, one hundred and thirty years before, Chen Tan, sole survivor of the six hundred passengers of the *María Ugarteburu*, badly burned but alive, washes onto the shore.

Now, as once again her body turns a somersault, Julia falls feet first and the full skirt of her maid's uniform balloons and then inverts like a blue tulip and in this way she plummets and plummets, tumbling thousands of feet, not from the second floor of her employers' mansion but from the Railroad in the Sky where, just an instant ago, Taciturno Huaman was tightening screws, turning and turning until he felt the metal girders pushing against him, tighter and tighter, for the screws would have to hold for generations to come – those were the words of Señor Henry Meiggs – *for generations and generations to come!* Up here their children and their children's children and their children's children's children would cross the mountains even faster than the chasquis on their dirt tracks – yes, they would think nothing of speeding along like gods through the clouds, far above where the llamas walk, yes! Above, even, where the condors fly! Yes, they were building the Railroad in the Sky or, for the less fanciful, el Ferrocarril Central Andino – and it would traverse the mountains! It would penetrate the mountains! It would scale and outreach the mountains, elevating the mere mortal traveller to where the breasts of the earth grazed the heavens!

With all the lofty talk of soaring through clouds, it was hard not to lose one's head as so many of Taciturno's workmates had done, dizzied by the whirlwind of human ambition and the nauseating effect of soroche at such high altitudes, which made the circulation sluggish and clouded the head and, in the blink of a sleepy eye, there was a teetering over the side of the railroad tracks and a frantic scrabbling for something sturdy and then a tumbling, tumbling into the ravine, away from the vast blue of the sky and down towards the river Lurín below. The falling man's companions could only watch as he became a blob and then a speck and then a distant, barely audible, pop.

Taciturno Huaman had often wondered how it felt to fall in this way. Was there a thrill to it? A sudden heightening of the senses to the sounds, the sights, the smells as the will resigns itself to the inevitability of the journey's end so that all that remains is to enjoy the trajectory? Or would there be torment? A desperation to survive and fight on? A refusal to let go? Sometimes his thoughts took on a more morbid bent, for he had known many of the fallen ones intimately and often imagined their mangled bodies, which had not been – which could not be – recovered, piled up on the riverbank, some half-eaten by pumas and carrion birds. They had, all of them, died with unfinished business – families and aspirations and dreams of returning home to a peaceful retirement without manual labour – and he imagined their resentful souls stomping back and forth down there, grumbling together about the injustice of it all, cursing the Railroad in the Sky and that damned Yankee, Henry Meiggs.

The questions of Taciturno Huaman about the nature of death by falling would not remain forever unanswered: on a winter afternoon in 1878, just a few days before the line to Chicla would be completed, Taciturno suffered an episode of fatal clumsiness, tripped on a rogue hammer, teetered right on the edge of the railway tracks and, for a few thrilling moments, contemplated the expanse of wide-open air into which he would then tumble. Before he reached the ground, where he would join the grumbling ghosts on the banks of the Lurín, he would watch his life flash, projected onto the dusty faces of the cliffs around him and onto the white underbellies of the clouds above. Peering down from between the girders of the railway were his workmates, wondering what it was that Taciturno was feeling as he descended.

Now Julia Álvarez Yupanqui joins Taciturno Huaman, hearing the air scream as it rushes past his ears, squinting at the receding faces of his fellow labourers, clutching the screwdriver he had been twisting moments before. She feels it in her hand, this screwdriver, rubbing against the calluses in her palm and the blisters on her fingertips where her prints have been worn away by the bleach with which she cleans the bathrooms and the steel wool with which she scrubs the pots and pans. She feels, too, the saw of Uriel Uybua – who somewhere deep within the house is fixing a door frame warped by the penetration of humidity – and the steel wire cutting into the fingers of her father, Julio Álvarez Mayo, as he lashes together four panels of straw matting that will serve as the walls of their home.

Now, for the first time since her fall began (mere instants ago, though into those instants several centuries have been compressed), Julia sees through her own eyes – the eyes of her infant self, seventeen years before, as she lay in a Moses basket nestled in the dust of Los Polvos de Nadie y Nunca under the shade cast by a threadbare jacket propped up on a bamboo post. Days before, Julio Álvarez and his wife, newly wed and newly parents, had heard rumours whispered on street corners: there was a patch of land, little more than a stretch of dust, over in Miraflores behind the Echeverría casona, which had been earmarked by that family for a cemetery. But what need had the dead for land? What was it with these rich people? Buying homes for relatives not yet dead for their corpses to inhabit!

Incensed by the insanity of housing the dead (while the living slept piled like rats!) and emboldened by the Revolutionary Government of the Armed Forces, which had taken over just two months before, the people had devised a plan, or so Julio Álvarez heard it said. There was to be a land takeover, and anyone who desired a square of land to call home should congregate on the dust plain in Los Polvos – that very space intended to be a neighbourhood for the dead – and bring with them whatever materials they could gather to build themselves a house.

It was there that baby Julia watched her father squat and squint, stroking his long, angular chin as he carefully assessed the ground before choosing the square of dirt that the family Álvarez would claim. The flat land would not do, he concluded, dusting off his hands, for it was buried far too deep in sand and ash: with the slightest gust of breeze, the foundations would tilt and slide and their home would be buried in dirt. Instead, he chose to build on the hill where the ground was rocky and where the slope came down in steps, and he chose the side that faced away from the sea, to protect his family from the ocean winds. There, as he laid the flattened cardboard boxes that would, for now, serve as the floor until he could raise enough funds to lay proper foundations, Julia's father saw in his mind's eye the home that he would build: the steel beams and walls of concrete and windows with actual glass, a door with a lock and a stone path and a facade painted hummingbird blue.

Falling, Julia saw her father's visions of the future from that December morning in 1968 – visions which he failed to see fully realised for he died before the house could be completed. Once he had been buried, it fell to Julia, the eldest of the Álvarez siblings, to make a wage because the windows were still without glass and the roof was still untiled and the twins needed new shoes before they started school in the autumn. And that was how Julia, aged only fifteen but claiming to be eighteen, came, seeking work, to the Echeverría mansion on the hill in 1984, the same month that the municipality of Miraflores finally recognised the shanty town in Los Polvos de Nadie y Nunca (and having not asked the residents what they wanted their neighbourhood to be called, it was simply named Los Polvos and would not be renamed for more than two decades, when an act of communal heroism earned the Polvorinos the right, in the eyes of the mayor, to choose a new title for themselves). When Julia presented herself at the door of the yellow house on the hill, mistaking her queasiness for nerves, she was hired on the spot because Carmen, the cook, could see she was a quiet girl, not given to answering back, and the mistress of the house took pity on her because of the scar on her cheek (which was not, in fact, a scar at all but a birthmark in the shape of a condor in flight).

It was there that Julia Álvarez Yupanqui met the monochrome baby with whom she felt an instant connection, perhaps because they shared the same taciturn wide-eyed glare and the powers of observation that enabled them to see beyond sight but which attracted the scowling consternation of the grown-ups that floated around them – all of the grown-ups, that is, except for Doña Consuelo, who insisted that the two girls, the maid and the baby, were gifted.

With her nose almost at the floor now, Julia thinks of that baby – the baby who is no longer a baby but a silent little girl who sees things and whom Julia calls Ojitos Negros – and she wonders where the child could be. On the journey to come, Julia will learn that there was something out of balance in the child's relationship with pacha, with space and time. The child's inner world was congested to overflowing and yet still greedy, sucking energy from the world of the living and siphoning it into kaylla pacha, the unseen realm behind the veil. It was not sustainable. The child would implode from the gravity of so much past accumulating in her soul. Her burden was not only her own but was tugging on the lives of others and Julia will see, in time, just how many it would affect, before long, if there was no intervention. For now, Julia does not know any of this. When she thinks of the black-eyed child, Julia only hopes that the girl is far from the gruesome scene about to unfold…

What is that sound now? It is only air rushing past her ears. Seconds colliding and erupting into flame. Years bleeding into one another. Decades tussling and epochs rubbing together, firing off sparks. The battle cries of convicts out on El Frontón and, perhaps, machine-gun fire from later tonight rattling backwards to forewarn us.

The spirits of the air begin to panic now and push their visions upon Julia without method, out of turn and frantic. She sees the vast waves of the Atlantic through the eyes of Fernandito Condorcanqui Bastidas as he sails, exiled, to Cádiz. She sees the square of Cajamarca as the conquistadors leap, shrieking, from behind columns towards the gilded litter of Atahualpa. She sees Uriel planing wood and Sarita Colonia languishing in her bed and Don Juan Uybua cleaning his blade.

What she does not see are the two black eyes peering through the geranium leaves or the beetle that scurries away from her shadow or the majolica tiles as the tip of her nose grazes the floor.

On the morning of Wednesday the eighteenth of June in the year 1986, when Julia Álvarez Yupanqui fell from the second floor of the home of her employers, she landed face first and from there everything followed: her spine compressed like a telescope retracting and her organs exploded in bursts of autumnal colour. The coroner who attended the scene would interpret the evidence set before him as indicative of suicide and, in the absence of any witnesses, the incident was recorded as such despite the protestations of Don Julio and Doña Carolina Echeverría, for if the death had been a suicide, the workplace insurance would not make a payout to the deceased girl's family. But to land face first, the coroner asserted, was incontrovertible proof that the plummet had been deliberate and intended to kill: what chance was there otherwise of landing in a manner so perfectly certain to be fatal?

Had anyone been there they would have known that the moment before she hit the ground, Julia exclaimed, *I can't believe it!* But, since she had died utterly alone, an assessment could only be made on the basis of the remains that now decorated the Echeverría house – the mess on the patio, the chunks on the grass and splatters on the facade of lúcuma yellow. No one knew about the anchoveta which had been in Julia's hand when she fell and which might have served as evidence that the girl had been up on the ledge of the second-floor window for some reason other than suicide.

FIVE

I have been here before. How is it possible? Have I only been walking in circles all this time, returning again and again to this same place? But I have been so careful – so methodical. Running my hands along the walls to direct myself in the gloom, I have kept track of the twists and the turns. I tell myself *There should be a left turn now, into the library* or *A right turn now brings me to the ballroom*, but I am always wrong. Where I expect a left turn, the wall gives way to the right. Where I expect a door frame, there is only unyielding brick. And where I expect wall, I find myself stumbling through a sudden partition. Nothing is as it was. But it is not possible for the house to have sprouted new rooms or reshuffled its walls: it is my memory that must be misdrawn.

So again I find myself here in the dining room, shuffling round and round the table in the dim light, squinting to try to see better, leaning against the back of a chair then reaching out with my fingertips for the wall, sliding along, patting the cool surface in search of light switch or door frame or shutter. All this time that I have been scrabbling in the darkness, I have not managed to find my way. And I have been calling and calling – for Q'orianka, for Tía Consuelo – but have had no reply.

Earlier, fleetingly, I thought I heard a little voice singing 'Happy Birthday', but it was only in my head – a hallucination, induced by the house and the memory of sudden darkness. When the Shining

Path stole our light, Julia and the other empleadas would light candles by which to see and Leandro, thinking it a game, would sing and try to blow them out and ask Carmen for birthday cake. It was his voice I heard. Thought I heard. In reality, no one was singing.

As I wander around, finding my way by touch and not by sight, I am alone. Only Inti-Killa calls out to me in his strangled screams, but always from far away no matter how much I try to follow and seek out his noise. The poor, darling, pathetic little monster. How long did it take for him to realise I was not coming back? Has he been screaming for me all these years? In London, I was certain I heard him sometimes, in the screech of underground trains coming to a halt or in the tormented squalls of midnight foxes. I believed, sometimes, that he had found me – that he had dragged his mangled form across continents to curl himself against my chest again and quiver there with his stertorous breathing. But he had not found me. What I mistook for his screams were always something else – the wind howling, car brakes squealing, a baby's cry – and then I would miss him and the space between my breasts felt hollow and cold.

I remember when Abue found the creature: it was a few hours old, hairless and still slick with maternal juices, dumped in a yucca pot by its horrified mother and left to roast in the sun. It was clearly a runt, just a tangled knot of livid flesh with bulbous veins, able only to squirm, restricted by the enormous weight of its two heads. Abue wrapped the thing in his handkerchief and took it to the kitchen, where he rolled it out onto a plate and summoned us all to inspect the curiosity.

We gathered around, enthralled by the ugliness of the creature splayed there like a plucked bird. Writhing, piscine, it painted hieroglyphs of blood and faeces on the china and from one head emitted murine screeches while from the other head it croaked in a broken little voice like a toad.

Carmen, the cook, was furious. 'Don Julio! You could at least have used a napkin! How can any of us ever eat off that dish again?'

'Is it a Martian?' Leandro asked.

'It's a cat,' I said. 'Look at its paws, its little tail.'

'¡Caramba! It's hardly more than a menstrual clot.' This was Tío Raúl's diagnosis, with the authority of twenty years of medical practice. 'Smash it and put it out of its misery.'

'Do not kill it!' Tía María Dolores smacked her son. 'It is alive now. Whether it lives or dies is in God's hands. Let us leave it and see what happens.'

'Without a mother it will die before nightfall,' Tío Raúl forecast.

But I was determined that the thing would not die. While Carmen and the men searched for an implement with which to kill the creature, I stole it – plate and all – and carried it to my room. With a warm, wet flannel I groomed the monster, wiping the slime from its chicken skin. Then, with a roll of bandage from Raúl's medical bag, I fashioned a sling and strapped the creature to my chest where, at first, it felt cold and clammy, like a dead thing between my budding pubescent breasts, but over the hours it began to draw from my heat and writhe and nestle. It nuzzled its heads against my ribs and tried to suckle, biting at my skin, sometimes piercing, drawing blood, leaving desperate little love bites that gave it no sustenance.

To feed it, I milked the mother cats that lounged around the patio lactating smugly in the sun and nursed the two heads through syringes that I stole from Tía Consuelo. When it grew a little, I fed it meat and fish that I saved from my own meals, chewed to a pulp, spat out and then rubbed onto the two mouths so the creature would get used to the taste.

In the beginning, too weak to carry the weight of its deformity, all the thing could do was squirm on its bed of torn-up rags in the corner of my room and squawk out to me its needs. When it soiled itself, I wiped it clean. When it was hungry, I put food in its mouth. When it was thirsty, I moistened its lips.

But slowly it gained enough strength in its limbs to carry itself clumsily around. It was then that the battle with itself began. Eating was a torment because, while both heads – locked at a forty-five-degree angle – jostled and strained against each other, the ants devoured its meal. When the croaking head wanted to sleep, the screeching head wanted to play; while this head preferred daytime, the other preferred night.

The only thing on which the heads seemed to agree was their devotion to the one who had rescued them. While none of the other kittens would play with it, hissing if it drew near, the creature fused itself to me. It stalked me devotedly around the house. Wherever I went, the two heads followed, butting themselves against my legs. When my family learned I was the one who had stolen the thing – for they had assumed it had been carried away and eaten by ants or perhaps by a large bird of prey – they were appalled. But by then the beast had grown fur – a mottled blend of ginger and grey on its body, with one head in either colour – and had a name, so it could not be euthanised. On Carmen's suggestion, I had named it Inti-Killa, Sun-Moon, and in the absence of evidence either way I decided that It was a He. I taught him to respond to Inki for short and trained him to sit on my shoulder, where he sucked on my earlobe and purred when my loved ones were near and hissed at those I did not like.

Today, as I have wandered in circles, getting nowhere, I have heard Inki crying for me from somewhere deep in the bowels of the house and I am gripped by a churning guilt for abandoning the creature that no one else learned to love. The night I left I remember looking up from the garden steps to see him sitting at the window, Inti sleeping and Killa watching me with wide trusting blue eyes.

My guilt feels like hunger, boring a hole so palpable in my stomach that I expect a gaping chasm to appear in my abdomen. But a yawning hollow in my torso would never placate the Tías: they would seek to fill it with marzipan fruits and paper flowers and icons of the saints. They would plug the hole, perhaps with a cage of Amazonian songbirds or an aquarium of tropical fishes. Lord, let us not tolerate the abyss within. Make me a walking display case for a howling menagerie.

Wail no more, Inki. Your mother has returned. I will find you. But first I must find my way out of this dining room that seems so eager to swallow me up. I must find a door, an exit, a source of light. I must go round the room and check again. Round and round and round.

Is it always this way with places we have loved? We visit them in our dreams – how many times? – and trace our way through the rooms in our mind. We imagine ourselves standing in the hall and feel the space around us. We know – we think we know – how many steps there are until the stairs and where exactly to turn to reach this room or that. We practise going through the place – here is the sitting room, here the kitchen, here the cupboard where we keep the coats. But there are details missing – the height of the ceilings, perhaps, or the size of the tiles. What colour was the paint in this dining room? And was the floor wooden or paved? I can't remember… I can't remember at all… In this darkness I cannot guess the colour of the walls, but I can bend down and feel the floor under my fingers… I can press against it with my palm and find out its nature by touch…

Yes. Tiles. Cool and smooth.

Yes, the dining-room floor is tiled – I remember now, sitting silent under the dining table, the cool ceramic pressed against my naked legs, hiding – but from whom? From doctors? No, not from doctors. From someone within the household… Yes, that's right: from María Dolores and her enormous wooden crucifix. Perhaps she is there now, the child, still hiding underneath the dust sheet, trying hard to sit perfectly still, to turn to stone, straining in vain to hear the approach of the hard-eyed Tía who moved around the house as silently as a shadow and carried a vial of holy water in her pocket so that, whenever she saw a cat, she could flick the cleansing liquid at it and proclaim in a sonorous voice that it was free of demonic possession. Whenever she crossed me in the hall she would make me recite the Nicene Creed on pain of a swipe across the calves with her rosary beads if I stumbled over my words. She made me anxious about speaking. Made me associate misspeaking with pain and shame.

In the distance – much, much further away than the far wall of the dining room – I see a flickering light approaching as if floating across a stretch of black water. Transfixed, I watch as it emits shards and planes of light and the air around it seems to warp and bend, buckle and collapse. They are coming for me. They are coming to distort things for me and fold me up. I will not let them. I will press myself against this wall and feel its firm coolness against my cheek, my neck. I will plant my feet firmly on the ground. I will not let them come and fold me into myself because, once it starts, the folding inwards does not stop: with the subsidence comes the slippage and with the slippage comes the infinite regress. I will not regress. I must not.

But it is not, thank God, they who come towards me out of the gloom – it is only Q'orianka, dressed in a long white nightgown, arms stretched out, palms up, a candle in one hand. Her braided raven hair, meandering serpentine over one shoulder, glitters with silvery strands that were not there when I saw her last.

'Niñachay.' She cups my cheek with one hand. 'You are here. And you bring with you your pequeño fish.'

In the iridescent light of her candle, the skin of the little pink fish has become translucent and I see its skeleton floating luminous in the dark, its dorsal fin pulsing electrically, its eyes two black holes.

'You see the fish?' I ask her.

She looks me up and down as she strokes my cheek with her thumb.

'You are dressed like a massacre.'

She is right. By her light I can see myself now, hair tangled and matted, skirt torn, blouse smeared with blood and greenery.

'Vomitastes,' she adds, wiping my chin with her sleeve and shaking her head.

The squall of Inti-Killa reverberates through the house.

'Inti-Killa has been screaming more than usual today,' she says. 'He sensed you were coming.'

'I heard the screams when I came in. Perhaps Inki did not want me to return?'

'He wanted you. But sometimes, niñachay, seeing again the ones we have missed is a torment. It exhumes pain from the bones.'

'I am surprised Inki is still alive.'

'I am not sure he is. I hear him always screaming but I never find him.'

She sets down the candle and tells me, 'Ven, niñachay.' She leads me through the house, which seems to obey her, rooms slotting back into their proper places, complying with the map inside my brain. I half-expect she will take me to the ballroom where she will sing 'Valicha' to me as she waxes the parquet in concentric circles while I lie in the centre and fall asleep under Noah's ark, hypnotised by the fumes of the varnish.

No, she does not take me there. Nor to the library, where the literary vandalism of the man in the library got me branded destructive. Nor to the kitchen, where Julia taught me to play cat's cradle with packing twine and Mamabue made shadow puppets dance across the walls with their hands. She takes me out to the patio, where night has fallen. But it was morning when I crossed the threshold – have I really been wandering, cyclically, this empty house since then?

As we climb the stairs, the moon casts its light in a silver beam on the many-headed fountain, redundant now. Its twelve monsters that always glistened, slick with the waters that never stopped running, are dry and cracked as they watch me, their mouths hanging open, empty, gaping – this one as if yawning, that one petrified in a tortured scream, another one twisted in maniacal laughter.

She's back.

God help us.

Took her time.

That's not her.

Of course it's her.

How can you tell?

Just look at her:
Covered in dirt. Caked in blood.
It's certainly her.

God help us.

She leads me along the balcony above the patio. We pass bedrooms upon bedrooms, each door firmly closed. What lies behind? I picture shrouded furniture and Limenian dust allowed to accumulate into mounds and dunes but, intruding on my desolate pictures, I see in each room a relative – a forgotten Tío or long-dead Titi – sitting, waiting, patient and pensive, on the edge of a bed, head hung, hands folded, or leaning back in an armchair, stroking their chin. They are waiting for me. They have been waiting all this time, for me, behind locked doors.

Abruptly Q'ori stops, fiddles with the bundle of keys hanging at her waist. She asks me about the house, whether it is being sold.

'I don't know,' I say. 'Not yet. Not today.'

'You are staying here?'

Perhaps Q'orianka does not want me here. Perhaps she prefers the solitude and not having someone else to look after. Will it be a problem to her if I stay?

'No, niña. Not a problem.'

Perhaps she already had plans? For after the sale of the house? Perhaps she has somewhere else she needs to be?

'No plans. Verdad is better for me to be here. My sister and mother live there below en Los Polvos. Here I am close to them.'

A shadow darts across the patio below – a cat, or a pigeon taking flight. Nothing more. Not a toddling infant rubbing her head, endlessly reciting *Sana, sana*. Certainly not a wailing jilted lover rending his shirt, ripping through the cotton like a madman and drinking himself into a stupor. Not an elegant Don and Doña floating from room to room in their evening dress seeking players for an eternal game of Dudo. It would not and could not be these things. It was a cat. It was Inti-Killa. It was a stray dog that has hobbled in to find shelter for the night.

By the wrist, Q'orianka pulls me into the room she has unlocked and, once again, into the darkness.

'No hay corriente en la casa,' she tells me. 'Tomorrow you will have to get them to switch on the power.'

I woke to the chattering of pigeons. The shutters had been opened and, in the axes of light cast by the morning sun, the dust particles were dancing. I had slept in a room I did not recognise, on a four-poster bed still draped with dust sheets, under a fur coat for a blanket and not in my own clothes. I vaguely remembered rifling around for something to wear, my hand falling on what felt like chain mail. I must have put it on, half-sleeping already, because it was wrapped around me now – a beaded evening gown, far too long for me, belonging to some willowy ancestress or other, still smelling faintly of coffee, cigarettes and Shalimar by Guerlain.

Wandering around the casona barefoot, dragging the beaded hems of the dress behind me, I searched for a place to wash, but, when I opened the taps, no water flowed – only a rumbling as if the very bones of the house were groaning. In the kitchen, the pipes clunked and chimed, while out on the servants' terrace, the outdoor taps spluttered, with great effort urinated an impotent trickle of tawny discharge, and then dried up altogether.

Q'orianka was nowhere to be found: not in the kitchen, where a chinchilla was taking a dust bath in a mound of kiwicha that had spilled onto the floor from a shattered Mason jar; not in the library, into which a stray dog, golden, with one ear torn and a weeping eye, had found his way and was now reclining on a writing desk, spreadeagled, licking a festering wound on his flank; not in the ballroom, which I found had already been claimed by the Pacífico foreman (confident, I suppose, that I would sign the papers without fuss) as a storage bunker for concrete blocks and pneumatic drills and enormous iron girders, which had been stacked into a pyramid directly under the chandelier.

They would be back today, I told myself. Mimi and Pulpo and the workmen would be back with the papers, certain that – as Mimi had prophesied – I lacked the fortitude to cope with a house where the pipes weren't working and the electrics were down. They would come with thinly veiled smugness and insincere sympathy – *Poor child, you just wanted things to be as they were* – and coax me into signing.

No. I would show them. When they came for me, I would not be in. Or, if they found me at home, it would be in the comfort of a house with lighting and running water: I would be reclining out on the patio, my hair freshly washed, a glass of something hanging lazily, precariously, from my hand, music playing from Tía Consuelo's bedroom window and the bubbling of the waters from the many-headed fountain heralding the return of power. *Oh, it's you*, I would say. *Well, good. I've decided: I think I'll stay awhile…*

I had to walk the length of the Avenida del Guanero in my abuela's shoes to hail a cab. Q'orianka having disappeared with my clothes, I had been forced to scavenge: the shirt, a man's, gently greying, I found hanging from the line on the servants' terrace; the slacks, mustard yellow, probably women's but ambiguous, folded in a trunk, the only item not gnawed to threads by moths. The shoes, maroon leather, tarnished buckles on the toes, had been kicked into a corner and there gathered a coat of silt and spiders' webs, and the hat, a cloche in pea-green felt, hung from a nail in the wall near the front door.

On the Avenida del Ejército I hailed a cab to take me to the power company's offices in Surquillo. As the driver pulled up outside the building, blocking the street instead of parking alongside the kerb, I reached out of habit for my handbag – but it was not there. Q'orianka must have taken it along with the rest of my clothes. I realised, stupidly, for the first time, that I had no money with me. No money, no cards, no phone.

Behind us the traffic was backing up, horns blaring, shouted insults, lights flashing. I patted myself down frantically. In the pocket of the shirt I wore, I found a couple of crumbling cigarettes and a crumpled business card for El Haití at Parque Kennedy. Weakened by decades of humidity, they disintegrated in my hands. The driver, impatient, turned in his seat to look at me just as I allowed the dust to fall from my fingers to the floor of his car. His body was wiry, his face angular. His movements were quick, like the jerks and twitches of a bird, not nervous but exaggerated, as if each gesture were born of a sudden flash of genius, unique to him, and had to be tested out immediately. He had a habit of suddenly flicking his nose with his thumb and simultaneously raising his eyebrows in a way that suggested he saw everything as a joke. A joke to which the rest of the world was not privy. He did this now as he watched me down the sharp bridge of his nose.

His air of rakish confidence unnerved me. I thrust my hands into the pockets of the slacks and there found a lipstick, a two-piece pack of Adams Chiclets and a five-hundred-inti note. I held them out to him in the palm of my hand, and as I did it, I had a sense I had done it before. I hadn't, of course. The slacks, the lipstick, the candies, the note – none of them were mine.

'Are you joking, señora? That note isn't worth anything.'

'It's all I have...'

Directly behind us a combi full of passengers waited, its engine shuddering; in the rear-view mirror I could see the llamador hanging from the doorway by one hand, cursing us with the other, hollering insults that reached us in snippets between the roar of the klaxons and the grinding of gears as traffic piled to a halt. From every side, heads and fists emerged from car windows and dark eyes watched us under furrowed brows. Men wiped the backs of their necks with rags and ladies in back seats fanned themselves while the little pink fish, grown to the size of a guppy overnight, swooped and tilted in my eyeline, darting in and out among the heads and eyes and shaking fists.

The taxista threatened to summon the serenazgo, and I imagined being hauled off to jail and not knowing whom to telephone with my one phone call, because how could I call Mimi and Pulpo, even if I knew their number by heart, without making myself play the role of naughty child? I knew no one's numbers here, except that of la Casa Echeverría, where the lines were still down. Would I have to ask the guards for a copy of the páginas amarillas, run my finger down the pages of Echeverrías and hope that someone was home? How awful to have to leave a message with an empleada – *Please tell Tía Nosecuentos to come and collect her incarcerated niece from Santa Monica de Chorrillos*. What humiliation. The Titis would never forgive me.

I patted myself down again, conscious it was in vain, but hoping that my fingers would brush against something I had overlooked. As if my skin might germinate coins under my clothes. *Here, señor. The fare has spawned from my body.* But no. Not today.

A crowd was gathering on the pavement to watch the chaos. The taxista began to wind down his window, his eyes fixed on a serenazgo a little distance away. I reached out and clutched his arm; I explained to him my predicament – the empty, power-less house; its imminent sale; my missing clothes; how long I had been away and how I had concocted this mismatched outfit from the cast-offs of my ancestors… If he could only be patient and wait for me here while I dealt with the electrics then he could take me to the Vivaldi and there I could pay him for his kindness. In dollars. I had dollars in the bags. Would that be acceptable? Should we say cincuenta dolares por su tiempo?

At the mention of dollars he paused, his hand sticking out of the window, poised to gesture for the serenazgo but not moving. I was always a terrible negotiator, starting where I would like to end up and then getting corralled into agreements that I could never abide. By the age of five Leandro had learned how to work me, outbidding me and tricking me out of toys and desserts and, no matter how much the Don tried to teach me how to bluff, playing endless card games with me at the dining-room table, I never got the hang of wrangling a deal.

The driver examined me through squinted eyes. Could I be believed? Was the chance of fifty dollars worth the risk that I was a swindler and would pay nothing? What was fifty dollars to him? We made the mental calculations simultaneously... What was the exchange rate? At three to one that made – how much? – one hundred and fifty soles. And how much must a taxista earn each day? Ten soles for a half hour's journey…if he works ten hours… two hundred soles…and how much does fuel cost these days? Then there's insurance, if he has any, and repairs and car depreciation and—

'You say you have dollars?'

'In my luggage, at the hotel.'

The combista behind us leaned on his horn with his elbow, emitting a dissonant, brassy blast, and drew the attention of the serenazgo. The combi passengers were leaning out of the windows up to their waists, shaking their heads, waving their fists at me, calling out—

'One hundred.'

'¿Perdón?'

'One hundred dollars. For my time.'

'I'm not paying you one hundred dollars!'

The taxista leaned out the window and shouted to the serenazgo.

'All right, all right! Seventy-five!'

'¿Qué demonios pasa aquí?'

The serenazgo leaned over, resting his hands on his knees, peering in through the window at me with one eye shut and one eye squinting. He was examining me as if I were a specimen behind glass.

'Please, señor!'

I begged the driver, hiding my face from the enquiring gaze of the serenazgo as if shielding my eyes from the sun.

'I said I'd pay you seventy-five.'

'Eighty,' he said, leaning his wrist lazily on the half-retracted window. He knew he had won. I was always a terrible negotiator. Nothing changes.

'Eighty, then.'

He smiled and nodded, told the serenazgo everything was fine, it was just a bit of confusion, the señora had forgotten where she was going, but we had sorted it now. There was no trouble. We would be on our way.

He parked down a side street, fixed the lock to the steering wheel and accompanied me inside the building of Inti-lectrica, taking me by the arm, feigning dedication and concern. He wanted to be *helpful*, señora: I'd been away a long time and Lima had *changed* a great deal. He knew how things *worked* in this city. He could make himself *useful*.

Of course, we both knew that above all he wanted to be sure I didn't try to fool him by running off. He wasn't one to be fleeced, to be left sitting like a fool in his car with the engine running, burning money as if it were nothing, waiting for someone who had no intention of returning. Within the hour he would abandon me of his own accord, declaring me a lunatic, relinquishing his claim to eighty dollars as hopeless. I feel guilty about it now: how much fuel did he waste to drive me around? How many passengers did he forego to wait as I dithered? No matter. He made his choice on the evidence that lay before him. And, for him, all the signs were there that I was mad.

*

'Do you have identity?'

Do I have identity? A profound question. All I wanted was the electricity turned on… I hadn't expected an interrogation, an exploration of the self. Do I have identity? Well, I – I – I –

The attendant was not patient with me. Her eyes, enormous, magnified behind thick spectacles, were restless, eyelids flickering as if she was struggling to hold them up under the weight of mascara that had congealed and turned her lashes to thorns, like the barbs on the lips of carnivorous plants. On her left eyeball, a red vein branched out from her iris, like a river seen from above – or a lightning bolt, angular, scratching its way. Back and forth, back and forth, her eyeballs shivered, distracting me from my thoughts, from my search for – what was it? – identity, she said.

'Your national identity document. Do you have it?'

She was vexed. It was a simple question. My DNI. Did I have it? No. I had never had it. My mother, presumably, had received it on my behalf, but I had never been given it. Had I? No. I was certain.

'You have no DNI? No passport?'

No, I have a passport, I assured her. But not on my person. It was in my bags, at the hotel. The Hotel Vivaldi. In Miraflores.

She rolled her eyes so far back that her irises disappeared. She reminded me just then of the paintings of saints in the throes of martyrdom, their eyes rolling towards the heavens. I understood her frustration: she was suspicious as I stood there attired like a dusty clown, nervously fidgeting, hands gesticulating wildly and then burrowing deep into my pockets, a man twitching jauntily at my elbow, I unable to give her any proof of my identity, not even able to tell her the address of the property because I knew neither its postcode nor its door number since I had never learned them. To my memory it had always been enough to simply cite la Casa Echeverría. *Ah, yes,* people would say, *the yellow house on the hill. Yes, yes, we know the one.*

'Vaya, señorita,' the taxista urged her. 'You know it; everyone knows it.'

But, no, she did not know it. La Casa Echeverría meant nothing to her. She was immovable, her fingers hovering over the keyboard, her lips pursed: she needed ID papers *and* the property address to be able to switch on the power. And really, señora, how was it possible I didn't know my address? Did I live at the property?

I tried to explain as I had done to the taxista – how I'd arrived the day before, no, that's not right, the day before that, to return to a childhood home without light, without water and—

She wasn't listening. She didn't care. She shivered her head as if trying to shake away the vision of something disgusting – a cockroach flying towards her, a weeping sore – and her eyes rolled back into her skull several times like a doll's.

The taxista took over. In his petition, he was glib – obviously so – but the rising and falling singsong of his voice and the mournful extension of his vowels made his expression quiver between plaintive and lyrical. *¡Ve-e-enga, señori-i-ita, sé bueni-i-ita!* Surely she would not, *señori-i-ita*, leave the woman without light, without power? How would she see? Or cook? Or contact her family, *señori-i-ita*, her children (he invented children for me) so far away in England?

Her reply came smilingly, her lashes flickering now not in impatience but flirtation. She fingered the ends of the red-white silk scarf knotted around her neck, rubbed the embroidered sun badge, the emblem of the Inti-lectrica brand, between her finger and thumb. They were playing a game, she and the driver – a game at which I was not skilled.

He continued: if he took me to the hotel to collect my passport, we could return within the hour. Surely then something could be done? Quizás, she replied. But she would need to see bank statements too, to be sure I could pay. And at any rate, we would have to be quick: they were closing in an hour. In an hour? Seriously? But it was only eleven in the morning! Yes, they were closing in an hour. It was Friday, and on Fridays they closed at noon. He was undeterred: but surely señorita could wait for us a little after closing time? Surely she could do that. As a special favour, for him? Otherwise the poor woman (I had become a 'poor woman') would have to wait until Monday, and certainly the señorita – the kind and lovely señorita – would not put the señora through an entire weekend without power?

They spoke as if above me, arranging my day, my comings and goings, fixing the matters I could not manage for myself. I stood with my hands clasped over my belly, protectively, ashamedly, like a schoolgirl awaiting punishment – like all those years ago when the nuns, the doctors, the Tías discussed me over my head as if I were absent, or the fact of my presence were no matter.

'You have to know how to work people,' the taxista told me as he led me back to his car with a hand on my lower back. Already he was too familiar, too proprietary. I seem to have that effect on people.

At the Hotel Vivaldi, he was less confident, loitering a few steps behind me instead of at my elbow the way he had before. His sudden tics turned to preening: he wiped his ear repeatedly on his shoulder, ran his fingers through his hair, examined his nails, jagged and tooth-cut. He seemed to want to hide his sandalled feet, positioning himself behind chairs, and vigor-ously rubbed his bare arms, exposed by the short sleeves of his button-down khaki shirt. As the guests came and went through the revolving doors, he would avoid their gaze, flick his nose and sniff.

The concierge at the front desk was the one I had encountered two nights before, no longer glassy-eyed with sleep but awake, urbane and smiling, attending to guests with fluid, practised move-ments, swiping key cards, pointing out directions with a flourish of the fingers, listening to enquiries with his head tilted at an empathetic angle, his wrists resting delicately on the edge of the desk the way my mother had taught us was the elegant manner to sit at table.

I waited a few steps away: far enough to give the impression I could not hear the conversations between the concierge and the other guests, but close enough to know they were all playing the game – making unreasonable demands with confidence, whether in the melodic inflections of Peruvian plaint or in the confident low tones of the North American businessman.

And then it was my turn to petition. I was here to collect my luggage: four suitcases, a carry-on. I forced a smile; the concierge did not. He turned his body slowly towards the computer but kept his eyes on me until the last second, when, at last, he suddenly snatched up his wrists and began to type frantically. He took my name, typed some more, furrowed his brow in concentration and occasionally flicked his eyes up to examine me, to examine the taxista behind me, then back to staring at the screen, which cast an anaemic light on his face.

'There is no record of you,' he said.

'But there must be.'

'There is none.'

'But I was here only yesterday…'

He tutted and ran a flattened palm over his slick, shining hair, side-parted in the old style. 1920s? 1940s?

'Room number?'

Of course, I had forgotten. On which floor had I stayed? And on which side? Facing the sea, certainly: I remembered speaking to the whale, but nothing that could give a more precise location. The concierge frowned.

Try another name, I suggested. I had given 'Rose Gest' the first time – the name under which I had, or thought I had, made the booking. Try Anaïs, I told him. Anaïs Gest.

A sudden spurt of typing. Manic fingers, frenzied appendages bursting from hands, wrists, arms that were otherwise completely still. Fingers that seemed to have life and will of their own, entirely apart from the rigid attendant whose eyes were fixed on me, interrogating, suspicious.

But no: there was no record of an Anaïs Gest either.

Try Echeverría, I told him. Anaïs and/or Rose Echeverría. I had many names, I explained – apologised. It was my parents' fault! They couldn't decide, you see, when I was born… I tried to make it light, to make a joke, laughing doubtfully, trying to imitate the singing cadence I had seen the taxi driver use with the electric girl. *¡Los padres! ¿No es así-i-i?* Instead, what came from my mouth was not the charmingly mournful lilt of the *taxista* but a quivering, squeaking glissando.

There was no Echeverría (Rose or Anaïs or otherwise) and there was no record of a Gest either, he said, so perhaps it would be best if the *señora* would stop wasting his time, so that he could attend to the other guests who were waiting, and he gestured over my shoulder at the huddle that was beginning to form.

You saw me, I wanted to say. I stood before you in my robe in the middle of the night and you looked straight at me. But, of course, he had not seen me at all – if he had, it was only as a fleeting figure in his dreams. Still, I wanted to grab his shoulders, pick him up from the floor and shake him until he saw sense. I had *been here*. It was fact, undeniable and true. I had placed my hands on this desk, smoothed out the guestbook, seen myself reflected in the mirrors. I had been here: I wanted him to understand that. To confirm it and, in so confessing, make it truer – make the past fact present and solid and incontrovertible. What could I say to him to make him understand? That I had cut myself on the key card, and that here, on my own flesh, I still bore the mark? That I had stuffed my pockets with the Hotel Vivaldi candies? That I had kissed the orchids…? Yes, the orchids: I had kissed them. I would tell him that. This wasn't the sort of evidence a fraudster would invent. Its implausibility would make it plausible…

I looked to the embroidered badge on his lapel to remind myself of his name – using names fosters trust, so I've been told – and there I read *Ricardo*.

Ricardo? Hadn't it been Javier two nights ago? Or was I mis-remembering? Perhaps it had indeed been Javier but was now, for some perfectly rational reason, Ricardo. Perhaps the name badges were entirely arbitrary – a moniker simply to give the guests an illusion of relationship. To give the guests something to call out instead of *¡Oye, camarero!* Or perhaps the tin soldier of two nights ago was Javier and this seemingly identical concierge was not in fact Javier but another (a Ricardo) and downstairs there were a dozen others, replicas, all copies, rotating one after another after another, each with different names to give the semblance of humanity – Javier, Ricardo, Héctor, Juan…

No, forget about the names. They are unimportant. What matters is the orchids, I told myself. The orchids: I had kissed them. But looking around myself I saw that there were no orchids in the foyer – only lilies. Flawless, milky white calla lilies towering out of tall, slim glass vases. They had not been there two days before: there had been only orchids. I was certain.

'There is no record of you here, señora,' he repeated, gesturing for me to step aside.

The taxista was furious, spasming wildly, heaving his shoulders and flicking at his nose, his eyebrow, his chin. Qué demonios was going on here? What the hell kind of a dodge was I trying to pull? If I was trying to learn the game of artimaña I was doing a pretty shitty job of it. Or maybe I was just loca, maniática, unhinged and unstable. Well, whatever was going on, he wasn't waiting around: he was leaving. And he did.

He had accused me of artimaña: of the art of manual dexterity. Of sleight of hand and cunning. But also of arte-manía, the art of mania, obsession and madness. For there is artistry to both. This was not the first time I had stood so accused – of lunacy and trickery, of guile and of hysteria – and I wondered, as I stood alone in the foyer of the Hotel Vivaldi, surrounded by lilies, not orchids, whether I had lost my sense. My sense of time, at least. Was it possible I had miscalculated? Was it possible I had been at the house not just one night but several? That the jet lag had got the better of me and I had slept through a number of days? But, no, the day today was Friday. And I had landed on (when was it?) a Wednesday. I could not, surely, have slept through an entire week?

The little fish pulsated in time with my heart, obscuring entirely, in a wash of salmon, the vision from my right eye. With half the world shrouded in pink, I struggled to walk straight, veering to my left, avoiding out of instinct that which I could not see, protecting myself from the unknown. In this manner, circuitously, I meandered towards the doors and, nauseated and unsteady, I watched them revolve several times before I could bring myself to pass through them into the street.

Once outside, I stood, ignored by the doormen and the valets, wringing my hands, my entrails writhing. *No luggage, no money, no papers, no phone.* I recited this to myself and, in its rhythm, there was some comfort. I repeated and repeated the words until they lost meaning: no longer ciphers of my hopelessness, they became empty shells of sound, a talisman, a spell, to ward off the panic that buzzed a little above my head. To busy my fingers – and to delay the tremors that I could already feel crawling down from my shoulders just a little way below my skin – I used them to tap out the rhythm on my thighs. *No luggage, no money, no papers, no phone. No luggage, no money, no papers, no phone.* To each finger, a syllable, until they had all tapped out an equal number of beats, and then I paused, looked around, started again. *No luggage, no money, no papers, no phone.* It was imperative not to mis-tap – to get the rhythm exactly right. I took it slowly; I concentrated. To go wrong would mean certain catastrophe, like stepping on a crack in the pavement. *No luggage, no money, no papers, no phone.* Take it slowly; get it right.

Until the sudden calling out of my name interrupted my focus and a man in a suit, a manager at the Hotel Vivaldi, tumbled out of the revolving doors to catch me.

His words staggered and slid over each other: he was so sorry, so terribly sorry, about Javier (yes, it was Javier after all!). He was new to the staff. He had started only a few days before and didn't yet understand the computer booking system. Of course I had stayed there, only the night before last, and my luggage had been taken care of, looked after so very carefully, so scrupulously carefully. Would I accept his apologies, señora?

It occurred to me then, as he stood before me gabbling, that I had been called señora all day today, first by the taxista, then by the electric girl, also by Javier the concierge, and now by this manager. I looked down at my hands to see if I was wearing the Napier engagement ring, an emblem that in the eyes of a Peruvian would transform me from señorita to señora, but no, I was not. My hands were bare. Scratched and scarred by key cards and thorns, but otherwise bare. Why then call me señora? Had I aged so drastically in my two days in Lima? Perhaps there was something in the air of the casa that had drained me. I had a sudden urge to see my reflection – to check that my hair had not fallen out, that my skin had not puckered and my eyes had not faded with the clouds of age. I touched my face with my fingertips, then held my hands out to examine them for wrinkles or sunspots or bulging veins.

Seeing me examine my hands, he apologised, corrected himself, called me *Señorita* Echeverría, and apologised again.

It must have been my clothes. In a shirt that had not seen use since the days of Herbert Hoover and a pair of slacks whose pockets had not been emptied since Alan García had been in power (the first time), I was a mishmash of eras and difficult to date. I could be seventeen or seventy-five. It was not his fault.

My bags. That's all I wanted now, I told him. Nothing else mattered.

'But señorita, we do not have your bags. They were taken this morning.'

'Taken? By whom?'

They were sent for, he told me. I had called the hotel that morning, early, and informed them that my relatives would be attending to collect my things and, a little later, the relatives had come, had signed a receipt and had taken everything – the suitcases, the carry-on...

I could have berated him. Could have demanded an account of the events and compensation. Filed a complaint with the Vivaldi head office in wherever. But what use was that? My luggage had already been taken, I guessed, by Mimi and Pulpo as a means of reminding me of my incompetence, my dependence. Without them I was helpless. Cast off. Utterly bereft, without luggage or money or papers or phone. And so I did not scold the manager. I simply let him thrust a copy of the receipt into my hands, and then I left.

I felt calmer as I walked back to the house, folding and refolding absent-mindedly the signed bit of paper in my hands. There was a perfectly rational explanation for it all: the concierge – he who had made me feel so worthless – was inept. The fact of my presence had not been erased from the face of time. I had not imagined my stay at the Hotel Vivaldi. My memory could be relied upon and so could the means of its corroboration – computer records and such. The occurrences of the past, the things we have done or not done, are not so easily malleable.

But if time does not bend, how is it that they can still all be sitting here at the dining table? How is it that the house's lúcuma facade, pristine in the morning, can be weather-beaten and crumbling by the afternoon? I left it, only a few hours ago, immaculate, the virgin paint unmarked, unspoiled. I returned to it and the shutters swung dangerously from their hinges, the paint peeled off in strips as large as handbills, while the roof yawned, black holes like missing teeth where the tiles had slid away and shattered on the dusty patio below.

From outside the gates, I looked in, mesmerised, enchanted by the house's decrepit splendour. Across and over and around the gates, the greenery had returned in force, closing the gap through which I had slipped not four hours earlier. Vines as thick as arms weaved in and out of the iron bars so tightly as to warp the metal into the serpentine curvature of human spines.

Tethered to the vines with a length of plastic ribbon knotted messily, hurriedly, was a plastic wallet stuffed with papers – the papers for me to sign, marked with heavy red X's where my name was expected, no, *demanded*. They had been here, then, and found me absent. Or perhaps they had not even been able to pass beyond the gates. I imagined them fumbling, frustrated at being beaten by foliage, kicking stem and root, resorting to abandoning the papers there for me to discover, bird-pecked and shit-stained.

I wandered for some time back and forth, back and forth, along the length of the front of the property, trying to find a way in through the undergrowth and, failing, I floated for some time around the abandoned building sites, where I found a collection of saw blades, worn, half-blunted and thrown aside into the dirt. With these, I hacked my way through the weeds and crawled into the grounds.

There, I found my belongings, thrown over the gates, piece by piece, strewn across the garden: underwear in the bushes, shoes among the geraniums, garments splayed spreadeagled across the grass, while the stray dog from the library, the gash on its flank still oozing, sniffed around. I watched the dog scrabbling, pawing at the lawn, scratching the tree roots a little. I half-heard the clattering of pots and pans and Julia's voice: *¡Basta! ¡Basta! Out of here!* But the dog did not hear her: he turned his ass to me and brandished his bulging testicles. Then he squatted and deposited an enormous pile of faeces, slick and oleaginous in the sunlight. He smelled it, satisfied, cast me a derisory glance with his healthy eye and then stalked away, balls swinging. Soon, then, there were flies – many flies – nestling in the shit.

Ani?

Ani?

Through the trees I heard a voice, distant but distinct. *Ani? Ani?* Only Rupert calls me that. He was there! He had followed me all the way from London. Just like him to worry, to check on me. Usually, I would have been vexed – he hadn't trusted me, had expected me to fail – but in that moment I was relieved. He would rescue me. He would sort out the electricity, the water. He would take care of the Tías.

I followed his voice through the garden. *Ani? Ani? Are you there?*

'Yes! Yes, Rupert, I'm over here!'

There was something strange about his voice, a new tone, something tinny and cold.

I searched for him everywhere, right the way around the house, all the time chasing his voice as it got louder, then thinner, closer and then distant. There seemed to be no logic to its fluctuations. He must be moving as well, I reasoned, and I called out to him to stay still, that I would find him if he stayed in one place.

At last I found him, hidden among the bushes. Not him, but his voice, calling from the mobile phone which had been flung, along with the rest of my belongings, into the undergrowth.

'Rupert? Hello!'

'Ani? Ani? Hello? Are you there?'

He couldn't hear me: the line was bad. It crackled and hissed and his voice faded away, then returned voluminous, rising and falling, metallic and harsh. I looked at the phone, turned it over in my hands. Was there a way to fix it? If there was, I wouldn't know it. I tried tapping it, shaking it, wiping the dirt from its smashed screen, and, on the cracked glass, I cut my finger: a tiny shard like a lightning bolt embedded itself in my skin. Disgusted, I flung the phone away and it bounced against the patio tiles and skidded into the wall of the house, silencing Rupert's voice entirely.

Immediately, I regretted it. Without power in the house, I could have used that phone. What would I do now over the course of an entire weekend? Without water or light or telephone line.

I floated towards the house, squeezing my bleeding finger to staunch the blood.

What would I do now?

The front door swung open without resistance. Had I locked it? No, I couldn't have, because I had not brought the keys out with me. Foolish! What if, on top of all the rest, I had been locked out as well? What then? Did I want to be homeless, prey for the roving delinquents and the rabid strays?

I scolded myself – a habit of mine. The theory being that by punishing myself I train myself to do better. Behaviourism, I think they call it. Behaviourism or, in some countries, Catholicism.

But the door swung open effortlessly and so the painful consequence of my stupidity was only hypothetical. In those circumstances, the behaviourism loses its sting, perhaps, and I might have reflected on this quandary if it hadn't been for the fact that, inside the house, the injuries of time had been undone.

The ashen sheets had been removed from the furniture, all repositioned to Mamabue's tastes. The electric lights were illuminated, casting a warm glow on the clay-coloured walls of the hallway. The dust had been swept and shutters thrown open; from the patio, the gurgling of the fountain licked the air. Everything was as I remembered it – as if, just behind a wall or door, Mamabue and others waited to welcome me back, their voices still warm in their throats, skin still stretched over their hands to touch my cheek or smooth my hair. As if Leandro could round a corner ready to kick my shins and start a fight. As if Inki might be perched on my shoulder, sucking at my ear, purring against my jaw.

In the light, I walked around touching things, making sure of their forms. It wasn't possible and yet – it *was*. It undeniably was, there, before my very eyes, igniting all my senses. It all was.

93

That is how I found them. Undeniably *there*, in the dining room, crowded around the table, every last one. Not just those I had known intimately (the Don, the Doña, la bebe Vittoria, the wailing lover), but also those whose presence had been fleeting (the musicians, the stonemasons, all the ones I never understood), all crammed in together, far too many to fit into that one room. When I opened the door, they all turned their eyes upon me and began to speak at once.

She's back.

At last.

Will she play with us?

Sana, sana.

What a mess.

¡Sana, sana!   *Sit and eat, querida.*

¡Sana, sana!

That is what I saw – and heard – only a moment ago behind the dining-room door against which I now lean. At my ear the little fish writhes and writhes. I hear it splashing. I have never heard it until now. I might ask myself against what, exactly, it is splashing, but does it matter? Because I hear it and its little bones clicking and clicking against one another as it moves. Behind this door, time has bent like a corkscrew to meet itself again. I have returned, a child on a carousel, to where I was before. It is not possible, and yet it *is*.

SEIS

When Julia Álvarez Yupanqui fell from the second-floor window of the yellow house on the hill, her spirit left her body, but it did not linger to join the spirits of the air. Instead it shivered across the majolica and down the hill, witnessed by the child crouching in the geranium bushes, and when it reached the street, it lifted itself, quivered a moment like a mamba balancing on the tip of its tail, and ascended. It rose up towards the sun and janaj pacha and the throne of the Lord God Almighty, which did not mean that Julia would never return to this world. That would happen later. For now, she departed.

As she rose, she heard, from inside the yellow house, shouts and panic. Family members emerged – Mamabue from the parlour, Carmen from the kitchen, Uriel from among the naranjos – seeking the source of the calamitous noise that had interrupted the quiet of their morning. While they gathered around the exploded remains of the maid, screaming and weeping, clamouring for a doctor, the child squatting in the geranium bushes crept away unseen, an anchoveta clenched in her fist.

But some of that child stayed behind. A slice of her was extracted. A portion of soul detached itself and burrowed like a sand flea into the earth. Another twenty-one years would pass before she recovered it. Julia Álvarez Yupanqui saw this as she shivered towards the sky, but there was nothing she could do because it was not yet her time to intervene in the affairs of the living. For now, her task was to observe – only to watch from a higher elevation the comings and goings of humankind across the Earth.

As she rose, the Earth fell away from her, as if she were a pinnacle towards which all land and sea was climbing. It seemed to her that the Earth had unfurled itself and now, no longer a globe, was nothing more than a sheet of cloth, a mapamundi pulled taut and pinned at its four corners. This map of the world radiated from her in all directions. She saw the land masses stretched tight – costa, sierra, selva, continents and isles – and from pole to pole she saw, imposed upon the map, the meridian of Tordesillas drawn to divide the New World between its conquerors, the east for João II of Portugal, the west for the Crown of Castile. All across both land and sea, the people's paths were etched, bright lines like shafts of light, crossing and criss-crossing, a luminous cat's cradle of the frantic quests of lives in search of destinations.

Superimposed upon the flattened Earth she saw Time, spread like an ocean, flowing this way and that, tossing up moments, driving them forwards on the crest of a wave then swallowing them again, pulling them back into the deep. Here, rising from the waters, she saw the first tentative caravels, soaring on the volta do mar, exploring the southern seas, ascertaining that the oceans were not – as had been feared – boiling hot or teeming with monsters. She discerned, among these caravels, the ship of Lopo Gonçalves crossing the equator, of Cristoforo Colombo aiming for Asia, of Francisco Pizarro drawing nearer and nearer, yes, all these ships drawing nearer and nearer while, on land, at the centre of the Tawantinsuyu, the Sapa Inka, Huayna Cápac, does not see what is approaching, does not see that a pachacuti is coming…

For a mere observer, it would be hard to say whether Julia Álvarez Yupanqui, dead and ascended into heaven, felt amazed by the sudden expansion of her sight. She gave no outward indication of surprise. In truth, it did not amaze her that she could, at once, discern the movements of the cosmos and everything contained within, seeable and unseeable, for it feels as natural to the ascended dead to see these cosmic things as it does to watch the movements of ants up and down blades of grass, their scurrying this way and that across kitchen tiles. But Julia saw and immediately understood the motion of space-time, because its currents were in constant motion, flowing, revolving, coursing and reversing not only from north to south and east to west but also from janan to urin and kaylla and tiqsi so that Time was above and below and before and behind, and what Julia now understood was that every point on the Earth had been and was being and would again be visited and revisited by the moments that had passed already, infinite times before.

Each of these moments, infinitely recurring, Julia could see in infinitesimal detail, for her panoptic vision was also microscopic, encroaching and receding, zooming in to examine the pigment of an iris, the jagged edge on a grain of sand, the pulse of energy across a neuron, and then her sight would soar away again to other histories and scenes. As she watched these moments play out over and over, mesmerised by their endless looping like a child lulled by the hypnotic reassurance of a zoetrope, she came to understand. And with this understanding came a quietness. It was not a quietness that would last. At the appointed time, Julia would be overcome – as all saints are – by a ferocious compassion that could not remain still, by a distaste for observation and a compulsion to action.

But this would happen later. For now, she simply watched.

She watched, time and time and time again, the progenitor of the Echeverrías set foot on American soil, and saw that he arrived weighed down by a spirit of deception on his shoulder. This is not surprising because, when the first Echeverría set foot in the New World in 1531, it was with an identity that was not truly his. His true names, the names of his mother and father, he had discarded – like a snake shedding its skin – back in Sevilla and left them lying somewhere in a gutter. He felt little affection for his provenance: the bastard son of a randy colonel and an impoverished washerwoman, the one thing about himself he truly prized was his ambition. It was an ambition that made him despise his mother and her hunched back, crooked from so many years of bending over a tub. An ambition that made him envy the easy insouciance with which his father breezed in and out of his childhood, always armed, sword by his side, always happy to eat the food placed before him, though it meant his son would go without dinner that night. In the end, it was an ambition that would lead him (when he came of age and received a sizeable one-time-only sum from his father with which he was instructed to 'find his fortune') to turn his eyes to the Atlantic and devise a plan to reinvent himself as conqueror and lord on a new continent.

So it was that, aged twenty-one, the washerwoman's son left the backwater Andalusian town in which he was born and began his journey to the coast. He did not know that the woman he left behind waited for his return. Would wait for the rest of her life, watching the horizon for his silhouette, with her olive-green eyes full of tears. But he would not come and so she would be forced to search for him, not in flesh and blood but by retracting deep into herself, curling smaller and tighter, compressing into the smallest particles of her being, retreating into the very nuclei of her cells and, this done, she retired from the world of the living so that she could resurface, generation after generation, vibrating in their bones and blood, in their skin and in their nails. Yes, many years later, she would return.

But he did not think of his mother. He would go to Cádiz, he had decided, and there he would find a crew headed for the New World and join them. But, such was his shame in his ancestry, the washerwoman's son did not believe that any explorer's crew would accept him, illiterate peasant that he was. And so, as he travelled to Granada, rattling along in the back of farmers' carts on which he hitched rides, he pondered his dilemma – how could a man leave his mother's arms a peasant and within the space of a three-day journey arrive at Cádiz a man of consequence?

The answer, he believed, was in his father's money, which he carried in a pouch inside the lining of his jacket. He felt the coins pressing against his chest, heard them jangling with every jolt of the cart, and despised them. They were the price his father had paid to be rid of him for good. Standing around the kitchen table in the cramped single-room shack where he had been conceived, the washerwoman and her son had watched the colonel as he laid out the coins. The father had engaged in an appraisal of his bastard son – looked him up and down, taken in his stature, the size of his hands, the angles of his jaw, the breadth of his shoulders. The father had inspected the boy, calculated his value, then measured it out in bits of copper and silver and a little gold. The humiliation was twofold: first, to be priced up by his father as if he were nothing more than cattle, and second, to be so poor and without connection that he had no choice but to scoop up the mounds of metal and thank the colonel for his generosity.

On that journey to Granada, the washerwoman's son felt hatred for his father rising so bitter and corrosive in his throat that he was possessed by the urge to toss the bag of coins into the dirt by the roadside. He had visions of rising to his feet in the moving cart and, with a flourish and cry of ¡Por Dios!, flinging the pouch away. In his imagination, he was a reckless man, heady and headstrong, confident in his ability to live off his strength and wits alone. In his daydreams he throttled bulls with his bare hands and leapt on unsuspecting women in the olive groves he passed. These imagined acts of unrestrained passion and extravagant contempt, he felt, suited him far more than his current attire of peasantry and meekness. Valour and excess coursed through his veins and now, at last, he was determined to find a way to dress himself in a glory befitting his temperament. Yet still, he could not find it in himself to cast away his father's money. Instead, he clung to it with a resignation that made him loathe himself. These two parts – the conceited and the obsequious – vied in him and soured his spirit.

As he watched the dusty mountains and ramshackle villages of Andalusia pass him by, he was conscious of a falling away in himself. Every vista he passed, he knew he passed it for the last time because, whether new life or death lay ahead of him, he was certain he would not return to the land of his birth. As he so reflected, the idea dawned on him to use the coins in his pocket to reinvent himself. This is what he did.

At the market of Jaén, he spent the first of his father's coins on new clothes – an elegant doublet, breeches and fine leather boots. The rags in which he had arrived he took into a backstreet and burned to cinders. At Granada, taking a siesta in the Sacromonte, watching the labourers constructing the palace of Carlos V at the Alhambra, he renamed himself: Hernando Echeverría y de Vargas. Lying there, between sleep and waking, he vowed that one day his progeny would be kings and queens in their land, living in a palace of their own, waited upon by servants. He would people a nation, and to this nation he would be both Abraham and Moses, yes, and Joshua too, *¡Por Dios!*, because not only would he father them and lead them out of indignity, he would also be the one to lead them into the promised land.

By the time he reached Sevilla, he had devised an entire ancestry of brave knights who had been warriors in crusades against the Moors and noblewomen who had left their fathers' homes to engage in illicit marriages, carried off by brave soldiers in the night. He could recount his genealogy to five generations and describe the family coat of arms in meticulous detail. But there was one last prop he must acquire for his act, and he knew it was in the slavers' square in Sevilla that he would find it.

As the man who called himself Hernando Echeverría wound his way across Andalusia, Julia watched his trajectory illuminated on the mapamundi: a bright white line, purposeful and glaring.

Simultaneously, another bright line was approaching, and the two would converge at Sevilla. This second thread of light originated in Málaga and from there had set out across the Alboran Sea only to be accosted and turned around again many times. These abortive journeys represented each of the tireless attempts to escape slavery undertaken by Hamet Alfarraz, passionate poet, learned astronomer and indefatigable escapee from the control of a torpid master – immeasurably his intellectual inferior – to whom he had been gifted by Rey Fernando II after the Christians' victory at Mālaqa.

Hamet Alfarraz was also named Hamet al-Rashid ibn Muhammad ibn Harun al-Farraz, for he was a rightly guided boy, son of Muhammad, grandson of Harun, though he had never known his father while alive. He had been born under an infelicitous star on the twentieth of August 1487, twenty-four hours after the city of Mālaqa had surrendered. Alfarraz would spend the rest of his life studying the constellations in an attempt to understand why fate had been so cruel. After the fall of the city, Fatimah Alfarraz, Hamet's merchant mother, had been seized with all her wealth and she and her unborn child earmarked as reward for some common soldier or other. They were given to one Juan Calvo, a man who did not understand either the injustice or stupidity of the concept of slavery for though he had been blessed with an enormous, expansive, gleaming forehead (a trait handed down from father to son for generations and which had gained for the family the dubious honour of their surname), he had not been blessed with a commensurate portion of intellect. It did not occur to him as he observed the infant Hamet lying sleeping that the human soul with all its passions and yearnings, all its immortality and ardour, its love and reason, hatred, vulnerability, nobility and cruelty was no more susceptible to possession than the movements of the planets, or the capriciousness of fate, or the regurgitations of time. As the sunrise of the twentieth of August 1487 reflected off his greasy, high-domed pate, there was, as ever, very little activity to disturb the stillness of the vacant terrain that lay behind that prodigious skull. Juan Calvo, also known as Cabezón, Baldy and The Forehead, had not grasped (nor would he ever) the most visceral of truths that a human is – must be, by very definition – free, and to call anyone a slave is a nonsense and a lie.

Still, under Castilian law, Fatimah Alfarraz was called a 'slave', and this brand purported to erase what had come before. Purported to erase that she had once been the subject of poems in which it had been written: *She is a long-stemmed flower* and *The gazelle of the market / is wrapped in sumptuous robes. / She has the heart of a lioness.* Purported to erase that she had once been known as 'The Saqr' because of the mark of a falcon in flight on her cheek and because she was a fearless businesswoman, renowned among traders across the seas. All her life, Fatimah had dressed well, walked gracefully. Inspired by her favourite poetess, Wallada bint al-Mustakfi, who had done the same, Fatimah had embroidered into her favourite coat two verses of her own writing. Into the right-hand side she had sewn:

By Allah, I am a strong tower, I walk tall and shelter my treasures.

And into the left:

I am a reed by the river, I bend to the meek with compassion but I do not break.

But now, in accordance with Castilian law, she was Baldy's slave, and a child born of a so-called slave would be one from birth. So it was that Hamet Alfarraz, who for nine months had grown inside the belly of a free Muslim woman, would emerge from between the legs of a woman purportedly owned and, still slick with maternal juices, the pair of them were forcibly baptised on the orders of The Forehead and given Christian names – Fatimah became Francisca, and the baby was named José Plácido – because The Forehead would not tolerate even the slightest vestiges of Islam among his household. To be sure, when Hamet's four half-brothers were born, The Forehead gave them all the name of Calvo and removed them from their mother's care so she could not surreptitiously raise them – these four boys in whose veins his own blood ran – as Muslims. While these four half-brothers had inherited Fatimah's dark, narrow eyes and though they shared their brother's low, thick eyebrows and sharp, high cheekbones, never mind that their chins tapered to the same pharaonic chin, it was on their heads that their father's same prodigious pate imposed itself, and with this gleaming pate came his same supercilious intellectual lethargy. These four Calvos were manumitted at birth and raised and educated by their father, while Hamet (the firstborn) was given to them as their servant.

In their public lives and according to the law of property, Fatimah and her son were Morisco slaves. But in private, Fatimah taught her Hamet to be anything he wanted. She instilled in him her values of adab and balāghah, of decency, decorum and eloquence. She taught him to read Ptolemy's *Syntaxis Mathematica* in ancient Greek and al-Sufi's *Book of Fixed Stars* in Arabic. She taught him to recite verses from the Bible in perfect Latin, and, in this way, mother and son would convince innumerable inquisitors that their Christian conversion had been genuine while, in secret, Fatimah taught her son how to preserve Islam in his heart and, in accordance with the Oran fatwa of 1504, to maintain a protective appearance of Christianity while fulfilling Islamic obligations in a manner unseen by any but Allah himself.

So, while he served his younger brothers, washing them and dressing them and sustaining their tantrums of kicking and biting, Hamet internally recited his ritual prayers. Though he was unable to perform the required rakats, in accordance with the Oran fatwa, he indicated with the slightest movements of his fingers or by flickering his eyes this way or that, the movements that he would have made had he been free to worship how he wanted. Fortified by his prayers, Hamet felt no bitterness for the younger brothers who despised him. He cared for them, even felt sorry for them and their inheritance of intellectual torpidity from their father. He understood that their precocious superciliousness was the fault of those who raised them: they had not had the privilege of a loving, guiding mother.

Then, in labour, expelling a fifth son fathered by The Forehead, Fatimah and the infant left this world. Without his mother and her conviction that he was destined to a higher calling, the adolescent Hamet grew restless. He saw no end to his servitude. Resentful, he found ways to undermine the master: he took to sprinkling sand into Don Calvo's hose and laughing as he watched the man scratching himself desperately like a flea-ridden dog. He sewed small, sharp rocks into the lining of his doublet so that, with the slightest movement, the man found himself stabbed by unseen assailants.

Aged nineteen, Hamet made his first attempt to escape and reach Fez and, though he did not manage even to board a ship, let alone leave the shore (for he was apprehended at the port by a friend of The Forehead), he had his first taste of freedom. As he left the master's house behind and wound his way through the streets subject to no one, answering to no one, aware no one knew where he was or where he was heading, he vowed that whatever might happen he would never again do anything but on his own terms.

That evening, after he was delivered back to The Forehead's house, he lost a tooth. It was a molar and it was knocked from his head by his brother, for it was that evening that The Forehead decided to teach his eldest son what should be done with a rebellious slave and demonstrated to him how to beat a man into submission with a poker. When The Forehead let the boy finish the job, he realised too late that the boy had too much enthusiasm for the task and, before Forehead Senior could intervene, Young Forehead had knocked the tooth from his half-brother's jaw. The sound of the molar clattering onto the stone floor and the sight of it gleaming there against the dark grey tile, pure white but rimmed with blood, would remain with The Forehead forever. He would remember it not because of any compassion or remorse it moved within him.

No, he would remember it because he knew that, should he ever wish to sell the runaway, a cursory inspection of the mouth by prospective purchasers would raise all kinds of uncomfortable questions. *Was it ill health or rough treatment that dislodged the molar? If the latter, for what was the punishment? For disobedience? Or sloth? Surely, either way, a discount is in order...*

No, The Forehead was not pleased by the loss of the young rebel's tooth. But he let his son keep it anyway, as a trophy. For Hamet, the empty space on his gum, into which his tongue would slither and probe, was a constant reminder – an exhortation – to try again for escape, if only to inconvenience The Forehead.

It was at the slavers' market in Sevilla that Julia Álvarez Yupanqui saw the bright lines of these two men – of Hamet Alfarraz and the one who called himself Hernando – converge. Echeverría was there to purchase a slave to take with him to the New World, the final prop in his charade of social importance. And Alfarraz was there for sale, at a bargain price, as his brother, into whose ownership he had been passed, had reached the end of his patience in dealing with increasingly elaborate and ever more successful escape plans. On his latest escapade, Alfarraz had evaded capture for ten whole days before he had been discovered aboard a pirate ship halfway across the Alboran Sea. For this, his brother had beaten him until they both were sweaty and exhausted, barely conscious, and still Alfarraz, with laboured breaths between the gobs of blood and phlegm he spat up, had sworn that he would not stop running until he or the brother died from the effort.

This was how Echeverría and Alfarraz came to be allied. No other purchasers would take the rebel slave– now infamous throughout the region for his recalcitrance – no matter how learned, no matter how skilled in oration and astronomy.

But Echeverría saw in this clever adventurer a chance at redemption for them both, and he offered Alfarraz a deal. In exchange for his allegiance, Echeverría would guarantee Alfarraz his release in the New World. In exchange for validating Echeverría's story of noble heritage and feats of bravery, Alfarraz would secure his freedom.

Julia watched them as they sailed, many months later, across the ocean on the caravel of the Pizarro brothers. They did not know then, but Julia did, that because of the scorn and the affection of a rebellious ñusta, daughter of the Sapa Inka, and because of the complex tapestry of the centuries, their children would intermingle so that it would not be clear which descendants were Echeverrías and which were Alfarrazes.

As Echeverría and Alfarraz approached the New World, their journey played out over and over on the zoetrope of Earth and Time that lay beneath the ascended Julia. She saw, infinitely repeated, this journey and others, like the *Andraste* on which Leung Huang thanked his lucky stars to have miraculously escaped the outbreak of dysentery that killed two hundred and seventy-four men whose corpses were jettisoned and floated, borne by the currents, to diverse shores. She saw, too, the journey of Elena, the soprano from Málaga, journeying to Lima to sing in a travelling revue and the young Colombe Fantonbleu, hand-picked by Enrique Echeverría as a bride for his son, and, later, Colombe's brother Gustave on his transatlantic liner with his books, beginning his quest to learn from his sister how to be a man – a quest that would end in his disappearance into the library of the yellow house on the hill, from which he would never emerge.

Time and time and time again, ad infinitum, Julia observed these journeys. She watched as Hernando Echeverría y de Vargas first placed his foot on American soil for the thousandth time and as Hamet Alfarraz followed, for the thousandth time, in his tracks. She witnessed again and again Leung Huang approaching the Chincha Islands on the tugboat from Callao, marvelling at how these mountains of frost did not melt in the American sun. And when Chen Tan washed up, six years later, on an empty beach outside Pisco, badly burned in the *María Ugarteburu* but alive, Julia saw this too, infinitely recurring.

So when Julia watched the *Nuestra Señora de la Misericordia* arrive in Cartagena, she knew already what would happen, for she had seen it countless times before. She knew that the emaciated pregnant woman with fever, who was being whisked away in the arms of the Jesuit Alonso de Sandoval, would not lose her life but that instead she would lose a limb, her husband, and her name. For while the woman convalesced in the care of the Jesuits at Cartagena, the father of her child, who had not fallen ill on the journey from Loanda, was sent onwards to Panamá, where he was made to walk across the isthmus and sold at market to a man who lived somewhere his wife and his daughter would never see. The pregnant woman, unable to communicate because she was delirious with fever from the gangrene that was rising up her body and because she did not know the tongue of the Jesuits, could not explain to those around her that she had a husband from whom she did not wish to be parted. By the time she came round from surgery, her husband was gone, as was her leg, and around her neck was a tin medallion. She was informed by a young ladino, interpreting on behalf of the Jesuit, that this medallion symbolised that she had been baptised and this had secured the freedom of her eternal soul. Her new name, now that she was a Christian woman, would be Ana Angola. What was more, she had been healed of her physical ailments and was ready to continue her journey to whatever destination God had in store for her. Since the Jesuit Sandoval had already prayed that God would send Ana into the hands of a merciful master who would have an eye for the physical and spiritual needs of his slaves, she need not go in trepidation, but with confidence in the providence of the Lord.

Overcome, but not by gratitude as the Jesuit assumed, Ana struggled to articulate, even inside her own mind, the questions she had to ask, such as when she might be reunited with her husband, what had happened to her right leg, and how it was that a man who cared so profoundly for the destination of her eternal soul could have so little concern for where her earthly body might end up. Had she asked, perhaps Padre Sandoval would have shared with her his vast musings on the topic of the enslavement of the African, which he had compiled into his treatise entitled *De Instauranda Aethiopum Salute*. As it was, Ana did not ask.

When the slaver – a Portuguese merchant named Pérez who also ran a roaring trade in gold and silver and Iberian textiles – sent his man to retrieve Ana from the Jesuits, he expected to collect a woman renewed. When Pérez had agreed with Sandoval to allow the sickly to be taken away from his ships and ministered to at the church sanatorium, he had done so less out of compassion and more out of a profitability calculation. He had weighed up the administrative inconvenience of the project, for records would have to be kept of how many slaves were charged to the Jesuits – their sexes, ages, characteristics and conditions. Against this, he had counted the benefits of receiving, after their period of convalescence, slaves who had been nourished and healed and initiated into the Christian languages and faith, all of which were grounds for the inflation of prices. On balance, he had felt the Jesuits offered him a profitable option.

But when Pérez's man arrived for Ana, he found her still emaciated and ashen. She had, the Jesuits explained, refused to eat. She was downcast and uncommunicative. She had made no attempts to learn a new language – neither Spanish nor Portuguese – and had only become animated when conversing in her own tongue with those from her own land. Otherwise she had withdrawn into herself. Her eyes seemed not to see the world around her but rather a world not physically present – perhaps an internal world or a metaphysical realm beyond natural human sight. She would curl her tiny, waning body into corners and, like one entranced, sit completely still but for her hands that moved constantly, fingers bending and flexing, prying and wriggling through the air as if caressing some invisible, beloved artefact. They moved keenly, artfully, her skeletal digits, with the dexterity of an expert – but an expert at what? No one could tell. What was she doing with those restless, relentless hands that never ceased? The Jesuits had discussed whether she might be possessed by a spirit that had come with her from Africa, and whether some sort of exorcism was in order.

Ana was not possessed. She had, however, turned her eyes inward and focused upon the needfulness of remembering. All this time she was silent, not speaking, not seeing the comings and goings around her. She was working inwardly, working intently and laboriously, on the artefact of her memory. Not only her memory, but the memory of her people. Back home, in the Kingdom of Luba, she and her husband had been respected young members of the Bambudye, the Men of Memory, whose task it was to preserve the stories and lineages of the Luba people through storytelling and dance, through song and the reading of the lukasa memory board. Now, on this new continent among these strangers with alien words, without tools or wood or beads with which to craft a physical lukasa, she constructed a lukasa in her mind. With her thoughts, she shaped it: she carved it with the legends of Kongolo and Mbidi the Hunter and also with the faces of the people she had known. She glued to it the smell of the earth and the texture of the tortoise shell and the fear of the journey she had just undertaken. Onto it, she poured the sound of her true name, not Ana Angola but Bulanda Ilunga, and with her fingers she beat upon it the rhythm of ritual. At last, painfully, with her own fingernails, she inscribed upon it the outline of her husband and, with her tears, she polished it.

As she added detail to the lukasa inside her, the external world faded. Solidity became as mist and in its place the artefact of memory became tangible: she could turn it over in her hands, feel its grooves and nicks at her fingertips, hold it up to her face and peer through its holes, for already it had holes, gaps in her knowledge where something was forgotten. Already she could not recall the sound of her mother's laughter – this was a memory that would return to her years later in a dream, her mother's merriment reverberating to her from across a vast ocean – and certain details of the lineages that she had been learning to recite. It was to fill these holes in her memory that she spoke so urgently to the other Luba she encountered along the length of her life. From them she extracted details, little things that they remembered, even the seemingly inconsequential, and meticulously, obsessively, she fixed them to the lukasa in her mind. Later, to her children, she passed on the lukasa, narrating to them the memory she had crafted in the hope that they would pass it on to their children.

But Bulanda Ilunga's children were taken from her young, before they had grasped the entirety of their mother's lukasa, before they had mastered their mother tongue. While Bulanda lived out her days in Panamá, her daughters were sold on and trafficked further south. They spoke in tangled tongues, blending Spanish and Guaraní and Portuguese and Quechua. With each successive generation, the lukasa was whittled down, a leaner, smoother imitation of the one that Bulanda had constructed. The holes became wider – wide enough, at first, for a needle, then a twig, then for a finger to poke through. But Bulanda's daughters and granddaughters were resourceful, and they plugged these holes with the materials at their disposal – with stories from other kingdoms and other peoples, invented in other tongues, shared from companion to companion. To their lukasas they added Viracocha and the Vírgen María, sahumerios and ekekos, chupacabras and hapiñuñu. Into the gaps they crammed the zamacueca and the alcatraz, the marinera and the lundu, the cajón, the flauta, the festejo, and the guitar… And every now and then, when there was a stubborn hole that nothing else could fill, they would dream they heard a voice laughing, echoing to them from across the sea.

All of this Julia saw, and as she watched she realised that she too had inherited a piece of Bulanda's lukasa. But for now she had no time to reflect, no time to turn over the lukasa in her hands. There were more moments to perceive, like the sale of Bulanda at the feria de los negros in Panamá City, which was the first time in months that Bulanda allowed her sight to be distracted from the inner world as her eyes darted back and forth among the crowds, looking for signs of her husband. Several times she thought she caught a glimpse of him, but these were only hopeful hallucinations that, as soon as they appeared, dissolved into the forms and faces of strangers. It was at this feria that Bulanda, now Ana Angola, was sold to a criollo agent who had been sent by his employer to purchase a lady's maid for his wife. Having been outbid on a dozen others, the criollo saw his chance at a deal when he spotted the clumsy stump that ended just above where Bulanda's right knee had been. On account of her missing leg, the criollo wangled with the slaver:

Two hundred pesos?!

Nothing less.

You're mad! What work can be extracted from a one-legged woman?

And the slaver replied with a few suggestions as to what exactly could be extracted from a one-legged woman: she was, after all, with child.

You're getting two slaves for the price of one, man!

Perhaps. Or perhaps I am buying only risk – she may well die in childbirth.

Ah, my friend, despite the leg, she is strong. Come see for yourself.

As the criollo led Ana Angola away from the market, she continued to sweep her eyes back and forth across the crowds, searching for her husband. She did not see him. He was already miles and miles away, to the south, on the Hacienda Echeverría near Pisco. Ana Angola would live and die in the service of the Panamanian criollo's wife, but many years later her distant descendant would find herself on that same hacienda near Pisco, carrying the unborn child of an Echeverría, himself the distant descendant of the man whom her husband had served.

Julia Álvarez Yupanqui did not stop to marvel at the entanglements of genealogies as Alfarrazes bedded Yupanquis bedded Echeverrías bedded Ilungas. She was watching, instead, the arrival of the first Americans trekking across Beringia more than ten thousand years before, and how they meandered south and west and populated the empty continent. She watched, too, the Polynesian explorers reaching the shores of the Tawantinsuyu in their voyaging canoes, exchanging their chickens for sweet potatoes and, many years later, she watched Thor Heyerdahl's *Kon-Tiki* sail west, carried by the Humboldt Current, as he aimed to prove that the Inkas had been mariners.

She saw, too, the micro-journeys: her parents' rush from the crowded corralón in the centre of Lima to the stretch of dust where they would claim their patch of land and raise four walls of straw matting for a home. From there, her own even shorter journeys appeared – her first steps across the cardboard boxes that served as the floor for the one-room shack; her goings back and forth to school, to the market and, eventually, to the yellow house on the hill where she would start work as an empleada aged fifteen; her plummet from the second-floor window one month before her eighteenth birthday. Yes, she watched her own final journey, falling interminably from that unlucky window, smashing repeatedly against the majolica.

Even this, her own grisly death, did not slow the roving of her all-seeing eyes, which took in the advent of air travel – the flight maps scratching across the skies, radiating from glaring cities out to the world's remotest parts. It occurred to Julia that, while living, she had never left Lima – neither by sea nor sky. Her whole life had been spent with her feet on the ground, until her death, when she had flown. Now, she watched the thousands upon thousands of passengers buzzing this way and that at unnatural speed across the heavens. She saw the flights of Professor Leonard Gest backwards and forwards from London to Lima, Lima to London, and how his black-eyed daughter followed in his tracks – Lima to London, London to Lima, always searching for something. A nameless, intangible, just-out-of-reach something. Belonging or sanity or restfulness or home?

Humanity, she understood, was restless. Itchy-footed, irascible, blighted by ennui. Like a child in the womb, humanity kicks at its enclosures. It writhes and wrenches like a tantrum, like a wasp caught in a web.

Because across the ether, through every particle of space and time, from uju pacha to janaj pacha, a voice reverberates, and it says, *Bear fruit and multiply, and swell the earth and subjugate her, and be masters over the fish of the sea and the birds of the skies, and over all the beasts that move on the earth.* And to the sound of this voice, under its compulsion, humanity beats on.

For this vagabond race, she felt pity and disgust. At last, the time had come, as it does for every risen saint – after millennia spent watching the migrations of man – for Julia Álvarez Yupanqui to be compelled into action. She had risen so as to see; now she must descend again to intervene. But in what had come before her, Julia found she could not partake; Pizarro and Atahualpa and Fernando II she could not touch. Try as she might to plunge herself into those moments, to go to Bulanda Ilunga's side as she convulsed with fever or to help Hamet Alfarraz cross the Alboran Sea, she was held back as if by an adverse wind. Like the dreamer who runs but never arrives, she struggled towards them but was borne backwards and away.

It was only in the events that succeeded her fall that Julia was able to participate. And, even then, only in the micro. To influence the decisions of presidents, the judgments of high courts, that was not allotted to her. For her were the small things, the daily, the quotidian miracles of little, forgettable people. Resurrecting the pets of children. Multiplying the pennies in the cup of a beggar. Printing the face of Christ on an old widow's toasted bread. Little alleviations in the journeys of the common man: this was the calling of Santa Julia Álvarez Yupanqui.

SEVEN

I panicked. Yes, I saw behind the dining-room door where they were all sitting around the table, the ones I am not meant to see. I saw them there, temporarily lost my mind, and called Doctor de las Casas. I was desperate, and his number was right there, written in thick black letters in Mamabue's leather-bound notebook, lying where it always did next to the telephone. The dialling tone soothed me. Sitting on the velvet armchair, I listened to it drone. It spoke to me of bees. No, not bees: flies. Yes, flies. Also foghorns.

It took me several attempts to dial before I reached de las Casas. The first time, with shaking fingers, I must have punched the wrong numbers, because I called some woman who was half-deaf.

'Busco al doctor de las Casas,' I said when she answered.

'No vendo,' she told me.

'¡No! ¡No! De las casas! Busco al doctor llamado de las Casas.'

'¿Qué? Speak up! ¿Qué casa?'

'My God!' I cried and slammed down the receiver.

With a fingertip I traced the number in the notebook again. A flap of sliced skin skidded along the paper and smarted, sharpening my focus. I whispered the numbers to myself, blinked to make sure I was seeing them clearly.

From the wall opposite the telephone, the portrait of Tía Paloma watched me sadly. During my childhood, my Tía Paloma was spoken about only rarely and always cryptically, with sentences that trailed off into silence: *When querida Paloma… If la Paloma had not… The real tragedy is that Paloma…* Tía Paloma was everywhere enshrined, her photograph displayed at least once in every room: her Communion pictures in the sala, her graduation portrait in the study, snapshots of her smiling with her siblings (my Mami, Tío Pulpo, Tío Ignacio Tercero) in canoes and on hammocks at various ages from infant to adolescent to young woman. She reaches a certain age (around the age that I am now) but then the photographs end. She vanishes.

I tried to ignore her eyes on me as I rehearsed the numbers. I would not mistake their order again. I must read from front to back – it is not hard. From the left of the page to the right, I ran my finger.

The second and third times I dialled, I lost confidence halfway, replaced the receiver, started again. I whispered the digits to myself before I touched each button and then said them again, aloud, as I pressed out the numbers – *one*, one; *nueve*, nueve; *tres*, tres – but immediately after pressing I questioned myself. Had I pushed the button that I thought I had? Had I missed out a digit? There was something sticky and humid about my brain and my numbers got tangled. I was getting overly familiar with the digits to the point of forgetting – what did a nine look like? Which was the two? Was that a one, written in the French style, or a seven? I always struggled with my mother's handwriting…

When I heard his voice, it startled me. I had dialled his number, certainly (I must have done, although I do not now remember doing it), but he answered so quickly there was not even a ring. I was unprepared.

He was unsurprised to hear from me. I was right to have called him, he said. When I left years ago, I had acted prematurely – we had not finished my therapy. Matters were unresolved. We had opened up issues, dug around, and not closed them. It was most unsatisfactory – perilous, in fact. How had I coped all this time?

Through repression, he could only assume. And repression is a temporary fix, Señorita Echeverría.

Yes, Doctor, I agreed. His voice took me back to being a child who was starting to succumb, to believe what the professionals told her – that she was not well. Yes, Doctor. Yes. If you say it, it must be. I nodded and acquiesced to everything he said. I had been wandering around all this time with my head sawn open and my insides precariously balanced. It was a wonder everything had not all spilled out of me, like a pot overflowing. But if only he would come tonight and help me…

Not tonight. He could not come tonight. Tomorrow, first thing, and we would pick up where we left off. Until then, I should try to relax. Curl up in bed. Read a book… No. On second thought, perhaps not, he said. No reading. He was remembering, I suppose, about the episode with the library books. About the man in the History section. About the ocean of torn fragments strewn about. No reading, Señorita Echeverría. Just sleep. Do not go back into the dining room nor, under any circumstance, up to the second floor.

If he had not said this, it would have been better. I had forgotten about the second floor and its west-facing windows that look out to the sea. About my habit of throwing open the shutters and standing on the windowsill, arms spread, a somnambulant condor child. About my claim that Julia called to me from the ocean – that she rose from the waves and whispered to me to come to her. I had not thought about the time she reached out her arm and it stretched for miles, right to my window, her cupped palm enormous, like a canoe hovering just below the ledge where I balanced. Forgotten how I had stepped into it and she had lowered me gently to the garden where Uriel found me in the morning, sleeping, sucking my thumb, one eye closed, the other wide open and staring at the sky.

All this I had disremembered until de las Casas reminded me. When he said not to go up to the second floor, he triggered something. Not memory. Not true memory, anyway. Borrowed memory, false, a bricolage of second-hand details. Of things I've been told – reports of what I did (that I am not wholly convinced are true) or of what I said (but have no recollection of saying). Of images plagiarised – yes, especially these. My vision of Julia rising from the waves, for example, is a pastiche of *The Birth of Venus*, except she wears the face of Sarita Colonia – that placid, inscrutable face that I have seen on a thousand detentes milagrosos and half a dozen murals – and is dressed in the pale blue pinafore of Miraflores niñeras. The sky behind her is not the guano grey of a Limenian afternoon: instead it is a wall of flowers, unreal in their vibrancy, like the too-bright artificial flowers sold cheaply in buckets by the roadside. Around her is the faded gold gloriole I know I have stolen from paintings of la Vírgen de Guadalupe and at her feet, crushed between two toes, is an inexplicable snake. Inexplicable for, as far as I know, Julia never had any interaction with a serpent.

This is how I remember her first appearance to me after her death. Or rather this is how I *imagine* remembering her. All I really know is that I have been *told* that I once *said*, when Uriel found me sleeping outside the house with all the doors and windows locked and bolted from the inside, that Julia had come for me and carried me through the air.

I cannot see how this can be true. It defies all sense and still I have constructed a memory around the episode, vivid and multisensory. It smells of fish and sounds like the calls of seagulls and the rush of water. But it is only a delusion.

And yet there were witnesses. Yes, the vieja in the mock-Tudor house, she saw it happen. Claimed to have seen it happen. Declared that she had watched the whole encounter from her bedroom window. Impossible, of course. But her empleada corroborated the tale and spread it around the families of Los Polvos and that was when the crowds descended. This I *do* remember with, I think, my own recollections. I have sounds and images, zoomed in, with heightened detail, that play incongruously spliced together – a foil windmill spinning to white noise from a transistor radio; a piece of frayed poly ribbon, purple, fluttering on the breeze; a car backfiring; a blind old man with arthritic hands laying a coin.

I thought about those crowds last night as I sat on a window ledge up on the second floor and looked out to sea. Yes, against the doctor's express instructions I went up to the second floor and, what is worse, more audacious, is that I sat so precariously and dangled my legs in the air, swung them back and forth, let my heels kick the crumbling lúcuma plaster and watched the flakes and dust rise from the side of the house in sepia clouds. It was a short-lived bout of obstinacy. How dare he tell me what to do. I'm a grown woman – I will do as I please. I imagined him pulling up to the house the next morning, seeing me there brazen as anything, legs swinging, bare toes stretched wide, me waving down to him, kicking my head back and laughing, not holding on, not even with one hand. *¡Buenos días, Doctor! ¡Qué locura!* The scene in my head was intercut with another, almost the same, but this time an enormous hand, Julia's hand, I suppose, was lifting me from the window and cradling me, depositing me safely before the doctor's car and he, baffled, falls to his knees, humbled, penitent, begging my forgiveness for years of disbelieving me. It was all true. All true. Forgive me. I was vindicated.

Then I lost my balance and the ledge disappeared and I had one of those sharp, bright, vivifying moments when you die and the sky is suddenly everywhere, white and wet and full of too much oxygen. These moments, instants in which you die and are resurrected (like when you nearly fall down the stairs but don't or when the car in which you ride brakes almost but not quite too late), prolong themselves between two heartbeats, the second of which takes lifetimes to come and is the incontrovertible proof that time flows erratically and unpredictably. That is how it was yesterday evening when the ledge disappeared and the ground disappeared and the sky took their place and I saw myself falling, every sense heightened, the world opening up and simultaneously closing in with the dizzying taste of air and light and the enormity of everything I had risked screeching at me that I was a fool; if I had fallen, de las Casas would have found me crumpled and concluded suicide and it would have been *they* that were vindicated – all those who for years called me crazy. *She was crazy after all. Crazy and with child. Qué tragedia.* But my hand, by some miracle, caught the lintel and I steadied myself, found my balance, and did not die.

That was last night. Since then, I have not slept. I was awake all night listening to the travesuras of the ghosts from my bedroom. I bolted the door, though I knew it was a futile defence: only the living can be detained by locks and bars. Had they wanted to cross over, they would have, but they did not enter my chamber. They were courteous and respected my privacy and yet still they kept me up with their conversations, their excitable hollering as they played at dice and cards, accompanied by the shrieking of opera music from the gramophone. The ghost of the jilted lover wailed, unceasing, and la bebe Vittoria dragged her pony on a string up and down the corridors, cracking her skull against table corners and then screaming, disconsolate.

Down the beach, the honk of a kazoo rouses me from my thoughts. An ice-cream vendor is cycling towards me, a blaze of yellow against the grey sky, the wheels of his cart-bike leaving three wavering tracks in the sand. He moves slowly, as if through water, legs heaving with each push on the pedals. It is hard work: his skin glistens with sweat. The tufts of black hair that protrude from under his yellow cap stick to the sides of his face. As he approaches, he fixes his eyes on me and I stare back at him, blinking into the light that breaks through clouds and shines around him like a halo, dazzling. For a second, blinded, I panic, think this is de las Casas in disguise looking for me, and my body tenses, ready to bolt. But then the bike comes to a halt, the man speaks, clouds veil the light, and the illusion is broken. This is not de las Casas. This is another man entirely, smiling, his tongue visible through missing teeth.

He is waiting for an answer, but I did not hear what he said to me.

'Disculpe, pero, no oí,' I say. Would he please repeat himself?

He wants to know if I will purchase something.

'Disculpe,' I say. 'No tengo plata.' I am sorry. So very sorry. I turn my pockets inside out to prove myself. I grovel a little for forgiveness.

With his cap he wipes the sweat from his brow, sticks the kazoo back between his lips, and carries on down the beach. I watch his back as he goes.

I am a mess. Not my clothes – for the first time since arriving I am dressed in my own things, and I dressed well today, expecting to see the doctor. Everything matches, down to my fingernails. I am 'put together'. Compuesta. Composed, like a painting. Yes, staged, like a vintage photograph. But outside the frame, underneath this headscarf, I am a mess.

All morning, everywhere I have been, I have seen de las Casas. Running along el Malecón, leaning out from a taxi cab, smoking a cigarette as he leaned from a third-floor balcony, the man was everywhere. But of course it was my imagination, my paranoia. I knew exactly where he was in actuality: on his way to keep my appointment with him at Mamabue's house. The appointment which I missed, am missing right now, in fact.

In the sunlight, my fingernails shimmer, a little red, a little pink. Almost pretty, if it weren't for how the polish has bled over my cuticles. My hands were too tremulous this morning: I could not keep the little brush within the lines. I had to repaint my right thumb three times because of the smudging and even after the last attempt, it came out too thick, too gloopy. But there wasn't time to paint it a fourth time: the doctor was coming. He would be there any moment. So now there are tiny bits of fluff in the lacquer, cat hair and other unattributable fuzz, almost imperceptible, but not entirely.

Disgusted, I get up and go to the water's edge, squat down and thrust my hands out of sight into the wet sand, which gives way with a satisfactory glug and then recomposes itself around my forearms, sucking at my skin like little kisses. This was how I played as a girl: banned from swimming in the sea like the other children, I amused myself with hunting the muy muys that lived hidden in the sand. If I dug into the grains, just-wet by the waves, the chubby, grey-white crustaceans would fill my hands. Desperate, always, to burrow into the beach and hide, the muy muys would frantically scuttle and tickle my palm with their scratchy little legs. I search for them now, wriggling my fingertips deeper, but there are no scrabbling bodies under the surface.

A little distance away, a couple of teenagers entangled in each other's arms watch me quizzically. What must they think? A grown woman, alone, squatting by the waves, elbow-deep in wet sand. When I try to release my arms, the beach will not let me go. It sucks me down as I pull against it and, surprised by its forcefulness, I lose my balance, my ankles buckle and I tumble onto my side. One of the teenagers, the boy, snorts and then lobs a shell at the water, showing off the strength of his arm. The girl squeezes his bicep. They have stopped watching me. I am not so interesting.

Perhaps that is true. Perhaps I could go back to the casa now, find the doctor standing on the doorstep and tell him, unequivo-cally, that I am utterly unremarkable, that I do not need his services because there is nothing, after all, to discuss. If he asks about the phone call, I will say, *Ah, the phone call!* and laugh jovially, *Jaja! Just a little trick, Doctor, to get you to come and visit. And here you are! You see? It worked! I wanted you to come and see how well I am. See how grown I am and how my fingernails match my scarf. Do come in, Doctor, and let me take your jacket and pour you a drink because I am not a child any more but your equal, an engaged woman with child. Quite capable of looking after myself. Quite capable.* I will lead him through to the garden and serve him sandwichitos and alfajores; I will wear sunglasses so he cannot see my eyes, but I will make humming noises and nod my head sagely as he speaks to show I am listening, and I will ask him questions, interrogative after interrogative, the way he used to do to me.

My arms are caked in sand up to the elbow, so I wade into the sea to clean myself. It is colder than I remember and makes me gasp. I feel its iciness in my eyeballs, like a brain freeze, an ice pick to the temple. As I rinse my arms, I realise I have forgotten to raise my dress, which, now saturated up to the waist, has wound itself around me and clings to my calves, my thighs and hips. It constricts my legs as I walk back out of the surf, and I imagine how I must look, shuffling like the straitjacketed lunatics in vintage horror movies. I am an asylum escapee – or a mummy, bound by my own garments. I fight the dress to untangle myself. Wrenching my legs against the sodden fabric, holding out my arms to keep my balance, I have a flashback to Frankenstein's monster lumbering through a shadowy laboratory.

The teenagers are watching me again and smirking, so I walk away from them, south, towards Chorrillos. It must be eleven o'clock by now. Doctor de las Casas will have given up waiting for me and driven away. No doubt he will invoice me for his time, but it is a small price for the satisfaction of imagining him standing at the gates of the casona, calling and calling with no answer, readjusting his glasses in frustration, sweating dark patches into his linen jacket, needing to pee but with nowhere to go. He, who is so fastidious with his time, has been kept waiting, and the thought of it is so delicious that I laugh out loud. An abrupt guffaw like a donkey's bray. My own voice, so unfamiliar and harsh, shocks me into silence.

I do not need de las Casas. I should not have called him. Panic propelled me last night, but now I can see that I am capable of counselling myself. Take la bebe Vittoria, for instance: I met her through the bars of my cot, I inside looking out and she outside, reaching in. My earliest memory is of her bright blue eyes fixed on me, shining through the darkness. Every evening we watched each other, wide-eyed in the gloom, until she or I fell asleep. Although my recollections of her are vivid, I can ask myself all the probing questions. Was she not, perhaps, to begin with, simply one of Tía Consuelo's porcelain dolls? With her wide blue irises and Shirley Temple curls, she could easily have been a muñequita, sat up on the dresser opposite my bed, her glass eyes unblinking, reflecting the moon's rays in the night.

And the dent in the skull? The incessant chanting of *Sana, sana*? How can that be explained? Quite easily: could the doll not have taken a tumble and the china brow smashed? Could my infant mind not have imbued that doll with life, breathed a voice into it and, mourning its destruction, resurrected it and given it a litany to repeat and repeat – *Sana, sana. Sana, sana*?

Yes, certainly, I have no need of therapy. I can self-diagnose – self-soothe – very well. I can inspect my own mind from several angles. Here, an alternative assessment, the Lacanian perspective: la bebe Vittoria was not an embellishment of a doll at all. She was the méconnaissance of an infant in the mirror stage – an imaginary Other, constructed as the 'ideal I', that is, me as I would have liked to be: a little gringita, the Shirley Temple sobrina the Titis would like to have had.

Yes, my self-analysis is thorough.

And yet…la bebe Vittoria seems not to have left me. What might that say about my self-concept? That I was never able to readjust the reflection of my ideal self beyond a flaxen-haired, sapphire-eyed toddler with an imploded cranium? What does it mean that she continued to follow me about the house well into my teens, with no sense of propriety, appearing in a room at wholly inconvenient moments – while I was on the toilet or taking a shower, underwear down, passing a menstrual clot or holding a mirror between parted thighs to examine my orifices? What does it mean that she has returned to me now that I am grown?

Some things should not be psychoanalysed. Some things are repressed for a reason. Better not to dig. Better to turn away, leave the scab in place.

I have wandered so far along the beach that the sand has turned to shingle and the jagged edges of stones dig into my soles. My feet are naked. Where are my shoes? I must have left them where I was before, back near the smirking teenagers. I am forgetting so many things these days. I have – what do they call it? – 'baby brain'. This little pink fish has given me baby brain. What a horrible term – as if pregnancy has lobotomised me and transplanted for my woman's mind that of a neonate.

It is a brutal thing, procreation. Utterly invasive. I read somewhere that the baby's cells can cross the placenta and, far from being contained, migrate around the mother's body. Foetal cells can live, entrench themselves, multiply in the mother's organs for decades. They have been found even in the brain! In the mother's brain! With what kind of influence on her thoughts, I wonder? What kind of presence is the child there – tender or malign? I find it horrific to be redesigned from the inside out by an alien presence, to imagine the thing spreading its tentacles throughout my body, stretching its fronds through the channels of my blood vessels, occupying every part. I cannot bear it. Foetomaternal chimerism they call it, as if a mother is a monster of the ancient world, a conglomerate of dissonant parts.

Now I remember: I gave birth last night. Or rather I dreamed that I did, because I recall looking between my legs and seeing the front half of a fish protruding, its eyes bulbous, staring up at me as it opened and closed its beaky, parrotfish mouth. Its dorsal fin was stuck inside me, digging into my pubic bone: there was no question of it emerging. We were fused together, a hybrid monster with two heads, one between the shoulders and one nestled in the groin, and I turned cartwheels over and over, walking now on my feet and now on my hands, each head taking precedence in turn. Behold the remarkable fish woman!

I thought I did not sleep last night, but I must have. The little fish is still here, frolicking in the waves that break upon the beach. I can see it in the corner of my right eye, a succulent little morsel, a pink worm writhing, with the seagulls circling and screeching above. Perhaps it will be devoured, a tasty little piece of bait. If I tilt my head so it is in my blind spot, then I cannot be held accountable if it gets eaten. One moment there – the next not. Nothing to be done.

The dead were always threatening to eat me. It was one of the first things the Don and Doña said to me the afternoon when I met them. Julia was not long dead, the patio where she fell, just outside the dining-room window, still smelled like bleach, but her devotees had already begun to gather, forming a line that snaked from the house, down the hill, along the Avenida del Guanero, around the Óvalo, and all the way to el Malecón. I watched them through the shutters as they lay flowers and crucifixes, statuettes and altar candles; I watched with envy as the ice-cream vendors sold them cones and ices at the foot of the hill. From my position at the window, unseen behind shutters, I alone among all the living was privileged with the secrets of Julia's devoted. I alone heard their susurrations, their tremulous singing, the weeping and cursing.

It was as I was hiding there, eavesdropping on the supplications of the worshippers, that the Don and the Doña first appeared to me. I heard them before I saw them. First a tinkling sound, like the ringing of distant wind chimes. Then a dragging, metal on stone, and a rumbling, intensifying to a crescendo that at its loudest drowned out the music from Consuelo's gramophone. At last there was silence, save for the rattling of dice that were jumping and then settling in two little clusters on the dining-room table, gathered and dropped by unseen hands.

She can see us at last.

¡Dudo!

> *No, truly. She is looking straight at us.*

¡Bueno, pues! She took her time.

> *Shall we ask her, just to be sure?*

¡Oye, niña! Can you see us, hija?

Yes, I could see them, barely. Sitting at the dining table, they hazed in and out of focus in the way of those little cartoons the oculist gave me to examine as he adjusted lenses imposed before my eyeballs. Shrinking and growing, now and then they flickered, like actors lost between frames of old movies. Even when they grew more distinct, their outlines sharp and defined, they gave the impression of being seen from very far off, although they were enormous: inhumanly tall, elongated figures, as if stretched, the tips of their heads grazing the ceiling, backs hunched, legs folded uncomfortably under the table.

They seemed to be made of bronze, sculpted to resemble humans but not quite succeeding, their figures pockmarked and dented, rough like the surface of coal. On their faces, depressions served for where the eyes would be, the nostrils too, reminding me of the indistinctness of seeing a face through a veil, a filter through which the only expression that could seep was mournfulness. When they spoke, the lips moved but the voice seemed to come not from the mouth – they had no mouths to speak of between those lips – but from somewhere lower, somewhere around the navel.

On this, the first meeting, they wore no clothes. Later they would acquire dress, but on this day they were naked. But, no, that word is wrong – I cannot say they were naked in the carnal sense. Their bodies were innocuous, the way a child might imagine the adult form to be. Male and female they were, but almost sexless and without genitals. She had breasts – deflated and nipple-less – which, along with a waspish waist, were all that could distinguish her body from his. And he, for maleness, could only boast a larger nose, a slightly more prominent chin.

Save your breath.

This is the pitiful zonza that doesn't speak.

'I am not a zonza!' I told them, and they were all of a sudden brightly lit and clear.

'So she *can* hear us!' the man said triumphantly, flinging his dice across the tabletop.

'But can she see us?' the woman asked.

'I can see you.'

'Tell me, hija, are you living or are you retired?'

'Retired from what?' I asked.

'Retired from living,' the man replied.

'Do you mean dead?'

'If we meant *dead*, we would have said *dead*.'

I thought for a moment. 'Does it matter?'

'Perhaps not. But you should make up your mind. Before the curse comes for you. There's a curse, ya tú sabes,' the man said.

'A curse?'

'Pues, sí. A curse is hovering all around this house,' the man said. 'You haven't seen it?'

Now that I thought of it, yes, I had seen it. I had seen it all my life but taken it for granted. It was a quivering quality in the air. A shivering aura that did not exist anywhere else. A sort of hesitant malignancy spectating on our lives, withholding its hand as long as it was entertained. This was why la Casa Echeverría could never have a quiet day, never be dull. This was why the Tías had to make such incessant drama, chillando y chismeando all day long, why the primos had to commit their endless travesuras and why the Tíos performed their borracheras with such gusto. Were we all nothing more than performers? Jesters enacting our skits to distract the curse from boredom, to appease it and keep its sting at bay?

'Vaya,' the woman said to the man. 'Por fin it speaks, this girl child. I told you it would! And all this time you thought it was a mute.'

The man shrugged.

'Better for you,' she said, fixing the two concavities of her brow upon me, looking down at me from her great height. 'We were getting bored with your silence. Vaya, so bored, in fact, that we have been debating whether we should just eat you.'

That was the first time the spectres threatened to consume me, but not the last. It was because of this threat and my fear of being devoured that I did not dare ignore them when they spoke to me, no matter whether they addressed me when we were alone or whether they demanded that I speak in the presence of the living. Whenever and wherever they confronted me, I answered, so, before long, I found myself sitting on the verandah of my first therapist, the one who said I was beyond help, who refused to treat me, and who gave me the statuette of Santa Christina the Astonishing for a talisman.

'Eh-sun-eh-scrin?'

A man touting a box of sunscreen blocks my way, his words tearing me from my memories. He jiggles a bottle of overpriced SPF50 in my face.

'Lady? Sunscreen?'

He thinks me a gringa. He has assessed the shade of my face and taken me for a tourist who has underestimated the strength of the Peruvian sun behind Limenian clouds and is now trapped down here, far below el Malecón, far from any subida, any bodegas. He grins at me and waggles the bottle this way, that way.

'The sun – you burn.'

I want to argue with him. Something furious rises in me, an acid from decades ago, refluxing from my childhood, from all the times the Tías called me blanca, palida, clarita del huevo and never let me bathe in the sun. While Leandro was tostadito, quemadito como un frijol, I was pale and had to be smeared in sunblock, draped under sarongs and confined to the shade of the sombrilla. My cutis was from the *English side*. It was my father's skin I wore, pobrecita – a delicate, Celtic skin, fragile like a fly's wing, no, like paper, rice-white and liable to float away, probably. I had a skin so light, they said, so blue-white it was almost transparent, a skin through which the veins could be seen, snaking across my body in hues of purple and turquoise. Dios mío, that Celtic skin! Practically invisible! (And in hushed voices, so I couldn't hear them: *Pobre niña, like Morticia Addams, like a little muertita! A brujita!*) What skin! Better slather it in protection. Weigh it down so the breeze can't lift it. Coat it so we don't have to see the child's organs through the cellophane epidermis she wears.

He's still there, grinning at me, shaking the bottle at my nose. I could explain to him… No, señor, I'm Peruvian, I could say. I don't burn. This is my patria: my skin can stand the light. I don't have to skulk in the darkness like a little cockroach, scurrying from shadow to shadow, or like a limpid nematode, coiling and recoiling in the bowel. My skin adapts. It knows how to protect itself. It darkens.

But I don't explain to him. I simply turn out the pockets of my dress and shrug apologetically. No money, no money, I say in English. He smiles sympathetically and makes a gesture over his head as if cowering from the sun, taps his watch, advising me it is almost noon. I should take shelter. I smile politely, nod, yes, yes, señor, I understand.

He is right. It is hot. I am thirsty. I haven't drunk since I left the house and my tongue is sticky against my palate. I need water.

I look around me and notice, as if waking from sleep, the brightly painted rowing boats being hauled onto the beach. This is the Playa Pescadores – a little inlet used by independent fishermen, right at the southern tip of el Circuito de Playas. I have never been here before, only seen it zooming past in Abue's Cadillac on the way to the regatta club. Far from Miraflores, I have walked a long way, past the Larcomar mall and the Rosa Nautica with its elegant pier, beyond Barranco even, and the Escuela Militar. Facing the ocean, to my right the cliffs of Lima curve towards La Punta, disappearing into the mist; to my left, rows upon rows of little boats in guava pink and uchuva orange and lime green. They have names like *Mama Qucha*,

Rosalinda, Diana de Gales. Behind the rowboats are little restaurants, a row of cevicherías sharing one roof of corrugated iron, menus painted onto flaking wooden boards propped up against a plastic garden chair. They are empty, save for the strays sniffing around and the owners who sit cross-armed and dozing in the shade. In all my years of driving past, I never saw the restaurants peopled, but then, fishermen keep different hours to the rest of us. Perhaps at night, before they launch at dawn, the places are teeming.

Behind the cevicherías is a high concrete wall, separating the fishermen's beach from the private Playa Uno of the Club de Regatas Lima. Behind that wall, there will be children, watched over by niñeras in pale pinafores while their mothers sun themselves or attend spinning classes in the private gym. The restaurants behind that wall will be full at this hour: men in cream-coloured chinos and starched polo shirts congregate there for lunch-hour meetings that will extend far beyond an hour. They will drink Cusqueñas and eat tequeños and order ceviches made, I suppose, with the fish caught here, at the Playa Pescadores, which has never occurred to me before.

As a child, it discomfited me, that wall – the wall that separated the regatta club from the other beaches. I could not articulate why, even after I found my larynx: there were issues wrapped up in that wall, social issues which I did not yet understand, but it all made me feel embarrassed. As a teenager I began to rebel, stopped going to the club with my family, stayed at home instead with Q'ori and Uriel, hovering near them as they worked, loitering with the awkwardness of a teenager, unsure whether I ought to offer to help, whether this would be an act of kindness, of friendship, or whether my offer would be offensive in some way, as if I were suggesting their work was easy, that anyone could do it.

I have to pee. My bladder is full to bursting, announcing itself without warning as a swollen, distended presence pulsating against the inside of my pubis, as a wrenching pain like a fishing wire hooked to my meatus being urgently reeled in, tugging there, below. That's how it is these days, with the little pink fish. De la nada, the bladder is full and demands to be emptied, immediately, without delay, on pain of urinary humiliation.

Behind that concrete wall, inside the club grounds, there are toilets upon toilets: in the changing cabins for each of the beaches, in the gym, by the frontón courts, at the end of every pier, in the restaurants and bars. Toilets placed strategically, anticipating members' every need right down to the urethra, to the rectum, lest their sphincters be inconvenienced.

In the past, I would not have thought anything of approaching the club gates, whipping out my carnet and crossing over. But today, I doubt security will let me pass. I can't imagine my mother kept paying my fee once I left. The gatekeepers used to know us by face and welcome us by name – *Bienvenidos, Señor, Señora Echeverría* – with a nod of the head and a swoop of the arm to part the gates for Abue's Cadillac.

Today, barefoot, with my sand-crusted dress, carrying nothing on my person – no carnet, no ID, not even a centavo – they would not let me in. Not even if I cited the family name.

But I cannot hold it in any more. The services at the Playa Pescadores are a rudimentary cabin, the BAÑO sign swinging from one screw. Inside, I can imagine it: the toilet bowl will have no seat. There will be no paper, no soap, a trickle of muddy water from the taps, but I can't hold it in. The little pink fish is wretched now, turning blue in the corner of my vision, gasping, pulsing in time with my bladder.

Gathering my skirts, I run into the sea, leaping over the incoming waves and, when I am waist-deep, hidden by the green-grey waters, holding my dress above the surface with one hand, I wriggle out of my underwear and release it from between my fingers. I see it, briefly, swirling beside my hip just below the water, a strange grey fish, before it is sucked away.

As I urinate, I fix my eyes on the horizon. There are trawlers there, disappearing and appearing into and out of the rolling fog, and planes cutting through the clouds. Ocean and sky blend into each other, an expanse of pale grey, shifting and swirling, phantasmal, like breath exhaled in winter, except it is summer and stifling. The air is close round the throat, clings to the skin.

As an adolescent, I developed the romantic habit of standing on the shore and looking out to sea, imagining myself being lifted by an unseen force. I would picture myself through another's eye, an external gaze, like a disciple witnessing a miraculous ascension. First my hair would rise and stand on end, then my arms would lift from the shoulders and reach towards the clouds. My spine would lengthen, my lungs inflate, my whole body relax, deliciously loose, until my feet peeled away from the sand, first the heels, then the arches and finally the toes, the tips detaching themselves from the earth without hesitation.

Then the perspective would be mine again: seeing through my own eyes, across the waters I would soar, faster and faster, waves rushing below me, the coastline of Perú receding into the distance, enveloped by mist and then gone. I would swoop past flocks of migrating birds, past gulls and pelicans, over pods of whales snorting and bellowing. Away, away I would fly until I reached another continent, until I spied the cliffs of Dover, which I imagined to stand facing the cliffs of Lima, an opposite shore, a parallel land mass, across the vast expanse of waters.

There, looking out to sea, my father would be standing, always waiting for me.

Of course, trace a line from Lima across the ocean and the finger hits Queensland, Australia – or possibly Papua New Guinea. Geography was not in my favour.

What is more, the father in my dreams was illusory, an exercise in wish fulfilment. My whole childhood, I blamed my mother for my father's distance, assumed it was she, with her dramatics and her mood swings, who had chased him away. I imagined him as a father who thought of me. A father for whom Leandro and I were the priority, not merely – as I later learned – the embarrassing vestige of an affair between a frustrated anthropology professor and a naive young woman more than twenty years his junior. We were his secondary family, his unintended and unwanted family, consigned to the margins, little more than a semi-interesting field project to occupy his mind on sabbatical years.

My real father, the one of flesh and blood, of meat and bone, lived nowhere near the sea, but miles and miles away with his wife and daughters – his original and preferred (his English) family – in a Victorian house in Wimbledon. That was where I went when I fled Lima after Abue's funeral and arrived in London with no one to turn to and nowhere to go except an address scrawled on the back of the formal and perfunctory airmail letters my father sent us on birthdays and Christmases. I carried one with me that day, folded in my pocket, and showed it to the cabbie after he had repeated three times the words I failed at first to decipher: *Whereyagawindarlin?* Pardon? *Whereyagawin?* Seven years at the British school in Lima had not prepared me for the miscellany of vernaculars I would find when I came to my father's land in person. I was not English. Not bilingual at all, but a foreigner squinting my eyes as I tried to read the cabbie's lips. *Where-are-ya-gah-win?* And when, just over a year later, I relocated to the north to join Rupert at his university, I was lost again, drowning in the vowels and cadences I had never heard before.

Oh, it's you. That is what my father said to me when he opened his door to find me drenched and friendless on his front step. *Oh.*

He had been waiting for, hoping for, his wife. A wife I learned existed only at that moment. A wife who had, a few days before, walked out on him, tired of being neglected for his books and his travels. In her absence, he had not washed, had not eaten in days. There were cold cups of tea balanced atop piles of books spreadeagled, spines cracked, pages scribbled with pencil jottings.

He ran his fingers through his hair several times as he tried to find a place for me to sit.

'It's not a good time really,' he said, avoiding my gaze as I stood dripping into the carpet. 'One ought to call ahead. Give notice.' His hands were shaky as he moved mess about, whether from irritation or exhaustion, I could not tell. He was not the tender father I had fantasised about, nor was he the intrepid adventurer his reputation proclaimed. Just a dishevelled, scattered, carelessly selfish man. He had no time for me. Had an article to finish. Was scratching his head over a catchy hook to open its title: *Something something colon butterfly symbolism in the pre-Hispanic necropoleis of South and Meso-America*. Did I have any ideas? Then, before I could answer, 'No, of course not,' he said. 'Never mind.'

He left me perched on the corner of an armchair laden with papers while he made a phone call in another room. I looked about the room, taking in the photographs of his wife and of his grown-up daughters, half-siblings I had not known existed, and their children, my father's grandchildren. Sitting there, I overheard fragments of phrases from his conversation: *Out of the blue...no notice...bad time... Please come...if you would...*

Within ten minutes, his best friend's wife arrived, olive waxed jacket thrown over an old pair of dungarees. As she shook her umbrella under the porch, she apologised for her appearance, said she and 'Rupey' had been packing. He was off to Durham in a few weeks, Rupey. The house was an awful mess. Terrible timing really. But never mind. Once he was off I could have his room as long as I needed it and, until then, Nouchka was still away travelling on her gap year, so I could take her bed for now. The woman pointed at one of the houses on the opposite side of the street and there in the bay window looking out was a young man, lanky and awkward, even at that distance, and he waved at me.

It was Rupert, with his eyes too close together, his nose too thin for his face and his fluffy, ridiculous hair that his mother used to sweep out of his eyes in a doting, devoted way. Dependable, kind Rupert who, that evening, accompanied me in my jet lag and stayed up late in the kitchen to ask me about myself over cups of cocoa in the half-light dribbling through the window from the street lamps. 'Gosh, that's brave,' he said when I told him I had left my home, my whole family, and travelled alone to an unknown place. Rupert, with his constellations of doting relatives, loyal friends, adoring cousins who all like him so much and revolve around him in a galaxy of devotion. To win friends Rupert need only flash that sympathetic smile or walk alongside someone in that slightly stooping way, hands in pockets, looking pensive, reliable, attentive. *He's such a sweetie*, everyone said to me – cousins, friends, classmates of his. *Just a sweetie*, and from the other side of the room he would dip his head and grin at me through tufts of falling fringe, knowing people were speaking enchantments about him. Before long he had pulled me into his world until I, like everyone else, was circling him, bending my life to orbit his. In the end, he embroidered me so completely into him that, when he proposed, I could not even begin to imagine how to unpick myself without unravelling every relationship, every connection I had made in England and leaving myself cut off and alone.

'That's Rupey,' his mother said, pointing at him in the bay window. He rubbed the back of his neck then gave a curt little wave.

It was less than an hour before I crossed that street with Rupert's mother, given away by my father to the Napiers, who fed me, clothed me, took me on weekends to their country home and then drove me to Durham a year later to join Rupert. I studied anthropology because even then, after all his betrayals, I wanted to impress my father. To find some common language. He never had time for me, though, and only saw me for the occasional Sunday roast with the Napiers, when he would ask me how my degree was going and whether I was in good health, like some distant uncle. But he finished that article about the butterflies found on burial sites. I read it in the final year of my degree and wrote a resentful critique of it in a footnote of an essay.

I remember all these things as my bladder unclenches itself, a fist unfurling in my pelvis, and I look across the waves and settle my eyes on the trawlers. I extend my sight no further. There is nothing like intense pain, extreme pleasure, urination, defecation, orgasm, to anchor the mind to the physical.

So I imagine nothing. No one waits for me on distant shores. No one pines for me. No ascensions or miraculous flying. Just standing chest-deep in the Pacific, naked to the waist, pissing.

OCHO

Santa Julia's first miracle was to rise from the waves of the Pacific and return to the land of the living. The second, witnessed from across the road by an old crone known as La Vieja and her nurse, was to save the somnambulant Echeverría girl child from falling to her death from a second-floor window. The third, unseen and to this day unknown by any but the recipient herself, was a miracle gifted to the old Echeverría cook, Carmen Navarro Thupa.

By the time of her third miracle, Julia had not yet been dead and resurrected for even one day, but the word had already spread that a new saint had been born or ordained or created by whatever means it is that spawns a saint. And then they all came, the pious, the desperate, with their petitions to gather around the foot of Mamabue's house and supplicate. They brought their offerings: incense and scapulars, votive candles, tea lights, paper flowers, foil windmills, soft toys with felt hearts between their paws, plastic plates laden with food, coins imbued with wishes tossed at the windows, enormous prayers scribbled on postcards printed with the young no-longer-dead girl's face and sold at two for one sol by her enterprising second cousins. Later, when the story began to circulate that Santa Julia was a saint for the masses (a saint acquainted with manual labour and ready to lighten the load of her flock), they brought the tools of their trade: tubs of Sapolio and bottles of bleach; dusters and chisels and plungers and wire; origami animals made out of sandpaper; spools of thread, thimbles, and tape of various kinds. They came with these, the instruments of their survival, to beg for her to bless them in their livelihoods.

And she did. But the first of the labourers whom she blessed was la cocinera Carmen, not out of pure altruism, but to rectify a wrong that she had unintentionally created not long before her death. It was a wrong that had deprived the old woman of the use of her right hand and put her at risk of dismissal, for though Carmen had fed the family since Abue was a boy, and though Mamabue had chosen to retain her services even when younger, more talented, more efficient women had knocked on their door seeking employment, it was too much to expect that they would employ a one-handed cocinera who could no longer actually cook.

The accident had come about during one of Carmen's storytell- ing marathons. It was by listening to her grandmother, Jueves Mayo Primera, that Carmen Navarro Thupa had learned to tell stories. Had she been able to finish her studies, Carmen would have writ- ten books. As it was, without a secondary education and without children or grandchildren of her own, Carmen satisfied herself with narrating tales to the strange little mute granddaughter of her employers. Anaïs (the girl who sat at the oak worktable staring into kaylla pacha, so that Carmen was unsure the child could even understand human language) would not remember the old cook's tales in later life, but she would remember the way they made her feel – transported and lifted, as if she were hovering just below the ceiling, watching from above how the salsa bubbled on the stove, how the ants carried away whole mountains of limes one by one, how the old woman's hands snapped the choclos, how the juice of ripe tomatoes spilled across her fingers.

Though the child never gave the slightest indication that she was listening, Carmen could not help narrating. There were stories inside her that could not be still, like bees buzzing in a jar. So, whenever the little mute entered the kitchen, clambered up onto one of the tottering walnut chairs and rested her elbows on the oak worktable, Carmen would begin, and as she spoke, her hands would move expertly, denuding artichokes, shelling scallops, peeling garlic cloves, kneading dough. Always, while narrating, Carmen Thupa's hands must be busy, so much so that if she had no food or kitchen utensil within her grasp, her fingers still worked, sometimes quivering and twitching, sometimes sensuously circling a thumb against a fingertip as if rubbing a sumptuous material that lay between them, then, suddenly, prying, stroking, probing the air as if eagerly and artfully examining an invisible apparatus. With these unquiet hands she told her stories, and every time she opened her marathon of storytelling the same way:

Dice que there was an old woman. ¿No es así, bebe?

She would wait for the little mute to speak, which the child never did, and then Carmen would continue:

Y dice que this viejita, she was on her way home from the market, where she had bought some eggs, when all of a sudden, so they say, there appeared a terrible, raging lion…

(And here, each time, the menace could be different: now a furious bull, now a writhing boa, now, if she delayed too long at her shopping and traversed the lonely roads outside the village after nightfall, she might encounter a hapiñuñu; sometimes, worst of all, the creature was a hybrid freak, with horns of goat and legs of horse, eyes of spider and teeth of lynx.)

…and this viejita, terrified, tried to run, but she stumbled, and in her panic she dropped the basket and dice que the eggs went rolling all around. Passing by, I stopped to help her collect these eggs. Now tell me, chiquilla, how many eggs did you salvage?

The strange little Echeverría never answered her question but just sat there, palms on her cheeks, closing first one eye then the other (a habit which neither oculists nor neurologists nor psychologists had been able to explain); in the silence that followed, Carmen – bent over the table peeling a camote with a carving knife or gutting a fish with her bare fingers – felt profoundly alone in the depths of her entrails because, back at home in Lunahuaná, gathered around the fire at dusk, listening to the huerequeques shrieking scandals between the trees, she and her cousins, her mother and her aunts, indeed all those who had gathered to listen to grandmother Jueves Mayo narrate, understood her invitation and would answer her:

How many eggs did you salvage?

I salvaged three.   *I two.*

I only one.   *I salvaged not a single egg this time.*

Each would share how many eggs she had helped the proverbial old woman recover – of course, what she meant by these was the number of tales she had prepared to tell around the fire that evening.

But in the vast kitchen of the mansion on the hill, when Carmen asked the black-eyed Echeverría child how many eggs she had salvaged, the answer was always a silence the cook would fill with her tales memorised from childhood, though each time a little altered, a little embellished. Sometimes, when she was feeling tired, her stories were a little tamed. Other times, when she had slept and eaten well, they were intensified by the modulations of her voice and movements of her body with which she could become anyone and anything, from the little stone kicked aside in the dirt, into which the soul of a dead man had been compressed, to the fearsome damned of uju pacha, tormented forever in vats of molten iron. Perhaps it was a blessing that Carmen Navarro Thupa had never finished school and become a writer, because the pen would have dampened her narrative – the paper could not have contained the characters she embodied: they needed audible voices cascading from a throat of flesh and blood, legs with which to leap onto tabletops and arms with which to cast trembling shadows onto whitewashed walls.

In those hours in the kitchen, Carmen told the girl about pacha, which meant space-time, and how time and space were one. How the land held time in its very fabric. She told about the mountains and how they held ancient time in their bellies, ñawpa ñawpa pacha boiling there, waiting to erupt like lava because new time was only old time regurgitated from underground. Yes, time is recycled just like water from a subterranean spring that becomes a rushing river racing to the sea then clouds and rain which cries into the soil and burrows deep once more, returning to the hidden realm. Or like life itself which, when extinguished, is buried and returns to the earth only to germinate again. Pacha is a spiral that revolves and revolves into infinity. Like a corkscrew, she said, taking one from a drawer and waving it in front of the child.

And Carmen told about the mountain spirits, the wamani, which ruled over pacha and how, during the dark and distant days called purunpacha, or Wild Time, Thunupa summoned the Andes out of the ground with his voice and banished into their cavities the ancient monsters of the world, and how, deep inside those cerros, rattling around among the bones of the earth, reside the spirits of the evil dead forbidden to enter the heavens of janaj pacha, always trying to escape and find their way back to here, to kay pacha, to recover their bodies and re-enter the world of the living while the Lord God's back is turned. She told her how, at the summits of the tallest alps, the hapiñuñu lurk, watching the mountain tracks, waiting for the solitary traveller so they, those malignant old hags, can snatch their victims between pendulous claw-tipped breasts, drag them to the snow-capped peaks and devour them. And she told the child of the journey to the beyond, of the long walk to Mount Coropuna, where the Lord sits in judgement; of the treacherous crossing of the Map'a-Mayo river; of the cities of dogs, of cats, of chickens and guinea pigs that must be traversed, at best, with the help of those creatures or, at worst, under the pain of their vengeance for a life lived in defiance of Mother Earth; of the fate of those who are judged unworthy to ascend to the heavens, those who are sent into the mouths of the mountains to burn or, worse, exiled to the land of the living to toil forever, banished to the Cordillera to pay for their evils by – pues, it sounds so simple – rolling a boulder to the top of Ausangate, that is all, but, hijita, they fall: the gradient is steep and the ice there is slippery and they never ascend to the top of the mountain, and the terrible cold, it bites their fingers and nips at their toes until the frostbite devours them, little by little. Their hands fall off first, leaving them only blunted wrists with which to push their boulders. Then their feet crumble away, and they hobble around on the bloody stumps, all the time screaming out in agony. Eventually they are just a head, kicked aside into the snow, wailing and wailing, their eyes rolling up towards the summit of the mountain, the point where salvation lies but which they will never reach… Some say, querida, that these heads can float, and, dice que, if you walk alone at night in the Cordillera you will see them, floating and screaming, searching for a body to steal to continue their futile labours…

And so, mi niña, if you know a person guilty of terrible crimes, of incest or murder or the destruction of nature, you must bury them face down, with a boulder on their back. This way, when the banished soul returns to collect their corpse, they will not find it. And without their corpse they cannot journey to the Ausangate to purge their sins: instead they will wander, a fleshless spirit, furious but harmless, through the world, unless, of course, they can find a body to inhabit, which sometimes they do: a bird, perhaps, or a beetle, sometimes a stone or a plant. Or, if they are very clever, they will look for a person. A person wandering alone. A defence-less young woman, too trusting. A child to take their place on the Ausangate. So you must be wary, mi niña, cunning and sharp, and never trust a wandering spirit that you meet on the path.

Then Carmen would pause to observe the child and see if her narrative had taken root, but the girl, like a statue, would stare into nowhere and show no reaction other than the rhythmic opening and closing of each eye in turn.

What Carmen did not know was that the girl was listening, and listening intently, not only to the old cook's narrative but to others as well. To the stories of the servant girls who gathered in the kitchen, unseen by any human eye but one – the right eye of the strange little mute with the inexplicable habit of slowly, deliberately closing one eye then the other instead of blinking both at once. These servant girls, who crowded the room preparing meals for unseen crowds, for opera singers, zarzuela dancers, wedding guests and scores of servants, filled the silences, for each had salvaged more eggs for the viejita than one could begin to count. So the little mute learned that, when Carmen grew tired, she could simply close her left eye and the kitchen would be filled again with the servant girls' stories: this one told tales of damned souls wandering the puna, endlessly searching for a crust of bread to sate their hunger or a cup of water to slake their thirst, never satisfied, for beneath their ragged sackcloth tunics were bodies of air and bone, hollow, through which their victuals slid to land in heaps of slime on the earth. This other told of processions of the dead, hooded and cloaked, with jaws that grind and chains that tremble, who come in search of the sickly and old to circle their home and prepare the way for the arrival of Death himself. And this one told of body parts hovering along the mountain paths at night and of the undead anthropophages who feast on human victims to try to eat their way back into the society of the living.

Each told a tale more hideous than the last, but the worst was a legend that they had all heard, all agreed was true, and which was proof irrefutable that the sins of the guilty could be visited on the innocent, the sins of the father on the son. This was how they told it:

Dice que there was a wealthy landowner – a man full of pride – whose stables were packed with horses and whose coffers overflowed with gold. He was a selfish man: he failed to give alms to the poor and did not treat his slaves with kindness and never left food on the dusty lanes outside the town for the hungry dead. Do you hear, querida?

But the girl sat silent, watching them with one wide black eye, holding the other firmly shut with her fingers. At the stove, Carmen tutted and sighed, shaking her head with pity for the poor child who had been born without intelligence, while all around her she could not see the servant girls that laughed and bustled.

The wealthy man, así dicen, had no wife. Instead he took for himself the wives of his workers with no care for whether these women wanted him or not. It came to pass that one of the women – the wife of one of his faithful servants who had worked for him with loyalty for many years – particularly pleased him, and he could not bear to share her with her husband. So, one night, the wealthy landowner woke his servant at midnight with all urgency, telling him, 'Come quickly! One of the horses has fallen into a pit and cannot escape!'

The servant, dutiful as always, leapt from his bed and followed the landowner out into the fields, the darkness illuminated only by the weak flame of his master's lantern.

'Give me a light, master,' the servant said. 'Give me a light so that I might see the way.'

But the master refused and told him, 'Follow behind me, and I will make you a path.'

And so the master led the faithful servant through the night.

When they reached the edge of the pit, the servant said to his master, 'The night is silent, but I cannot hear the sound of any fallen horse. Give me a light so that I might see through the darkness.'

But the master refused and told him, 'Come closer, and I will light your vision.'

So the servant came closer to the master and peered through the gloom and said, 'I am searching hard, but I cannot see any shapes through the shadows. Give me a light so that I might search more carefully.'

But the landowner insisted and told his servant, 'Look! There!' Then he pointed his finger towards the cavernous deep of the pit and, as the dutiful servant leaned over the edge, the wealthy landowner pushed him over, and the servant tumbled down. As he fell, the sound of his bones cracking and shattering could be heard like gunshots resounding across the fields – or they would have been heard if anyone had been awake to hear them. They say, no es así, that if you go to the wealthy man's hacienda today, you can still hear the sound of the servant's bones cracking like gunshots in the night.

Here, the little girl would raise her eyebrows and blink a few times to alleviate the stinging of her corneas, caused, perhaps, by pity over the fate of the doomed servant, or perhaps because of the sharp vapours of the red onions Carmen sliced to accompany every meal.

But the servant was not yet dead, the servant girls told the child. The landowner could hear him whimpering at the bottom of the pit. So the landowner grabbed a shovel and filled in the pit until, by daybreak, all that could be seen was a circle of fresh earth in a field. Beneath that circle was the servant, buried while still alive.

In the morning, the servant's wife woke to find he was not there and she raised the alarm among her friends, but the husband was nowhere to be found.

'He has abandoned you,' the wealthy man told the wife, and he brought her to live inside his grand house. Some months later, the servant's wife bore a child, a daughter, and the wealthy man – infuriated by the child's screaming – sent mother and daughter away, paying for their meagre survival in a small hut in a village several hours' journey from the hacienda.

Now, the wealthy man also had a wife and she gave him a son and the wealthy man was proud of this son, who was as headstrong and stubborn as his father. But the son would never do as he was told by his mother or his tutors: instead he would escape the hacienda on horseback to wander around the countryside, playing tricks on the labourers and flirting with the local girls.

At last, when he was fifteen years old, the rebellious son met a young woman who beguiled him more than any other. Though she lived far from the hacienda, he would steal away before daybreak to hide among the bushes and watch her bathing in the river.

Now the servant girls would giggle and pinch each other at the waist, waving maize leaves flirtatiously like fans and winking at the Echeverría child with knowing smiles. But the child did not smile back: she simply stared at them with her one open eye. Sometimes she heard her name called in exasperated tones from somewhere far off in the house or perhaps between the naranjos in the garden, and then she would hide under the table, hugging her knees, staying very still to be sure not to betray herself to those who might come searching...

At around this time, the hacienda began to be menaced by a terrible monster that roamed at night. Some said it was a huge black bird with a piranha's teeth in its beak. Some said it took the shape of a llama and that they had seen it silhouetted on the crests of hills against the face of the moon. Others said it appeared like a lumbering tree on legs. But all agreed on the noise it made as it stalked the darkness: it cried out qar-qar, qar-qar, qar-qar. It was, without doubt, a qarqacha.

The rich man disbelieved the stories of his workers for, unlike his servants who slept in huts outdoors in the fields with flimsy doors of rush, he slept safe and warm behind the strong stone walls of the farmhouse. So he ignored the claims until the monster began to attack his livestock, slitting their throats in the fields, gutting them messily, leaving trails of bowels along the hacienda's pathways and courtyards. Then the rich man began to sit awake at night to listen, and, at last, one evening, he heard the cry coming from the bedroom of his son.

Dagger in hand, he summoned his mastiffs and sprinted to the son's bedside only to find that the boy was not there! The bed was empty! Furious, suspecting his son of sabotaging his own father by attacking the hacienda's livestock, the rich man waited in hiding outside the hacienda for the return of the boy but, overcome by fatigue, he fell asleep.

Early the next morning the rich man was woken by the rays of the sunrise to see his son slipping away from the hacienda. So the rich man roused himself and followed the boy, intent on discovering his mischief and punishing him.

He followed the boy for several hours until he reached the river, where he watched his son meet with the girl who was his lover. Secretly, he watched the couple bathe in the river and, afterwards, how they lay together in the long grass and made love.

Then the rich man knew the cause of the qarqacha for, looking at the girl, there could not be any doubt that he was her father, but it was too late. His son and the girl had already consummated their relationship. There was nothing to be done.

Sometimes the servant girls, in swooping past the transistor radio, would interfere with its signal and Carmen, her fingertips wet with lime juice or fish sweat, would become frustrated by the white noise that crackled across the kitchen and would try to turn the knob with her knuckles, her wrists, even her elbows, cursing the house for its radio reception that, despite the casona's elevated situation, was so unreliable. Meanwhile, around her, the servant girls continued, undisturbed by the radio's hiss, hearing instead the soprano voice that rang out from Tía Consuelo's gramophone or sometimes from the very vocal chords of Elena Echeverría herself. And they continued to tell their tale:

So the rich man sent his son away – far away from the hacienda – to work in some distant part of the country. And the son's lover stayed behind, broken-hearted, with no knowledge of where her beloved had gone.

Many years later, the wealthy landowner died and was buried. Because the servant women knew the things that he had done in life, they took every precaution with his corpse. With knives, they scored his palms and with a branding iron burned the soles of his feet. With pliers they tore his fingernails from their beds and plucked the lashes from his eyes. Then they had their men bury the corpse face down in the ground, with a boulder on its back.

The rich man's widow, terrified by the stories she heard of his wrong-doings, agreed that she and all the women with whom he had sinned should be protected lest his soul return to sweep one of them away with him into the beyond. After the burial, all the rich man's women gathered together in the dining room of the farmhouse, ready to remain there for ten days, protected by a perimeter of crucifixes, shutters closed, illuminated only by the flames of burning candles, rinsing themselves hourly in holy water. Meanwhile, the men took it in turns to watch over the rich man's grave, night and day, to be sure that his soul could not return to recover its body.

Now, the rich man's son returned to the hacienda as soon as the news reached him of his father's death, but he was so far away that he arrived after the burial had taken place. So distraught was he that he insisted he should be allowed to watch the grave alone, to mourn and say his goodbyes to the old man in privacy.

The following morning, when the servant-men arrived to relieve the son of his watch, they found that the young man was gone and the mound over the grave sunken, collapsed back into the earth. Frantically, they dug at the grave and there they found the body face up, the boulder removed and – worst of all – the corpse picked at, as if by sharp teeth, with great chunks bitten out of its face, its arms, its torso... Terrified, the men ran all the way to the village to summon a priest, but when they returned with the holy man, the corpse was nowhere to be seen, the grave entirely empty.

For you see, querida, the young man had exhumed his father's corpse and devoured it, and this was the old man's punishment because of his terrible evils, for allowing his own son to mate with the daughter he had sired in adultery and who was the fruit of his murderous lusts.

And they say, mi niña, that, if you visit the hacienda, the monster is roaming still, shrieking qar-qar in the night, devouring any who dare to walk out after dusk.

They say that the soul of the father, damned forever, wanders the fields, moaning in agony, for he feels even in his spirit the pain of being continually digested – eternally chewed and torn by the teeth of his son, the qarqacha.

Their tale told, the servant girls would pause mournfully where they stood, reflecting on the pitiful fate of the damned. Still, the little Echeverría would not react: she would only mechanically release her fingers from her left eyelid. Stiff from being held down so long and so firmly, the flap of skin would stick a few moments to the eyeball before slowly peeling itself away and retracting back into her skull.

This tale of the wealthy landowner and his qarqacha son was the one tale Grandmother Jueves Mayo had not told young Carmen. The first time Carmen heard it was when she was already very old, in the kitchen of the yellow house on the hill. She heard it not from the servant girls (unseen by any eyes but one), but from the seventeen-year-old not-yet-Santa Julia Álvarez Yupanqui, who was amazed that the old woman, who knew all the tales there were to tell and even added to their number, had never heard this ubiquitous story. One quiet morning before dawn when all the Echeverrías were still asleep, while Carmen stood peeling the breakfast papayas with a carving knife, young Julia leaned conspiratorially across the oak worktable and, eyes wide with the mischievous pride of a novice schooling the master, told the tale which she had known by heart since infancy.

As Carmen absorbed the words, something vital and brittle shattered inside her. Later, when reflecting upon her reaction to the tale, Carmen would say that it was because she had heard the tortured scream of a loved one, but all Julia saw was that the old woman jumped and her usually dextrous hands fumbled, causing her to drop the carving knife with which she had been peeling the papayas. The knife spun in the air and then the blade, now turned towards her, sliced through the old woman's right hand, severing not only flesh and sinew, but also the median nerve, so that even after the curandero of Los Polvos (for Carmen had forbidden Julia from summoning any doctor connected with the family) had stemmed the bleeding, disinfected and sewn shut the wound and bound it in cloth, the thumb would never work again. If the old woman had been seen in the private clinic of her employers, could her hand have been saved? But she insisted that Don Julio and the mistress must not be woken lest they see her injury and deem her no longer fit for service.

To help the old woman hide her new impediment, Julia colluded in the lie that the bandage hid nothing more than a dog bite, and from that day on she rose earlier every morning, long before dawn, to complete all the washing and chopping and peeling needed for the day ahead. It exhausted her, this early rising to undertake another woman's job before she began her own duties: of waking the children and bathing them; of taking them, washed and dressed and breakfasted, to their mother; of laundering the clothes and hanging them to dry; of ironing and starching and darning and folding; of polishing the silver and defogging the glass; of disinfecting toilet bowls and descaling taps and rinsing the bathtubs, the bidets, the sinks; of inspecting corners and cornices, skirting boards and architraves for poisonous spiders or roach eggs; of sluicing the majolica and wiping down the shutters and running a rag over every last horizontal surface; and, of course, of sweeping – insistently, tenaciously, unendingly sweeping – the dust.

Several times Julia was tempted to confess all to Mamabue and implore them out of mercy to retire old Carmen, but with a pension to match her current salary or, at least, a portion of it; Julia, from her own wages, would offer to supplement the difference in the monthly sum. But then she would carry out the calculations silently in her mind as she dusted and swept, exhausted, distracted, her mind far from her task as she worked and reworked the numbers, limbs moving through the chores from muscle memory but without intent, and then Julia would realise her plan was not feasible, for she had younger siblings who needed shoes and books and feeding and the windows of the Álvarez family home were still without glass and the roof was still untiled and she knew that the old woman's nephew relied on the contributions she made to be able to continue his studies at the National University of Engineering. No, there were too many lives contingent on the current arrangement, and too many futures poised on leaving things as they were.

To make matters worse, refining and purifying her guilt, Carmen had developed the habit of wailing in her sleep. Julia did not understand it then, but once she had died and ascended into janaj pacha she would learn that to Carmen the loss of the hand was not just the loss of an appendage with which to peel and dice and stir the meals of her employers or to comb her hair in the morning or to turn the pages of her Bible at night. Carmen's hands connected her to a long line of memory from which she had been severed when the papaya-wet blade cut open her palm and sliced her median nerve and, though she did not understand this consciously, her spirit knew it, and this is why she wailed in her sleep.

Santa Julia understood all this when, from her elevated position above Space and Time, she would see Carmen's inquisitive hands fidgeting on the wrists of an emaciated pregnant Luba woman in Cartagena and also on the wrists of that woman's daughters and granddaughters spread across the continent. With those same hands two hundred years later, twin girls born on a Wednesday in August would learn to crawl across the dusty vineyards of a hacienda in Pisco while their mother picked Quebranta grapes. These identical restless hands on identical restless sisters would conduct identical relentless work for seventeen years until, one Sunday afternoon, the right palm of Miércoles the Second was branded by the master in punishment for tripping on a stone and spilling her vat of grapes, while the hand of Miércoles the First was left unscarred. It was the scar of Miércoles the Second that was held aloft in a courtroom to convince a judge of the guilt of the master. Under the Royal Decree of 1789 on the Education, Treatment, and Occupation of Slaves, a master could choose sanctions from among imprisonment, shackles, chains, beatings with a mace, confinement within stocks (albeit not by the head), and scourging not exceeding twenty-five lashes with such instruments as will not draw blood or leave grievous bruising.

But, as evidenced by the burn scar on Miércoles the Second's right palm, Enrique Echeverría had not restricted himself to the sanctions set out in the Decree and had inflicted cruel, unusual punishments such that Miércoles Segunda was manumitted by the court while Miércoles Primera had to remain enslaved.

So it was that the hands of Miércoles Segunda would clutch her carta de horría, the letter freeing her from slavery, as she made her way to Lima, while the hands of Miércoles Primera would remain behind and, later, swaddle the daughter who had been fathered not by her husband, sent away to the islands of hell, but by the master who had branded one sister and brought the other into his farm-house for his pleasure. The illegitimate daughter, on account of being born on the first Thursday in May, was named Jueves Mayo Primera and she, too, had inherited Bulanda Ilunga's inquisitive hands. These hands, when they were just fourteen years old and unhardened by manual labour, would find their way inside the trousers of a boy she had met by the river with whom she felt an irresistible connection, a closeness that was more than physical, and there, by the river, they did things together of which their mothers would not approve. Though this boy would disappear from her life, she never forgot him and out of love for him she never married, instead dedicating herself to the telling of tales for which she was famous. These tales she told while gesticulating urgently with those turbulent, relentless hands – hands also inherited by her daughter, Augusta, and with which her daughter waved her goodbye as she departed Lunahuaná to work as a lavandera in Lima, collecting clothes from the grand casonas of Miraflores and laundering them in a wooden vat in the alley of the crowded corralón where she would live and work and die prematurely, leaving her own daughter nothing more than restive hands as an inheritance.

While living, burdened by the guilt of the accident she had caused, Julia colluded in the old cook's charade until the exhaustion of completing two women's jobs led her to plummet from the second-floor window that fateful morning in June 1986. Thereafter, Santa Julia was able to intervene in a more effective way to relieve the old woman's pain, not by healing her hand (the power of miraculous healing was not in her gift), but by continuing to orchestrate the washing and peeling and chopping and stirring.

The morning after the death of Julia Álvarez Yupanqui, Carmen – now facing life at the casona without her faithful accomplice and friend – descended the house towards the kitchen utterly hopeless, cradling her right hand in her left, willing the nerve to repair itself, praying that the thumb would find some animation. Of course, she found that try as she might the member would do nothing but flop listlessly and uselessly from her wrist.

She was ready to turn herself in to her employers, to confess all, but then she pushed open the door of the kitchen and saw in plain sight the third miracle enacted by Santa Julia. The carving knives whipped through the air, peeling and dicing papayas that rolled without support far above head height. Oranges and lemons hovered in a neat row, waiting in line to juice themselves in the fruit press. On the stove, a pot of strawberries simmered for jam, a pan of rice pudding stirred itself. On the oak worktable, three headless chicken carcasses strutted in a circle rubbing one another with seasoning while on the floor around them were the heads that had already been chopped off and the mounds of feathers that had been plucked by some unseen force. In the mortar, the pestle ground the ají and the ajo. In the oven, fifty flawless karamandukas were baking. In the fridge, ready-made, were guacamole and salsa Huancaína and rocoto salsa and pico de gallo.

In the months and years that followed, the Echeverrías were often known to comment that despite the tragic loss of Julia (the best maid they had ever had), their one consolation was that the food produced by la cocinera Carmen, both in terms of quality and quantity, had never been better. The old woman had reached her peak at the age of seventy-six and she would, defying all sense and reasonable explanation, sustain her pace of production well into her eighties, even after she lost her sight due to cataracts and even after she was so overcome by tremors that she could not pour a glass of water without wetting the whole tablecloth. The Echeverrías often asked themselves how Carmen did it, but they were never allowed into the kitchen during the hours of meal preparation to find out. The old woman, in return for an endless supply of delicious meals, had only two requests: that she receive her wages on time and that her territory be respected. It was a small price to pay. In this way, the Echeverrías ate well and Carmen Navarro Thupa was able to put her nephew, Augusto García Navarro, through his degree in architecture at the National University of Engineering.

Eventually, as Santa Julia's fame grew and she became inundated with prayers and petitions, there came mornings when Carmen would descend to find the utensils resting in their places, the food inanimate, the kitchen entirely unmoving. Over time, such mornings became more frequent, until the day when Santa Julia visited the Echeverría kitchen for the last time, never to return again. Then the family had no choice but to retire old Carmen, and Q'orianka took her place.

Upon enquiry, the Echeverrías found that Carmen had no children, no living siblings (for her sister had lately died), no next of kin who could house her. Her nephew was now studying in Europe and had no income beyond a small university stipend. The Navarros of Lunahuaná had not heard of Carmen, and they could not trace any Thupas in the region, which (though they did not know it) was because Thupa was a name that Grandmother Jueves had chosen at random, not knowing the real surname of the handsome boy she had loved by the river.

So Mamabue let the old cook keep her small room and there she lived out her days, muttering to herself, leafing through her Bible pretending she could still see to read, mostly sleeping, clutching and clawing at the sheets with her left hand, wailing so loudly at night that the dogs of Los Polvos would howl along with her and keep all the residents of the Avenida del Guanero awake. Once in a while, her wailing would fall silent. These were the times when she was dreaming about that morning when she witnessed the third miracle of Santa Julia – then she would laugh and laugh and her mirth infiltrated the dreams of the slumbering Echeverrías.

NINE

Sin duda alguna, you will break his heart.

The Wailing Lover, El Gritón, hangs sloppily from the chandelier, prophesying over me as I peer between the shutters and watch
Rupert. He is beyond the gates, looking up at the house from the
twilit Avenida where I left him. He examines without affection or
familiarity, like a surveyor assessing structural integrity. Or like a
tourist, half-interested, half-disappointed, inspecting some great
monument that looked better in brochures. What is he seeing?
Are the walls pristine or peeling? Lúcuma or some other shade?
Are the shutters, from where he stands, secure or swinging loose?
Every time I see this house, it changes, ageing and transfiguring,
sweeping backwards and forwards across the decades as if time
were a wardrobe of costumes to be donned and discarded, or as
if the present, the past, the future were painted scrims, dropping
from the flies, appearing and disappearing as the light changes.

What does Rupert see as he stands squinting up at the house
where we, peeking through the shutters, watch him?

Like all women, you are sinister and unfeeling.

El Gritón interrupts my thoughts. The fingers of his left hand,
inhumanly long, wind round and round the neck of a half-empty
bottle of Portón while with his right hand he scratches my back.
His fingers, spindly and articulated like spider's legs, leave red
tracks on my skin. He is drunk. He was always drunk, alternately

157

skulking in corners and sobbing and then leaping into open spaces and roaring his resentment against womankind. Jilted! Abandonado y rechazado by a woman whose name he had forgotten but who had been, sin duda alguna and without question, the love of his life, his soulmate, la única.

Without doubt, it was the heartache that killed him, he told me the first time I discovered him folded up like an accordion in the liquor cabinet – it was the heartache, sin duda. Yes! Indudablemente! Beyond question! In a way, if you think about it, niña, she was the murderess who put me in this state. He let out a tortured snort – the sound of air escaping a withering balloon – and plunged his head and neck, right down to the shoulders, into a bottle of scotch.

After I had seen him once, I could not unsee him, could not ignore the stench of alcohol and stagnant breath that wafted from him, and, worse, could not unhear him and his wailing without end, his embittered assertions that all women were vipers, walking snake pits, empty shells of tits and nalgas but, inside, no heart.

I say it now, once and for all, you will destroy this man.
He lets out a scream that sets every windowpane and glass in the house to ringing, high and sharp like the prefiguring of disaster. When I used to live here, some of the Tías could hear it: they would cock their heads to one side and comment on the piercing tinnitus that had suddenly afflicted them. Es la electricidad, someone would say to comfort them. Nothing more than the electricity humming in the walls. But it was always El Gritón, vibrating the glass with his grief.

Outside, Rupert is speaking on the phone, left fist on hip, pacing back and forth. Who is he speaking to? Mimi, probably. The one who summoned him here from across the ocean – traidora, metiche – alarming him with news that I was incapable, unstable, living in squalor, alone and pregnant. Yes! Pregnant! He couldn't believe it. He was hurt. I could see it as soon as the taxi pulled up by the gate and he was there, sitting on the kerb. We blinked at each other through the glass of the cab window. I thought he was a hallucination: all day I had been seeing Dr de las Casas in the faces of strangers, the back of his head among crowds of tourists, the flash of his briefcase between the bodies of cars backed up on el Circuito de Playas, and now I was imagining Rupert here, thousands of miles from where he must actually be – London, in his office, staring at his computer, firing off emails.

Even as he stood and came towards me, opened the car door, paid the driver, I watched in a kind of stupor. The sun had soaked my brain; I hadn't drunk anything in hours. I was thinking through a gauze, with everything diaphanous and glaring. In a moment he would change colour or turn into a plant or bark at me and become the golden, torn-eared stray with the oozing flank.

No, it really was him.

'Your Aunt Mimi called,' he told me. 'She was worried about you.'

I straightened myself up, ran my hands over my skirt to smooth it, wondered whether he could tell I wasn't wearing underwear and had peed in the ocean.

'She needn't have worried you,' I told him, the English clumsy on my tongue. Since arriving, my tongue has been reshaping itself – that is how it feels. My palate, the position of my teeth, my vocal cords all feel different. I've been dreaming in Spanish, the way I used to. There's something cumbersome about English sounds, the proliferation of consonants, the way they aren't separated by vowels that open the mouth and bounce the tongue between syllables. It's like mumbling. Like being so ashamed of what you're saying that you daren't even part your lips. 'I'm fine. It's all fine. Everything's under control.'

I should have told him, he said. He would have helped me. He would never have let me travel alone if he had known…

'That's why I didn't tell you,' I said. My mind chewed over his words. He would have *helped me*. He wouldn't have *let me*.

'Let's go inside,' he said, 'to talk.' That's when I noticed that the casona had changed utterly since the day before: from weather-beaten and dilapidated it had morphed again. Shutters had been reattached and sanded down, the facade had been re-rendered, the winding path weeded and washed until gleaming. And the yellow house on the hill – it was not yellow any more, but green. A guacamole green, with the shutters painted the orange-red of rocoto salsa.

Had the taxista parked in front of the wrong house? Was this another street entirely? But no, this was Mamabue's casa, discoloured and gaudy in colours that I had never seen it painted, yet underneath its garish paintwork, it was still the same.

What was he seeing? I asked myself then, as I ask myself now. A yellow house or a green one? Decrepit or unsullied? And what would he see if I brought him inside? Would the lights be turned on and the water running? Would the parquet be polished, the majolica gleaming and the smell of neroli curling through the halls? Or would all be dark and dusty, sheet-draped furniture looming like bulky ghosts, ants marching along the walls? If he entered, would he condemn the house, put his foot down and take me away?

No, I said, a little too urgently. We should go out. He should see the city a little. I know a lovely spot. We could get a drink. See some Limenian sights. Have a stroll, if he wanted.

This man loves you, and you dissimulate.

El Gritón has wrapped the fingers of his free hand around my torso and is beginning to squeeze. I can feel the knobs of his knuckles pressing between my shoulder blades and just underneath my sternum.

When he learns how much you lie to him, it will poison his soul.

'Your problem is that you expect too much of people,' I tell El Gritón, extricating myself from his grip.

I hear my words as if ventriloquised at a distance and feel the keen eyes of de las Casas on me, as if he were watching me from behind a one-way mirror or from above, through the clear plastic of a Perspex cube in which I scurry, a lab rat, and complete tasks for him in return for little treats. I sense his analysis of me. I watch his notes appearing in the air in his angular, black script: *Cynical lack of trust. Fear of intimacy. Inability to commit.* I see him sitting in his armchair, humming critically, scribbling and scribbling about me.

With thumb and forefinger, I pick him up by the collar and visualise dropping him into the hollow of a Russian doll, see him curled inside there, foetal, peering up at me. I twist on the lid – it squeaks – and I close him inside. Then I put the first doll inside another and another and another, layer upon layer, locking him deeper and deeper until I can barely hear the scratching of his nib on paper.

She's seeing things.

She's always seeing things.

Loca, loca, loca.

'Unless you want to be next, les convendría to shut your mouths.'

They fall silent. El Gritón, still hanging from the chandelier, begins to stretch languorously and viscously, his nose, his eyes, his lips melting like wax towards the floor, features extending and blending together, bursting into Technicolor and bleeding. I want to stretch out my hands and run them through the colours, swirl my fingers through the mess and make curlicues and filigrees. But I don't. I keep them to myself, bury them in the folds of my skirt.

This is exactly why Rupert could not have come into this house. How could I even be sure if, stepping across the threshold, we would arrive in the same place? What if he had crossed into the immaculate house and I into the derelict? Or, worse, the other way around? What if he had found himself alone in this place of melting, expressionist drunkards and tiny psychoanalysts without me here to reassure him, to guide him in the etiquette of coexisting with the dead? Separated in space and time, how could I have found him again? And, upon finding him, how would I explain the things he had seen and heard in my absence? No. It would be best if Rupert did not enter Mamabue's house.

Instead we went to the Parque Kennedy and sat at a bistro table under the awning of El Haití. We sat in silence at first. We watched the people walking past. Tourists buying chullos from stalls on the pavement. Brujas accosting passers-by with offers of palm readings, love spells. Cambistas in high-vis waistcoats, wads of dollars, euros, soles wedged behind elastic belts and into deep pockets. Drifting from the amphitheatre, the tones of a salsa band intermingled with the noise of traffic, the claxons, the grunting of engines. Between the trees and buses, we could snatch glimpses of people dancing: young lovers with pelvises pressed together, middle-aged ladies with ample bosoms waving their arms and laughing, old men leaning on walking sticks, bending their knees in time with the beat, updown updown updown updown. Watching – pretending to watch – justified our silences. We were – we hoped that we seemed to be – absorbed in observation, comfortable in our quietness.

Then, suddenly, he reached out to hold my hand. I moved it away, used it to lift my glass, pretended I hadn't noticed his attempt at affection. He asked where the Napier ring was – why I wasn't wearing it. Not safe, I told him. Not safe to wear such an expensive piece of jewellery outside in Lima. It satisfied him, my reply. Another lie. It assuaged his fears. We should get an alternative, he said. Something less ostentatious. Something *cheap and cheerful*, to wear while I'm here. He'd heard gold was good value in Perú. All right, I said. We could do that.

Most of the tables were filled with limeña ladies, more-than-middle-aged. Chanel perfume in the air. Everywhere terracotta nails drumming the tabletops. Handbags strapped to chairs with safety chains, just in case – the economy is good, but you never know. Waiters in white shirts and bow ties bobbed in and out between the tables and the potted palm trees. The room, mirrored like a 1920s dance hall, wine glasses hanging upside down above the bar where a young muscular man was chopping pineapples. He caught me watching him and raised his eyebrows. I looked away. Looked at Rupert. Tried to affect a look of love. I'm with this man.

'Mother is very hurt,' he said at last. 'She can't understand why you didn't tell us and just ran off.'

'Well, God forbid I offend your mother,' I said.

'That's not fair. She cares about you.' And to prove it, his mother had sent me a gift, a parcel wrapped in pastels with a label: *For the Napier baby.* They were booties – little woollen booties that had been Rupert's, knitted by his grandmother.

'Very nice,' I said, laying them on the tabletop while the little pink fish, with no feet to speak of, bobbed about in the corner of my vision.

'I just don't understand why you didn't tell me,' he said.

And what could I say? How could I confess my ambivalence about the pregnancy? The utter lack of candyfloss happiness that one is supposed to feel (or so I've been led to believe) when a foetus has lodged itself inside one's abdomen. How could I explain that, seeing the two pink lines that afternoon of my graduation, I had been appalled by the notion of having a *Napier baby* – a baby who would be three quarters English, barely Peruvian at all, and sur-rounded by *his* web of connections, knowing nothing of my family, my culture. That I had a presentiment of how, with each genera-tion, the slice of Peruvianness in my children's children's children would halve and halve and halve again, a quarter, then an eighth, then one sixteenth, fading smaller and smaller, pruning me away.

'You don't need to worry,' he said when I didn't answer, taking a pen out of his jacket pocket. 'About the finances, I mean, if that's what you were worried about. I'll take care of you. And now it doesn't matter that you haven't found a job. You can look after the baby. And you don't need to feel bad about the money.' He began scribbling calculations on a paper napkin, listing numbers down two columns, his salary, his investments, then subtracting, applying percentages. 'I've got my trust fund, and my parents will help us, and you're bringing this inheritance money from the house, so you needn't feel like you aren't contributing.' He looked up from his jottings through a fuzz of hair and smiled, raising his eyebrows, holding my gaze as if seeking my approval.

Behind me, two men sat smoking and gossiping in loud, gruff voices. They spoke with all the confidence and entitlement of the miraflorino – no hedging, no modulation of volume, but a stirring, zealous conviction, growled from the back of the throat, passionate, like two preachers delivering noontime sermons to each other face to face across the table.

¡Pues, sí! That's what I told him. Le dije, ¡Pedro, eres un imbécil!

¡Así es! He is useless! Idiota.

Idiota total.

But didn't I tell you ya? Así te lo dije. Te dije, don't trust Pedro. No me jodas. It was I that told you.

¡No te hagas, Jaime! Go to hell.

Go there yourself.

All the while, as they called Pedro an imbécil and damned each other to hell, they sat together, elbow to elbow, drinking their coffee and puffing on cigarettes.

A child approached our table. He was maybe six or seven. His toes – crooked, dusty, ragged nails – spilled out over the front of his flip-flops. His shirt was misbuttoned. His black hair lustreless. His dark eyes wide.

'Money, mister. Money, lady.'

With one hand, he gripped the edge of the table, dirt under his fingernails and encrusted in his cuticles. The other hand he held out to us, flat and insistent. There was grime in the creases of his palm.

Across the street, a young woman was watching – younger than me. Strapped to her back with a grubby cloth was a baby. Or rather the outline of a baby – I could not see its face. The woman's expression was mournful but not urgently so. She looked straight at me and seemed not to see me at all, as if I were transparent, a pane of glass or a puff of air. I had the feeling of being erased, forgotten, a phantom but she…she and her mournfulness, her unblinking eyes, the form of the burden on her back, were so incontrovertibly solid, so undeniably here.

It would be wrong to call her a beggar. She was not begging. Nothing about her expression implored me. She was simply watching. Waiting to see what I would do. Give the money or do not give it – she was completely resigned to our choice. To our whim. Yielded, utterly, to our inclinations, as if she and we inhabited alien worlds and the road that ran between us was an impassable chasm. As if nothing she could do would have any bearing on our decision – give the money or do not give it. She was merely spectating, a bystander.

Rupert looked to me. *What is the etiquette here?* he seemed to ask. *Do we tip the street children?* He was deferring to me as the native. As someone local. Someone who knew the rules.

When I was young, when the street children were everywhere, crowding the Cadillac at every traffic light, thronging us on the pavement, knocking at the door at Christmas and Easter and most Sundays, I learned that there were two responses. The women gave them money. A few moneditas from their purse, handed over with gentle, humming voices: *Ten, mi amor. Tan pequeño. Dios te cuide.* Or, from the little ones that sold caramelitos outside the supermarkets, the women would buy the treats – lemon drops, Adams Chiclets – and then hand them back to the children, saying, *These are for you, mi amor. You enjoy them.*

Then, the men would tut and shake their heads. They would point to the mothers, sitting together in groups on the grass of the central reservation, babies strapped to their hunched backs. *See there*, they would say. *See their mothers, sitting there, lazy, on their asses?* Then they would tap their watches. *See the time it is*, they would say. *These children should be in school, learning, getting an education for a better future. But you! You do-gooders give them money and their mothers take them out of school to beg. ¡Es abuso! Child abuse, es esto! Stop giving them money, and their mothers will send them to school.*

The women would wave their hands in the air, swatting away their husbands' criticisms. *How can children study without food? Without shoes on their feet? Without paper and pencils? Let us put food in their bellies first.*

Then the men would grumble about food stamps and the racket of beggar kids for hire and the campesinos breeding like rabbits. The women would curse the male race who lead young girls – only children themselves – astray and then abandon them as soon as their bellies bear fruit. Then the men would execrate the Church and its medieval stance on contraception and the women would throw up their hands saying that El Señor would come to judge the living and the dead and how could they stand before him, they who were mothers themselves, and say they had refused a child or a mother in need?

Now they looked to me – Rupert and the little boy and the woman across the street and generations of Tíos and Tías watching over my shoulder to see what I would do. And, as if that weren't enough, also God in heaven! The little pink fish, as always, was eyeballing me. Give the money or do not give it – what is the etiquette here?

My hands moved instinctively to my purse, but it was not there. Once again, I had nothing on me. I took Rupert's wallet – Aspinal of London, leather, embossed in gold with his initials. Folding it open, I noticed its skin, creased and wrinkled with lines, with hatch patterns and criss-cross marks like those on my own hands, like those on the palm of the begging child, and I marvelled at how humans think so little of wearing dead things, marvelled at how easily the deceased accumulate around the living.

I rifled clumsily through the contents – dollars, euros, pounds – did he even have soles? The child had no use for foreign currency. Should we change some notes with the cambistas? No. No time. The child was here now, hand outstretched. At last, I found some soles. Denominations of two hundred and one hundred…nothing smaller. Unzipping the coin pouch, I poured change out onto the table: a dozen queens' heads rolled out. British coins. Nothing useful. Nothing for the boy. Still, he got up on tiptoe, examined the coins but waited, obediently, to be handed his share.

Staring at the notes, I faltered. The Tías usually handed over *moneditas*. A sol or two in spare change. Never notes. Almost never, except, perhaps, to the *mendigos* outside the church – the really needy ones. The ones without limbs or eyes. The ones who had begged there for decades and grown old and withered under the bucayo trees, some selling little candles, embroidered prayers on scraps of cloth, statuettes of saints, others too ailing to craft, able just to sit, arms outstretched, muttering pleas to God and passers-by. To these, whose need produced in me a terror that gripped my bladder like a crushing hand, the Tías might give a bill of ten soles at Christmas or on Good Friday. But to the children, they gave *monedas*.

As I dithered, a waiter emerged, tray of drinks balanced on one hand; with the other he gripped the boy by the shoulder and steered him away from our table, speaking in a low tone. *Away from here, boy. Estás fastidiando. You're bothering.* The child shuffled away, not lifting his feet from the pavement, heels hanging over the back of the soles of his flip-flops.

I chased after him, bent down to his height, thrust the two-hundred-sol note into his fist. *Thank you, lady,* he said flatly. He showed no other reaction – no surprise at the amount, no joy. Perhaps he does not understand how much it is, I said to myself. He is, what, six? Seven? A sense of monetary value will come later, when innocence is lost. Across the street, his mother moved parallel with her son. She blinked at me – did not smile, did not nod in thanks. Give the money or not – she would have offered no judgement either way.

I folded the wallet closed, straightened up, felt disappointed, even irritated. I could have turned the child away, given nothing. *No tengo monedas*, I could have said, and it would not have been a lie. Did they not understand what I had given? Did they not know the protocol? I remembered the way the mendigos outside the church had joined their hands as if in prayer and bowed their heads in gratitude to my Tías. *Gracias, señora. Dios le bendiga.*

Then I self-corrected. Two hundred soles was hardly a life-changing sum. How long would they eat on that? Who did I think I was? Some sort of saint?

I let them go, watched them walk away on opposite sides of the road, the boy's little fist gripping the red note, crumpling the paper in a dirty palm.

Back at the table, Rupert praised me as he pushed his wallet back into his pocket.

'That's why I love you,' he said. 'You're so kind. You're going to be a wonderful mother.'

I didn't answer. Undeserved praise makes me anxious. It feels like cheating or stealing. It makes me feel compelled to confess things – misdemeanours I have committed, or flaws in my character – to redress the imbalance.

I blame the father.

Why?

When a girl has poor self-esteem it's always the father's fault.

The Don and the Doña sit face to face in a pair of wicker rocking chairs far too small for their elongated forms. The light of the evening creeps between the slats of the shutters and falls across them in diagonal lines of pale blue. They look now how they did when I first met them, like something mined or excavated from chasms. Their limbs, keen as rapiers, cast shadows like pylons against the walls. Over the coming days they will grow. Feeding on my attention they will fatten and take shape, sprout flesh, humanise. They will don clothes, take on hues, light as well as shadow, and make demands, stitching themselves to me, leaving bite marks on my skin, claw marks on my face.

She didn't give to the child out of a sense of charity.
Pues, no.
    Why did she do it, do you think?
She is afraid of judgement.
    But the judgement of whom?
The judgement of those who watch her.
    Including us?
Pues, sí.
    ¿Cómo tú sabes?
See how she avoids looking at us and pretends not to listen?
    Ya veo.
She pretends. But she is listening.
'We don't do that here.'

It was one of the noisy miraflorinos from the table behind us. A sturdy man, tall, his shirt unbuttoned at the top to reveal a tuft of greying chest hair. His face was tanned – but in the sun-spotted way of skin that would have preferred a shadier climate – and framed by a short, boxed beard, well-trimmed, grey flecked with white; his eyebrows, thick, were still black. On his wrist he wore a gold watch with roman numerals and three sub-dials on the face. He leaned towards us, his hands placed on our table, fingers spread. His cologne was dense and acrid, applied with too much confidence.

'You should not give them money. No here,' he said to us, in English. 'Is all right for you tourists. But we live here. You give money, they keep coming. We need places to go where we relax without always being begged. You see? Otherwise they become crowds, like flies around the meal.' He raised his eyebrows at us, paternal. 'I say this to help you.'

Then he patted Rupert on the back, rejoined his compañero, and left.

I felt embarrassed. The man had called me 'tourist', called out my ignorance of local custom, exposed me in front of Rupert as extranjera, a gringa, someone not from here, while Rupert, in these last five years of our relationship, had thought of me as Peruvian, introduced me as his *Peruvian* girlfriend, shown me off under this label like some rare specimen he had collected. Now someone senior, more knowledgeable in the field, a connoisseur of Peruvianness, had looked me over, examined me, and found me lacking. Counterfeit and phoney. A cheap imitation, nothing more.

It was not the first time. Like the sunscreen vendor on the beach, or the waiter who had handed us menus in English and to whom I had made a point of handing mine back: I'd like a Spanish one, I told him, English for the señor but a *Spanish* one for me. It was only a matter of time before the pedestrians in the street, the llamadores on the micros, the cambistas on every street corner, would turn to me and start chanting *¡Im-pos-to-ra! ¡Im-pos-to-ra! ¡Im-pos-to-ra!*

Outside on the Avenida, Rupert has not stopped talking on the phone. Surely he cannot be speaking with Tía Mimi *still*? Qué tanto could they have to say to one another? Perhaps he is updating her on our conversations. After all, she was the one who told him I was staying at the house. She telephoned his workplace to communicate how worried she was, yes, how absolutamente angustiada – overcome with anguish – she was that I had insisted on sleeping in these crumbling ruins without running water, without light, without so much as a box of matches and all this while eighteen weeks pregnant!

'I have water,' I told him. 'And electricity.'

'But your aunt said—'

'I took care of it,' I said. 'I got it all switched back on. And Q'orianka is with me.'

He wanted me to stay with him. He had a suite at the Vivaldi, had booked two weeks off work: we could make a holiday of it. A 'babymoon' was his term. I could show him the city – *your* city, he called it – perhaps we could travel; he wanted to see Machu Picchu, the Nazca lines, the Islas Ballestas… We could go to Mimi's office tomorrow, sign the papers, and then relax…

Yes, Mimi had told him about the papers, the expediency of a quick sale, the need not to lose our buyers. She had told him the price per square metre of land on the Avenida del Guanero. He was amazed! *I had no idea Limenian land was so lucrative*, he said. *We could invest here ourselves one day. But not yet. Not with the baby…*

Ah, yes, the baby. The baby was behind all his reasoning. I should sign the papers, *for the baby*. We could use my share of the sale price to buy a home, a large detached one in the country, with a garden, something spacious and airy, *for the baby*. That way we could keep his apartment in the city as – what did he call it? – a 'pied-à-terre' for work, and, for the long term, as an investment, a little nest egg in the London property market, a college fund, perhaps, or an inheritance, *for the baby*. It was only later that I realised, in all our conversation, he had not once asked me how I was, how I felt about it all.

He had it all planned out very well, *for the baby*. Impeccably thought through. How much input had come from Tía Mimi, I wondered. How much had she advised him how to persuade an expectant mother? How to capitalise upon the maternal instinct that would be simmering in her belly by now, eighteen weeks into the gestation?

'I won't be signing the papers tomorrow,' I told him. 'I can get a better deal. I've had a lot of interest from – other buyers. One in particular – a lady…a hotelier who wants to convert it. It's very fashionable now, in Lima, to buy old casonas and make them into hotels.'

He listened, hand near his mouth, index finger resting on his lips, his other fingers curled against his chin. He listened as I lied, and it surprised me how easily the untruths came, how smoothly and sweetly, like algarrobina, they flowed.

'I even have drawings,' I told him, 'that she commissioned from her architect, for what she would do to the place. Her ideas, you know.'

It took no effort at all. I felt shame, yes, but a contained sort of shame, comfortably concealed behind a breezy demeanour. What does this say about me, this faculty for invention? This knack for telling stories – falsehoods, I should say – with convincing details and compelling quirks?

'She plans to turn the ballroom into a restaurant.'

Rupert was impressed. He praised me. Said how quickly I had moved. He hadn't thought so much could be done in so few days. But, if this woman was willing to pay more, if she had the funds and was serious, then certainly we should pursue the deal. Create a bit of a buzz. Drive up the prices. 'We', he said. *We*. And *we* should discuss it with my aunt and uncle, tomorrow...

No. *We* would not do that. *I* was handling it. *I* would bring the offer to Mimi and Pulpo when *I* was ready. I didn't need his help. I was perfectly capable of doing it by myself. Why did he always think me so incompetent? So needy of him to rescue me all the time? I could do it – I *would* do it – myself.

'All right,' he said. 'All right.'

I wonder now, as I watch him talking away, rubbing the back of his neck, pacing this way and that, whether he has seen through my untruths. Maybe he is telling Mimi about my little inventions, reassuring her that he will try again tomorrow, that he will convince me within the fortnight. They are in cahoots, perhaps, to bend my will to theirs. *We should approach her gently*, they are saying. *After all, she's pregnant. She has baby brain.*

I am paranoid. He wouldn't speak that way about me. He isn't speaking to Mimi at all. It is a work call. That's it. He is making the most of the time zone to liaise with his North American associates. Back in London he is always sitting up late into the night – into the early hours – to talk with New York and Chicago and San Francisco. Yes, he must be speaking with the States.

Or de las Casas.

'What?'

He could be talking to de las Casas.

El Gritón is back, reconstructed, misassembled – body parts stuck on jauntily and wrong, cubistic, like a Picasso painting – but all in one piece and leaning breezily against the door.

We watched him when he arrived.

'You did?'

He spoke to de las Casas.

They spoke for a long time…

Rupert did mention meeting de las Casas when he arrived, said the doctor had been waiting for me all morning in the heat, that the two of them had worried for me, considered summoning the serenazgo, but then called Mimi and Pulpo and several primas, none of whom, of course, had known where I was. Rupert said the doctor had asked to be notified when I was found safe and sound.

That could be it. He has called de las Casas to let him know I'm all right. Or rather that I'm not all right at all. That I'm losing it. That I'm insisting on living in a tumbledown old mansion without water, without light, making up stories about non-existent buyers, refusing to let go of the past, talking with dead people and hiding from the world behind dusty old shutters. In turn, de las Casas is filling him in on my long and colourful history, breaching every tenet of doctor–patient confidentiality, warning him to stay away from me, to watch for the signs of madness that run in the Echeverría line, to keep a wary eye on the child when it comes, lest it be afflicted too.

She lacks capacity, de las Casas will say to him. Utterly lacks capacity to act on her own behalf. You must intervene. Involve a doctor…a lawyer. Get power over her affairs. Yes, apply for a poder from the court, as a matter of urgency.

He is looking this way, right at this window. I dart away from the shutters and press my back against the wall. Did he see me?

From that distance, between the slats, could he see me watching and mistrusting him? The little fish remains at the window, darting up and down excitedly, slashing her tail this way, that way. Certainly, she is a she. Through her translucent skin, just behind the gills, I can see a tiny cerise heart, throbbing. She is besotted. She has the Electra complex already. How dreadfully predictable. What a cliché.

DIEZ

The queue of the devoted wound around and around the hill and spilled out onto the Avenida, snaking all the way back to the entrance of Los Polvos. Holy news travels fast. This particular announcement (of the arrival of a new maid-saint) had originated from the lips of Anny-Lu Higa Ito, who had been raising a glass of water to the lips of her patient when she saw through the open window a pale grey figure, the outline of a child illuminated and almost limpid in the moonlight. She recognised the creature as the mute child from the Echeverría house and wondered for a moment whether the child had died and this was a yūrei. It was well known, after all, that death frolicked in the Echeverría mansion – in it, around it, and especially underneath it, where the restless bones of los muertos rattled and simmered and threatened to bubble over into the land of the living.

As she tilted small sips of water into the old woman's mouth (the old woman known as La Vieja), Anny-Lu watched the moonlit figure leaning half-slouched, like a puppet on the side of a chair, over the ledge of a second-floor window, the delicate evening breeze only slightly disturbing the limp black hair, barely perceptibly fluttering the edges of the ivory cotton nightdress. It did not occur to her to be alarmed for the safety of the pellucid being. Anny-Lu was only half-awake so it did not strike her as perilous for an undead child to float ten metres off the ground. No, Anny-Lu was not perturbed.

She just calmly carried on watering her old lady and watching the teetering yūrei.

But the anguished scream and sudden jolt forward of her elderly patient summoned Anny-Lu back to full consciousness and in that instant of clarity she registered the wide-eyed expression of terror on the pale child's face: this yūrei was not dead but very much alive and she was falling forward, falling away from the window, yes, falling off the same ledge from which Julia Álvarez Yupanqui had slipped and died only hours before, as if the Echeverría child were trying to chase the maid into the afterlife.

It was all instantaneous: the old woman screaming and lurching forward; the nurse losing grip of the water glass and it tumbling from her hands; the child plunging into the night. Anny-Lu knew that within the instant there would be devastation (eruption of guts on patio and shattering of glass on tile), but instead there was a prolonged, incandescent emptiness. A stretched-out nothingness in which everything was sliding away, not just the glass and the child and the old woman but also the two houses standing face to face on the Avenida and the Earth and the universe in which it hung – everything was dissipating away from her and all that was left was a delicious lucidity, an illuminated sense that all was one. That Anny-Lu was the child and the child was the glass and her blood was the water and water was moonlight and all the edges were blurred and indistinguishable in this Now in which Time had both stopped and infinitely stretched itself. There was no Anny-Lu. There was no Me or Not-Me. There was only a consciousness (her own or universal, she could not tell) through which there was a continual flow of awareness, ever-changing, like a blank screen onto which images were continually being projected and now they had suddenly stopped. Or perhaps they had not stopped. Perhaps now, in one saturated instant, all the images of all time were being projected at once, their combined wavelengths converging into a white light. Then Anny-Lu understood that there was no use trying to cling to the fixedness of things. That there was no fixedness. There was only impermanence. Only flux.

An hour later, racing from house to house in Los Polvos, Anny-Lu would try (and struggle) to articulate the illumination she had experienced. It was an unutterable thing, entirely eluding all vocabulary. In fact, when she came to think of it, she realised she could not even clearly remember what it was that she had felt or understood in that resplendent emptiness one hour before. The best she could do was to recount a description of the fall of the yūrei-child and the moment that the old woman had lurched forward and the glass had fallen and then how, just when she had expected blood and shards and disaster, instead the glass had bounced off the tiles as if it were a rubber ball and rebounded right back into her hands, water undisturbed and, in the same instant, instead of the Echeverría girl plunging to her death, she had simply suspended in the air and hung there, slightly curled, foetal, like a comma or a shrimp, as if from an invisible fishing line dangled from the hands of a giant.

Anny-Lu would recount how, seeing the child dangling against the sky, she had sprinted from La Vieja's bedroom, down the stairs, and burst out into the Avenida. It was there that she had collided with Julia. Yes, standing in the lamplit Avenida, looking exactly as she had in life, dressed in her pale blue work pinafore, without a scratch or bruise on her body, was Julia Álvarez Yupanqui, not made of air or vapour but solid flesh and blood, resurrected.

The people believed it. After all, Anny-Lu and Julia had been well acquainted in life. The day that Julia's parents had stuck their bamboo post into the dust and claimed their land on Los Polvos, Anny-Lu had also been there, claiming her patch of land a few metres to the south. When Julio Álvarez had wet his index finger with spit and run it through the dirt to draw the perimeter of his family's new home, it had collided with the moistened index finger of Anny-Lu, who was doing the very same thing. They had looked up at each other with narrowed eyes, prepared for a conflict.

The land grab had been promoted through rumours, quiet words in eager ears. It had been sold as an act of solidarity among the proletariat: if we act together, they cannot resist us. It was an undertaking of communitarianism and collectivism. But it also wasn't, for although they had arrived as a mass, the land-grabbers were now busy asserting their borders, demarcating perimeters, assessing how much earth they could claim without attracting the censure of their neighbour. From each according to his ability, to each according to his dream. Here they were, Julio Álvarez Mayo and Anny-Lu Higa Ito, wet fingers colliding in the dust, backs bent, parallel to the ground, necks craned up and narrowed eyes fixed on each other, the perimeters of their future homes intersecting.

To take something for oneself. This was what the people understood General Velasco had promised. When he had declared that land would be for the peasant and that he would enact its immediate expropriation, the people had understood that the land would be theirs. Had the general not said that the land should be passed to those who work it? Land to the tiller. Campo to the campesino.

On this promise, the people in the mountains and in the fields built their hopes, sinking their hands into the dear earth knowing that, since time immemorial, it had been theirs *morally* speaking but now, at last, it was also theirs *legally* speaking – or it would be once someone in government had finalised the paperwork because, of course, there were procedures and red tape. First the land must be passed to the Revolutionary Government of the Armed Forces. Then a justiprecio must be paid to the old hacendados – for certainly they must be compensated for their loss, though many said this was like compensating a thief. But then at last, surely, the sharing out of the land would begin? Soon someone official would come with a piece of paper delineating what was whose and who had what.

They dreamed of their own farms, of strips and fragments of land they could make their own and name after themselves – la Granja Tercero; el Rancho Quispe. Patches of earth that would feed them and where, when they died, they could lay their bones to stay close to their children. They did not know then that they would have to wait a little longer for their strips and fragments of land, or that the glorious objective of the revolution had not been, as they had believed, to take from the master and give to the peasant (that 'land to the tiller' had not meant the literal land to the literal tiller) – no, they had misunderstood. The glorious objective had been cooperatives, yes! Not a free-for-all but 'legal entities functioning as democratic corporations' with boards and councils and committees and branches elected by the members with powers to approve and powers to invest, to veto and appoint, to demote and distribute and regulate and undertake countless other functions of an administrative nature…yes, they had misunderstood the revolution, but it had all been there from the beginning in the fine print. The president himself had made it clear: *Cooperativisation in favour of the workers, with the guarantee that the new enterprises will function as one sole unit.*

The problem was that, listening as they had with their ears at the door of the hacendado's study, the workers had heard the President General's speech in scraps and snatches from the wireless – had heard him condemn *the iniquity of ploughing the land of others*; had heard him promise that *the Peruvian peasant will no longer be disinherited*; had heard him bequeath to them *the right to the fruits of the land that they work* – and from these fragments they had designed the agrarian reform in their own minds and foreseen an outcome that was not intended by the collectivists at the presidential palace who sat drawing and redrawing red lines across a map of the nation.

In the cities, too, the people said the President General was behind them, that he would not only turn a blind eye to the invasion of vacant land but would support them. He would make sure the new barriadas got public services – water and light and refuse collection. Why else had he expropriated the industries? Surely to ensure that Perú's industry was for the Peruvian!

Land to the tiller! Perú to the Peruvian! This was what repeated in Julio Álvarez's head that morning like a liturgical chant. Land to the tiller. Perú to the Peruvian. Now and forever, por los siglos de los siglos, Amén, as he crouched in the sand of Los Polvos, glaring into the narrowed eyes of a stranger whom he did not see as an inheritor of this brave new revolution because she was not, in his eyes, Peruvian.

Julia Álvarez Yupanqui, then only an infant, lying in the shade cast by her father's jacket which hung from a bamboo post, sensed the tension between her father and the stranger, and the anxiety made her bowel convulse so that she filled her diaper with a pungent orange diarrhoea. Seconds later, the stench of the baby's faeces reached the nostrils of Julio and Anny-Lu. Their fingers still touching, their eyes locked together, they smelled the shit together and, instead of launching into a confrontation, they laughed. They uncurled their spines, stood upright face to face, and together walked over to where the baby had begun to wail.

All around them the bustle of land-grabbers arriving (hollering and hammering and the clanging of pickaxes). The grey sky, low as a ceiling. Squawks of buzzards circling overhead. And Julio and Anny-Lu standing above the baby, looking down at her scrunched-up face, her tight-balled fists, the dark mark on her cheek that then looked like a misshapen egg but over the years would become a condor in flight. The father looks with panic at the woman. He explains he does not know how to change a diaper. His wife is not here: she is with their friends, fetching building materials, and she did not leave the baby supplies with him.

From her nurse's kit, Anny-Lu fetches bandages, tears them into rags, moistens them in sterile water and cleans the shit from the child's buttocks, thighs, back. *You are a mother?* the father asks her. *No, I have no family*, she tells him. *You have gentle hands*, he says. She replies, *I am a nurse*.

Yes, Anny-Lu had known Julia Álvarez Yupanqui her whole life.

She had been a beloved aunt, almost a second mother. If anyone would recognise Julia Álvarez Yupanqui without any doubt, it was Anny-Lu. There was no way it had been a case of mistaken identity. So it was taken as gospel when Anny-Lu raced through the entrance to Los Polvos crying the good news that Julia had returned, and not as a yūrei, not as a condenado or a ghost. She had returned in power, for Anny-Lu had seen with her own eyes how Julia had miraculously saved the mute Echeverría girl-child from death.

The good news spread through the pueblo jóven, each inter-preting it according to their need: the new saint held all knowledge and wisdom in her gift. *The new saint could predict the future. She could raise the dead and rescue the living. She could grant the deepest desires of your heart.* Induced by the promise of prayers granted, the Polvorinos abandoned their tasks and plans for the day, gathered up implements of worship (their rosary beads and votive candles, ekekos and huacos and agua de kananga, bivalve shells from the beaches of the north, stones from the heights of the Cordillera) and marched to the front of the yellow house, led by Anny-Lu, who pointed out to them the spot where she had found herself face to face with the newly born maid-saint.

Anny-Lu told those nearest in the gathering crowd how it felt to look into the eyes of a saintess. As she told the story, her narrative began to change her memory of what had happened. The revelation she had experienced – it had happened not up in La Vieja's bedroom but right here in the street, face to face with Santa Julia. The clarity, the illumination, the white light had been emanating from the face of the resurrected maid herself. She had the power to stop time, to reverse gravity, to manipulate the laws of nature, to reveal the hidden secrets of the universe. It had all been Julia.

She misremembered a conversation between them: she thought she recalled asking the saintess why she had been sent back.

I was not sent. I returned of my own volition.

But why?

I returned to help my people.

Who are your people?

All those who call my name.

But Santa Julia remembered the encounter differently: no conversation, just two women (one living, one more-than-living) standing in silence, looking into each other's faces. This is not to say they did not speak, or that it was a lie for Anny-Lu to say that they had spoken. There were infinite iterations of the encounter that inhabited the space between those two houses on the Avenida. There were the iterations that had taken place already, all those now confined to antiquity, in ñawpa ñawpa pacha – confined but still there, recurring and recurring. There were also those iterations which were now below their feet in urin pacha, reverberating and knocking against the foundations of the houses and the roots of the bucayo trees, preparing to rise again. Also the ones behind the veil, in kaylla pacha, invisible but inhabiting that same space under the street lamps of the Avenida. And there are the iterations taking place this very moment, even now, in that exact spot, the ones that they remembered and the ones that they did not remember because they were versions of events that branched off into contingent timelines, hypotheticals, conditionals, abstractions expressible only in modal verbs and subjunctive moods. In all of these pachas, it is certain that, at least once, the two women had had the conversation Anny-Lu remembered.

Meanwhile, Julia did not remember speaking to Anny-Lu. As she remembered it, the two women had been silent, Anny-Lu dumbstruck and she, the resurrected Julia, speechless with awe because in that instant she had been learning that now, as a saintess, when she looked into a human face, she knew immediately everything about the world that lay behind it – everything about that person's life. Their fondest and most traumatic memories. The keenest wishes of their heart. She knew how that life had begun and also how it would end, knew all the things that had happened to its distant ancestors and also all the things that would happen to its most distant descendants. She would win her fame as La Santa de Los Polvorinos for her everyday miracles (making a seamstress sew twice as fast; making a carpenter's skin impenetrable to splinters), but the true miracle, the one about which no living person would ever know, was her ability to see, as she walked among the people, the histories that tethered them together. Her sight could make bounds across the centuries like a stone leaping as it skims over water.

So, in Anny-Lu's face she saw Haruto Higa disembarking from the *Sakura Maru* at Callao in 1899, and she saw the seven hundred and ninety-one other Japanese men who had arrived with him, induced by the promise of good work, room and board, and the prospect of sending fifteen yen back home each month. She saw the papers, the contracts, the charter parties drawn up by businessmen and lawyers, through translators and interpreters, between government ministers and ambassadors. Drawn up without regard to the wishes of the men themselves. Drawn up to stipulate that the men would work ten hours a day (or twelve, if indoors) for four years in the employ of the Morioka Emigration Company and any or all of said company's heirs, legal representatives, successors and assigns. She saw these contracts now, languishing in forgotten corners of old mansions, stuffed into the drawers of the library in the yellow house on the hill.

She saw, too, the haciendas and factories across the country to which these Japanese men were sent, including the Hacienda Echeverría, where Haruto Higa and two dozen others were put immediately to work harvesting the Quebranta grapes that would pay for seven hundred and fifty thousand Andalusian azulejo tiles. She saw those tiles now, decorating the yellow mansion's Sevillian patio. They were the same azulejo tiles which Julia Álvarez Yupanqui had spent so many hours of her life mopping and polishing, and the same tiles onto which her insides were painted the moment of her death.

Julia saw all of this. Saw the lines and lands and lives that connected each soul to every other. She saw, too, the burdens of guilt and blood that yoke genealogies together, for within a month of arriving at the hacienda, Haruto Higa and the two dozen would be on the verge of death, prostrate, delirious with fever, fighting for their lives, eyes glazed, bodies flopping around like rag dolls.

A doctor was summoned. Eberth's bacillus, he said. Very little could be done. The British had lately created a typhoid vaccine, but it was not for men such as these. The first imperative was to quarantine, lest the other plantation workers (or worse, the managers, administrators, the patrón's agents) also be infected. As for the patients themselves, many were too far gone to be worth treating. A majority would die of the complications that were already taking effect, evident from the jaundice and delirium they were exhibiting. For others, symptomatic relief might be found in antipyretic drugs, but these were expensive. Just as effective in reducing fever was hydrotherapy. That is to say, one might try, in the first instance, cold water treatment, which the foreman did, standing at the door of the men's dormitory every few hours and hosing them down.

Despite the foreman's assiduous efforts, seventeen of the two dozen died and were buried on the outer edges of the hacienda in shared graves, unmarked. Julia saw these graves and the men buried in them and the parents they had left in Japan who would never receive news from them so would not know whether to wait or to mourn. She saw, too, the lives that might have been, had they lived. The children they might have had, and the grandchildren. She saw these lives unlived rising from the unmarked graves as curling vapours, writhing and fretting, breathing down the neck of history, chattering about what could have been, what should have been, what ought not to have been. She saw them twist and twine together, filigrees of smoke like tentacles of octopuses crawling across the sky. They joined with other un-souls, the vestiges of lineages cut off reaching back from pachas that almost were. They coalesced, mingling into clouds that rolled across the mountains, over the Nazca lines, migrating north from Lake Titicaca or south from the ruins of Chan Chan, pushing towards Lima where they thickened to fog – the fog of thousands upon thousands of un-souls pressing down upon the city, clamouring, shouting their stories and shrouding the sun.

All this Julia saw in Anny-Lu's face when they stood eyeball to eyeball on the Avenida del Guanero on the resurrection morn as, by some unfathomable provenance, Anny-Lu Higa Ito was not among these un-souls curling in the neblina. Haruto Higa, in the first of a lifetime of lucky escapes, had not been buried in one of the unmarked graves but had survived the typhus, fled from the hacienda, and made his way to Lima. Now, penniless, unable to afford a trans-Pacific boat fare back to Japan, Julia saw him stumble into the alley of a callejón on Jirón Ucayali, begging for food. A hungry man begging from other hungry men. It was there that he met a young woman squatting around a tub, washing clothes. She had an air of someone else from somewhere else, the way the face in a painting recollects, from a distance, the face of the person who inspired it. The resemblance was impressionistic, fleeting, as if the likeness were a perception only, distorted by a veil that might be pulled away at any moment and nobody who looked at her could ever say of whom it was she reminded them, but she certainly reminded them of somebody they had known.

When he saw her, Haruto had the feeling that he had met her once, many years before, though this was impossible because he had been in this country only a few months and she had undoubtedly never been in his. What he and countless others saw in Augusta was the trace of another woman from many centuries earlier, a woman who had long since died but who could not rest because her son had left home one day and disappeared. Here she was in Augusta Thupa Mayo, in the olive green of her eyes and the long, sloping curve of her eyebrows. She was in the broadness of Augusta's brow and the tapering of her chin, in her widow's peak and the curve of her back when she sat at the tub, washing, washing. They washed together, agitating the waters with Augusta's urgent, restive hands.

With these hands Augusta Thupa Mayo shared her lunch with Haruto Higa that day in the crowded callejón – a lunch given to her by Aurora Montealegre, her employer, purchased from Señor Tan, whose food fed most of the inhabitants of the crowded alley. A particular favourite among the working community of the calle-jones, his signature dish (rice, onions, tomatoes, parsley sautéed in a bittersweet sauce with, if he could acquire them, cheap cuts of meat), was quickly becoming famous. Even some of the fancy limeños, the young ones, bohemians in particular, had started to venture onto Calle Capón, in spite of its reputation for delinquency and disorder, to taste the dishes of Señor Tan or El Quemado as they knew him, because his face was badly burned. His meals were being referred to now by the collective name of *chifa* because the people often heard him shouting this word to his sons whilst they cooked. Of course, the people were mishearing: Chen Tan was not saying chifa but 'Chī fàn'. But rumours of the delicious chifa would spread so that when los Tan opened their first restaurant twenty years later, above its doors the words *Chifa Tan* would be emblazoned in red and gold lettering.

Augusta Thupa Mayo shared her chifa with the hungry man who was begging in the alley, though it was the only meal she would get all day – that day a meal without meat, only rice and vegetables and bittersweet sauce. She shared even though she was sick and needed the sustenance because she saw in Haruto the same desperation and loneliness she had felt so often herself. They ate together, sitting on the ground, their backs against the washtub, communicating through gestures and smiles and comfortable silences. In the soapy water was a set of bed sheets, soaking to remove urine stains. They were sheets that Augusta had collected before sunrise from one of the maids at the yellow house on the hill. In that house lived a child (she had caught a glimpse of him at the window once) who was still at the age of bed-wetting, so the Don and the Doña were having his sheets laundered daily. These predawn trips from Ucayali to the Avenida del Guanero were exhausting: Augusta felt fatigue saturating her very skeleton, though she did not dare tell Doña Montealegre for fear of losing her job. But meeting Haruto Higa had given Augusta an idea that would alleviate both of their troubles. Later that same day, she suggested to Doña Montealegre that if this Japanese man did the collections and deliveries, it would give more time for the girls to focus on the laundering.

In this way, Augusta Thupa Mayo provided Haruto Higa with the second of his lucky escapes. His third would be almost but not quite getting gored by a runaway bull at the Plaza de Acho. His fourth, the time he leapt out of the path of a speeding automobile on the Avenida Abancay (but his wife did not) and his fifth, in May 1940, when the anti-Japanese pogroms led his neighbours to torch his home but he crawled out alive and unburned. His last lucky escape came three years after that when the government came for his son and took him away, yes, sent him to a place called Crystal City that Franklin Delano Roosevelt had prepared. But the government did not take Haruto. *You can stay, old man*, they said, and they left him standing there, watching his son being led away in his pyjamas, his daughter-in-law wailing by his side, while little Anny-Lu slept in her cot. What could he say to her? What could he do?

In all his years of collecting and delivering laundry at the yellow house on the hill, Haruto Higa did not and would never know that the clothes he collected belonged to the man who had bought the right to four years of his life in the same way that Augusta Thupa Mayo did not know and would never know that the shirts and trousers and handkerchiefs she laundered, brought to her from the yellow house on the hill, were the clothes of her own father, whom her mother had made love to by the river at Lunahuaná. Nor did she know that the urine-stained sheets she washed had been pissed on by her little brother or that, after she died so prematurely, her own daughter, little Carmen, would have to go to work for that same brother and spend her entire life in that man's mansion until she would die in a small, single bed in a small, single room in its attics with the one consolation that her wages from this house had put her nephew, Augusto García Navarro, through architectural school.

PART II

ONCE

After she had performed the third miracle of the breakfast, the dead and risen Santa Julia Álvarez Yupanqui emerged from the yellow house to walk amidst her queueing devoted. She saw among them many faces she recognised: faces she knew from her own life in Los Polvos but also faces she recognised from her observations while she had been above the world in janaj pacha, and it was difficult for her now to distinguish which faces she had known in life and which in afterlife. She felt that there had been a blurring. A blurring between the things that had happened to Julia, daughter of Julio and Merly Álvarez, and the things that had happened to Santa Julia, the risen. The sense of lives arranged in time (a sense of past, present and future) had been utterly exploded. All she knew for certain was that there were those whom she could help and those she could not: some lives she could reach out and touch and others she could see and smell and hear but they were blocked from her as if behind a pane of rippling glass.

She moved among the devoted who, after Anny-Lu had told them about her encounter with the saint, had cut open the padlock on the casona's gates and spilled into the gardens. They were gathered in crowds under the naranjos. Some of the youths leaned against the tree trunks with their arms folded, unsure what to expect when the dead returned to life, trying to look casual but scanning their eyes here and there, expecting light because that is how resurrections were depicted on the religious postcards and calendars their parents affixed to walls. Other young people partnered up, embracing and nuzzling behind foliage or around the corner of the house, the heat of romance intensified by the trespassing and the proximity to their parents. Those better versed in the rituals of worship identified the spot where Julia had met her death (the cleanest tiles, the ones that smelled most strongly of bleach) and erected a makeshift altar out of two crates balanced on a wheelbarrow and draped with a sheet.

To the altar, Hilario García García, a schoolteacher at Escuela 5086 Santíssima Madre, donated a book. It was a beautiful volume with creamy paper, cloth binding, a purple ribbon to divide the pages – a book he had purchased with a semester's savings to reward himself for staying at Escuela 5086 when he had been offered a job at the local American school where the salary was higher and the children cleaner and there was never a shortage of pencils. This book, in which Hilario García García was the first to write, became the petition book of Santa Julia in which pleas were made and answers acknowledged.

Eugenia Sánchez, who was known for keeping a pristine house, donated a bowl of potpourri to the altar, and José-Maria Villanueva (who had not been seen at church for years on account, it was assumed, of the rumours), brought to the altar a dozen votive candles. Alessandra La Bocona Flores (who was such a blabber-mouth that people said her tongue was as quick and bald as a skink) donated an enormous faux-gold vase, a dozen fabric roses and a large, varnished wooden crucifix emblazoned with plastic gems.

By the time the altar was laid and adorned, more worshippers had arrived from other parts of the city, worshippers who did not know the name or provenance of this new saint but who had heard – on the combi or at the market, shouted from a balcony or whispered across a municipal office waiting room – that something miraculous was happening over in Miraflores. These newcomers formed a queue towards the back of which was a woman named Juana Jimenez Loayza who, that very morning, in a distant part of Lima, had heard a rumour that her brother had been executed the night before during the struggles at El Frontón penitentiary. It was being said that dozens of prisoners had died in a massacre, possibly more than a hundred, mostly shot in the back of the head by soldiers, but others said there had been grenades and knifings too. It was difficult to know what had happened because the president had not made a statement and Juana only heard whispers and hearsay. But it was likely that her brother was dead, for it was being said that the soldiers had not left alive anyone accused of sympathising with Sendero.

Juana was coming now to the birthplace of this newest saint to ask her for help in recovering the body of her brother. It would be tricky. The authorities did not know her as his sister. In fact, almost nobody in Lima knew her as the sister of an accused terrorist incarcerated at El Frontón because when Juana had left Accomarca ten months before, she had not been called Juana Jimenez Loayza. She had been known by another name – a name she had shared with her brother and which she had left behind along with her home and town and the bodies of her relatives buried in the ground. She had followed her brother, a supposed subversive, captured by the armed forces and brought to Lima for incarceration without trial, and on her journey she had invented a new identity for herself. It was this identity she had given to the landlord of the callejón where she had used the last of her money to rent a space to sleep for the week. It was the identity she had given to the owners of the bodegas and kioscos she had traipsed around looking for a job. It was the identity she shared with the family who, for some time before her arrival, had been renting a space to sleep in the same room where she now found herself. For her safety, and for theirs as well, it was best to deceive them. They had three small children. The mother was still breastfeeding the youngest. They were all relying on the casual work the father could find as a handyman. This family could not afford to be suspected of fraternising with terrucos. Still, she felt guilty for lying to them, especially when they shared with her their evening meals of bread and broth.

Looking into Juana's face, Santa Julia saw these meals and, running concurrently, the massacre at Accomarca. She saw the sky turn red with a sunrise that bathed the morning as if with blood. She saw the twenty-nine soldiers of patrol units Lince 6 and Lince 7, led by Sub-Lieutenant Telmo Hurtado, approaching the village. She witnessed how they entered the huts by force, hauled the schoolteacher into the street, and also his wife and children, and shot them all in the back of the head. Santa Julia saw how they rounded up the villagers (for an assembly, they said, to be counted) and marched them to an open plain at Llocllapampa. There, the soldiers beat the men and boys with their fists and rifle butts and with their boots kicked and stamped on them before locking them into one house. All of this Santa Julia observed through the eyes of Juana Jimenez Loayza while she narrated her memories over lunch to the evangelists who had brought her food and water.

Santa Julia also saw how the soldiers of Lince 6 and 7 dragged the women and girls, with no discrimination as to age, into the brush and raped them. And she saw all this through the eyes of those villagers who had escaped and hidden among the bushes – saw it all but also heard it through their ears, the screams and wailing and the explosions of bullets until at last the women and girls were also locked into a house, not the house where their men and sons were being held. Then, finally, Santa Julia saw how the soldiers shot bullets into both houses and how the bullets found their destinations in the flesh of the imprisoned and also how the soldiers threw grenades until the buildings caught alight and the houses burned to the ground with sixty-nine villagers, living and dead and halfway between, locked inside them.

Yes, sixty-nine villagers were killed at Accomarca, and Santa Julia knew the faces and the lives of every last one, including the thirty children who had been among them.

Throughout all of this, Juana Jimenez Loayza (whose name at that time was not Juana Jimenez Loayza) had been hiding in a tree just outside the plain of Llocllapampa, and she hid there among its branches the rest of the day while the houses burned and the soldiers sacked the village, looting and stealing anything of value, until at last, late in the day, Lince 6 and Lince 7 left, led by Sub-Lieutenant Telmo Hurtado, but even then Juana did not dare to climb down, though her arms were sore from clinging to the bough on which she lay, and though she had pissed herself in fear, and though she was hungry and thirsty. She stayed up in that tree until nightfall when, by the light of the flames rising from the burning houses, she saw others emerge from the bushes – a handful of her neighbours who had managed to escape. Together they walked through the silent village, avoiding the pools of blood and entrails, too shocked and too tired and afraid to speak or cry or make a sound. Silently they floated around the empty village like ghosts, more dead than alive, yes, more dead because to witness so much violence and murder, to witness the souls of so many being torn from their bodies, is to be infected by a little of that same deadness that seeps into the body and displaces some of the life there. Yes, if a person witnesses enough death, the life inside can be entirely displaced until the person is walking around an empty shell, a condenado, a body without a soul. This is mancharisqa.

The survivors had tried to bury their dead, but without coffins and without individual graves, because how could there be individual graves for bodies so charred that they stuck together, or for unidentifiable pieces of carcass? For an unknown leg or an unrecognisable ribcage? For chunks and scraps and slices of people? So they buried them all together with the best dignity they could provide, and all of this they did with their own hands because the soldiers had taken all the tools from the village in their looting. Somewhere among this pile of bodies were the parents and grandparents and siblings and cousins of Juana Jimenez Loayza, all except for her brother who had been arrested some weeks before and taken to a prison in Lima far away. Juana had followed him towards the coast and now she learned that he too, the last of her kin, lay in another pile of bodies, a pyramid of human carcasses, out on the island of El Frontón, executed as a Senderista, though he had never been a Senderista, just a tragic case of mistaken identity. This is what her brother had sworn from the start and maintained even until the last moment, when he begged for his life.

Now Juana was coming to the shrine of this new saint to beg for help in recovering the body of the last of her relatives. But Santa Julia already knew that Juana would never recover her brother's body. Of the ninety-seven bodies that would be found at El Frontón, only four would be released to their relatives. The rest would be buried in secret locations around Lima, among them Juana's brother, whose spirit would wander the city in search of his sister, but he would never find her (not in this world at least): he would ask the people whom he passed (both the living and the dead) whether they had seen Antonia Palacios Pérez, but nobody knew a woman by that name because Antonia Palacios Pérez was no more and in her place was only Juana Jimenez Loayza.

There was nothing Santa Julia could do to answer Juana's prayer, so instead she performed the best miracle she could offer. She took Juana's little bolsa of cancha, merely a handful of toasted corn wrapped in a polythene bag, and she blessed it and multiplied it so that every time Juana put her hand in her pocket it seemed that there was more corn than there had been before. In this way, all that day, as Juana shuffled forward in the interminable queue to petition the santa (whom people around her were now saying had lived in Los Polvos and so was certain to grant the petitions of those in need), Juana did not go hungry. Not only could she fully satisfy her own hunger, but the bolsa of cancha became so full that it began spilling out of her pocket and she was obliged to share the kernels with her queue-mates, filling their cupped hands, passing the bag around, encouraging people to help themselves.

But the cancha was salty, sating hunger but inciting thirst. *Do you have water?* the people began to ask. *Does anyone have water?* Yes, someone had water. Just a small plastic bottle, five hundred millilitres, nothing more. But he was willing to share. Have a sip, he told the woman next to him, and she did. You too, he said, and the next person also drank. In this way the cancha and the bottle travelled together and they never ran out. The more people ate, the more the corn multiplied. And though the people drank, the meniscus of the water never lowered.

Soon news of the miraculous bag of cancha and the never-ending water spread throughout the whole queue, and people began to laugh and worship, saying, *Surely this is a powerful saintess who cares about the needs of the poor.* And when the bottle of water had been passed all through the queue, right from the front all the way to the rear and at last back to its owner, the water level had not changed. And the bag, when it returned to Juana's hands, was still full to bursting, fuller than it had been when she first bought it at the bodega.

The bag of cancha would never empty. It would remain full in her pocket many years later in 1992 when Sub-Lieutenant Telmo Hurtado was charged and tried in a martial court and three years after that when he was absolved. The kernels would still be over-flowing in the year 2000 when Hurtado exiled himself to the United States and even more so in 2011 when he was extradited back to Perú. When she sat to give her testimony to the Comisión de Verdad y Reconciliación in 2002, the bag would bulge reassuringly in her pocket and years later in 2016, as she sat in the public gallery during the second trial of Telmo Hurtado, she would share those miraculous kernels around with her fellow justice-seekers.

The miraculous cancha of Juana Jimenez Loayza was with her for the length of her life, and it won her many friends. With it she was able to feed the hungry and share a meal with beggars. It allowed her to strike up conversation with strangers on the micro, which is how she met her husband, and to keep the bellies of her children full when money was tight, as it was after her husband died.

On the day that the saintess first blessed the bag of cancha, Santa Julia already knew that all this would happen, and she said to Juana (although Juana could not hear her) while gesturing to the people queuing all around, *Behold, this is your mother and this your brother. Here is your father and here your son.* For Santa Julia had looked into Juana's face and understood that this woman who had seen the purest evil that could hide in the heart of man and who had lost every last one of her relatives and was now quite alone in the world needed, above all, to find kindred spirits in her fellow humans.

It was closeness with his fellow man that was also needed by Bartimeo Cabana Puyucahua, a man whom few miraflorinos had taken the time to know but many recognised because they had passed him every Sunday of their life as he sat on a bundle of blankets outside the Iglesia Santa María Reina, leaning against the metal railings, his legs terminating in two stumps at the thighs where his cotton long johns were tied into knots. He would sit with one arm outstretched, palm facing the sky, the other arm amputated at the elbow, a wide toothless smile on his face, milky eyes staring into the distance and a polystyrene cup placed a few feet away where churchgoers could drop their alms because they could not bear to approach him on account of the smell.

Today he had been brought by some of the young novices of the church, who carried him in his blankets as if in a hammock. Their superiors would have been appalled to know that they had brought the man to the shrine of an uncanonised folk saint. They would have said the gesture was an act of paganism and that the women had not yet grasped the difference between superstition and true faith. Still, the novices had heard rumours of folk saints with power and since Bartimeo could not take himself to the shrine and since he had no family or friends to take him either, they had determined to carry the man themselves, but wearing gloves so as not to have to touch his soiled sheets and standing always upwind of him.

All around, the other petitioners moved away as Bartimeo lay back in the hammock of sheets and stared at the clouds in the sky through the fog of his cataracts. Santa Julia was able to see through his eyes now and, simultaneously, through his healthier eyes the evening his mother had abandoned him outside a church in Puno. Terrified, only an infant, he had sat outside that church without making a sound all night (a night when the temperatures fell well below freezing) and when he was found in the morning, the frostbite in both his legs and in his right arm was so severe that it was clear neither legs nor arm could be saved. That morning, too, he had lain back on some blankets while a sister stroked his forehead, and the off-white ceiling at which he stared had looked to him like clouds.

Julia was also able to see through the misty eyes of his many-times-great-grandmother Josefa Puyucahua, watching the dismembered limbs of her executed children swinging gently from the queuña tree at Pampamarca. Julia was struck by a sudden wish to stretch out her hand, pluck the two legs hanging from the branches and bolt them to the stumps of Bartimeo, but Josefa and the tree and the dangling limbs were behind the pane of rippling glass through which she could not reach. It seemed to her there was a kind of sick joke, a deliberate cruelty, in Bartimeo's family tree that there should be so many limbs severed from bodies and now this body so desperately in need of limbs.

All she wanted was to put the people back together again, matching them with their lost limbs as if they were pieces of a bloody and sinister puzzle. But healing was not in the gift of Santa Julia. Instead, what she did for Bartimeo was clean his sheets. The sheets on which he had sat and slept and been dragged from place to place had not been washed in years: he had no one in the world to wash for him. Years of dust and dirt from the Lima streets, years of food spillages and bodily fluids, had accumulated in those sheets. Now Santa Julia cleaned them, loosening from between their threads the particles of grime, the absorbed filth, the eggs of microscopic bugs. She lifted away the stains, revived the original colours of each sheet, mended the seams and the threadbare patches. She also cleaned Bartimeo, unclogged the pores of his skin, blew off the dirt and dust, slicked away the sweat and encrustations of effluvia. All of this she did in an instant, a mere blink of an eye, but it was some minutes before anyone noticed. Of course, as is often the case, the first to look – to really look – and see the newly clean Bartimeo was a child, a little boy, who slipped from his mother's grasp, approached the old man without timidity, and held out a foil windmill so Bartimeo could blow it and make it spin.

Miguel Ángel Ribeiro Yupanqui, eight years old, almost nine, had come with his mother and aunt and elder brother to the shrine of this supposed new saintess of the people. His mother and aunt had their own specific reasons to be there. But Miguel Ángel had not come with any particular petition in mind, so he spent his time in the queue trying to decide on a prayer to present. A dog: he was going to ask for a dog. A puppy with floppy ears and golden fur. His parents had always refused to get a dog; their lives were far too busy, too precarious, to worry about an animal. There were enough starving strays in Los Polvos, they said, to bring another pobre criatura into the town. But Miguel Ángel believed in miracles, and a miracle could convince his parents that they were not too busy or too poor for a dog.

They both worked, Óscar Ribeiro and his wife Alba, he in short-term roles at various trade unions, she as a childminder, but not for the fancy families, not wearing pastel-coloured pinafores and pushing expensive North American buggies around fenced-off play-grounds in gated communities. No, she looked after the children of the working Polvorinas, the women who rose before dawn to go and scrub floors, wax legs, stack shelves, peel potatoes, tint eyelashes, wipe tables, work as cashiers, gut fish, sell artesanías, run market stalls or do errands for tips. Alba Yupanqui Collo was the woman who raised the babies of the community so that the other women could earn. They would bring their infants to Alba's house, where she would feed them and clean them and tell them stories of the glorious future that was approaching.

Yes, Alba Yupanqui Collo believed in a glorious future. Hers was not a distant belief, not a vacuous faith pendent upon a deus ex machina or a promised but always receding return by a god who seemed to have forgotten his appointment with humanity. Her belief was firm and sure because it was founded on action, for she was part of the glorious revolution that was beginning here in Perú but would before long bring a pachacuti for the whole world.

True, there would be resistance. She, her husband and their comrades had already faced resistance. There would be sacrifices. And blood, unavoidably. There had already been blood. And she could not deny that the blood that had been and was being and would be spilled was a great price to pay. Especially that of her own people... But all great things come at great cost. When they asked her, this is what she explained to her sons, especially the elder, José Antonio, who was pushing back now that he was in high school, slamming newspapers down on the kitchen table, demanding to know how anything could justify the killings, the bombings and burnings.

You think there are not killings in the capitalist system, mi hijo? she would ask him. *You think people do not die now?* She would drag him outdoors and point out the mendigos, the beggars and barefooted children. *People die, mi hijo: hold that very clear in your mind. You can kill a dog by shooting it, or you can kill a dog by starving it. Both ways, the dog dies.*

But José Antonio was not convinced by his mother's arguments. He could no longer look the other way when a crate appeared in the house and he knew that underneath the straw and apples were pistols and machine guns. He struggled to believe that any ends could justify such means. Were there not other methods? Other ways to make their voices heard?

Alba would laugh and place her palms on her son's cheeks, running fingers through his curls to push them away from his eyes. He would see, she told him. This was merely a necessary night of struggle so that the sun could rise on a better world. When the red dawn finally came, he would understand. She was fighting so he would not have to. *Let me take the night watch, mi hijo, so that you are well-rested and strong for the day.*

For now, his role in the struggle was to study, to become someone useful to the new democracy that was approaching. They would need intelligent young people to rebuild the nation: engineers, scientists, architects. José Antonio did not tell her that he had no interest in these professions. He wanted to be an archaeologist.

José Antonio, too, had come to the yellow house on the hill that morning, but not with his aunt and mother. He had come reluctantly with his girlfriend, Susana. José Antonio had found the whole thing absurd on the one hand, and macabre on the other: how could people believe that Julia Álvarez Yupanqui was a saint? His own cousin! A saint! She was no saint. He could vouch for that. Just a regular girl. But the people were idiots who would believe anything.

Even if you don't believe, Susana had said to him, *come and pay your respects.*

Now, as he approached the altar (the two decorated crates balanced on a wheelbarrow), he felt compelled to pray, just in case. And he asked Julia to protect his father, to bring him home safely. For the past seven months Óscar Ribeiro had been held at the prison on El Frontón. All this time, since his father's arrest, José Antonio had heard whispering at night. In the evenings, after he and Miguel Ángel had gone to bed, his father's friends would come and gather around the kitchen table to consult with Alba. These men, the ones his father called *comrades* and *brothers in arms*, the ones he had grown up calling *Tío*, would whisper about a prison revolt. José Antonio heard only snatches of plans, but he gathered that there would be hostages and lists of demands. The release of political prisoners, above all. And he heard his mother ask,

What if the worst should happen?

The worst?

What if the government responds with excessive force?

It almost certainly will.

And what then?

José Antonio held his breath to hear above his brother's gentle snoring.

In that case, camarada Alba, your husband will have given the greatest sacrifice for the sake of the people's struggle. And the State will have demonstrated publicly what we have been saying all along. That it is unfit to rule, intent on genocide, and must be overthrown for the good of all.

Yesterday morning when José Antonio had risen, he knew that the worst had happened, because one of the Tíos was in the kitchen and the Tíos never usually came in daylight. So now he begged, *Prima Julia, if there is any way, any way at all that you can bring him home alive, let it be. Let it be, let it be, let it be that he is not dead.*

Alba Yupanqui Collo was not there to pray for her husband. She knew already in her heart that he was gone. He had paid the highest price for revolution. It was a price he had for years been preparing himself to pay. No, she had come to accompany her sister, to see whether the rumours were true that Julia, their own little Julia, was being venerated by the people.

Usually, Alba had little time for religions. In her experience, saints and gods and angels did little for the people who turned to them.

They were the circus of shiny shit and migas used to distract the people from their suffering. But if Julia – her beloved niece, sensible, careful, methodical Julia – had become some kind of saint, then she would be a saint that Alba had time for. Julia had always been clever, but so uninterested in abstractions. She concerned herself with the day-to-day, with the practical needs of the hour before her, with putting food in front of her siblings, packing their schoolbags, combing their hair. She was unostentatious. She was practical. She never complained about how much her parents asked of her in helping to care for the little ones, never lamented how much she had to give up when her father died and she had to go to work. It seemed never to occur to her to think *It's not fair* or to imagine what could have been, what should have been, or to compare herself to others. Julia had always done what was needed, and so it was for Julia, as much as for her own sons, that Alba wanted so desperately to succeed in the revolutionary struggle.

As Alba shuffled forward in the queue, one hand on Miguel Ángel's shoulder, the other arm wrapped around her sister's waist, she spoke to Julia wordlessly, internally. She asked Julia to bless the revolution. She trusted that Julia, from wherever she was now standing, could see the needfulness of overthrowing the current order and ushering in a new democracy. But, from where Julia was standing, right by her mother's side, what she saw was rather different. She saw a little boy with dark curls clutching a foil windmill, wishing, wishing, wishing for a puppy. She saw, too, that this little boy had just lost his father, though he did not know it yet, and she saw that his father's body was lying, bloodied, in a pile of corpses at El Frontón penitentiary, eyes wide open, staring at the grizzled, Limenian neblina that chattered all the time about pachas that could have been in the voices of souls that could have been if things had only been different.

Julia saw that before long Óscar Ribeiro's spirit would crawl out of his body, squeezing itself painfully out of the orifices, and would stand for a long time, arms crossed, staring at the pile of corpses, examining the limbs sticking out at strange angles, the eyeballs turning grey, the pools of blood and entrails sprawled out where they shouldn't be. And then Óscar Ribeiro would ask himself *Was it worth it?* Truthfully, from where he was now standing, he wasn't sure. But what was done was done, so he turned his back on the corpses and walked away, through the courtyard, through the prison walls, out across the rocky shore of the island and over the sea. He walked on the waves. He could have walked west, towards the ocean – the great expanse of blue where sea and sky blur together, the place where the sun sets – but he walked east towards the coast and the city where his sons were praying for his return, and where his wife had already released him to the hereafter.

All around the water-walking spirit of Óscar Ribeiro were dozens of others, all walking away from El Frontón towards the shore. When they reached the land and began to crawl up the cliffs of Chorrillos and Callao and Miraflores, hundreds upon hundreds of others joined them. The city was full of the wandering dead searching for family, searching for resting places, seeking absolution, paying their penance. Some came to demand justice, others to mete it out. Many were simply lost, walking in circles, around and around. Julia could see them all. She could hear them too, asking, *Have you seen my wife? Have you seen my son? I have lost my legs, have you seen them? Which way to the Palace of Justice?* But there were too many questions and too few answers, and all the time more ghosts were added to their number and, with them, more voices, clamouring all the time. There was always the incessant chattering of clouds, the neblina pressing noisily down over the city, and the chorus of the dead, the complaints of the living, and the traffic (the klaxons and growling of engines, the wheezing exhaust pipes), now and then the explosions of car bombs and rattling of gunfire over which the wealthy in their mansions simply turned up the radio or television from which the jingle of irrepressibly hopeful commercials played in a loop over the cacophonous city with

¡Feliz navidad para todos! ¡Feliz navidad para todos!

¿Si mata cucarachas, qué no matará?

La mejor es Blanca Nieve.

¡Siempre Coca-Cola!

Alba Yupanqui Collo trusted that, wherever her niece was now, she would understand the importance of the revolution. But, whether she had come to believe in the revolution or not, Santa Julia had no power over such things. She had no power to dismantle governments or win wars. She could not tear down powers or raise up new ones. What she knew, from her time ascended into janaj pacha, from her observations far beyond the Earth, was that these things took care of themselves. Empires fall and rise and fall again. Powers swell and bloom then shrivel, are buried and germinate again. The exalted ones are eventually laid low. Every emperor becomes a corpse and rots alongside the beggar. As the hero dances, a snake waits in the bushes to bite his heel. The order of the world is pachacuti. Always, a pachacuti is coming. The wheel is turning, inexorably turning, and will return to its starting point, so the Earth revolves around the sun and the stars turn in the sky and, yes, revolution is inevitable, but not necessarily the revolution Alba had in mind.

Even now that she had died and ascended into janaj pacha and returned, resurrected, to the land of the living, Julia Álvarez Yupanqui had no power over any of this. All she could offer were the little miracles. She could blow on Miguel Ángel's foil windmill and make it spin. She could bring to yap around José Antonio's ankles a flea-ridden yellow dog that would follow him home and insist on staying so that not even Alba could bear to shoo him away because, as it turned out, a little creature to care for was exactly what she needed to distract herself from the grief that gnawed at her intestines when she woke and saw her husband's shirt hanging on the back of the door and knew he would never be back. It was the stinky, mischievous, scratchy little dog that kept her company at night when the bed felt too wide and too cold. It was this same dog that comforted her sons when, two years later, she was executed extrajudicially with a bullet in the back of the head and dumped from the cliffs onto the beach at Chorrillos.

These were the miracles of Santa Julia, small mercies, little alleviations in the lives of her devoted: combi tyres that never deflated, tubs of boot polish that never ran dry. To the mother with young children, school shoes that grew with their feet. To the carpenter, tools that could not be blunted. For the children who begged on street corners, smiles that the tourist could not refuse. And, for the hungry, toasted corn that proliferated inexplicably and was now being passed down the queue from person to person, cupped hand to cupped hand, from mother to son, boy to anciana, preacher to penitent, pedlar to pimp, seamstress to smuggler, fisherman to thief, cambista, combista, Senderista, militar, ciego y calvo, pobre o perdido – all accepted the toasted corn and shared it on.

The smell of the kernels drew the turkey buzzards. They glared down from the walls of the casona, ancient-looking, dinosauric. The Echeverría cats, too, were emerging, slinking in and out of the worshippers, batting with their paws at the pieces that fell to the ground. In the trees, rosaries and scapulars had been hung from the branches and tinkled against one another, chattering like wind chimes. Now and then, the sun emerged from behind the neblina to make the rosary beads glint and sparkle in the foliage and in the scintillating light they cast, people sat in groups, wrapped in ponchos and shawls, laughing, sharing cancha, playing music, tickling charangos, pursing lips over quenas. In one clearing, within a circle of spectators, a couple danced a marinera in jeans and sneakers (though some said the woman should have removed her shoes). By the tool shed, a girl gave birth and praised Santa Julia when the child was not born, as she had feared, with seven heads (one for each of the men that had forced himself upon her). At the gates, an old man fainted, fell, hit his head and swore he could see Santa

Julia reaching out to him from among the clouds. By now the tourists had also arrived, as had the hawkers, ice-cream vendors with their cart-bikes, palm readers and tarot witches. There were even newspaper crews and television cameras sent to take the heat off the government ministers (who were beginning to think they might have responded to the prison riots with a little too much force).

From a window on the first floor, some members of the Echeverría family were peeking down through the shutters. What was to be done about this invasion? About the hundreds of feet trampling the lawn? About the looting of the orange trees and the teenagers copulating in corners? This is exactly what they had feared, what several of the Tíos foresaw back in 1968 when the president had been yanked out of bed in his pyjamas and led at gunpoint to a plane that would take him into exile. Their fears were confirmed a year later when the land rush descended onto Los Polvos. Then, like today, they had watched from the windows and said, *It will start with the empty lots, but they will come for our houses. Just you wait! They will come for our houses before long!*

And they were not wrong, because within a few months, one insufferably hot Wednesday in February 1970, the Ministry of Agriculture for the Revolutionary Government of the Armed Forces (and this had, of course, been a different revolution, not *the* revolution Alba believed in) sent a pickup truck to the hacienda at Pisco. It drove right across the courtyard and burned a set of brown track marks into the grass. From that truck two heavy black military boots thudded against the ground, marched to the front door, and kicked hard.

The farmhouse itself had not been included in the expropriation papers that arrived rolled up in the fist of the booted sub-lieutenant. Nevertheless, the family (Ignacio the Second, his wife and their children) found themselves marooned in their vast casona surrounded by vehicles they could not drive, livestock they could not slaughter, crops they could not harvest, and vineyards on which they could not set foot (for everything, every last item, from the wine press to the toolbox, was property of the agrarian reform and you must not touch, *señor patrón*, the property of the revolution!). Finding their new situation intolerable, akin to being imprisoned within the four walls of their own home, they fled to the city to take refuge in the yellow house on the hill.

Now, sixteen years later, huddling around the yellow house's shutters and looking down on the invaders who snaked around the hill under the naranjos, along the Avenida and into the distance, Ignacio Segundo told the rest of the family: *You see! You see what we told you! They are coming to take the house! They won't be satisfied until they turn the whole country to hell. First the agriculture, then the industries, and now our very homes will go to shit.*

Should we call the police?

There might be terrucos down there.

The police? The police, she says!

The police don't care a cucumber about us!

Come now, papá…

Where were the police when they came
for our farmhouse?

Tranquilo, papá.

I'll call the serenazgo.

What can the serenazgo do?!

Call the army! It's Sendero, sin duda.

We need the army.

The army is busy, Mamá,
dealing with these riots in the prisons.

Call the army, she says!

As if it wasn't the army that took our home!

Cálmense, please.

There are no terrucos down there.

¡Ja!

They're just people in search of hope. *¡Ja!*

> *Lord knows, the people need*
> *hope right now.*

Would you listen to our son, Isabel?

> *I know! I know!*

Un rojo. We've raised un rojo.
> *¡Papá!*
You'll see. They've come to take from us.

> *They've come to shoot us in the head.*

But the worshippers were not Senderistas, Reds or terrucos. They were not here to take from the Echeverrías, or to shoot them in the head. They were here to petition the santa: to ask for school fees for their children, for healing for their parents, for a new job or blessings on their exam results, for the winning lotería numbers, for a husband or a wife or safe passage to the United States. No, the worshippers had not come to oust the Echeverrías. They had their own troubles to preoccupy them, and they believed the santa would alleviate their suffering.

Margarita Montealegre Belén had no interest in Santa Julia. She put no faith in saints. She put no faith in anything except herself and activism and progressive social policies that would better the day-to-day lives of the poor. This was why she had founded the Federación Popular de Mujeres de Los Polvos, the Fepomup, to help the women of the young town organise and lobby for what they needed – childcare, a community kitchen, a medical post…

Margarita knew, as she weaved in and out of the queue that snaked around and around the hill, that the petitions of the worshippers would go unanswered. There was no one listening to their prayers. The skies were devoid of ears. But she believed it was important to go where the people were so here she was, stopping to shake a hand, to ask a question, to hand over a leaflet and to urge support for the Vaso de Leche programme which would require the municipality to provide every child with a carton of milk each day at school.

For some time, Julia walked unseen alongside Margarita, all the time looking into the young woman's face. A dawn was breaking behind this face, a beautiful dawn, and Julia had seen it before through the eyes of a woman two hundred years dead, standing just inside the Portada de Maravillas, all alone in the wide-open square, within the walls of Lima for the first time. Repeatedly, urgently, this long-ago woman kept pressing her burn-scarred palm against a pocket sewn into the folds of her dress, touching there just to feel the reassuring crackle of her letter of freedom. She needed to know she hadn't lost it, that it hadn't fallen out or disintegrated into dust. She knew what could happen to those who lost their papers, had heard tales about people being snatched from the street as they walked along and, unable to prove their free status, being sold back into slavery. But her carta was still there. She could feel it through the fabric and make out its four corners, its flat edge pushing back against her fingertips.

Yes, Miércoles Agosto Segunda was free, but she stood in the Plaza de Armas that morning at dawn as if made of stone, paralysed by too much emotion, the sadness of leaving behind everyone she had ever known, the fear of beginning again in a foreign place, and the vertiginous relief of being (Lord, was it actually true?) *free*, but also by the guilt that she alone out of all her brothers and sisters had been the one to benefit from the manumission. She could not fathom from where she would pluck the strength to start again, alone, for how could Miércoles Segunda live without Miércoles Primera when the two had shared a womb, shared a childhood, shared every crust of bread and cup of water, every sunrise and sunset, every dream and every fear?

The cathedral, stoic and silent, saw the girl standing at its foot and whispered something to the palm trees. The palm trees heard the cathedral's whisper and passed it to the wind. The wind carried the message up to the mountains that guard the north side of the city (the Hill of Willows, as it is known, and the Daffodil Mountains, which are the toes of the Andes stretching out towards the inner regions). Then the mountains whispered back a message for the girl. They said, *Turn to us, turn to us*, and she did, just as the sun burst from the horizon and painted the hills with gold, the Peruvian daffodils catching the light. Then Miércoles Segunda understood that she needed a new name with which to face the day so she called herself Aurora Montealegre and, with a new name, felt braver.

Some years later, Aurora returned to Pisco with the sum she had saved to purchase her sister's freedom, but her sister had grown tired of waiting for her and had made a new plan: she had petitioned to the court for a licence to marry Domingo Julio Tercero in accordance with the Royal Decree stipulating that slave marriages must be encouraged to avoid 'fornication and illicit relations'. When Aurora went to the hacienda, she found that Miércoles Primera was a mother and pregnant, so her value was now well in excess of what it had been. Aurora would have to work harder, much harder, to be able to afford the price of her sister's liberty and that of her children, but every time she returned to the hacienda at Pisco, each time with more money than the last, Miércoles Primera's value would increase and increase until one day Segunda returned for the last time to find that Primera was no longer there, for she had been sent away by her master and he would not reveal where she had gone.

Frustration with chasing a receding goal was something Margarita Montealegre Belén understood well. Every time she applied to the municipality of Miraflores for something (electricity lines, sewage pipes, milk for the schoolchildren), there was a new reason it could not be done, some bureaucratic obstacle disproportionate to the task at hand. This particular form needed stamping or, if it had been stamped, it was with the wrong seal by the wrong teller at the wrong window and by the time the right stamp had been acquired, the form had changed – you don't need that form, you need this one and its five appendices. That particular fee needed paying or, if it had been paid, needed evidencing with a receipt, but not that receipt, a different receipt of a different colour with a different signature. Regulations and procedures would come scuttling out of corners like cockroaches. She seemed to spend her life with the notary public and, inevitably, the bureaucrats at the municipal office were never satisfied with what the notary had done (*he has made a mistake, you need to go back*) and the notary would insist that it was the municipal employee who was mistaken (*they're all incompetent there, tell them to check again*) so round and round she went, ferrying papers, sitting in waiting rooms, getting behind on her university work.

You see? Alba would tell her. *This is why your suave-suave pacific methods do not work. You try to ignore that there is a class war being waged. But the bourgeoisie are waging it against you. With their rules and regulations and procedures, they are slowly killing you, Tita, as they have slowly killed us all for generation after generation.*

It was some years now since Margarita and Alba, old friends from their days on the fringes of the Communist Party, had been estranged. For Margarita, it was prudent to stay as far away as possible from Sendero, not only because, as an izquierdista, the government would see her as a terruco, but also because Sendero were targeting any leftists who did not align with their vision. She knew that *El Diario* had marked the Federaciones Populares de Mujeres as revisionists and enemies of the revolution. She knew that Sendero intended to silence them and put an end to their activities by whatever means necessary. As for Alba, she had grown tired of trying to recruit Margarita to the struggle. If Margarita wanted to continue chasing her tail, let her do it. Alba had no energy left for people who insisted, through their continued compliance, on endorsing the imperialist apparatus of the State.

But today, for the first time in years, Margarita and Alba met face to face and just for this day they put aside their differences because someone needed them. Merly Yupanqui Collo, leaning on her sister's arm, had reached the front of the queue and stood now before the altar of her daughter, the one they were saying had died and resurrected, the one they were calling Santa.

Since she had heard the news that her daughter, seventeen years old, had fallen from the second-floor window of the yellow house on the hill and exploded all over the antique majolica tiles, Merly Yupanqui Collo felt as if her throat had closed. Not a sound would emerge, not a wail, not a word. She felt desiccated: her gullet was a dry twig; her vocal cords were strips of straw. Her very bones were wispy, just sticks threatening to snap.

She had buried her daughter that morning and had not said a word. The priest had tried to condole with her, but she replied with silence. The mourners had prayed and she could not even say *Amén*. When her sister had brought the mortician to her home to ask what arrangements she desired (*What sort of coffin? Lined with which fabric? What colour flowers?*) Merly had been speechless, only licking her lips because of the insupportable dryness. No one had thought to bring her water. They just rubbed her back and made arrangements and stroked her hair and put the little ones to bed while she sat on the couch and wondered since when she had had sand on her tongue.

Now, held up by her sister, Merly placed her hands on the altar and smoothed the tablecloth. Among the flickering candles and heads of flowers, the plates of bread, cups of wine and coins piled upon coins, someone had placed a photograph of her daughter. Merly felt ashamed because she had not thought to do so herself. What kind of mother cannot cry for her firstborn? What sort of terrible mother was she, dry and hard and unfeeling as rock?

Unseen by any, Julia Álvarez Yupanqui, the one they now called Santa Julia, stood face to face with the woman who had once been her mother and it was like regarding a mise en abyme – in her mother's eyes she saw her own face in the eyes of which was her mother's face in whose eyes she found herself again and so on and so on until the end of the world. If you go to Lima now and stand on the mount just off the Avenida del Guanero, you will find them still, these two women, standing cara a cara, contemplating each other, meditating one on the other, world without end, Amén.

Julia Álvarez Yupanqui, or what remained of her, wanted to fall into her mother's arms and cry and cry. To cry about the injustice of being dead and the inhumanity of slavery and the pile of bodies at El Frontón and the melancholy of frustrated dreams. This is what Julia Álvarez Yupanqui would have done. But the days of Julia Álvarez Yupanqui were over. In her place was Santa Julia, hearer of prayers and granter of petitions. Except that Merly Yupanqui Collo was praying for the kind of miracle that Santa Julia did not have the power to perform. Merly was praying, silently, inwardly, but fervently and repeatedly, for her daughter to come back to life. She prayed for broken bones to be reformed and scuttle back together, for mashed flesh to knit and spilled blood to flow into the veins. Please, please, let the frozen heart beat again.

What Merly Yupanqui Collo did not understand was that her prayer, which she uttered this very moment silently in the recesses of her soul, had already been heard. It had (just now but also a thousand thousand years before) risen to the heavens and been heard by the ears that listened there and they had reached back into the past and plucked her daughter out of death and brought her back to the land of the living. Merly's prayer, before it had ever been prayed (and also at the same time and many times again), had already come and was coming and would again come to pass.

But Merly did not know this, and so it could not comfort her. She continued to stand, heavy and silent as stone, before the altar. Her sister by her side turned to Margarita, and neither knew what to do for this mother who was so blocked she could not cry.

The miracles of Santa Julia are not spectacular. Face to face with a mother (her own mother) who could not grieve, Santa Julia reached out and with one finger pushed against the woman's forehead to unbalance her. Like a statue, stiff as a corpse, Merly Yupanqui Collo teetered a little, back and forth, back and forth, before collapsing to the ground.

In that instant, the people in the queue rushed into action. The ones nearby surrounded her, pushing Alba and Margarita away in their eagerness. Others began to clamour that a woman had fainted. Get help! Get help! Was there a doctor in the crowd?

No doctors! She needs water.

Someone bring water!

And sugar! She needs sugar!

Not sugar! She needs salt.

Salt?

Yes! Salt! Salt! For the blood pressure.

In the muddle, somehow the bag of cancha found its way into Alba's hands and she shoved a path through the strangers that had bunched themselves around her sister. Simultaneously, elsewhere in the throng, someone thrust the bottle of unending water into Margarita's chest and she, too, began fighting her way towards her fallen friend.

In the mouth of Merly, mother of Julia, the salt and water mingled. They washed across her tongue with a taste like the sea. She swilled it, this ocean inside her, filled with grit and ghosts, around and around her teeth and gums, and it stung. Then she swallowed, and she felt suddenly full. Full to overflowing with salt water that threatened to split her open if she did not, at last, after too many hours of dry and brittle silence, cry.

Then Merly, mother of Julia, finally wept. Her llanto was so vehement, so plaintive and unconstrained, that it silenced the crowd, their songs and instruments falling to the grass. It horrified the tourists and turned the television cameras to scrutinise her face. It rose to the windows of the mansion where the Echeverrías ceased in their squabbles and looked down, open-mouthed, appalled: some

at the thought of what the city would say when they saw a griev-
ing mother wailing on the casona's doorstep; others heartbroken,
wondering what they could do. Should they go out there? Take
her something from the pantry? A hamper of non-perishables? A
panetón?

Before they could organise themselves, Carmen was at the doorway. She was apologetic, she did not mean to disturb, but did the
family know that little Anaïs was outside? *What? Again? What do
you mean Anaïs is outside? How could she be outside?* Carmen came to
the window, pointed down to the garden and, sure enough, the girl
was down there, still in her nightdress (because, in all the uproar
of the invaders, no one had thought to bathe her, dress her – it was
usually Julia who did that). She was standing a few paces from the
wailing mother, black eyes wide open, skin pale and clammy. She
looked sick. She looked, in truth, muerta.

Yes, Anaïs looked muerta, and this was not surprising because,
when she had seen Julia fall, a portion of her soul had extracted
itself and the earth had snatched it up. Now, the girl (half-dead,
hollowed out) had come outside to recover this lost part of her soul,
or rather she had come outside to find *something*, because she had
a sense that a part was missing within her. But instead of her soul,
she found Julia, dead and resurrected, standing on the front patio.

And, of course, Anaïs could see her.

TWELVE

I woke at midnight to the clattering of small hard things on the bedside table. I watched them dance in the darkness, small cubes of osseous white ricocheting jauntily off the wood, and thought at first that they were dice tossed in the ghosts' never-ending game of Dudo. Then, as my eyes found their focus, I saw they were not dice but bones – sheep knuckles and human molars with which the Don and the Doña were playing at jacks.

She's awake.

Ya veo.

She'll be off to scratch at walls again.

Most probably.

She's losing grip.

It is evident.

I ignored them, didn't rise to the provocation. I don't have time to waste on fruitless argumentation. It is night, and the nights are not interminable. This is when I work now. The clickety-clack of bones woke me at the perfect time: late enough that Q'orianka and Uriel would be fast asleep, early enough that I had several hours of unbroken productivity before the sun rose.

I got up and went to the mirror. There, a lemur confronted me. The lemur was me and I was not surprised. I have not taken a stable form these past few days. When I lifted my left arm I found that it was still a decorator's brush – one of those with the long

218

handles for painting high ceilings and hard-to-reach places – and my right leg was now a broom (wooden, with horsehair bristles), though it had been normal when I went to bed. It didn't matter, I told myself: broom for leg – brush for arm. It would make the night's work easier.

My tasks now consume my body as well as my mind. The other day, before the reunion at Tía Mimi's apartment, I set myself the goal of making pie de limón. A perfect, authentic pie de limón the way Mama used to make it would prove to the aunts and primas two things: first, that I was competent, that I had everything under control. And second, that I was a true limeña. A genuine Echeverría. Granddaughter of my grandmother. Denizen of Miraflores. That I understood the components of the Limenian family gathering – dress code, menu, etiquette.

I have rehearsed the rituals in my mind since my fracaso of an appearance at prima Mimita's impromptu reunion. Like mother, like daughter – she likes her reunions, likes playing hostess in her apartment with vista al mar and roof terrace. She turned up here, at Mamabue's house, the evening of the day I escaped de las Casas. Rupert was still out on the Avenida, talking away to Dios knows quien on his mobile phone. I was here in the house, hiding behind the shutters, watching the little pink fish succumb to the Electra complex, dorsal fin pulsing, heart thumping behind quivering gills. That was when she, primita Mimita, skidded up to the gate, tinted driver's-side window rolled down, enormous black tyres throbbing under the gleaming white hulk of her Mercedes, a behemoth of a car, *un Jeep*, one of those monolithic cuboids designed for the Great Plains and rough terrains, not city streets, and yet all the miraflorinos drive them, air con blasting, one hand on the wheel, the other smoothing hair, adjusting Ray-Bans.

At first I did not know her. She was a conglomeration of parts: gently rounded brown shoulder protruding from a white Bardot blouse: long hair, castaño, lightened by artificial means and blow-dried, carefully tousled, twisted and sprayed into beach waves; painted fingernails with white tips; a long, shimmering limb stretching out as she emerged, engine still running; block heel of her leather mule sandal hitting the ground and reverberating through me. She leaned forward, took Rupert by the forearms, made effortless air kisses and then didn't release her grip, green eyes rolling under black butterfly lashes, delicate gold chain glinting against her collarbone. I watched her painted mouth, pink lips making shapes, bright white teeth flashing when she laughed.

I noticed, suddenly, that I was imitating her. Behind the shutters, I was tossing my hair, laughing soundlessly with my head thrown back, gesticulating with palms up.

Loca.

Loca loca loca.

And this time it wasn't the ghosts who were saying it, but me. The ghosts were simply watching, mouths fallen open.

Bien bien loca estoy.

All at once, Mimita was on the path, climbing the cracked steps, confidently placing her feet in the spaces between the criss-crossed vines. She had no fear of falling. She trusted her feet to bear her up, even balanced as she was on her polished toes – trusted the earth to hold her.

Her arrival took me by surprise, gave me no time to prepare. I opened the door and she snatched me, dragging me into the cloud of her perfume (fruity and floral, too sweet, empalagoso to the point of dizziness). She gripped me so close that I could smell the powder of her blusher, the hairspray, the top notes of hair salon and coconut body oil, the accents of Mercedes leather seats. *Naaaniiii-ta!* she cooed at me, elongating the syllables.

Nanita. No one had called me that in years. Nanita (short for Anaïs) and Mimita (short for Miriam) had been thrown together as children on the basis of age and gender since she, the only daughter of Tío Pulpo and Tía Mimi, had five older brothers who tortured her, and I, Nanita the Strange, had been prescribed living human children by the doctor to draw me out of myself and my obsession with dead people. So Mimita and I would be plonked together in the centre of a room while the adults lined the walls and – paternalistic, observant – watched us play. Under their noses, obediently and self-consciously, we invented stories with the lithe-limbed, blonde-haired dolls placed before us, carefully avoiding the scandalous storylines of the telenovelas the Titis watched in the afternoons – stories of surreptitious pregnancies and indecorous love affairs, of unwitting incest and jealous murder plots. No, Mimita and I played cautiously under the eyes of the elders with the dolls that, later, our brothers would steal and take out to the garden, strip naked, make to perform indecent acts and then leave hanging by their hair from the naranjos.

Now Mimita was here, poised on tiptoe, one leg crossed in front of the other, speaking in rapid Spanish, voice so much sharper than I remembered it, syllables tripping one over the other faster than I could catch them. Why couldn't I make sense of her garbled sounds? I ferreted around among the vowels for something firm and realised she was eating her consonants – all the dentals, swallowed entirely. The plosives barely there. Aside from the fillers – *Eeeste* and *Pueees* – which she paused over, extended, intoned melismatically, her words eluded me. I tried to read her lips. She hardly moved them.

Later that evening, at her apartment, primo after primo would speak to me the same way, running their vowels together, comién-dose los consonants, commenting on my own Spanish, how clear it was, how well articulated, tan bien pronuncia'o, like Real Academia Española Spanish. How-it-should-be-spoken Spanish, they said. I knew what they meant. That I spoke Spanish as if I had learned it in a classroom. I had lost my Limenian accent, while their own accents, I thought, had migrated northwards, towards the Caribbean, imi-tating, a little, the Spanish of Latinos in the States, algo cubano, algo dominica'o. Some – the ones who had studied their bachelor's in Florida – had picked up the miamense accent. Others, who had studied in New York, spoke a little boricua. All spoke with such insouciance, not carefully, as I did. I took great pains to find the right word, stress the right syllable, use the correct gender, verb tense and mood. But they had nothing to prove. They code-switched to Spanglish without shame.

¡Oye, Paquito! Pásame los hielos del freezer.

Mira, Flaquis. ¿Desde cuando estás tan gorgeous?

Le estoy enseñando a Papi como bajar songs al iPod.

¡Pero, relax, pues! Take it easy, my brother!

Yes, entirely sin vergüenza, because no one would think that *they* had forgotten the right vocabulary. Shamelessly they slid from one tongue to the other, talking about *jangeando* and *Googlear*, *parquear carros* and *chequear los facts*, stringing together Spanish clauses with English conjunctions, *but* and *so* thrown in among the *estes* and *pueses*. But when I tried to do it, I got it wrong. People flinched, hesitated and looked at me blank-faced, without comprehension. I learned that 'well' could not replace 'pues'. Nor could 'then'. And while computer could become computadora and calculator could become calculadora, hoover could not become hooveradora. Nor was vacuumadora acceptable. They corrected my Spanglish. Primos smirked at me, threw their arms round me, squeezed my shoulders, jovial but pitying. Leave the Spanglish to the Americans, they laughed. Spanglish is not for the British.

So I stuck to Spanish. Just Spanish. But by then some of my Tíos were already concerned that I was losing command of my tongue. They listened intently as I spoke, watched me with narrowed eyes, monitoring my lexis, my syntax. I began to panic, stopped extemporising. I planned my answers before I said them, no longer listening to what the other person was saying, just rehearsing my own speech. Words over which I had never worried became unfamiliar, didn't sound right. It felt as if language were something precarious. Slippery. At all times, I was teetering on the edge of something drastic. An abyss. Shadows moved within it, shadows of words I could not grasp.

They gave me such strange looks that night, my Tíos, as I spoke, as if I were babbling nonsense like a baby. I heard my voice from very far away. I was a ventriloquist's dummy, mouth moving, wooden lips clacking together, but hollow and voiceless. Or rather voiced by someone else. They regarded me with confusion. Looks of bafflement and pity until I wondered whether I was speaking any language at all and I fell gradually silent. Tíos patted my knee affectionately. It'll come back to you, they said. It'll come back. And it suddenly occurred to me how hard it must have been for Q'orianka to learn Spanish when she came to work with us.

Standing on the doorstep, one golden leg crossed in front of the other, Mimita had stopped talking at me. She was waiting for my reply. Reply to what? I hadn't listened, had no idea what she had asked me. She looked at her watch. Her eyes flickered over my shoulder to the dark hallway behind me. I tensed, defensive. I would not let her come inside.

'Just an impromptu gathering,' she said. 'Informal. At my apartment. Nothing fancy. A few primos. A few Titis...Tíos.' And she flicked her wrist to straighten her watch.

I couldn't, I told her. I had so much to do. Like what? she asked, incredulous. As if it was unthinkable that *I* could ever be occupied. She said I was on vacation. Said I should *relax*. Rrrrelax, she said, with the alveolar trill, castellanified. I should *Rrrr-elaxarme*, which is even more relaxing than Anglo-Saxon relaxing.

I had things, I told her. *Things* to do. Another time, I promised. Next time, for sure.

No-no, she said and twitched her finger at me, back and forth. She wouldn't take no for an answer. I was coming. Get into my car. I'll take you. I'll bring you back. Rupert's coming. Everyone must meet Rupert. He's familia now, after all. Come-come. She liked to double up her words like this, it seemed. No-no. Come-come. Ven-ven.

I would change first, I told her, gesturing at my clothes. I was in the same outfit I had been in since the morning, except for the knickers, cast out to sea, and my shoes, which I had lost on the beach, and also my headscarf – where had that gone? Had I left it at the cafe? And then it occurred to me, I had gone to El Haití with Rupert barefoot. Had he noticed? Had other people noticed? Perhaps not. My skirt was long, after all – almost floor-length. And even if they had noticed, perhaps they had put it down to some adorable quirk. A hippy, eco-chic styling choice. Yes. That's it. I could pull that off. There were hippies in Lima too. But not among my family. I would need shoes for a reunion. Bare feet would attract questions...

'Nonsense,' she said. 'No need to change. It's just an informal thing. A little thing.'

'I've been at the beach,' I said, by way of excuse and apology.

'So have I,' she said.

Of course she had. She'd been at the Club Regatas, while I'd been outside, excluded, wandering around the fishermen's beach. She, just beyond the wall, on Playa Uno, had been frolicking in the waves, or reclining on a fluorescent towel, drenched in tanning oil, turning over at twenty-minute intervals, adjusting the strings around her hips to ensure even toasting. Then she would have gone in to the salon, had a shower, a massage, a mani-pedi, quick blow-dry. I remembered the ritual. As a teenager I had been initiated into it, taught how to hold my hand still as the girl oiled it, how to calculate the right tip, folding the notes and tucking them into the girl's apron pocket. She was always a girl – a chica – even when she was forty years old and married with children, even if her children were all grown and she had grandchildren. Always a chica.

I've been at the beach was no excuse for imperfection.

But my skirt, I insisted, looking down at it, smoothing it. My skirt was dry, but the sea salt had made it crunchy, scratchy with sand and bits of shell. I smelled like the ocean. Algal. A trace of something fetid. The pee, perhaps? I had peed in this skirt. They would smell the ammonia on me. I needed to wash. I felt unclean. I needed to scrub myself, tame my hair, check my make-up, reapply my face at least. It would have melted off by now – my make-up, not my face. I had a sudden impulse to raise my hands to my cheeks, my chin, my forehead and pat them to check they were still there, in the right places and proportions. But I didn't. I kept my hands at my sides. Your face is still there, I told myself.

But my make-up needed checking. It was smudged, possibly. For all I knew I had lipstick on my teeth, eyeliner on my cheeks. I turned my hands over to inspect them and saw that the nail polish had chipped. I had only just painted it on this morning! Already I was falling apart!

Ya-ya, she said, dismissively waving her hand in the air.

Ya-ya, I thought. Such a versatile word. *Right now*, she meant, *OK-OK! Whatever-whatever! Enough already!* It meant that what I wanted didn't matter. It meant, rrrrelax. Stop being dramatic. Hurry up and vamos, ya. *Ya-ya, Nanita. Ya-ya.*

Sitting in the back of her SUV in my pee-skirt, knickerless, shoe-less, picking at my nail polish (in vengeance letting the red flakes litter the pristine footwell), I listened as she and Rupert chattered in English. He sat beside her in the front. It would have been rude otherwise. She was not our taxista. I sat in the back, listening. She drove one-handed, flicking through the radio stations, flicking her hair. When she hit traffic, she would flick down the visor and check her eyelashes in the mirror. She would flick her wrist to straighten her watch. Flick, flick, flick. Sometimes our eyes locked for a moment. Her English reminded me of cats purring, a little lion's roar. The hairs on her forearm stood up from the cold of the air con. They caught the light – blonde, almost white, bleached by the sun. Mine were black. I became painfully aware of them, rubbed my arms with my palms as if the friction could rub away the hairs.

I was still gripping my forearms with my hands, spreading my fingers wide as if that could hide the shamefulness of my black fuzz, when we reached her apartment. The lift took us directly into her living room, where bifold doors opened onto a roof terrace with a view of the sea. There, at least a dozen aunts and uncles and probably two dozen primos greeted me with a cheer and an opening of many arms. It was confusing. Who was I meant to embrace first? There were too many limbs held aloft, too many faces. Rupert had none of my hesitation. He was already shaking hands, patting shoulders, thumping backs, giving air kisses to other easy, breezy, golden primas. *Hello, hello*, voices were saying. Or rather *Jello, Jello*, the 'h' turned guttural, rasped from the back of the throat.

Miriam's apartment – or, I should say, *the apartment in which Miriam lived*: it belonged to Mimi and Pulpo, who had bought it for her to live in (and as an investment property, because Barranco was up-and-coming these days) – unnerved me. The resemblance was uncanny. Easily, so easily, it could have been Rupert's place. I froze, gormless, staring at it all: the black quartz kitchen worktops and bright white high-gloss lacquer cabinets with no handles, all on magnetic catches, the blood-red coffee machine, flat-screen TV, black American-style fridge-freezer with buttons that pinged when you pressed them for filtered water or ice, cubed or crushed. In my mind, for a moment, it *was* Rupert's place. It was all some elaborate trick. *Surprise!* You're home! Ta-da! Distance is no distance now, in this globalised world where kitchens here look like kitchens there, where an apartment is an apartment is an apartment. Everything from the white walls to the white-grey laminate flooring to the black metro tiles in the bathroom…everything that was hers here was also ours there.

I felt dizzy, as if I had been on a carousel, riding too fast, and then been thrown off it in the exact place I boarded. Travel and travel and travel and you return to where you started. Or maybe you don't, but how would you know? Because everywhere's the same.

I overheard a Tío discussing this very thought with Rupert, gazing out at the sunset from the roof terrace, each with a beer in hand. From here, we could be anywhere, Rupert said approvingly. Any modern city in the world. Yes, the Tío replied, chest puffed with pride. Any metropolis. We could be anywhere, truly.

I felt sick, thrust out a hand and steadied myself on the kitchen worktop. I needed to find the bathroom, and instinctively I knew where it would be. There was one in the hallway, a guest toilet, immediately to the right of the front door. With a push I propelled myself from the quartz counter and straight into Tía Mimi.

She didn't pester me about Mamabue's house. She made no mention of the papers. She wanted to know why I wasn't wearing shoes. Didn't I know how dirty the streets of Lima are? Didn't I know about dog faeces and parasites that burrow into your skin and live in your insides? *Por Dios, Mimita*, she cried out to her daughter. *Why didn't you tell the girl* (the 'girl'!) *to put on some shoes?*

Mimita turned around from where she was standing with her back to us, talking to a small cluster of primos, hands clutching a pisco sour. She looked at my naked feet with narrowed eyes. Instinctively, my feet shrank in shame.

'Why aren't you wearing any shoes?' Mimita asked me.

Why wasn't I wearing any shoes? *Why aren't I wearing any shoes?* I wanted to scream at her. *Because you didn't give me time to put myself back together. You turned up on my doorstep – Mamabue's doorstep – with your ya-ya and your ven-ven and you didn't even give me a second to put something on my feet.*

Now everyone was involved. The scandal of the naked feet had spread throughout the party. The room was silent. Had someone turned off the music? Everyone – even Rupert – was looking at my feet. My tiny, shrunken, denuded feet.

¡Pero, pobre niña! Doesn't she have any shoes?

¡Por Dios! Give her some shoes!

Shoes, my God! Shoes!

An uncle was already unlacing his brogues but his wife batted him on the knee with her clutch bag – *¡No seas imbécil, Héctor! She doesn't want men's brogues!*

In the corner, a debate was under way.

In many cultures it is customary not to wear shoes in the home.

In what cultures?

I don't know! Asian cultures…

In some places they wear house shoes.

Zapatillas.

Exactly.

What's wrong with slaps?

Slaps?

She means flip-flops. Hawaianas, you know.

¿Hawaianas?

¿Qué Hawaianas?

It means chancletas, Papi.

Chanclas. You know.

Thongs for the feet?

Exacto.

Those aren't shoes. They're obscenities.

They're for the beach, Papi.

Then let them stay on the beach.

Mimita grabbed me by the hand and led me from the room, like a mother with a disgraced infant. She took me to her bedroom, sat me on the bed and opened her closet, where at least two dozen pairs of sandals, courts and stiletto boots were neatly lined up on two long shelves. With her back to me and hands on her hips, she surveyed her belongings. She was debating, I suppose, which pair she could trust to a sticky, ammoniacal creature like me. What if I destroyed them? What if I peed in them like an untrained puppy? How do we house-train the bizarre little idiot, she was thinking.

At last she chose a pair – navy canvas espadrilles, a little frayed, scuffed at the toes – and stood in front of me cradling them.

In a voice of strained patience, she said, 'Nanita, why didn't you wear any shoes? You should have just said you needed to put on some shoes.'

So simple. She made it sound so simple. *You should have just said. You could have just said.* Why do I complicate everything? Why make everything so circuitous and tangled? Making sure you are dressed is easy. Saying what you want is easy.

She left me to put on the shoes and shut the door behind her.

I went to her en suite, sat down on the toilet, gathered myself. Gathered the disparate parts. Waited for my heart to slow. The little pink fish was not a fish any more. It was a jelly with long, slender tentacles, glowing filaments floating in filigree patterns, parachute head billowing in the air currents.

My skin felt tight. It was the salt water and sun. My nose felt too small. No, it felt too big, as if my face were stretched over it too tightly. If I moved it at all, made any sort of expression, the skin would open right down the middle and all my insides would spill out like rice pouring from an overfilled canvas sack as it splits.

Mimita's en suite was lined with her potions. Oils, emollients, splashes and suspensions stood along the counter in translucent bottles printed with promises: *Revitalising – Calming – Rejuvenating*. Bathing as a kind of alchemy or rebirth.

I decided that I would rinse away the sea and salt and start again, clean and smooth and fragranced, so I stripped naked and stood in the shower cubicle – walls on three sides with a glass panel at the front, like those boxes they sell dolls in, with the see-through plastic. I thought about this as I stood under the shower. I turned the water on at a temperature on the cusp of scalding and stood under it for a long time, watching the room fill with vapours. Around the spotlights in the ceiling the water particles became visible and I watched their swirling patterns until I felt half-hypnotised. The little pink fish was frolicking in the humidity and I wondered how long it would take before the air was so filled with water that I would drown.

I peed in her shower and immediately regretted it. What if they had people monitoring for this sort of thing, like in swimming pools where the water turns purple if there is urine? Any moment the pee police would come knocking, demanding to know who had peed in the shower. What kind of animal pees in the shower? It's disgraceful.

There was nothing to dry myself with – just the bath mat (I wiped my feet on that) and a little hand towel that became saturated after two squeezes around my hair. I would have to drip-dry. Is that the term? Drip-dry? Air-dry? Or is that for clothes or plates? In any case the air would have to dry me, so I remained naked and sat on the toilet to put on the shoes, which had ties – two long ribbons of fabric on each espadrille. They were to be woven around and around the leg in some elegant fashion. But how? Around the ankle in criss-cross patterns, ballerina-style? Tied with delicate bows at the back? I tried this. The straps wouldn't hold: they kept slipping down, inexplicably unwinding until they lay, untied again, on the floor. My body was wrong, my ankles too thin or skin too slippery – whatever it was, the ribbons would not stay up. I tried winding them higher up my legs in a manner reminiscent of a Roman gladiator. I wrapped them around my thighs, tightly, squeezing the flesh, like a tourniquet: meat, trussed with kitchen string. Round and round I wound those straps, but they went on and on – were they growing? Endless lengths of ribbon proliferated from my hands – until I had bound my legs entirely and still more fabric lay in a coiled heap on the floor. I kept on weaving – up, past my thighs, my hips, plaiting the four cords together – but no: there were no longer only four. They had bred, issued offspring. There were at least six, perhaps twice that. Innumerable bands of fabric to plait and weave until I was bound, encased in wicker. I was a mummy, bandaged, lying wriggling on the floor because I must have managed to confuse the straps from each shoe and crossed them over, tethering my legs. I had fallen. Straitjacketed, effectively – now even my arms were bound.

And then I realised that the ties from the shoes had become interwoven with the lappets dangling from the head of the little pink fish, now a jelly. I was entangled in a web of sandal strap and tentacle and the jellyfish was lashing me, whipping its tendrils around and around my body. It would suffocate me. I would die here in its strangling arms.

There was a knock on the door.

'Nanita, are you in there?'

I didn't respond. The little pink fish froze, floating immobile in the air.

'You're taking a long time, querida. ¿Estás bien?'

This was another voice. There were two shadows visible in the crack under the door.

I forgot my words – just said, 'I… I…'

More voices.

Is she sick? Perhaps she's sick.

Yes, ask her if she's sick.

'Are you sick, querida?'

'It's just the fish,' I blurted out.

The fish? What fish?

What did she say? I can't hear.

Something about fish.

Qué fish?

I don't know. Maybe she ate fish?

Food poisoning? Maybe she has food poisoning.

Ay, Dios. She's always sick, this child.

She's pregnant. Maybe it's just las nauseas.

Is it the pregnancy? Ask her if it's the pregnancy.

'Are you pregnant?'

Not 'are you pregnant', imbécil! We know she's pregnant.
Say, 'Is it THE pregnancy?'

'Is it *the* pregnancy?'

I rolled my eyes with such force that my body followed and I found myself flipped over onto my belly.

'I'm fine,' I called. 'I'll be just a moment. I'm…freshening up.'

'She says she's freshening up,' the voice reported to the others. There was some muttering, an overlapping of disparate conversations, and then the shadows at the door moved away. The little pink fish, bashful, retracted its tentacles, releasing me.

After some time, Rupert rapped on the door with his *rat-at-at… at*, the final beat assertive, familiar, even when he had knocked on the doors of our lecturers' offices at university. Sometimes that final knock had overlapped their 'Come in' and Rupert would enter, I loitering behind in the hallway, and the professor would be a little flustered at having been interrupted by the beat of a confident fist.

'Ani? Are you all right?'

Something tangled tumbled from my mouth.

'Are you vomiting? Do you need help?'

At university, he had always been the one to hold back my hair when I drank too much, coming into the women's toilets with me, laying down his jacket so I didn't need to kneel on the sticky floor with my bare legs. Rupert had been friends with a clan of rugby lads, overdrinkers, though he had never been one to binge or sing shouty songs in public. He sat among them, smiling, unflustered, as everyone around got messier and messier, louder and sweatier. I tagged along on those nights and took far longer than I should have to learn my limits, to police my boundaries, so most weekends started with Rupert pulling my hair back as I heaved, threading it into a ponytail, concerned, parental.

'Ani? Ani?' From the height of his voice, it seemed he was kneeling, bringing his mouth close to the keyhole.

'A towel,' I told him. 'Bring a towel.'

He left me to fetch one and, when he returned, I opened the door a crack to receive it and then he waited for me, sitting with his back against the door, but we didn't speak. *He is a good man*, I told myself as I got dried and dressed. *A good man. You could do worse.*

When I emerged, teetering in the espadrilles too big for my feet, I was led by many hands to the sofa. I was to rest, they said. I was not allowed to dance – everyone else was dancing now. I was to sit, quietly, conserving my energies until the taxi came to take me away. They didn't want me here any more, terrifying everyone with my eccentricity. They wanted me gone. Take her away. Take the strange one away.

I was sitting next to some prehistoric Echeverría. I vaguely recognised her as a cousin of my Abue's who had been ancient when I left years ago and was even more so now. I tried to speak to her, but she didn't look at me – just kept staring straight ahead with wide, wet, milky eyes and a mouth that opened and closed, opened and closed. A bone in the side of her face clicked every time the jaw fell open and clicked again every time it shut. Click-open; clack-shut. Click-clack. Click-clack.

In my childhood, my family danced to live music. For big gatherings, they hired musicians. At smaller reunions it would be Tío Raúl on the guitarra, Tío Paco on the cajón, Titi María Dolores's rasping, melancholic voice; together they would perform a vals criollo or a marinera and the oldies would dance in one another's arms while the young parents danced with their little ones and the teenagers lurked in corners examining their nails and asking to listen to the radio. Now María Dolores refuses to sing – says she will only perform religious hymns for the glory of the Lord – and her sisters try to persuade her but she will not be moved. And Tío Raúl's medical practice has taken him away to the States – and Tío Paco is dead.

Now the family danced to the music on Mimita's iPod – reggaeton, mostly, which made the oldies frown. They looked on with furrowed brows and murmured as the young ones pulsed and twitched. The movements were too sexualised, the old ones thought – they didn't realise that the young ones were self-censoring for their benefit, observing a respectful distance between bodies, gyrating shoulders more than hips, dancing low but keeping their legs together, only just separating their knees, never moving violently enough to spill the champagne in their flutes. They didn't smile as they performed – at best, they smirked. Mostly they frowned, especially the women, and looked at things slantwise, out of the corners of their eyes, usually downwards, towards the floor. It was the faraway scowl of the MTV video vixen, as if dancing is a painful and solitary act, something enforced but not to be enjoyed. Something awkward to watch.

At the iPod, Tío Pulpo was admonishing his daughter. *You know how your mother hates this noise. Your tías are not enjoying this. Don't you have something lighter? Any Milly Quezada? Juan Luis Guerra?*

Sí, Papi. Claro, Papi. What would you like?

They conferred over a more appropriate song. Something the oldies could dance to – a cumbia or a merengue.

I stood up to leave, but a cousin pushed me back down and sat next to me, patting my knee with her palm.

'You poor thing! ¡Pobrecita! With las nauseas, I suffered terribly. Ay, how I suffered with the nauseas carrying my children. Especially with the girl – my daughter.' She waved her hand vaguely in the direction of a heap of children piled in the corner of the room, sleeping. The mass undulated as one with their soporific breathing, inhaling and exhaling in unison. Around them a ring of nannies in beige pinafores watched blank-eyed. 'Yes, I was tortured by the nauseas. And daughters are the worst. That's what they say: boys make you look better, feel better. But daughters, ay Dios! Daughters destroy you. Rob your health. Rob your beauty. My hija drew grey hairs from my head, I swear to you. She still does. I have to dye my hair every week from all the greys! It's all her. She's a terror. So fuerte. A strong character, that child. But yes, carrying a daughter makes you sick and ugly – that's what they say. I guess yours is a daughter, primita. You look so pale. But don't worry. It passes. My God, I thought I would die from all the nauseas, but it passes. I have three now, so I know. But no more. I've told Rodri, three and no more. Three is enough. Three is too much.' She smiled, then she turned her eyes, blank and glazed as marbles, to stare blankly at the mound of breathing children.

The oldies were up and dancing now, sashaying around the room in the basic merengue step, their bodies lithe, weaving in the Cuban motion. They smiled, waved, and called out to one another over the music, winking at me. They grabbed the young ones, laughing, and made them dance too, and then Rupert was among them, trying to copy, marching just off the beat, lifting his knees too high, hitting the floor with his heels. *No, hijo, dance on your toes. On your toes!* Crouching on the ground, on elbows and knees, two Tías were pressing with all their might onto his feet, trying to keep him from lifting them off the ground. In front of him an old Tío was pounding out the beat with his walking stick – *Pam! Pam! Pam! Pam! No, hijo! You are dancing up, like you wanna lift-off like a rocket ship. You wanna dance low. Drive your toes into the ground. Like you a snake that wanna burrow.*

La cosa es que his brain is in his knees.
You wanna get him moving the hips, Papi.

¡Oye, Nanita! How can it be that you never teach your novio how to dance, ah?

'We will have to throw you a baby shower,' the mother-of-three said, still staring dead-eyed at the babies and patting my knee mechanically. 'Perhaps we should ask Mimi and Pulpo if they can host it at the hacienda. They've turned it into a beautiful country home. Just beautiful. You remember the hacienda, right, Nanita?'

I threw up right then. Right there on the sofa, I projectile-vomited onto the ancient Echeverría woman and the mother-of-three cousin. Neither reacted. One just click-clack-click-clacked with her mouth.

The other rose very slowly, held her arms up like a zombie and blinked. I continued to sit on the sofa, my cupped palms filled with orange, quivering vomit.

This was why I had to make the pie de limón for the next reunion. A pie de limón would make amends. A pie de limón would prove I could behave in an appropriate fashion. So when Tía Mimi phoned a few weeks later to say there would be a gathering, I went straight to the sideboard where Mama kept her recipe cards. They were there. Or what I want to say is that their remnants were there. Between the tarnished silverware and the English china, shreds of card lay in piles like confetti. Mice – I suspected them first. Or moths – do moths eat paper? Then I picked up a handful of the confetti and saw that the rips were too perfect to have been done by mouth: they were deliberate. Painstaking. Words had been torn apart with care.

Undoubtedly it was the ghost of the library who must have emerged; tired of desecrating novels and reference volumes, he had also set about decimating Mama's recipes. All these index cards, written in her hand, documenting her life's archive in hosting and housekeeping – destroyed. But what was there to do? Should I sit there and wail about it? Cry like a Magdalena over a bit of torn cardboard? Nada que hacer. I swept the fragments into my palm, carried them into the kitchen and laid them on the oak worktable. I was tempted, on the way, to sprinkle them over my head like some sort of nymph at a saturnalia. Like a bride rejoicing under the rice thrown by adoring friends and relatives.

Instead I laid the pieces out on the worktable and with my fingertips moved them about. There were several recipes, both savoury and sweet, which made the task more complicated. I came up with idiotic suggestions (beat the / beef mince / with the / ground garlic / and sugar / until / forming stiff peaks / Add the /

juice of a dozen / eggs / and / parboil the / limes / Garnish with / coriander / cinnamon sticks / and black olives) and also with saner suggestions that accorded with my memories of the pie de limón, which I knew would need a biscuit base, a centre that involved lemons and condensed milk, and a meringue topping. See, I told myself. You know things. You know how to do cooking.

I was able to form an index-card-sized recipe on the worktable. There were gaps – holes with missing words where the wood showed through – but my logic filled them. That is the law of closure: the mind perceives the incomplete as whole. The mind perfects the flawed. We close the circle and square the square. That must be what Rupert does with me, I suppose – fills in the gaps, glosses over the chasms, squares the circle and rounds off the corners. What am I saying? Does that make sense, what I said? I don't know. Perhaps it does not matter.

The process started well. I sent Q'orianka out with a list and, when she returned, I lined up the lemons and eggs on the counter. I put out the vanilla biscuits and butter, ready for melting. I weighed the sugar. I had found a couple of tins of condensed milk in the pantry. Also an antediluvian potato. It was so old it had shrivelled almost to the size of a small nut, but it had put out roots – a mess of long, enormous, twisted roots. Firm roots, almost like bark. It was a nest – or a crown of thorns. It had put out these tendrils, I suppose, in search of water or nutrients. The endeavour had robbed the spud of all its vitality and shrunken it, reduced it to a wrinkled, perverse little nugget. But those roots! Glorious roots! It was a monstrous thing now, so majestic I was scared to touch it, so I closed the door on it. I left it there in the darkness. I repressed the potato.

Crush the biscuits. That's what the recipe said. Batter the biscuits with an implement. A rolling pin tends to be the preferred tool, but anything hard and relentless will do. Leave them in the packaging and beat them to a powder. No, not quite a powder. Beat them to a crumb. I melted the butter over the stove, made the biscuit base, pressing it down with a metal spoon so as not to burn my fingers, and put it in the refrigerator to cool. I separated the yolks from the whites successfully; when the eggs cracked, not even the slightest shard of shell got into the mixing bowl. I was on a roll – a domestic goddess, a fifties housewife, smiling as I baked. It was going so well. Swimmingly – isn't that what they say? *Swimmingly?*

It was all going swimmingly until my fingers turned to egg beaters. I looked down and there were five egg beaters – the old-fashioned ones with rotating handles – sprouting from the knuckles of my left hand. The right one was the same. At first I thought, Oh good. This will make preparing the meringue easier, and so much quicker. I could make two pies de limón! Or half a dozen and really show the primas what I'm made of!

Then I realised I didn't have any fingers left with which to turn the handles on the tiny egg beaters. I held my hands up before my face and contemplated the issue – wondered if I could manoeuvre them with my toes, the way armless artists paint with their feet. But no, that takes skill and practice, years of training. I didn't have that sort of time. I considered using my mouth, but it seemed risky allowing that many rotating blades so near to my face.

So I sat on the floor and waited, egg-beater fingers in front of my eyes, flashes of light glinting off the metal. Night came before my fingers turned to flesh again. I missed the party. But I finished making the pie de limón! Yes, I baked it and put it into the refrigerator. A woman should always have something baked in the house, ready to serve to unwanted guests. The Titis always used to say that. No – that's not right. Not unwanted guests. Unexpected. A woman should always bake something and have it ready, in case of *unexpected* guests. Except it isn't always the woman who bakes it. Usually it is her chica. The empleada does the baking and the woman – the hostess – does the serving.

I am rehearsing these little details in my mind while I work at night. All the time that I am painting and sanding and scrubbing and scraping, I am reviewing the social niceties, because of the baby shower, which will not be taking place at the hacienda as Mimi and Pulpo suggested. It will take place here, on my insistence: 'Come and see the house,' I said. 'It is looking better than ever.'

Mimi's voice fell silent on the end of the line and, after a pause, she said, 'But, querida, you know we have to sell the place eventually.'

I made myself very nervous after that conversation. I realised that I had to find a real buyer. Otherwise soon they would start all over again with the insistence that I leave the place and come and stay with one of them and let the house be razed. So I called an estate agent from one of the high-end agencies that sell properties around the world. She walked around the house with her notebook and pencil and I followed behind, chiming in, telling little stories, drawing attention to the features. She made scribbles in her book, raised her eyebrows at the ballroom's mural ceiling, flicked the lights on and off several times with her shellac nails, knocked on pipes and listened to their replies, and tested the sturdiness of the bookcases in the library.

The house, as a house, was unsellable. That was her verdict. She called it a *burden fettering prime real estate*. Land is expensive in Miraflores, she explained, but it is not, in global terms, desirable. No one with enough money to buy this land would want a house like this when they could raze it, build upwards, make a killing selling the apartments, and then buy a home abroad in Los Angeles, Miami, London. The future was up, she said, moving her index finger upwards as if pointing to the sky. The future was not in sprawling houses like this one. There was no market in casonas any more. Her advice – sell the land by the square metre and forget about the house.

That was when the tremors began, or rather contractions. I thought at first, when I woke, that it was the house juddering, trying to shake me out of it, but the convulsing was inside me as if I had swallowed the casona and the casona had, in turn, swallowed my foetus in an infinite concentric pattern – house swallowing human swallowing house until eternity. I told Rupert not to worry but he insisted on flying out and, when he was here, he made me see an obstetrician who said it was false labour, rehearsal contractions so that my body could prepare, but this did not explain how the house had got into me.

The doctor did an ultrasound and I was anxious that the screen, instead of showing spine and femurs and human organs, would reveal joists, girders, ceiling tiles. But when the sonographer showed us the baby from different angles, she said *Here are the kidneys. Here is the spine. Here, you can see the little heart pumping.* What I was seeing looked like a langoustine with a human head – an enormous, bulbous head inside of which there was another langoustine with a human head. But there wasn't. The sonographer informed me that what I was seeing there was the foetus's brain (not one langoustine-twin having eaten another langoustine-twin).

My mother-of-three cousin telephoned to ask how it went, and I told her all the appropriate lies: heard the heartbeat, cried with joy, loved her so much I wanted to eat her and so on. None of which were true. I didn't even hear a discernible heartbeat: just a series of marine sounds. The distant rush of the sea. The thumping whirr of a propeller going around. But when the sonographer said, *Isn't that beautiful? Your baby's heartbeat!* I said, *Oh yes. So beautiful.* Rupert was crying and the sonographer offered him a box of Kleenex, then offered them to me, so I took one and pretended to dab my eyes as Rupert blew his nose.

After the appointment, Rupert said my stress levels were too high. That I should stop pursuing the hotelier and take the original deal Tía Mimi had arranged with Edificios Pacífico. This was the right thing to do. *For the baby.*

I do wonder, in the daytimes when the sun is out and there is light, whether I should give it all up, for the little fish. I could come clean. I could confess it was all a lie. Let the bulldozers come, and go to confession. Say some prayers and pound my chest. *Por mi culpa, por mi culpa, por mi gran culpa.*

But I do not want to relinquish the lie, and how can I confess before a priest about a lie that is ongoing? Such an act of insincere repentance would be a mortal sin for sure. And if we die in the commission of a mortal sin we are doomed to damnation, so I must be very careful not to die.

You don't get a say over when you die.

Pues, you get some say.

Not in this house. There's a curse, ya tu sabes.

So I have made myself very nervous and my cravings have become very strong. The cravings began abruptly, soon after the little pink fish turned to jelly and, since then, they have got steadily worse. They come at night, mainly, and there is never anything in the house to sate them. That evening, after the estate agent came, I couldn't sleep because of the intense antojo to eat something burnt. It didn't occur to me straight away that this is what I wanted. I lay in bed rolling my tongue around and around my mouth, salivating, puzzling over what it was I wanted. Something bitter. Ashy. Very dry. The colour black was important. What food is black? I couldn't think. The image of tar sprung to mind, and it was appetising. But tar? Tar is not food! What was like tar but not tar? Treacle! My stomach contracted and I gagged.

She's retching.

What's wrong with her?

Pregnant.

Again?

'I can't sleep. I have cravings.'

Well, eat, pues!

'I don't know what I want.'

Drink?

The wailing lover extended a bottle of pisco to me from where he reclined on the ceiling.

Drink helps.
She can't drink! She's pregnant.

Something sweet?

I gagged again. 'Nothing sweet. Certainly nothing sweet.'

Then what?

'Something bitter.'

They tried to help, bringing me food from the pantry – olives, cacao with no sugar, peppercorns, coffee grounds. I nibbled at them with the edges of my teeth, dipped my finger into the coffee and tested the flavour with the tip of my tongue. Nothing was right. Nothing helped.

Who does she think she is?

The Don was irritated. He loomed over me, his stretched form curving in a perfect Gaussian peak up to the ceiling and then down to my bed, where his face almost touched mine.

What do you want, hija?
Let her be. It's not her fault.

She is spoiled.

I got up, switched on the lamp, rubbed my face. My fingers were just fingers. My feet, also, just feet. I walked to the kitchen and wandered around without ideas. A craving is not hunger. If I had been hungry, I could have eaten and been satisfied. A craving is not like this. A craving is a kind of madness. A sharp sort of discomfort – an obsession over an intangible substance. No, not over the substance itself but over the feeling we imagine we will get (imagine with a sort of reverse déjà vu, because we will know it when at last we have it) when we ingest that thing – that noumenal entity that cannot be fully grasped or articulated. But the entity itself is not what we desire. What we desire is the *reaction*, the way our body will ease itself smoothly out of the sharp nervousness that has overcome us in the maddening pursuit of trying to perceive exactly what it is that we want. We mould our senses around the amorphous yearning, try to draw on memory – on smells and flavours, on textures even – to figure out exactly what it is that we are missing. And then we find it. And we devour it. And we realise that the nirvana we were anticipating does not arrive. There is relief, yes, of a kind. But the sharp discomfort is not entirely removed – it just retreats. It backs away into a corner of the skull and skulks there, itching, itching, until the next moment we should become aware that we are missing something.

I don't know what I'm talking about. I say 'we' but I haven't the slightest clue what anyone feels other than me.

I found my temporary relief from the craving that night: burnt matches. I sat in the parlour and struck the little splints against the matchbox, one by one. Holding them upright, breathing in their smoke (aromatic, a little sweet), I watched them burn – watched how the cobalt flame consumed the shaft, how the orange tongues licked the night, and how the pale wood shrivelled and deformed. I let them burn almost down to my fingertips, then I blew them out and waited for them to cool. The charred stick that remained looked, with its shrunken, pockmarked head, like the Don and Doña's pinched, charcoal forms. In the palm of my hand I could imagine it was them that I held and not a wasted matchstick. Then I tossed them into my mouth and they disintegrated to ash on my tongue.

It isn't always burnt things I crave. Sometimes I want blood – the taste of redness. The first time, I thought it was meat that I wanted. It was a sweltering night and, between the strangling heat and the oppression of the little demon on my shoulder clamouring for something red, I couldn't sleep. In just my knickers, I went down to the kitchen and stood in the cool, stale light of the open refrigerator. I stared at the raw, plastic-wrapped steaks, considered frying them, imagined the heat emanating from the stove, and recoiled. I could eat them raw, I told myself. What harm could it do?

E. coli.

Faecal matter.

Parasites.

Instinctively, in my entrails, I knew it wasn't the meat itself that I wanted. It was the blood in the meat. In fact, I didn't want the meat at all. Just a cup of blood, in a wine glass, probably. It was the keen taste of metal I sought. A stiff, ferrous drink. Neat. Or perhaps with ice. No, no ice. Ice would dilute the ferocity.

Since there was no cup of blood in there, I shut the fridge door and stood in the darkness. Now I understood how it felt to be a vampire – jittery, unpredictable. The image appeared in my mind of me as a qarqacha, drinking blood straight from the slit throat of a llama. I batted it away.

I sloped around the ground floor, running my arm along the walls behind me to cool myself. Then something nicked me, scratched my forearm almost but not quite enough to split the skin. I went back to the spot and felt around in the gloom for my assailant. In a slant of moonlight I saw it – an iron nail, protruding, inexplicably, point first from the plaster. I scratched it out, scrabbling at the wall until it was loose enough to pull the nail free. It was dull but not rusted, flat-headed with a smooth, angular shank and a long, sharp point. I put it in my mouth.

I didn't eat it. It would have sliced my guts to ribbons. I just suck on it, occasionally, while I work, whenever I'm craving iron. I'm very careful – it tests my resolve – because I know I must not bite it or chew it, I must turn it over in my mouth slowly, lest I scratch my palate or chip a tooth. When I need to swallow, I have to rest it carefully under my tongue. It settles my nerves to have something so precise, so meticulous, to focus on.

Knives, too. I suck on these because the flavour of the nail is dirty while the taste of the knife is keener. *Don't lick your knife*, the elders used to say to me as a child. *You'll chop your tongue off, or slice it in half like a snake.* I remember this whenever I run my mouth around the knife as if it were an ice-cream cone.

My work is hard. Q'orianka and Uriel try to dissuade me from it, which is why I work at night. Alone. They say that they can do it in my place. Say that in my state – that is, I assume, pregnancy – I should not be exerting myself. They insist on it. The thing is, they do not do it right. The redecoration must match, exactly, how the house was before. That is the only way I will convince a buyer to take it on, to leave the house intact. If they only see it as it was in its glory days. I told this to Q'orianka and Uriel. They remember how it was, they say. They can work from old photographs. But I, only I, know exactly, because I see it how it was in the flesh. I wait for it to appear in its best form – for the exact epoch I desire to come around again on the carousel – and then I can get busy matching paint colours to the walls, to the shutters, to the architraves and skirting boards. I don't have long. I have to work quickly, frantically, because some nights the house is very restless and it moves rapidly from age to age, as if what I see is nothing more than a slide show being cycled through on a magic lantern by a disinterested child. Click, and the scene changes.

The speed of it all makes me edgy. The speed and the unpredictability. The lack of control, I suppose, is the issue. Whoever controls the magic lantern has no concern for my well-being. So the cravings worsen. As well as burnt matches, iron nails, I eat other things now. Chips of plaster that I scrape from the walls. The powder that emanates from the wood when I sand it. Little stones that birds drop as they fly overhead. Teaspoons of dirt from the garden. My stomach is a construction site. An army of tiny people could build themselves a house quite comfortably inside there. I am a mise en abyme.

TRECE

On the third day after Julia Álvarez Yupanqui fell, the XVII Congress of the Socialist International was in its second day of proceedings in the historic centre of Lima under the banner of 'Peace and Economic Solidarity'. The congress was inaugurated by a speech from Alan García, the president of the Republic, who condemned the communist extremists at the El Frontón penitentiary who had sought to topple the Peruvian state and humiliate the government in front of their international guests with their totalitarianism and prison riots; he condemned the international media that had spread sensationalist news about the state of the nation to dissuade the foreign delegates from attending as a means of frustrating the socialist cause. He stressed that, in response to the unrest, he had created 'a peace commission made up of men of good faith' who had gone to the prison 'to beg, to implore the prisoners to avoid bloodshed'. But attempts at peace had failed and, regrettably, there had been deaths.

But *this is not the brute strength of a dictatorship*, he said.

It is the moral strength of the people.

Authority and *law* and *nationalist*, he said.

And *popular authority born of suffrage*.

This is what was declared by the president of the Republic to socialists from around the world.

Meanwhile, the bodies of the dead prisoners (so many, more than two hundred, among them Óscar Ribeiro and Arturo Palacios

Pérez) were being or had already been occulted – kicked into vast ditches or doused with kerosene and incinerated – so that the international journalists who had accompanied the congress would not find evidence of the scale of the massacre.

No exploitation, no hate, no injustice, García said.

On this same day, the third day after the family maid fell from the second-floor window, Anaïs began, finally, to speak. Then the living Echeverrías celebrated. After all these years of worry that the child had problems (that she had been afflicted by the family curse and was going to die young or had been born with the taciturn temperament of an Anglo-Saxon), maybe she was going to be all right.

They did not know what it was that had made the child suddenly start speaking. All they knew was that they could breathe a collective sigh of relief because the child had, at last, spoken. And not just spoken once! She was a little parrot now, talking fluently. Yes, she had found her tongue, and it was tireless. The unblocking of the girl's speech had been like finding the end of a ball of yarn and now all the tightly furled thoughts compressed inside her mind were loosening and unravelling. She was hitting all the benchmarks that, according to the therapists and physicians, are to be expected of a four-year-old: definite and indefinite articles; the use of adjectives; simple sentences with subject, verb and object (direct and indirect); coordination and some subordination of clauses; the ability to use question words to elicit information; and – most important of all – the ability to sequence both in terms of space and time through appropriately used prepositions, *above, below, behind, meanwhile* and *then* being, they said, some very positive indicators that Anaïs was grasping how the world around her worked.

Some of the family wondered whether the girl's sudden loquaciousness was a miracle from Santa Julia. Such things were possible, were they not? Perhaps the intruders from Los Polvos were right. Perhaps a new saintess had been born right here on their doorstep. It would certainly make sense that Julia (*Santa* Julia now) would have left a parting gift for the child. She had been so fond of Anaïs, after all. It was possible. More than possible. It was almost as certain as the gospel.

It was not possible, said others, like Tío Raúl, who railed against the naivety, *¡caramba!*, the utter stupidity, of the Polvorinos who would rather put their faith in tales of fairies, in putative magic, than in hard work and science. These were the same people who went to curanderos and witch doctors instead of proper physicians. The same people who paid their diezmo to the Church, *¡caramba!*, when they could barely put food on the table. It was Medieval Thinking. And this was why the country was jodido, yes, utterly and spectacularly fucked. A porquería de país because the Peruvian is an imbécil who would rather let himself be duped time and time again than get up and do something about it.

Since the influx of worshippers had begun, none of the family, living or retired from living, dared leave the boundaries of the house. It was getting claustrophobic. Everyone was out of their minds with too much feeling – out of their minds with grief for Julia, of course, and with pity for her widow mother, but there was also anxiety, so much anxiety, that there might be Senderistas on the lawn, and what if they battered in the doors or exploded the naranjos? What if they murdered the cats and strung them from the lamp posts on the Avenida as they had done with those poor dogs? And imagine, *my God!*, if they battered in the doors and held them hostage in the house, killed them right here in their own home, slit their throats. It could happen. These are the kind of barbarities they committed, after all. And weren't the Echeverrías exactly the sort of people los rojos hated? Enemies of the people? Class war and all that. Tío Ignacio Segundo's horror stories about the Reds were putting everyone on edge. Tía Consuelo had barricaded herself into her room and was wailing incessantly for her healer, while Tío Raúl was in a state of apoplexy over Medieval Thinking (the nation's in general; Consuelo's in particular) and the two were triggering each other in a vicious feedback loop of mutual irritation and misery.

To make matters worse, with Julia gone, la Casa Echeverría was in disarray. The ants were already out of control, marching shamelessly across worktops and up walls, totally ignoring gravity, even parading across ceilings, utterly contra natura. The cats were starving, inconsolable. The Tías were sneezing, clearing their throats with guttural shouts, wrapping their necks in silk scarves because all the dust they were inhaling was going to give them tonsillitis or bronchitis or Dios sabe what other kinds of -itis. *Oh Julia, Julia, why did you leave us?*

For her part, Julia was glad to be free of the locura of the yellow house and its maddening restlessness. How many times had she jumped at the aggressive way the cupboard doors would fly open or slam shut by their own volition? Or how the electric lights came on and off without (living) human intervention? How infuriating to shut the door to a room having just cleaned it, polished it from ceiling to floor, every corner, every crevice, having swept the floor and varnished it, arranged all the chairs and ornaments just so, and then, when the latch had clicked shut behind her, to realise she had left behind her rag or mop and, upon reopening the door, to find the room dusty, draped with cobwebs, walls peeling and furniture dormant under sheets as if abandoned for years. How disconcerting she had found it in the beginning. The first time it happened, not long after she came to work at the casona, a vertiginous dizziness blossomed behind her eyes, the floor seemed to give way like a trapdoor and she had to grab the door frame to stop herself from falling. It was true, then, what people said: that the Echeverría house was cursed. Or perhaps not cursed, but certainly only precariously attached to the time and space in which it was built.

Julia had opened doors to all sorts of strange visions. She once opened the ballroom to find an entire opera being performed there and once entered the library only to be screamed at by a man with a French accent and ragged clothing who insisted that she had to leave. Sometimes she opened a room to find it had not been constructed yet: there was only sand and a vision of desert. One particularly disturbing morning when she had gone down to the Avenida to take out the garbage, she turned around to see that the entire house had disappeared. Not only the house, but the top of the hill, too, was gone. In their place was a pile of bodies, bloodied, dressed like pre-Hispanic soldiers, armed with spears and shields. Then, just as suddenly, the house, the hill, the gated garden all blinked back into existence and it was as if nothing else had ever occupied this space in the universe before.

Within a few months, Julia had become used to the unreliability and learned how to manage it. Should she open a door to a room different from the one she had just left, she need only close it again, wait a few moments, and the house would recalibrate. She assumed the metamorphoses of the rooms did not happen to anyone else – Don Julio and Doña Carolina had never complained of rooms uncleaned. Or, if the room transformations did happen to the Echeverrías, they never spoke about it and so Julia suspected that perhaps it was a shameful secret they hid, a taboo, and she ought to pretend she had not seen what she had seen.

Yes, there were many things in this awful house that Julia had pretended not to witness, like the inadequacies of Señorita Katarina, the mother of Ojitos Negros. When la Katarina threw pebbles at Julia's window at three in the morning, sneaking back after a night at the salsodromo, Julia would creep down the servants' stairs and let her into the kitchen through the service door, all the time lowering her eyes, making herself anosmic to the smell of pisco sweat, turning a blind eye to the leaves in the señorita's knotted hair, the salt crystals around her navel or the fact that her denim skirt had shifted around so that the zip was at the front. Julia pretended not to mind when Katarina threw an arm around her shoulders and slurred how great it was to be friends with the empleada, though they were never friends when the señorita's old school friends came over and they lay out on the patio at noon, painting their nails, smearing themselves with coconut oil, yelling for sandwiches and Coca-Colas with lemon and ice. Indeed, Julia feigned indifference when Katarina clicked her fingers at her as if trying to recall her name or referred to her in conversation as *comosellama-la-whatshername?* and then, as she and Uriel carried out the patio furniture, Julia kept a straight face while Katarina boasted about the English professor, Leonard Gest, who had proposed marriage to her and that soon he would take her to Europe and she would be done with this pigsty of a country forever.

But Julia knew, which the shimmering, long-legged school friends presumably did not, how this professor came and went, drifting in and out like a bad breeze. He would suddenly call de la nada, casual as anything, and ask in his too-smooth, whisky-on-ice accent if Señorita Katarina was at home. For a few weeks he would take her here and there in his chauffeur-driven car, give her little presents that glittered in Katarina's ears, on her wrists, around her neck, and she, in return, would sneak him into the casona at night (usually into one of the unused servants' bedrooms) and Julia would pretend she couldn't hear the bedsprings creaking or how, in the subsequent quiet, Katarina would ask him about the future and why he wouldn't come with her now to look at Anaïs sleeping. His daughter was so beautiful, a muñeca, and he would fall in love with her if he would just look at her. But the professor always had excuses. *In the morning*, he would say, promising to meet the child – but first he would go and buy a gift. How could he meet her without a gift? So he would leave at dawn and Julia, as she took out the garbage, would turn her back towards where the señorita and her professor stood on the corner of the Avenida, pecking at each other's necks like hungry birds.

All morning, the señorita would hold out hope, instructing Julia to put Anaïs in her prettiest dress, dropping hints to the girl that someone exciting was coming, that a gift was on its way, but then noon would arrive and the professor had not come. On those days of disappointment, Katarina would come to the kitchen with a bottle of pisco and an armful of limes and say, *Carmen, let's make sours*. That way, by the time the phone rang (as it inevitably would) she was too drunk to care about the message: *The professor called to send his apologies. He was at the airport, called back to England for urgent business.*

Those evenings at dinner, as they cleared the plates, both Julia and Carmen would have to pretend they could not hear the pontifications of the elders about Katarina's folly in continuing to be this Englishman's plaything when he clearly had no intention of marriage (and why would he marry her when he was getting her milk for free?). Look at Julia! Younger than you and already working! Making herself useful. Work dignifies the man, Katarina. *Well, I'm not a man.* You know what I mean. Julia is wise and you are foolish (Julia stacked the plates, kept her face still). *Julia has to work because she is poor.* Arrogant child, Katarina! You take all this for granted, but you don't know how quickly money can disappear. Death, sickness, war can take it all away in an instant. *You think I don't know that?* We give you all of this (hand waving in the air to indicate *all of this*) and we can take it away like *that* (click of the fingers). *Are you threatening me?*

Then the screaming would start, the plans to take Anaïs away to England, the counter-promises of disinheritance, while Carmen and Julia waited behind the doors. Julia wondered whether rich people really thought that their home help did not hear or if they simply did not care what others thought of them. Perhaps it was only the opinions of the poor that did not matter to them. Because, in the end, what difference did it make to the Echeverrías what Julia thought?

Julia wanted to tell the señorita to forget this Englishman, to listen to her family and study, but it was not her place to share such thoughts. She was paid to clean, not to dispense advice, but she thought, just the same, how wasteful it was, with a fortune at her disposal, that the señorita had not used it to pursue a career while Julia, at fifteen, had dropped out of school to work so that the younger Álvarezes could study. Sometimes Julia wondered, as she polished the curlicues of the chandelier and rubbed wax into the antique furniture, what if their births had been reversed? What if Julia had been raised in this house and Katarina out in Los Polvos? Was it necessity that had made Julia and the lack of it that had formed Señorita Katarina? Who would she, Julia, have turned out to be if she had been born Julia Echeverría instead?

Don't even wonder, was Carmen's sharp advice when Julia shared her musings one afternoon in the kitchen. *What profit is there in wondering? You were born to your family, and she was born to hers. That's all there is.* Julia did not share her what ifs and hypotheticals with Carmen after that.

There were other things, too, that Julia did not share, like the knowledge of where Anaïs was hiding when the doctors came calling. Like the loss of Carmen's right hand. And like the desecration of the books in the library, which she discovered for the first time when it was snowing. Yes, she had stepped into the library and snow was falling. At least, that was how it seemed. It was hard to see at first because the electricity was out – another transmission tower somewhere had been bombed – and the library snow was illuminated only by the wan light of the moon and Julia's candle. The flakes floated as if afraid to land. Julia held out her hand to catch one and she was surprised to find it was not cold. Nor did the flake melt in her palm. She wondered, for a moment, whether the house had accelerated her into the future. Hundreds, perhaps thousands, of years had passed. An ice age had fallen. Human civilisation with all its modern comforts (roofs that excluded the elements, electric lighting) had long been forgotten, and it was perfectly natural for snow to fall in Lima.

No, Julia, these things do not happen. She looked down at her open hands and, inside her palm, the snowflake was still intact, curling slightly at the corners. It had writing – black letters, typed – and the edges were serrated, as if they had been torn. The flakes floating down were fragments of paper, snippets rent from the texts to which they belonged, from journals and encyclopaedias, fashion plates, novels, volumes of poetry and historical tomes, and those scraps had been flung into the air and now carpeted the floor with debris.

That night she ran through the house, her shadow elongated and deformed by the candlelight, chasing her. Then she stood, pigeon-toed, at the door of the master bedroom. She had never knocked on this door before. The room was out of bounds except during breakfast, which was the allotted hour for its cleaning. She had not seen her employers in their nightclothes: they descended in the morning always fully dressed, hair coiffed, perfumed, wearing formal shoes (he in brogues; she in a low block heel). Now she would disturb them unawares and perhaps they would be angry. But this could not wait until morning.

Don Julio came straight down (in his pyjamas, white with blue stripes, and bare feet slipped into unlaced brogues) and with his torch he stood wide-eyed in the doorway of the library. For several minutes all he could do was walk around the mound of paper flakes, then he squatted, took up a handful, and let the pieces fall through his fingers like sand. *My grandfather bought these books*, he said. The grandfather clock in the corner of the library chimed midnight and the old man sat on the ground, leaning against one of the stacks.

It was hard for Julia, only sixteen, to know what to say to this man, her employer, who was old and rich. She had not seen him like this before. Now, as he sat on the floor, legs bent at the knee so his flannel pyjama trousers pulled up away from the ankle, she could see between trouser hem and black brogue a few centimetres of shin – pale, almost translucent (like baking paper, she thought) – and upon it, a network of prominent, vulnerable blue veins. She thought, but she wasn't sure, that he might be weeping. It was hard to see in the darkness.

Don Julio, are you all right?

Yes. Forgive me. It is no grave thing.

Can I bring you something?

No. No.

Would you like me to keep the fragments, Don Julio?

They are only material things.

But you are sad.

Ay, pues. Water gone by does not turn the mill.
What profit is weeping?

Shall I sweep?

In the morning, when there is light.

But they did not move from that place for some time.

Julia was thinking of her father and of the night he had left. It had been a night like this – a blackout across the city; rumours of a bombing somewhere; the men of Los Polvos, with torches, escorting the women home from the gates of the young town because the street lamps were dark and it was easy, without light, to lose your footing on the steep stairways that wove in and out of the houses under construction. Most of the dwelling houses of Los Polvos still lacked electricity, but there were now street lamps and the community hall had indoor lighting with switches and power sockets. Usually, Julia would take her younger siblings and cousins there to the homework club run by the Fepomup so that they could read and write with proper lighting, but tonight they were studying at home, illuminated by several candles. Her mother had not returned from work; her father was not due back until morning from his night shifts at the Inti-lectrica plant where he worked as a guardián. Like most nights, it would be Julia's task to put the younger ones to bed, to ensure they brushed their teeth and combed their hair, to pack their schoolbags and warm Merly's dinner of rice. But tonight Julia would burn the rice because her uncle Óscar would knock on the door and she would open it to find him standing with his hat in his hands. *When is your mother due home?* She will return soon. *Good; let's sit down.* Tío Óscar, what has happened? *I will tell you when your mother is home.*

Merly hit him when he told her. Hit him and hit him until her palms were red and sore, her body drenched in sweat and hair fallen in clumps out of her hairnet. Then she collapsed in a heap and moaned: *You and your death cult, Óscar. You killed him. You and your death cult have killed him.*

> *I told him not to work there, Merly.*
> *I warned him.*

You killed him, Óscar.

> *Hermana, I had no idea.*
> *If I had known…*

Get out of my house.

How similar that night had been to every other apagón that came before it; how similar to this night – another blackout, another bombing, another family, probably, had lost someone. A father? A mother? A salary lost. A child going out to work. The story repeated itself, family after family, endlessly into the past and endlessly into the future. How similar each story was to the next, but for Julia that night had been the worst, the night to end all nights it seemed at the time. But the morning had still come, the sun had risen, and plans had to be made, which is what had brought Julia here to the yellow house on the hill (the place where she would die, though she did not know it then) and to this papery old man crouching in the darkness crying over shredded books.

Julio Echeverría was not crying because of the books. He was crying because, with the chiming of midnight, he had realised that it was now his birthday and it occurred to him, as it did each year on this date, that he was another year older than his father would ever be. He wondered, as he did every year on this day, whether when he got to heaven (if that place existed or, if not, in whatever realm is the place they call the *Más Allá*, the *More-Over-There* or the *Further Beyond*) his father would greet him as a young man while he, the son, would be tired and withered.

Padre Alfonso preached that in heaven all were young, but Julio Echeverría was not sure why there was such desperation to be young in death. To die young was not a Romantic ideal to be venerated. He knew this too well – too painfully well. When Padre Alfonso promised reincarnation in heavenly, youthful bodies, the thought of regressing to an earlier self gave him vertigo: it would be a kind of brutal surgery, a violent slicing back, because the self was comprised of concentric rings, each larger holding the smaller in a close embrace. Like a tree with its layers cultivated painstakingly slowly, season after season, each ring being added almost imperceptibly but, in the end, evincing a lifetime of careful growth. That is how he imagined it: self, inside self, inside self. To hack away the outer layers would risk cutting the inner ones, too, because they were one organism, and even if the excision could be made cleanly, the younger layers would be left raw and exposed in a world that had changed since their day in the sun. So, yes, inside him were all the iterations of himself that had existed, the young ones as well as the older, but he had no desire to strip any of them away. They were all him – cumulatively.

Therefore, when Julio met his father again in the further beyond, he knew he would have to be his whole self, with all the rings that had held him together until The End, just as his father would be the exact age that he had been when he died, ring within ring within ring, and his Paloma would be the age she had been (twenty years, two months and thirteen days) when she departed. So, when he saw her again, she would be exactly as she had been, but he would have aged because this was the curse of so long outliving the ones you love and, even so, there was no glamour in the dying of the young.

The next morning, as Julia was sweeping up the paper mountain, some of the elder Echeverrías walked past, saw the carnage and became furious, demanding to know how the books had been damaged. When Julia said she did not know, that she had discovered them this way, the blame fell to the girl who was brought down from her room, stood in front of the mess and scolded. Did she not understand that these were expensive books? *Of course she does not understand. The child is clearly a zonza.* Listen, niña, these are old and valuable books that belonged to your great-grandfather. *She doesn't know what you're saying.* How can she be made to understand? *Punishment is the only way.* Then Katarina, to prove that she was not a silly mother but capable of discipline, spanked the child's bare bottom in front of everyone gathered there. After that, Julia knew better than to report the discovery of shredded fragments in the library.

The way they treated Ojitos Negros was the main thing Julia had pretended not to see and not to hear. Every time the child had been dragged by the armpits from among the broken doll parts in Doña Conseulo's closet to be plonked before a new white coat, Julia had pressed her lips together, gripped her hands more tightly around the handle of her broom, and pretended to scrutinise the spiders' webs on the cornices. Julia pretended not to see how the child curled up on that stool, crunched her legs into her chest, raised her arms to her face. She had to look away when adult fingers were used to prise open the jaw or tilt back the head, to hold open eyes and restrain limbs.

Later, Julia would take the girl to the kitchen, sit her on the worktop, wipe away the silent tears and feed her agua de azahar on a teaspoon. What else could she do? She knew that Don Julio and

Doña Carolina (the ones Ojitos Negros called Mamabue) were just as distressed by the demonisation of the child, but neither would interfere with the wishes of the child's mother, who had threatened countless times to remove the girl, to move away as far as England. Like Julia, Mamabue would arrive after the event and try to smooth away the trauma with soft words and teaspoons of treats – manjar blanco, mazamorra morada. Mama would place her warm palms on the little one's cheeks or, if the girl's hands were shaking, she would clasp them between her own and press them tightly. Then, kneeling before Anaïs, face to face, Mama would intone *tranquila* over and over, but elongating the i (*tranquiiiiila, tranquiiiiila*), her voice rising and falling in a calmative glissando until the child's breathing slowed and she became limp and sleepy. Then Abue would carry her upstairs to bed, where Mama would change her, handing to Julia the sodden day clothes and receiving from her the girl's cotton nightdress. Julia arranged the shutters, lit the pungent incense stick that would protect the child from mosquitoes, smoothed the pillow and turned down the sheets. Then, as Anaïs lay back, somewhere between dreams and waking, Mama stroked her forehead, while the music of Tía Consuelo's gramophone, small and distant, hung gently in the room and sang of jasmine and roses and riverbanks and high domes. Julia would render herself invisible as she made the final arrangements to the bedroom (night light plugged into the wall, stuffed animals arranged cosily on the chaise) and would shut the door soundlessly behind her as she slipped away.

Yes, in life, the Echeverrías had had her service. Now, in afterlife, it was the Polvorinos whom Santa Julia wished to serve. There were pressing concerns for her to address, like at the municipal office, where she rearranged paperwork so that Margarita Montealegre Belén's petitions were always at the top of the pile and the requests of the wealthier neighbourhoods (for the planting of more flowers or the repainting of sidewalks) were moved lower. In Los Polvos itself, she performed little miracles to alleviate the day-to-day struggle, heating water on the stove a little faster, multiplying grains of rice in a sack, mending a sewing machine here, a flat tyre there. Occasionally she heard snatches of sound carried on the breeze from the yellow house – the retching and squalling of dramatic aunts and hungry cats, the night-time laughter of a lonely old cook. But she had no intention of returning.

And yet, when she looked into the faces of her devoted, she was reminded again and again that persons – lives, histories – could not be so easily disentangled. In the scenes that emerged from behind the veil, from the unseen realm of kaylla pacha, she began to see that the futures of the Polvorinos depended on the fate of the yellow house on the hill. They were inextricably bound together, but in a way that she could not quite decipher. All she knew was that it had something to do with Ojitos Negros. Whenever that child was involved in the future there was a blurriness. The futures she saw, instead of having the brightness and definition to which she had become accustomed in her miraculous expanded vision, seemed to warp and bend when they approached Anaïs Echeverría. The closer they came to her, the more scrambled the visions. The sounds of those futures turned to static, fragmented, garbled voices in alien pitches; and where Santa Julia should have seen Anaïs herself, there was instead a black hole, swallowing all that approached.

So she went back inside the yellow house and looked into the face of Anaïs Echeverría. She had expected to see, as she had seen in the faces of the petitioners who queued in the garden to worship her, the faces of other Echeverrías. She expected to be able to witness, as a bystander, lives being lived by the girl's ancestors, all out of reach, beyond help, untouchable behind the pane of rippling glass.

Instead, looking into the child's face was like looking down a deep well at the bottom of which were scores of ancestors, crowded, pushing and jostling each other, peering up the well shaft and calling out to her for attention, for intervention and help. *Don't leave us down here! Excavate us!* Now and then one of them managed, inexplicably, to scramble some way up, splaying their legs and arms across the diameter of the shaft, scrabbling like a spider, up, up until they slipped, lost footing or strength, and tumbled down again with screams of frustration.

How was this child possible? How had she not yet exploded from the strain of so much internal ancestral commotion? Maybe the melodramatic aunts were right. Maybe an exorcism was needed.

Relief over the inexplicable or miraculous healing of Little Black Eyes did not last for long in the Echeverría house. One evening, as the family sat around the dining table eulogising Carmen's latest masterpiece (conchitas a la parmesana followed by parihuela), the child suddenly climbed onto the table and stretched her body out across it as if to sleep. No, she lay her body out as if she were a human sacrifice splayed on an altar, reaching out with her arms and legs, disturbing the plates, bowls and glassware so there was red wine staining the tablecloth like blood, while the shells of scallops and mussels went clattering about, scattered with the crab pincers and the whole langoustines that scuttled to find their way, along with chunks of cod flesh and livid squid legs, into the child's hair. Lying there awkwardly among the sea life and debris of broken crockery, she looked like something dredged from the deep. The adults had risen to their feet and looked down on her with bemusement that turned to horror when she sat up suddenly, stretched her arms out towards empty space and said, *Come, Julia, take me to bed. I am sleepy.*

My God! What is she saying?!

She's talking to Julia.

Dead Julia?

Of course, dead Julia. What other Julia?

She is possessed! ¡Dios mío, la niña! Demon-possessed!

Qué, possessed? There's no such thing.

Call a priest! Ay, a priest!

A priest, she says!

Call Padre Alfonso!
Maybe Julia is here…

Ha! So we have ghosts now?

Does she have fever?
Maybe her brain is swollen…
¡Ay, Dios!

OK, tranquilos, all of you. The girl is just tired.

It might be a psychosis. I know a guy…

Qué psychosis? What does that mean?

That she's loca is what it means.

I think that's unhelpful language, Mamá.

I'll call de las Casas. Everyone wait here.

A panic. A screeching of chair legs on parquet. Tíos clambering over each other to reach the phone and summon their physicians. Up the stairs, the languid child was carried by the arms and legs, mother weeping into her wrists, Mamabue ashen with grief, a dozen Titis in their wake sobbing, sobbing. Santa Julia walked alongside the funereal procession, seeing visions of countless futures being sucked towards the ailing child, the scenes distorted, stretching and then slipping away inside her – lost forever, she feared.

The doctors congregated in the hallway to disagree about what was wrong with the child. Some blamed hallucinations and early-onset psychosis, suggesting medication or talking therapies. Others said that this was a perfectly untroubling example of imaginary friends in infancy and the child should be left to grow out of them alone. Padre Alfonso and the nuns came too, and favoured spiritual interventions, or at least the acquiring of a father for the child. Tía Consuelo and Prima Almendra had other ideas and summoned their shaman, the one who could cure all ills with her knowledge of secret magic, whose name was Qhawa Pachari, and she arrived in the night with her medicine bag and amulets, her pendulum and her talent.

It is said that Qhawa Pachari was touched by lightning. That this was what gave her the sight of the healer. That she could conduct the shoqma con cuy before her breasts had budded and had predicted more deaths than years she had lived by the time her first period arrived. She could tell with almost infallible accuracy, simply by feeling with her fingertips the belly of the guinea pig, whether she was facing a case of hap'iqasqa or a simple headache, whether the patient had been blown by an ill wind from a passing ancestor or had merely eaten a bad piece of fruit. And when she sliced open the rodent and began to examine more closely its entrails, then she could forewarn patients of ailments that had not yet even begun to manifest, so early were they in their development, and in this way she had saved the lives of countless men, women and children, and prolonged the years of the elderly far beyond even their most optimistic expectations.

When Qhawa Pachari entered the child's room, she thought at first, on account of the smell and wide vacancy of the eyes, that the girl had already died. But no, she was not dead, though there was deadness in her. Towards the bed, the old healer shuffled, hands outstretched, arthritic fingers feeling the density of the diseased vapours around the bed. She opened the shutters, letting in the light from the street lamps so she could conduct a physical examination. She lifted the girl's nightdress and placed a palm on her chest. The little one was flushed with fever, doubled over, foetal and moaning with pain. The old woman could smell from the rancid sweetness in the room that there had been vomiting, but there was none of the spiciness of diarrhoea in the scent and, since her eyes were still glistening under their lids and her tongue was still wet, it was clear the girl had not lost so many juices as one would expect from an infection of cólera.

Even by sight, the old woman knew that there had been soul loss, certainly, for in all her days of healing, Qhawa Pachari had not come across any other person whose presence she felt as at once so flimsy and at the same time so heavily burdened. She suspected, already, some sort of hybrid complication, the comorbidities perhaps of one or – God forbid it – more of her spirits being removed through mancharisqa, another, perhaps, grabbed by the Earth, and, from the mournfulness in the child's eyes and the manner of writhing, perhaps even some sort of ancestor sickness inherited at birth – some vengeance enacted from way back. There was no doubt that this was a complex case and needed careful handling. But she should see first what the cuy indicated.

Under the watchful eyes of the two distressed aunts, Qhawa Pachari stripped the child naked and rubbed her all over with the body of a quivering guinea pig, massaging the child with the creature, gripping the rodent in her hooked claws, clamping its neck still between her index and middle fingers and pressing its mouth shut with her thumb lest it bite. As she worked, she could hear the call of a qarqacha. It seemed to be coming from inside the child herself. And she wondered what manner of evils had taken place in this family.

When she slit open the rodent in the child's chamber pot and, by the light of a candle, examined its viscera, it was all as bad as she had feared: mancharisqa, hap'iqasqa, machu wayra, uraña – the list went on and on. Rarely had she seen such disastrous entrails. She would have to be scrupulous in disposing of the carcass when her work was done, lest the child's ailments swing back and afflict the old woman herself – she was now far too old and tired to bear such an assortment of evils. Yes, she would bury the corpse remotely, far away from this house, far away from the city, distant even from the roads out of the city, for there was no knowing how resilient these maladies would be.

What can be done? the aunts wanted to know. *What can be done to save her?*

There are several things I can do, Qhawa Pachari replied. *But there is someone in this room capable of far more than me.* It was at Santa Julia that she was looking when she said this, though to Consuelo and Almendra it seemed that she was speaking to the air.

Ayawasca is a herb whose name means soga de muertos, or 'rope of the dead ones', because it connects the worlds of the living with the dimensions of the spirits. It is also known as Sampedro because when St Peter lost the keys to heaven the Lord told him to take ayawasca to help him remember. With ayawasca the curandera fortifies herself to see more clearly if she needs to battle a spiritual opponent, find the location of a recurring dream or receive revelation from the universe, and on this occasion Qhawa Pachari took it to release her sombra so that it could journey with Santa Julia into the uju pacha within the hill under the yellow house. The old woman believed that here was the most expedient place for Julia to begin her attempt to heal the child stricken with a soul sickness that would hold not only her in its grasp but would also block the Polvorinos from reaching their fate.

Above ground, Tía Consuelo and Prima Almendra were feeding the child teaspoons of soil from the garden where Julia had fallen, because so doing could help the patient reconnect with the earth that had stolen her soul. But Qhawa Pachari believed that this child's case was more serious, so it was necessary to cross over, or rather *to go under*, into the realm of below, within and before.

When they fell through the soil and dropped down inside the hill, at first there was no sound, just the skirmishing of strange bars of light in darkness. These bars of light gave out no illumination and made no impact on the darkness around them, which was profound and penetrating; rather they seemed (if it is possible) to swallow the light and leave the darkness only darker. The bars of light, Julia realised, were bones that belonged to skeletons in movement, dancing to the silence – no, there was now the tumult of percussion: beating of heel of hand on drum, fingers and wrists on wood, thumping of feet on earth, whittled stick on cowbell, palm on thigh, dried rice and beans in jars, clicking bone in socket. A pulsing rhythm, tripping. A visceral language, repetitive and hypnotic – it drew Julia as if dreaming, lifted her off her feet and swept her, blue pinafore billowing, on undulating crests of noise. The music put out tendrils, wrapped itself around her limbs, her waist, caressed her face, carried her horizontally deeper into the hill.

She saw around her the dancers – dozens, thronging the space with nimble, half-rotten bodies: a leg might have a thigh of flesh but a bare tibia; chest might be clothed in muscle and skin but the pelvis bare bone, or vice versa. There were faces half-fallen from mandibles and scalps swinging loose, attached only by a thread of skin. And yet theirs was a joy – an arm-looping, pelvis-twisting, foot-stamping joy Julia had not seen before and would not likely see again. They danced like ones untouched by gravity, with weightless feet that stroked the earth in flight but barely landed as if borne by strings, gambolling marionettes, limbs unbound, joints in complete rotation. Some of the dancers, it seemed, had surrendered to the effects of time, because there were dislocated bones scattered about, some turned into instruments (femur to flute, metacarpals lashed together into zampoñas).

As she floated closer, the darkness began to open like a flower and Julia saw that the dancers had an audience of animals: a tortoise with the head of a parrot, a condor with the head of a horse, an enormous Technicolor snake in the process of swallowing another, smaller, fluorescent snake which was swallowing another, on and on, until the smallest snake was the size of an ant and still Julia believed the pattern must go on forever.

A hovering sphere was being tossed among the dancers. From bony hand to bony hand, this white sphere flew. It glowed slightly so that Julia wondered whether it was a star or a moon, but it was etched with tremulous scarlet lines like rivulets, so not the moon – perhaps another planet, where the water ran red? Then the sphere turned, and Julia saw it was neither star nor moon nor planet but an eye. An enormous eye that was all too familiar. Yes, this was (horrible, too horrible!) Anaïs's eye with which the decomposing dancers were playing catch, tossing it from skeleton to skeleton, laughing all the time.

Julia wanted to reach out and retrieve the eye, but it could not be done, for, presiding over the carnival, was the wamani of the hill. By the standards of wamanis, he was not large, but he was certainly too powerful for Julia (even dead and resurrected), and it was clear that he would not react kindly to interference. Centuries of rancour sat on his craggy face. Clinging to his long black hair were hundreds of cadavers, their bare bones clattering with each movement of his great head. And up and down his arms, scurrying without rest, legion scorpions, cockroaches, and all manner of scuttling things.

You have come to take back the animu, he said, voice like an approaching earthquake.

Julia replied that this was true. There was a child suffering, dying perhaps – a child who had been born on this hill and who, therefore, was his ward.

That child is no ward of mine. He lifted his hand and indicated the bodies all around him, dancing, rotting. *These are my offspring, not the family that parades above ground – them I do not recognise.*

Señor Wamani, allichu! Julia begged, and she told him that there existed a whole people, generations upon generations, whose futures were contingent on the healing of this child, dependent on her soul being freed from this hill so that she could move on. *Surely, Señor Wamani, the Polvorinos are your children? Surely you acknowledge that they are your own?*

But the wamani was resolute. He would not release Anaïs's animu from his control and send it back to the land of the living.

FOURTEEN

I am a cow. It is a cliché, but there is no other way to describe what has happened to my body, so here we are. I suppose it is the baby, but the other mothers I see at the breathing classes I go to all look tiny-tiny and when they make us get our bellies out to measure their circumference with bits of coloured string the other women are all stony abs protruding in a sort of rectangular fashion whereas mine is an absolute globe and the nurses praise me and rub my belly as if I were an ekeko or some sort of deity of plenty, as if I might sprout a thousand breasts and grant wishes out of them in return for offerings of food.

I don't understand. Are the other women not giving birth to humans? Sometimes I imagine them dropping a litter of tiny things – walnuts mainly. Just dropping a litter of walnuts out of their vaginas and those walnuts go clacketing all around, joyful at the prospect of life, rejoicing in their tiny voices. Somehow, those walnuts are wearing shoes, though they have no feet. Nor do they have heads. Whereas I am giving birth to a child the size of an elephant, apparently. And when she learns to crawl I will have to ride on her back like some sort of exotic queen. How else will I keep up with her? It is important, I am told, to supervise infants at all times, especially when they start crawling or toddling, in case they fall down the stairs or, in the case of my gargantuan infant, off the edge of the continent.

I am monstrous. My child is monstrous. What is to be done? At my last obstetric appointment, the nurse gasped when she measured my belly. She said I would need further examinations, scans, blood tests, and if the child was too large, a vaginal birth would not be safe.

Rupert asked me to translate for him – he has returned to Lima now and is insisting on staying until the birth, nagging me every day about leaving the casona to stay with him at the aparthotel he has rented. 'What is she saying?' he asked me. But I mistranslated for him. I did not tell him about the potential complications of giving birth to an elephant. Otherwise he would worry more, nag me more, insist on taking me to weekly medical appointments which would mean needles in my arms and straps around my belly, hooking me up to machines that would bleat at me like manic computerised goats. So instead I told him everything was fine. That my enormous belly was a good sign. Healthy belly. Healthy baby.

In the taxi back to the house, Rupert was all nuzzling, telling me how beautiful I was, how beautiful Our Baby was. Yes, everything was beautiful-beautiful. He kept lifting my hair to kiss my neck and tell me how in awe he was of my body and the miracle of life and in the end I asked the taxista to pull over because I had to vomit. When he pulled over I jumped out and ran off into the Inka Market, where it was easy to scurry away among the stalls, bobbing between vendors and tourists. I could hear Rupert calling out for me, but it was easy to lose him, get to the back entrance, and hail another cab to take me home.

By the time Rupert got back to Mamabue's house, I was in a cool bath Q'orianka had run for me, because the heat was getting insupportable. Rupert burst in, demanding to know why I had run off. Because I needed space. Space! he said. Space! This is what he does when he is angry, taken aback or incredulous. He repeats the last word I say. I suppose he expects that I will then explain myself, so he cries, Space! Space! And then I might say, *Yes. Space. Because I was feeling overwhelmed by your excessive attentions.* And he would cry,

Excessive attentions! *That's right: I am uncomfortable with affection because I find myself grotesque and any evidence to the contrary will lead me to believe I have to revisit the self-image I have cultivated over more than two decades of life and, frankly, I don't have the energy.*

This sort of illuminating and productive interchange, however, never takes place. Instead he cries, Space! Space! and then I either mimic him in a scornful tone (which means he cannot in turn repeat my last words or we would simply be parroting each other – *Space? Space?* Space! Space! and so on – endlessly, forever, until the end of the world) or I roll my eyes and walk away. But on this day, I was in the bath, slippery and naked, acutely aware that my now ginormous breasts were bobbing around like buoys and that I had not had a wax since my arrival in Lima. The hairs of my pubis were waving in the scummy bathwater like anemone tentacles.

I told Rupert that whatever his problem was, it would have to wait until I was done, and he said, Oh did I want Space? And I said, *Yes.* And then he sat on the toilet and stared pointedly at me, and I pretended not to care, tipping my head back as if to relax further into the bath, but really he was making me feel like I was naked, more naked than I already was. As if everything about me were exaggerated. As if I were a woman from a Botero painting.

But I remained calm and said, *Rupert, please. This can wait until I'm out of the bath.* Wait. Wait, he said. He felt like he was always waiting for me. Waiting for me to call. Waiting for me to feel better. Tiptoeing around my moods. Well, he was tired of waiting. We had to talk.

All right, I said. *All right!* I surged out of the bath like a whale rising for air. Bathwater everywhere. Breasts and enormous pubic hair everywhere. *All right, let's talk now!* I looked around the room for a towel. No towel. Obviously I had forgotten to bring one. I stormed past Rupert, into the bedroom, water dripping everywhere, cascading onto the parquet.

(*¡Por Dios! The parquet!*

Quick! Fetch a mop!)

I rifled among the bedclothes for a robe, a kimono, something to wear. Rupert followed, ranting about something at my back. For God's sake where were all my clothes? There was nothing but bed sheets. All the time Rupert was going on about the house. More specifically, *This Nonsense With The House* – he emphasised each word, pausing in-between, as if I'd lost my sense. Wasn't it time I gave it up? This nonsense?

Nonsense? It was me repeating his words this time. He thought this house was nonsense? I was facing him now, leaning a little forward from the waist in the manner of clichéd anger, arms stretched out behind me (palms forward), face screwed into a Commedia dell'Arte mask (enormous nose, probably), pendulous hapiñuñu breasts pointing down. He thought *my* house was nonsense? (This isn't *your* house.) Whereas Casa Napier was what? A perfect paradigm of rationality?

It would sound better if you completed the alliteration.
A perfect paradigm of puh-rationality?

Pues, no, that's not a word.

You think I don't find your family crazy sometimes? What's my family got to do with anything? Don't bring my family into this. *You don't think your family is a bit kooky? A bit kooky-dooky?* (And I spun my index fingers in wheels by my ears to indicate lunacy.) Kooky-dooky? He repeated my words again, derisive.

The boy's right. That's not a word.

Fuck you, Rupert. Fuck *me?* Yes, I said it. And what's more, I told him, I wasn't leaving this house. I wasn't going back to his family or England. I was staying here. Right here. And I pointed at the ground below my feet.

I flung open the double doors of my bedroom and went out onto the balcony overlooking the Sevillian patio. He followed me out, seemed not to have heard what I had said. Are you serious? Fuck *me? Yes, Fuck you.*

Q'orianka was down on the patio, pulling weeds. She looked up, startled. What kind of creature was I now, in her eyes? Bearded legs apart in a pugnacious stance, hands gesticulating wildly, wet hair plastered to my face, tetas al aire like a wiry demon-hag. A wild pishtaco. Beware me: I will feast on your fat. Especially now that I am so enormous.

I was my mother, I realised. Tearing screaming through the house. Rampaging. Throwing things. Letting it all out in front of the empleadas. Shameless. People say that in parenthood you become your own parents. Even if they are dead, they rise behind you and gobble you up. And here I was, being my mother, unstable, shrieking, voice of a screaming cockerel, face of a snarling dog. I didn't even care any more that I was naked. Let him see. Let Rupert see what he had done to me with all his sex and his nuzzling. He had turned me into this: a zombie of my mother.

Rupert apologised to Q'orianka. She waved as if to say no importa, it's all right. *Don't apologise for me*, I screamed at him. What was his problem? He had started this whole thing. He was the one who wanted to talk right now. *So now we're talking. Like this* (I indicated my naked body with my hands). We're not talking: we're yelling. *Yelling/talking: potato/pope, what difference does it make?* What the hell are you saying? If he knew Spanish, that would have been a funny joke. But did he know Spanish? Did he? No. Had he taken the trouble to learn it? No.

I threw open the doors of the next bedroom, Tío Ignacio Segundo's childhood room. Weapons everywhere. Guns, rapiers, cannons. Some fantasy, some real – too many real. This was how family tragedies happened. A couple in a fight. A conveniently placed knife. A husband staggering along the balustrade with a blade in his gut. A long-drawn-out death accompanied by mournful string music, a coloratura soprano singing portamento. ¡Triste! ¡Triste!

A crime of passion. That is what I would have to say. *A crime of passion.* Q'orianka would have to testify: she had witnessed it. She would say that the señorita (*Señorita?* the attorney would ask. Yes, señorita, because she was unmarried. *Unmarried, but with child?* Yes. *Aaah.* Hums of disapproval. That explains it.) lost her temper. The Señorita was provoked. It would not look good for me: women losing their temper, hysterical, do not fare well.

I was rifling around in Tío Ignacio's wardrobe for clothing. I found a dress shirt and some wool slacks (mid-twentieth-century, rat-pack-gangster trousers, wide leg with the crease down the middle) that smelled of naphthalene. I pulled the clothes off their hangers as Rupert continued haranguing me. He was saying something about buying a house. Something about good schools and catchment areas. I jumped towards him and let out a gruff sound from the back of my throat, somewhere between a bark and a cough. It startled him. He stepped out of my way and I left the room, slamming the door behind me to block his exit.

By the time he got out, I was halfway down the stairs to the patio, pulling on the wool trousers as I went, kind of hopping, my feet slippery with bathwater on the marble stairs. Ani, be careful, he said. *Don't tell me to be careful. I'll be careful when I want to be careful. It's my body, Goddammit. If I want to break my neck, I'll break my pinche neck, and nobody can stop me.*

Está loca.

She's not loca: she's angry.

Pues, as they say: mad.

Mad as in angry and mad as in mad.

By the time we were both on the patio, I was dressed, but the slacks were too big for me. I had to hold them up with one hand. I looked like a clown. Plus, they were itchy: wool plus heat plus bathwater. But I didn't want to scratch myself in front of Rupert, so I was making tiny jerking movements inside the trouser legs, trying to relieve the itch by rubbing my skin against the fabric, which was a doomed plan from the start, because the scratchy wool only made the sensation worse. It became a prickling. Then a stinging. I was probably developing hives down there. Uglier and uglier by the second.

You want to raise a child in this environment? That is what he asked me, gesturing around at the scenery. A backdrop of decay. Yellowing weeds grew between the mosaic tiles, reaching up in lament. Along the back wall was a pile of junk: a pornographic ceramic huaco with a cracked erection; a metal jack-in-the-box, half peeking out from under the dented lid; a pile of yellowing newspapers. The fruits from the trees, unpicked, rotted on the ground where they fell in explosions of juices and colours and seeds. The columns, lined with cracks and pockmarked, drip-painted with pigeon shit, some crusted and grey, some glistening yellow-purple and slick, still, just percep- tibly, sliding gently southward. Irreparably weathered, the fountain, its twelve monsters toothless and aged, and the fine, grey dust of Lima powdered everything with its thin gossamer of transience.

A few hours later, I lay alone on a recliner on the patio, wrapped in a sheet, and it all looked the same – the weeds, the shit, the broken-dick huaco. But there were also birds: yellow canaries, colibrís, lime-coloured parakeets and enormous macaws diving into the terrace to feed on the rotting fruits. Occasionally they stopped, peered around and sang. This is what I wish I could have shown Rupert when he asked, You really want to raise a child in this environment? I wish I had said, *You don't understand how it feels when the pretty birds sing.*

Instead I said, *All I know is I don't want to raise a child with you*, and at that the very casona gasped. All the doors gaped in horror. Rupert dropped his arms. Not dropped. They didn't fall off his body onto the floor. They were not props. They were his own arms. He lowered them. And also his voice. Sotto voce, now. Dolente. *You didn't mean that*, he said.

¡Ti amo tanto, tanto!

Uriel appeared from somewhere, carrying an uprooted lemon tree that had dried out and died. Its roots were desiccated, its leaves anaemic and crisp. The fruit on its branches had withered into shrunken stones. It was an obvious metaphor, worthy of the stage. He crossed the patio, upstaged us for a moment, then exited to the front of the house.

Rupert said he thought I needed space. I resisted the urge to reply with sarcastic surprise. This was no time for irony. Did he want me to return his ring? He did not. Things were not over between us. This was a difficult time. We would overcome it. (From somewhere else in the house, a tenor sang an aria. Tremulous crescendos. Doleful piano. Expressive strings. ¡Ay, dolor!) He was returning to London and would wait to hear from me. He would wait until the end of the world (or some such mawkishness). Take care of her, Q'orianka! (Q'orianka had appeared from the wings, or rather from the kitchen. She nodded.) Kisses on either cheek. Goodbye! Goodbye! Farewell, my darling! Both my darlings (he said with a hand on my belly).

And then he left, to rapturous applause. *Bravo! Bravo! Bravissimo!* No applause for me, of course, who – as it turns out – was the villain after all. No roses flung in adoration from the balconies. No shower of petals raining down.

It takes practice, querida mía, to be the ingénue.
It is hard to be the ingénue when you are a cow. The quadruped is never the heroine. It can only get worse for me. I am too big now, and too misshapen for my own clothes. It did not even occur to me when I packed my suitcases with enough clothes for a year that I would soon not be able to fit into most of them, and possibly never again. My old body is gone. It is a kind of death.

One morning (I can't remember how long after Rupert left me), I woke and found myself on my back, four cloven hooves straight up in the air, an enormous bulbously veined udder stretching from navel to perineum, and I screamed. I tried to scream, I should say, but instead there emerged from my throat a bestial noise – a long, bovine vowel, emitted from the same place where vomit comes from, but as if the vomit were paused there, somewhere around the tonsils, and abandoned. It was a disgusting sound. The sound of an aborted attempt at a purge – of quasi-catharsis, the contaminants lifted but not quite extracted, blocking the oesophagus, the airways. And it just kept coming, that bestial, pharyngeal sound.

I repulsed myself and started to cry, tried to roll over but couldn't. I was immobile for a very long time, lying there, weeping with the shutters closed. The bovine form persisted: it persisted longer than any of the other forms – the lemur, the egg beaters.

Yes, this body of a cow, it lingered. I was certain this was the end of Anaïs, certain that in a few months, someone would wonder, *Whatever happened to that poor pregnant girl?* and would come looking, push open the crumbling doors of the casona and step out into the decrepit courtyard to find an anaemic Friesian heifer munching on the weeds, ruminating, driblets of part-digested gunk oozing from her jowls, her tired, filmy eyes expressionless, fixed on the sky and pats of stinking excrement exhaling their fumes. *Poor cow. How did you get here, cow?* They would gift me to a country family who live on a farm with five or maybe six children who would pat my rump and all day long I would stand in their field, chewing the cud, crying silently into the sod. Maybe they would summon a vet and say, *Look at our cow. Why does she cry?* Maybe the vet would prescribe an ointment for the eyes which they would rub into my caruncles, holding my muzzle tenderly. They would say, *Isn't she a sweet cow, our cow? Isn't she tame?* And I would resign myself to this life, forgetting day by day that I used to have thoughts that were, in their fashion, intellectually complex.

I lay there helpless, dolefully lowing until Q'orianka came running, wrapped her arms around me and rocked me gently. She led me to the bathroom and lowered me into shallow, tepid water. With a sponge, she cleaned the chunks from my hair and my chin. Then she dried me and dressed me and fed me broth with a spoon, and all I could do was spiritlessly let her tend to me. Like a child, or a doll, I was listless.

It was later, when I came back to myself, that I realised she had dressed me in maternity clothes – a large smock dress with a pussy bow at the neck. Attire for an overgrown baby. Gingerly, I got out of bed, all the time feeling like my body was a thread that might snap. I groped my way out of the room – not because it was dark, but because the house seemed to be tilting – and down the stairs, along the loggia, taking care to stay out of the sun, which was too glaring, too much of a threat. I reached the kitchen, where Q'orianka was de-leafing culantro. An enormous pile of it. The smell was spiralling and fluorescent. I fell into that neon spiral – descending, descending. When I reached the bottom of my fall, I found I was sitting on a chair, Q'orianka putting lime on my tongue. It worked. The acid brought me back.

She told me, when I asked her, that they were my mother's clothes, the ones that I was wearing. In her bedroom, folded in protective paper, my mother had kept all her maternity wear with the intention that I should use it one day. Sorry, what? Had I heard her right? Yes, I had. I felt hurt. Not as myself – it was a nice gesture, a sentimental act, that my mother had thought of me in this way. I felt hurt on my mother's behalf. I imagined her kneeling, her bare shins against the parquet, naked feet (inexplicably, because my mother always wore shoes, indoors and out) and her face soft, contemplating the shift dresses and capacious blouses as she folded them carefully, smoothing the creases, nestling them in tissue paper. She missed me. She was regretful over all the lost time. Her hair was greyer, her eyes duller. God, I miss her, deeply.

But this is not the mother that I had. This placid, remorseful woman on her knees, this woman who enacts nostalgic rituals in advance, who sows the seeds of future, dewy-eyed moments to share: this is not my mother. She is an invention. She is merely the idea of a mother I wish I had based on things I have witnessed – films I have seen, interviews I have read in which celebrated people reminisce about pleasant mothers with soft hands who smelled like roses, whose bedrooms were bathed in a peach gossamer haze. Compelling, intoxicating, but utterly fictive.

My mother was a woman of intensities, a junkie of only the most potent emotions: it could never be irritation, it had to be fury; never sadness, only abject despair. I do not believe she felt love. Or, at least, her love was not the tender, respectful kind, nor the kind that casts serene smiles across a comfortable distance. My mother was either completely on top of me or completely gone, smothering or disappeared. It was she who did the disappearing – not me. I was always here, waiting, terrified that she might not return, or that, if she returned, it would be for Leo and she would leave me behind. With me she played a painful kind of peekaboo. I would ascertain that she was there. Check again: she was there. And now? Still there. Then suddenly – absent. And absent and absent and absent. And, when I had mourned her, just about got used to my solitude, *haHA! Peekaboo. Mami loves you. Mami adores you. Mami wants you right here in her arms always-always, amor de mi vida, reina de mi corazón, chiquilina bella.* Hers was not the kind of love that releases others. It was an irate, unpredictable love: an ardour that might throttle you in your sleep just to breathe in your scent as you died, just to drink up your breath, your very essence. That is how it felt: as if she wanted to gobble me up.

And yet Q'orianka was not lying. I went up to my mother's room to check for myself. I stood at the door and pressed my palm against it as if my hand were an ear or a stethoscope. I wanted to feel the room before I entered, to check whether it was weeping or breathing, had caught fire or fallen into an abyss. My mother's room was off limits to me as a child, in case, I suppose, I went in to destroy things. She used to lock it with a key. I was, after all, the library vandal. I ruined things, was calamitous and delinquent. When I was sick in the night, I went to Mamabue's room or even to the maids' corridor, but never here. What was the point? When I had knocked on this door in the night, had there ever been an answer? I'm not sure my mother was even in there. Perhaps at night she turned into a bat or a dove and flew out of the window.

Now, though, the door was unlocked and the knob in the shape of a lion's face turned fluidly in my hand. My arm leapt away as if run through by electricity. Release! Release! But the act was done. The door was falling open, floating away from me. If I wanted to close it again, I would have to step into the room to be able to reach the handle. Who knew what might happen when I crossed the threshold? If I stepped forward, I might fall into a chasm, because I made a wrong decision. I might tumble back into that moment almost two years ago when Tía Mimi called me and I ignored the phone.

It was afternoon, early summer. I was in Rupert's apartment studying, or feigning study, finding excuses to let my attention flit. I was alone. Rupert was at work, I suppose, but it was early in the day, well before lunchtime. I knew as soon as the phone rang that something was not right. By this I do not mean to suggest some sort of clairvoyance. It was nothing like that. But it was rare to have phone calls at the apartment during working hours. Those who called us, called *him*. His parents, his sister. Friends with stupid names (Oggie. Minty. *Ya-it's-Taaaarquin*. That's how he always said it. Hello? *Ya-it's-Taaaarquin*.). The Napiers and the idiotically titled friends had Rupert's office number because they knew he worked late, so if someone was calling early and calling *here*, it was out of the ordinary. But perhaps I am embellishing the memory with an import I did not give it at the time. Perhaps I thought it no grave thing. Sometimes telemarketers called at that hour. Wrong numbers, also.

How I remember it, though, is that the instant the phone rang, I jumped and then sat immobile, staring at it, waiting for the shrill tocsin to end. The expanse of room between the telephone and where

I was sitting seemed to warp and curve. The very air swelled under its reverberations. I could never answer that call. Not in a thousand years could I cross that gulf and lift the receiver from its stand.

For millennia, it rang. Then all at once it stopped, Rupert's voice was announcing we were not home, and then Mimi was talking at me. *Hola Anaïs.* (Pause.) *Soy tu Tía Miriam.* (Miriam. We never call her that.) *Eh – call me when you can.* (Pause.) *As soon as you can.* (Long pause.) *I will try with Leandro.* (Tío Pulpo indistinct in the background.) *OK, mi amor. Chau.* (An almost imperceptible sigh.) *Gracias.* (Silence.) *Chau.*

That is when I actually knew. My quasi-premonition of ill news around the ringing may or may not be my invention. But Tía Mimi calling herself 'Miriam' and leaving a retentive voice message to call her – this made things clear.

For some hours, I pretended the call had not come. I faffed around in the flat. I got up, made tea, sat down, forgot it, tipped out the cold tea in the sink, wiped it down, then the counter, also the cupboard doors (inside and out). I went for a pee. Whilst I was there I thought, Let me sort the laundry. Took it down to the laundry room and put on a load to wash. I leaned against the cuboid of the washer, looking into the circle of glass as if it were a porthole on a ship. A ship on a sea where everything was swirling. Should I go back up to the apartment? Find the address book and Mimi's number? Dial it? Learn what it was she had called to say?

I could already imagine what it was. What else? It had to be about my mother. Was she sick? It had to be serious, hospital-serious, or she would have called me herself and left a recording as she usually did, a recording I would delete a few days later, after Rupert asked me if I'd heard the message and whether I was going to return the call. But now Mimi was calling. And instead of calling her, I watched the clothes lolloping in the washer drum. Then I went for a walk outside in the bland vicinity of Rupert's apartment block. Bought a coffee, because people buy coffee, then gave it to a homeless man because I do not drink coffee. I did hours' worth of pointless tasks to postpone the inevitable. Ran superficial errands. Picked up stamps, kitchen roll, an extra value pack of sponges. When I returned, Mimi had left further messages on the phone. *Niña, call me. It's important. I can't get hold of Leo.*

Leandro went to the funeral. He was in Bogotá doing something consultancy-related. He just hopped on a flight. That's how he put it. Hopped. They offered to hold off the burial for me. But no. I said I had exams. That was true – I did. But that was not the reason not to go. I believed it to be the reason at the time. Reflecting on all of it from this distance I understand that the reason I abstained was because I was afraid she would confront me. My Mami, that is. On some level I expected her to be here, ready to scold me: *Qué te crees, hija, ignoring me all this time like this? Don't you know I gave you light? Your own mother. Your only madre, who gave you light!*

Yes, I thought (I hoped, maybe? And wouldn't that be strange, after all this?) that she would be here in this house waiting, still, and that the waiting would be indefinite, stretching and stretching into I don't know what. But also I feared that she might not be here, the way that Mamabue had not been here after they died. All these other dead ones hang around here. They float about and drive me crazy with their noise. But the ones that I could really do with seeing, the ones I would give – my God! – just about anything to see again for even the tiniest fraction of time, why do they never come?

I had banked on an indeterminate number of years in which to design exactly what it was I needed to say to my mother. To articulate something not yet fully comprehended, something I still cannot express, to tell her that there was a deep void in me that she had put there. How much hurt she caused me. *I want you to know that once you did this thing and it affected me so much.* I did not know the substantive content of the conversation, but it would start with *There is something I want to say.* Which is still true now. There is something I want to say.

How much time do we think we have? It goes and goes. I really believed that rite of reconciliation would come. I trusted implicitly in some semi-distant but reachable moment when we would enact a reunion. Part of me, I think, still believes that it will come because it cannot be that she is dead, truly dead. And isn't this my main trouble? My limitless ability to defer. To put off what must be confronted. Mañana, mañana. There is always tomorrow. There is always another day, a better opportunity. Always a mañana, mañana. Until there isn't.

There have been no tomorrows with my mother for almost two years now. It is time to face facts. I was beginning to understand this as I stood in the doorway to her room, the print of the lion's face still in my palm. *Mami? Are you in there?* No, she was not in there. Some dead ones stay and some dead ones don't. There is no logic to it. But I – I was living and I departed. When I left Perú, I abandoned my mother and Leandro and Inki, the house and all the retired. Such things are unforgivable.

My mother's room was preserved. Her bed was made. In the corner, the areca was lush and tall. On the dresser, her cosmetics, perfumes, cachivaches were ordered carefully. They had been kept clean. There was no dust in this room. In the wardrobe, her clothes had been hung inside clear plastic garment protectors. These were acts of devotion. Someone had gone on loving her after her death. Who? Tío Pulpo? Mimi? One of her cousins or a friend? Q'orianka, perhaps?

I realised I knew so little about my mother's life. Not just the life she had lived since I left, aged almost eighteen, fleeing the aftermath of Abue's burial. I knew almost nothing about anything: where she went to school, what music she liked, where she met my father (on a mountain somewhere – that I know). I ran my fingers over her possessions – the silk scarf tied to the bedpost; the bottle of Jean

Naté; a box of Chiclets on the bedside table; the frames, so many frames, and, within them, pictures of Leandro and me as children, some pictures of her with us, her head thrown back laughing, eyes creased, arms around each other, hair tousled from play or beach wind. I don't remember these moments. Even when I inspect the photographs for clues, I don't remember. Were we happy, sometimes? I suppose we were.

What is more, it was true that my mother had kept all of her maternity clothes in a mahogany chest at the bottom of her bed. Just as Q'orianka had described, they were folded, preserved between sheets of tissue and guarded by naphthalene balls. How could this be the same woman who had once given away her grandmother's ermine coat because *We should keep nothing! Keep nothing! Give it away to those who need it most! We arrive with nothing and take nothing with us!*

We were on the Avenida Larco not long after the Tarata bombing when she said this. It might have been that very week, in fact, because that harsh reminder of the war that had descended from the highlands had placed my mother in the grip of Life. *We have to live*, she kept telling me. *In the face of everything – we have to live!* It was more than Blitz spirit. It was a mania. Her terror throbbed so palpably under her conviction. Mostly I remember her wide eyes as she said it. *We have to live. Look at everything. Don't dare to blink. In a second it can all be gone.*

She seemed intent on living her whole life, every last experience – but it had to be Today. This second. She swept me up in her whirlwind. One day, she hailed a taxi cab and made the man drive us out to the countryside. It must have cost a fortune. She had to see trees, she said, and breathe mountain air. She had to see hummingbirds and cantuta flowers, right now, before it was too late. She did not take me out to the wilderness. She took me to La Cantuta, the country club, where there were guards on the gates checking DNIs and car registrations. We got ice cream, though it was a cold day, and sat wrapped up in our coats by an outdoor chimenea.

I had forgotten this, but it is true. We had happy times, although always tinged with peril, always as if only *right now* existed, poised on a knife edge. A moment ago had fallen away, a second from now did not yet exist, and if we leaned too far this way or that, if we shifted our eyes even the tiniest bit towards the past or future, then our weight would follow and we would lose balance and tumble, tumble, tumble down. The happiness always had to be wrung out to the last drop because, any instant, it could be snatched. Paloma taught her that. That is what she used to say: *Paloma taught me that.*

On another of the days that week of the Tarata tragedy, Mami took me shopping. She bought me extravagant things – dresses, velvet gloves, a silk kimono for dressing, just like hers. *We can be twins, Nanita!* We had turrón de chocolate with two spoons (see how I am remembering things now!) and chantilly cream. We clinked glasses. She was laughing.

At the end of the afternoon, as we stepped out of the pastelería (hand in hand, perhaps?), we encountered a mother and daughter. The girl was about my age, selling coloured plastic whistles, dressed in trousers too short for her legs and a stained T-shirt, faded blue. Across the chest, Mickey and Minnie Mouse posed in front of the Magic Kingdom castle, a well-used and now discarded souvenir from some other family's holiday in Florida. I remember little about the mother, except that her hair was in a low ponytail and she wore a zip-up fleece. Navy? This was the woman to whom my mother gave Bisabuela Elena's ermine coat, which, just that morning, she had taken from Elena's wardrobe, declaring that beautiful things should not be stored away in a cupboard, rotting. They should be worn; they should be gozado – enjoyed, revelled in, relished down to their last vestige. No matter what Abue said, she was going to wear it. Punto final.

Now, out in the street, Mami dropped the coat off her back and flung it into the arms of a stranger. *Give it away! Give it all away!* In my mind's eye, she is a ballerina, en pointe, arms flourishing as the coat flies through the air, her face turned away in disgust at the superficiality of luxurious things. *That coat could feed a village. That coat could solve world hunger.* The woman stood with her arms out, rigid, holding the coat aloft, my mother exhorting her to put it on.

What was this woman going to do with such an item? She could hardly wear it. Sell it? But what establishment would let her trade an ermine coat? There would be questions, suspicions. Lima is like this. How had she got such a coat? Did she really expect one to believe she had just been *given* it? These sorts of enquiries would be made – if they even let her in the front door. It would be like the time my mother took the two little boys into Wong. She had spotted them hawking cleaning cloths in the car park and been overcome with sorrow. She had to buy them presents, toys from the first-floor children's department, whatever they wanted. The security guard stopped us at the door, said the boys could not come in. He did not say why, but it was probably because they were poor. With their ragged clothes and falling-apart rubber sandals they would make the patrons uncomfortable, make the shoppers feel they ought to buy them things – food, clothing. In a country where the poor are everywhere, they need to be kept at bay. That is, I suppose, the rationale. Otherwise what will happen? They will be everywhere, reminding us of their needs, their wants, of the fact that we have (inconceivable!) too much, more than necessary, and that we could, just imagine, share a little. So the walls go up: the wall between the regatta club and the fishermen's beach, the wall between Los Polvos and the casona. And security guards defend the entrances of shops, even supermarkets. Especially supermarkets. It happens everywhere, of course – not just Perú. It happens in London too. People get accustomed to their own particular brand of walls that keep out the poor.

Perhaps I should not say *poor*? Should I say, instead, *of humble means*? *Economically disadvantaged*? *Children with Emerging Economic Capacity*? But that is how it was. They were poor, these boys outside

Wong. And poor people did not go *into* Wong, which is what the security guard was really saying when he stopped us at the door.

Then my mother kicked up a fuss about ignorancia-sin-vergüenza and the manager let us do what we wanted, what *she* wanted. She bought the little boys cars. Nothing for me, though. I already had enough toys, she said. Now, looking back, I understand that she was right.

This day, the day with Elena's coat, Mami schooled me in giving to the poor. She took my wrists and made me hand my bags (filled with dresses, velvet gloves, lace ribbons for the hair) to the woman's daughter. My mother, with her own hands and a firm grip, guided my arms and held me by the elbows until I released my fingers from around the twine handles and dropped them into the other girl's grasp. As we walked away, Mami asked, her cheeks wet with the silent tears of a saint, *Don't you feel it, Nanita? The joy of giving away? We don't need it. We don't need any of it.*

A few weeks later, when the Tarata bombing was receding into history – but no, it was not receding into history for everyone. For some, for the ones who died (I cannot remember, now, the number), Tarata could not recede because it was the end of all things. The final chapter. The end stop. For their families, its legacy was (still is) the empty chair, the silenced voice, the absence so present it seems to beat, breathe and observe. There was a little girl only a couple of years older than me who lost her leg – for her Tarata was not receding. It was always present, embodied, even now, perhaps, if she lives.

But for us, the Echeverrías, as for so many other privileged families, Tarata was receding and normal life was reimposing itself. Around that time, there was a commotion in the house about a string of pearls. The empleada was questioned and she, in turn, pointed the finger at me but was nonetheless fired for the offence. In the end, it was remembered that the pearls had been kept in a pocket in the lining of the ermine coat and there was an epic battle as

Tío Ignacio lectured about the value of a dollar and Mami screamed about privilege and death and the End of the World, throwing her hands into dramatic shapes and slamming things until somebody, I don't know who, said that things would be different if Paloma were still here, and then there was a lot of crying.

For some reason, the string of pearls struck me as very sad. Whatever happened to that coat? Had the woman pawned it? Dumped it by the roadside? About the coat itself, I didn't much care, but the pearls inside the coat, forgotten, unwittingly parted with, now lost forever – they struck me as unspeakably tragic and I pined for them, as did the Doña, who took the whole saga inexplicably badly and roared around the house like a trueno, even as my mother maintained that the loss of the pearls was not important. In life there were other, more devastating losses. At the time, this sounded like a threat. On reflection, I think she was alluding to Paloma.

I found Tía Paloma at the bottom of my mother's baúl. Or rather I found belongings of hers, items I recognised from the photographs: bits of clothing, a crystal rosary, a pair of bowling shoes stored carefully inside a shoebox. There were also other things I did not recognise: a book of handwritten poems, a tiny gold bracelet, a miniature bottle of Cacharel's Anaïs Anaïs. My mother had squirrelled them all away.

Who was this Mami I was discovering? I did not know this woman who held on to things, who ruminated on the past with affection. Had this been her all along, and I had simply failed to see? Or had she changed?

That evening, I saw my mother everywhere, in all the shiny objects of the house – in the curved silver bosom of the sugar bowl, in the steel blades of the knives and the round heads of the ladles. I saw her in the gold frames around the Cusqueñan paintings of saints, in the faces of coins, in door handles and iron nails, the nibs of pens, the lids of copper cooking pots, and in all of the mirrors. Mostly, she was going about her business, gliding about the house doing little jobs, straightening a picture here, hammering a nail or whitewashing a wall there. Now and then she would look over at me and smile vaguely. She was pregnant in all of the reflections, draped in her hand-painted silk kimono, turquoise with pink and purple orchids, green leaves, petals falling gently to the ground.

Spectres of my mother began to proliferate. I started to hear an infant screaming from another corner of the house. I assumed it was just la bebe Vittoria and that it would soon fade, but the screaming only intensified. The baby I found, lying in an empty bassinet, swaddled in pinkish sheets, was my mother. How I knew she was my mother, I cannot say: I knew it in the way of dream-knowledge. It was self-evident, the premise on which all other dream-action can proceed. This distressed baby was, certainly, my mother, and I had to soothe her, burp her, rock her to sleep. She appeared, too, as a little girl, running laughing through the orange grove, pursued by my Abue (younger, taller, dressed in slacks and lace-up brogues). They ran past and did not see the couple copulating under the trees – my mother and father, naked in the moonlight. It was day when I saw them, but they were still in moonlight. And my mother had my body – my pre-bovine body. It disturbed me to know that our thighs, our calves, the smalls of our backs were all identical. Twins across the decades. I wondered whether this is how I look when I orgasm. Appalled by the notion, I turned away and fled back into the house.

I saw her once or twice with me in her arms, a baby that was crying without crying, mouth open without sound, face wet with tears and wrinkled in distress, taking great heaving breaths, lungs emitting a strange clicking like a beetle and nothing else. My mother, in her silk robe, marched about the house with me, rubbing my back, patting my little bottom, stroking my forehead with her thumb. Nothing worked. Nothing soothed me. Once, I think she may have looked at me, straight at me, as if to say *You see now? It was not so easy.*

Most often, she appeared with her sister, my Tía-that-never-was Paloma. With Paloma, my mother appeared at all the ages of youth: infant, child, adolescent – but never adult. Never grown. When they appeared together, Paloma was always half a decade older, but so patient with little Mami, never vexed to have her near. It was evident how they adored each other, always hand in hand, arm in arm, heads together, hair mingling, raven curls falling down their backs as one mass, dancing together in the ballroom, toasting their skin together, slick with oil, out on the patio. There was laughter between them, a golden, tinkling laughter, like the high notes of a piano.

There was also weeping, accompanied by visions of the house filled with flowers, lilies and dusky roses, an open casket in the ballroom surrounded by pale blooms. And my mother, everywhere, hiding and crying, holding on to her sister's things (bits of clothing, a crystal rosary) and crying. Unlike with the visions of the baby, I could not comfort her. This adolescent mother of mine, thin and lost, was out of reach to me. I realised again how little I knew her. But I wanted to know about her, I ought to know, so I telephoned Señor Sepúlveda, the lawyer, the one who had been pestering me about my mother's will, the one whose number I had kept folded up in my wallet for almost two years. I telephoned and told him he should come with the papers.

He seemed unsurprised, as if he had been expecting my call and knew the whole time that I would yield. He probably thought it was the money that had lured me, and that greed, in the end, had outranked pride. It insulted me, this presumption I assumed he had made about my purported avarice. I wanted to correct him, to explain that there were more spiritual motivations behind my change of heart. These were matters of the soul, not of the wallet. In fact, he could take the inheritance money and give it all away – I almost said this. Just transfer it all to an orphanage or a hospital or some other worthy cause: I don't need it, don't care about it at all.

Then I caught sight of my mother. She was standing at the other end of the hall, hands on her hips, one eyebrow raised, a little smirk, and I thought about the ermine coat, the pearls in the pocket, and I thought *de tal palo, tal astilla*, but I must have said it aloud because Señor Sepúlveda said, 'Excuse me?' down the phone.

He would come that evening. So soon? Yes, he had time, he said. He would prioritise me. Perhaps he thought I would change my mind and he would have to spend another two years chasing me, sending headed letters via international mail, leaving expensive voicemails on our answerphone. Perhaps he had never had such a difficult inheritor to deal with, never met someone so reluctant to accept what had been handed down to them. Perhaps he had—

'Hello? Hello? Señorita Echeverría?'

My mind had wandered off again, right there on the phone with him. I apologised, said I would be in, waiting for him that evening. And I was. I didn't run off, didn't escape to the beach shoeless or half-dressed. I waited patiently and impressed myself with my maturity. I was an adult now – a woman with child. I could liaise with lawyers.

Just as he said, he came after dinner, carrying a manila envelope of papers and a leather box file with a lock on it. I showed him into the library, where we sat facing each other on either side of a Victorian writing desk. Q'orianka brought him a café con leche and some galletitas on a silver tray. I had a manzanilla and stirred it sedately with my teaspoon. *See?* I said to myself. *See how calmly I stir my tea.*

He spoke to me in legalese, mostly about money. He explained that he was the executor of my mother's will and that she had stipulated for everything to be split evenly between Leandro and me, that her main asset was her share of the house, which gave my brother and me each an ownership over one sixth of the casona, the other owners being my Tío Pulpo, who owned one third, and the surviving partner of my Tío Ignacio Tercero, a man in Miami whom I had never met, who had probably never seen the house, but who also owned a third. There were also liquid assets – that is to say, cash. Leandro had collected his half of the sum already.

Wait, I said. Leandro had already collected his share of our mother's cash?

The lawyer said yes, this was correct.

When?

When he was in Lima for the funeral.

Leandro had, during the two or three days he was in Lima to bury our mother, pocketed his inheritance? I felt disgusted. Indignant. Is that why he had come? Not to bury her but to pick at her bank account like a vulture? Was everything about money? Or maybe his girlfriend had been behind it – Floozy or Tilda or whatever her name is – so they could afford their Canary Wharf apartment. Yes, that must be it. Honestly, what audacity. To go to the lawyer's office, dirt from your mother's grave still on the soles of your boots.

But who was I to judge? I had not even acknowledged my mother's death, let alone attended her funeral, and did not even know where her body was buried. Thankless daughter. Sanctimonious monster of a woman.

Sepúlveda was still talking. I had missed some things. It took me a while to catch up with the conversation. Chattels. Movable assets. Her possessions. She had said nothing about these, which, apparently, was a little unusual. Ordinarily his clients liked to leave objects of particular importance to specific relatives, but my mother had not done so, which meant it was left to my brother and me to split them between us. We would have to agree. If disagreements arose we could involve lawyers, but he advised it was best not to do so. Disputes cost money. Then he said some things about taxes. Some of the duties on inheritance and property sales were cheaper for Peruvian residents. And something about the number of days, percentages. I don't know.

I had become distracted by the leather box file, because in one corner there was a label, written in my mother's hand. It said *For*

Anaïs. It seemed to me an auspicious object, this box file that the lawyer pushed across the table in the flickering light of the library chandeliers, as if this was a pivotal moment in the narrative of my life. This was, surely must be, the introduction of an enchanted talisman that would break the curse over my life and heal me. I felt myself watching the scene from above. There ought to be ambient music, something suspenseful but tender: the soft rumble of timpani drums; rippling notes on the piano like the twinkling of lights on crystal; some gentle strings, a mournful flute, the pensive notes of a clarinet, perhaps some choral voices singing elongated, open-mouthed vowels in portentous voices.

But there is no symphony accompanying life. There was only the lawyer's voice. It was saying that my mother had left this box for me. He did not know what was in it. It was mine now. And here was the key. And then he left.

I looked at the box for a long time, sat in the library and just watched it, turned the key over in my hand, contemplated the lock, but did not join them together. It was dark outside. Utterly night. My head was swimming with tiredness, and around it circled the little pink fish – no longer little, no longer a jelly, but now the size of a shark with an enormous rapier for a nose.

No lo puede abrir.

She is afraid.

Pues, of course she is afraid.

Sitting opposite me, where Sepúlveda had been, was my mother, but not really. She was not there the way the retired from living were there. I had put her there with my mind. Out of memories, I visualised her. It was not something I had done before. It felt a little discourteous, to steal her form in this way and place her here when, in reality, she was somewhere far away, in heaven, perhaps, with

Paloma, or on a mountain somewhere in the Andes with my father, living a happier time. But the Mami here now was only a shadow, an image of herself, not the real thing. She watched me patiently. I asked her once, ought I to open the box? She smiled, raised a hand to her throat and touched her larynx. She could not speak.

No tiene voz, la madre.

Above me, the retired from living discussed my predicament. What if I opened the box and it was everything I had ever needed? Apologies and explanations, declarations of love unconditional and a mother's blessing to go on with my life and be happy. What would I do with such vindication? Simply lay it all to rest and go on as a well-adjusted human being? Such things were possible, but were happy endings desirable?

But she's a masochist, this one.
She could never be happy with a happy ending.
It would leave her empty.

Or what if inside there were instead castigations? Reams of letters confirming my mother's hatred of me. What would I do with those? Or, worse, what if it was empty? A box of indifference. A scorning from beyond the grave.

I shook the box: it was not empty. I heard the dull thud of papers inside – photographs? Letters? A treasure map? Yes, a chart that would lead me across the city, perhaps, gathering clues – little riddles that would send me on a quest across the country, delving into archives, discovering myself along the way. There would be a series of tasks, monsters to overcome, and at the end there would be an invitation – *Meet me under the queuña tree* – and she would be there, my mother, not dead after all! It had all been a ruse! A clever ploy to bring me back to her after all this time.

I was getting delirious. Tonight was not the night for the task. In the morning, with a clear head, I would open it. And, venga lo que venga, I would face the contents of what my mother had left for me. For better or for worse.

I placed a palm on the box, stroked its soft leather. Hasta mañana, Mami. In the morning we will discuss. Then I turned out the light, shut the door to the library, and went upstairs to sleep.

But I cannot sleep.

QUINCE

Pitaq chay warmicha?

                                 Amigu, which young woman?

This young woman here, walking.

                                Brothermine, I do not know.

    Maymantam payri?
    Where from is she?

           Payqa Limamantam, ñañay.

Let us watch, hermanukunay, chay warmicha from Lima come.

At the gates of Los Polvos, the only home she could remember, Julia began her journey. She stood for some time at those gates, looking out across the main street, Avenida Esperanza, which had once been just a dirt track through the sand but was now paved with tarmac, not laid by the municipality of Miraflores but by the Polvorinos themselves in an act of mink'a, a tradition of reciprocal labour and devotion brought with them from the highlands. Avenida Esperanza was still without a sidewalk, framed by two stretches of dust on either side, because sidewalks were not important yet. There were other priorities. Running water, sewage pipes, a medical post…

As Julia walked, she could see to her right, climbing up the north side of the Mound of Defeat, the houses of the earliest Polvorinos in various states of construction, including the homes of Anny-Lu Higa Ito and of los Álvarez, those who had been her family in life.

The houses were painted in hopeful colours – chirimoya green, cocona orange, the fierce pink of the pitaya. To her left, criss-crossed on the sandy flatland, was the rest of the young town, laid out in a grid system designed by the first Organising Council of Los Polvos, which had been keen to prove its critics wrong, to prove that their town would not be characterised by chaos, lack of foresight, lawlessness. For this reason they had prized their grid system with its lettered avenidas and its numbered calles, each block a precise location code – cuadra 1A, cuadra 2A, and so on. Many years later, they wished to give their roads new names, names with stories and emotional depth (names that they already used in the Polvorino vernacular – Álvarez Street, the Fishmonger's Block, Avenida Túpac Amaru), but the municipality blocked their applications for reasons that were never entirely clear, so the young town was still a soup of letters and digits.

Julia turned onto Calle 6 and, all the time heading north, she performed little miracles for her neighbours as she went. Passing the Escuela 5086 on cuadra 6C where Hilario García García was teaching English and her little cousin Miguel Ángel was crying quietly for his father, Julia blessed the colouring pencils so they could be sharpened and sharpened but never grow shorter. At the kiosco of La Bocona Flores, right as that busybody was about to speak plagues of the new people who had just arrived (a young family who had fled to Lima to escape the violence in Oreja de Perro, that region known as Dog's Ear), Julia gave the woman a vision that played on the surface of her cup of maté, of the torturous ditches of the Malebolge where the hypocrites walk heavily, painfully, weighed down by helmets of lead; where the falsifiers of words languish, deformed, in great heaving hospitals with much wailing; and where the sowers of discord and strife, those who open rifts between people with their machinations, are perpetually being torn apart, limb from limb, head from neck, bowels from torso, piece by piece by piece. Terrified by the scene of dismemberment and the promise of coming judgement for the looseness of her tongue, La Bocona Flores snapped shut her teeth and vowed never to gossip again.

Along the eastern edge of the market, Julia walked, and there she brushed past la cocinera Carmen, who was buying a side of beef for the Echeverrías' dinner. As she passed by, Julia gave Carmen's shoulder a squeeze and that small act of affection filled the old cook with the warm glow of friendship so that, for several days, she did not feel quite so alone in the kitchen of the yellow house on the hill.

On past the newest of the homes, where the refugees from the conflict raging in the highlands were living crammed into huts of rush matting, insomniac because of the nightmares that played and replayed in the dark. Their nightmares had been dreamed up two decades before by a professor from Huamanga who called for revolution and, as he told his followers, revolution would come only with blood. Yes, blood would be spilled on all sides, but fear not, he said. This blood would be glorious, rivers of it flowing to baptise the nation and stain red the flags that would herald a new dawn – the dawn promised by glorious Marxist–Leninist Mao-Zedong-Thought. This was his promise, his call to arms to those who called themselves comrades of the Shining Path. Only by cleansing the nation of imperialism through the baptism of blood and the purification of fire would a new age begin. From these comrades the people fled. But also from the soldiers who came in retaliation, mandated to annihilate the terror in the Andes, and who saw in the villagers – all the villagers, even the children – the faces of terrorists who must be wiped out. And so these soldiers set about saving the nation by raping and shooting and dynamiting and burning, because terrucos were nothing but dogs.

From all this the people had fled from the highlands and set up their shacks in Los Polvos. Among these ramshackle refuges Julia tarried longer, cleaning a nose here, picking lice from hair there, chasing away a rabid dog that threatened to attack, and finally fortifying the broth being cooked on a camping stove, adding to it vitamins and minerals and flavour that it could never have contained by natural means. But she knew that these were only temporary fixes – more was needed, something more sustaining.

Onwards again: she entered upon the cemetery – three white-washed walls standing parallel. Each wall, constructed of concrete, contained one hundred and forty-four recesses, long cuboid-shaped hollows into which a coffin could be slotted. Shelves of muertos, one of them Julio Álvarez. She pressed her palm against the stone slab that sealed his niche, serving as his tombstone. Unable to afford any kind of engraving, the family had simply written in black marker his name, birth date, date of departure. Julia rectified this now, wiping away the paint and instead etching the epitaph into the stone in letters of gold. She did the same on her own tombstone, which was a few paces to the right, and here she left a message for her family – *bienaventurados los que lloran, porque ellos recibirán consolación.*

A little further, at the northernmost tip of the town, where there were still patches of unclaimed desert, expanses of sand where garbage was heaped in piles (worn tyres, corrugated metal, plastic wrappers and polystyrene packaging, the rubber soles of old chancletas, tin cans, lengths of frayed rope, the detritus of Polvorino life, uncollected by the municipality despite Margarita Montealegre's repeated applications for refuse collection), she passed a group of boys kicking about an almost flattened football that, in the blink of an eye, Julia inflated; the boys thanked her by making the sign of the cross and blowing a kiss at the sky.

Having stepped through the outer fence of the shanty town, Julia headed east along Avenida Angamos and then took the Vía Expresa north towards the old town. The traffic raced around her, but she did not mind it. On all sides, she performed her miracles, topping up fuel, inflating a tyre, unsticking a sticky gearbox, all right there on the freeway at rush hour. She did not discriminate by class or race or severity of need: whether it was for a frantic miraflorina running late for school pickup or a street performer in desperate need of tips to feed his children, Santa Julia extended a hand. When Julia was near, the passing drivers felt inexplicably more generous – instead of turning away to fiddle with their car radios, they wound down their windows, handed over moneditas in exchange for little candies, trapitos de limpieza, flimsy plastic whistles that they would give to their children that evening after work and then regret immediately so that, once the little ones were asleep, they would have to creep in, swipe the whistle from the bedside table and throw it in the garbage.

On her way along the Vía Expresa, she passed a young Haruto Higa riding in the other direction on his bicycle, weaving in and out of the traffic with an enormous bundle of laundry on his back. Also the entire cast, crew and orchestra of *Lakmé*, headed towards la Casa Echeverría in a convoy of horse-drawn trams with cellos, bassoons, trombones and music stands sticking out of the windows and piled in heaps on top of the roof while, right behind them, a cavalcade of Spanish men wearing doublets and cuirasses and capacete helmets was riding into battle.

This was when Santa Julia understood that in Lima time is like a fog that permeates everything. Any moment, past or yet to come, can descend as a mist and mingle with the air of the present so that all is humid with the vapours of time. It clings to the hair, penetrates the bones, moistens the clothes of the citizens, leaving everything always a little damp. The limeños breathe it daily, creeping down from the mountains or rolling in from the sea – lost time. The city is steeped in it, moistened by it, dragged down into it and, simultaneously, borne forth upon its crest. Which is why, at the same moment Julia saw around her the streaking forms of speeding traffic, the tall brutalist blocks of late-twentieth-century towers, the solidity of concrete bridges and tarmacked highways, she saw too the barren dust plains of what had once been an almost uninhabitable desert. On those dust plains, she saw the lonely huacas of the Ychma people whose villages clustered in the valleys of Lurín and

Rímac and whose great city was at Pachacamac. Simultaneously, on those dust plains, she saw the gold-drenched armies of the Sapa Inka Pachacuti invading and defeating the Ychma and also, some years later, the meagre troops of Francisco Pizarro riding out to meet with the auca camayoc of Manco Inka.

So many armies, all battling on the same plain, bodies strewn across the dust and the Vía Expresa, bleeding into the ground, maces and swords slicing through flesh, spears and clubs smashing bus windows, catapults and arrows whistling through the air, through the bonnets of cars, through the skin of warriors from centuries ago. So much fury spent, so much blood spilled, and for what, Julia asked herself. For claim to the land? But the land belongs to itself, and though the wamani might choose to show favour to this tribe over that tribe, though they might bless and feed and bear fruit for those who settle on the Earth's skin, they can also choose to demolish and destroy. With the wayqo and the temblor, the drought and the flood, the land can punish those who live upon its back. Men forget this – forget entirely the agency of the Earth – and assume that they can lay claim to it by skirmishing on its surface. Men forget, but the Earth reminds them.

All this Julia thought as she watched those armies warring on the desert plain and as more were added to their number with the bombings and the shoot-outs, the explosion at Calle Tarata and its one hundred and eighty victims, the intimidations of mafiosos charging cupos on their turf. All these belligerents, warring for centuries, Julia saw as they intermingled, turning against each other in the confusion, Pizarro's men duelling with pandilleros, riot police attacking Ychmas, the auca camayoc battling Sendero, bodies colliding with bodies, torsos splashing together, falling to pieces, blood raining down in scarlet drops.

Some of these bodies will be taken outside the walls of the city, piled together in mass graves and covered with dirt. One of these mass graves will be found centuries later by archaeologists at Puruchuco; another, further south, will become known as the Mound of Defeat and, many centuries later, a young man escaping his father's control will build a house to rival all houses on this mound, and his wife will paint this house yellow like the flesh of the lúcuma. From this house a young woman will fall and die and rise again and this woman will have the power to give hope to the poor and the powerless. But for now, the bodies lie haphazardly on the desert plain below the Vía Expresa and Julia, realising there is nothing she can do for these men, moves on.

She exits the freeway and swerves past the Palacio de Justicia, where the souls demanding to be heard (souls like Óscar Ribeiro and Arturo Palacios Pérez) cling with desperate fingers to the walls, crawl up the columns with elongated digits, rattle at the window bars and crouch in the pediments. The building is infested with the clamorous dead and yet the living cannot see them, cannot hear them. On the steps of the palace, Julia stops to whisper a word of encouragement to a young lawyer, a trainee from the University of San Marcos who is thinking of giving up because the white men at the firm treat him like an upstart cholo, but Julia knows that he must not give up because, many years from now, he will represent victims of the butcher called Telmo Hurtado, among them Juana Jimenez Loayza, whose parents Hurtado killed and whose brother, Augusto, squats on the roof of the courthouse among the pigeons, waiting to be avenged. Into the ears of this dejected young trainee, Julia whispers encouragement and then slips away onto the Avenida Abancay, heading north.

On Abancay she passes an automobile accident – a Ford convertible coupé overturned on the road, mangled together with a milk cart, leaving one dead donkey, one dead woman, five dead men. Among them is Eugenio Echeverría who is also, simultaneously, in Chinatown, where Chifa Tan still stands on Calle Capón and where Chen Tan and his sons feed their lomo saltado to the hungry and also to the wealthy bohemians who have acquired a taste for the oriental (silk robes, Ming vases, hand-painted sideboards decorated with peonies, dragons, fan-tailed fish). Eugenio's Ford Model T waits out on Jirón Ucayali, chauffeur behind the wheel, while he sits indoors eating wantán and drinking pisco with Mariátegui and César Falcón and the violinist Luis Cáceres as well as a throng of visitors from Europe, among them the ballerina Norka Rouskaya, who tonight (on a whim of inspiration and mournfulness) will dance with duende to the *Marche Funèbre*, naked in the General Cemetery of Lima, an act that will see all those who watched thrown into jail by morning (for indecency and the desecration of the dead), but not Eugenio, whose father will pull some strings.

Julia moves on, heads west, passes the laundresses of Aurora Montealegre who still wash in the alleys, passes the palace of Torre Tagle, where Ignacio Echeverría is taking a siesta in a hammock. She does not stop. She moves on to the Plaza de Armas, where the cathedral is both standing and not yet standing, in various stages of construction, where Miércoles Agosto Segunda is wondering what she should name herself as the palm trees whisper advice, where the delegates of the seventeenth congress of the Socialist International are getting into their black sedans and driving away, satisfied with themselves that their work here is done, and where Francisco Pizarro is declaring this place the City of Kings. By his side is Inés Huaylas Yupanqui, his first wife, whose name before her baptism was Quispe Sisa, half-sister to the last Inka Atahualpa, whom Pizarro killed.

Still Julia presses on, lifting her skirt above the water as she crosses the Río Rímac, passing the guitarists playing in the Boulevard of the Barefoot, where the sculptures of the zodiac look down and bless her as she goes. Onwards still, clambering up the rocky face of the foothills outside the city, she curves her spine forward to gain her balance as the ground grows steeper. Up here, beyond San Juan de Lurigancho and the overpopulated young towns of the North and East Cones, the houses grow scarcer and the paved roads disappear without warning into dead ends of sand where buses are left abandoned, inexplicably, on the dunes. There are billboards on stilts, onto which the municipality pastes instructional health announcements – *No littering! Washing hands saves lives! Water is health!* But there is no running water up here and posters for Coca-Cola are plastered on the walls of most of the bodegas. Up here, Santa Julia tarries, blessing the bottles of soda that the babies drink because it is cheaper than cow's milk, much cheaper than formula. She injects those bottles with something of sustenance, a little calcium, a little iron. Where she passes women knitting, she blesses their alpaca wool and their fingers so that the women marvel at the infinite capacity of their yarn and of their stamina – neither runs out, not even once they have knitted jumpers and chullos for all of their grandchildren, their friends' grandchildren, the grandchildren of strangers…

Just before she reaches the end of the straggling village, an emaciated golden dog approaches with one ear hanging from its head by a scrap of skin. She takes pity and pours water from her palms into the dirt for it. It laps gratefully. She caresses its head, careful to avoid the precariously swinging flap of ear.

But Julia cannot stay here. She has to go on because while she delays, Ojitos Negros is living with only half a soul on account of the mancharisqa she has suffered. So Julia moves forward and upward, beyond where humans dare to dwell, out onto the puna, the flat, wild, open grasslands where the condemned ones float. Underneath her feet, compressed into pebbles, the lost ones cry out to her as she walks, their faces emerging from the stones with sharp teeth and woeful eyes. Here and there, among the clumps of grass, are human heads – the remains of the damned who have been dismembered by the frost of the snow-capped peaks as they carry out their penance of pushing boulders up mountains, and they have tumbled down here, bouncing and rolling to the puna where they wait for redemption, wailing for all time. By these, Julia is at once repulsed and moved to pity, but she cannot help them.

They must wait until the judgement day. Above her, circling menacingly, the falcons and vultures observe – a lone girl on the puna at twilight will not survive for long. Down there, there are pishtacos, handsome white men with kindly blue eyes and golden hair under their wide-brimmed hats. They are at once elegant and rugged: tall, skilful riders of muscular horses, dressed in jackets and boots and gloves, all of soft leather, and they speak with smooth words as they jump from their steed to greet a lady. They say to her *princess* and *bella querida* and pluck flowers from the ground to stick in her hair. Beware the pishtaco, for he eats human fat: in his boot he keeps knives to slice flesh from bone. From the branches of trees, he hangs human steaks to drip from them the lipids he then stores in his hip flask and drinks on his journeys across the plains. Men, too, he will eat, but he prefers women, in whose breasts and buttocks and thighs the fat is abundant and sweet. Where the pishtaco roams, the buzzards follow to pick at the bones he leaves behind.

On the horizon, Julia sees a group of white men on horses. The dust rises around them in clouds of grey. Can a saintess be murdered for fat, she wonders, but she need not be worried: these are not pishtacos, they are visions of the past. They are Pizarro and Echeverría, riding through the Tawantinsuyu almost five hundred years ago. As they ride, they help themselves freely to the food that grows in fields and orchards. They avail themselves, also, of the women. All along their trajectory, they swoop down upon women collecting firewood from the brush, women herding livestock in the fields, women sitting together in the shade of trees, weaving. It was these last women, often found in large groups, who became the invaders' favourite prey, because among these gatherings there would be women for all tastes (young and old, scrawny or plump, the kind that screamed and the kind that cried, the kind that fought back or the kind that went limp in the arms) and because, by descending upon these, there would be enough partners to go around them all.

Pizarro's men (pishtacos after all, but of a slightly different sort) wasted no time in developing a fail-safe method for their binges. By working together at the opportune moment, surrounding the women with their horses and brandishing their steel weapons, they could startle and scatter them, sending them running across the fields. Then it was easy enough to pick them off, one by one, grabbing them by the waist and carrying them into the bushes or behind a rock, paying no attention to their cries and, when they were done, leaving them crumpled in the dirt, showered with the dust kicked up by the hooves of their horses.

Now, on the puna, Julia is enveloped in that same dust and, unable to intervene, she grabs handfuls of stones and earth and lobs them at the riders. But they leave no impact, just sail right through and land with thuds and hissing around the semi-transparent bodies of the women left lying on the ground.

It is over. She must continue. Julia lifts herself, brushes the soil from her pinafore and continues her walk further into the mountains, past Accomarca, where the houses burn as Antonia Palacios Pérez hides in the trees, past the bridge of Challape where the railroad in the sky is being built as Taciturno Huaman tumbles tumbles tumbles down to the river below, and past Josefa Puyucahua, standing staring at the queuña tree where the limbs of her children creak on the boughs.

Throughout the night, Julia walked. She dared not stop and sleep because she remembered Carmen had told her that those who sleep unprotected on mountain trails are liable to be eaten by the anthropophagi – the hungry dead looking for warm bodies to consume so they can eat their way back to the land of the living. Julia was not sure whether now, as a resurrected saintess, she was still edible – was she dead or alive, both or something else? But why take the chance? Better to keep walking. Walking and walking until she had completed her quest.

Onwards, until the glittering of dawn at the horizon, its light painting the sand a rippling amber. But when Julia moves closer, she sees it is not the dawn at all: only the scintillating light cast by a litter plated with gold lifted by six strong men carrying the ñusta Chimpu Yupanqui back from Cajamarca where she was traded in ransom by her brother, the Sapa Inka Atahualpa, in return for his freedom from the Spaniards, those foreign men who bark like dogs. Now, and also four and a half centuries earlier, she is in the custody of her husband and his caravan of soldiers and explorers, holy men and slaves. She has promised to lead him to a place where the ground is fertile and the mountains so filled with treasure that one tap on the rock and the gold spills forth like a waterfall. In fact, she has no intention of leading him there. Instead she has a plan to take him on an endless, winding journey to nowhere. Over the mountains, through the forests, across the deserts, she will lead them, on and on and on. All the time, ahead of the caravan, she sends her chasquis, who know the Tawantinsuyu from north to south and east to west. They know the shortcuts and, with their nimble feet and immunity to soroche, they can outpace even the Spaniards' horses.

Through her chasquis, Chimpu warns the towns and villages up ahead: she alerts the women to stay indoors (for she has learned about the horseback ambushes conducted by her husband's men and, yes, by her husband too). She advises the priests to empty the temples, to stash their sacred objects, to hide or to bury, if possible, the huacas. And she instructs the men, in the most stringent and absolute terms, not to fight back against the requerimiento that will be read aloud to them by the fat one cloaked in black with the pair of wooden sticks in his hand. She warns that the fat one will yap at them with doglike sounds that they will not understand. He will bark and bark, on and on, and it will seem interminable. But they must not laugh or scowl or turn away, for though it might sound like the meaningless baying of the zorro, he speaks most earnestly about the beliefs of these aliens – the beliefs that underpin their very world. The fat cloak speaks on behalf of the most high and powerful priest of their temple, and on behalf of their king and their coya, and on behalf of their god, the creator of their janaj pacha and their urin pacha, which are both old and have seen five thousand harvests, and on behalf of a man called Stone who is also called Potato whose head is kept on a chair in a place called Roma but who also wants to place his chair here in the Tawantinsuyu, and for this reason the aliens have come, although she has not yet seen this chair. Although this might sound like nonsense, laughable even, they should not mock the fat man cloaked in black, for behind him will be men with long knives made from a foreign metal, and they will not hesitate to use these knives on the slightest provocation. She knows, she tells them, for she witnessed with her own eyes the barbarity with which they killed her brother, even after he paid them the agreed ransom in full with a great deal of silver and of gold. These dogmen do not understand negotiation or diplomacy. They have no concept of promise or agreement. They understand only violence and greed. They are savages.

Therefore, when the fat one cloaked in black is barking, they should stand still and silent and let him finish. He will teach them about their lords: the father one who was also creator, the airy one who was also a dove, and the one who was son and who had died on a tree. At this last in particular they must not scoff, for his name is sacred. She warns them that her brother scoffed at this son lord, laughed with contempt at the weakness of a god that could be killed by his own people. This was a weak god indeed! A quivering god! And to be killed on a tree, like a mere fornicator, like a whore caught in adultery hung from a tree at Anta Caca! For this mockery (and for gold) they had executed him.

In truth, the ñusta was not certain the insult to the son lord had been said by Atahualpa at all. She was not there, she did not hear it, and she knew that the mischievous and slippery Felipillo had served as translator and might have deliberately contorted the messages between the parties. But the foreigners claimed a grave insult had been paid to them at Cajamarca, and this was the story they had scratched onto the pale leaves on which they carried their memory; she could not refute it to their faces because that which was scratched was sacred to them.

Julia stopped in her tracks as the glittering caravan passed by. As these two women crossed each other, space-time curved upon itself so neatly that it almost tied itself into a bow, for Julia at this moment had not yet been born. How could she have been when the woman from whom she would descend was here, still a girl, unmarried, a virgin? And yet Julia (unborn) was indeed here, having lived and died, ascended into janaj pacha and returned to the world of the living. In this same instant, Chimpu Yupanqui, long since dead, buried in the ground, flesh melted from her bones, teeth aged and yellow, was alive, fresh, the vitality of youth blazing through her veins. They saw each other only briefly, their paths crossed, and then they carried on their way, Chimpu and her golden procession slipping over the crest of the next hill and taking with them the light so that the night became dark again and there was only the glow of the celestial river to guide Julia towards her destination.

Onwards she travelled, past Cusco, where Túpac Amaru, the last Sapa Inka, is paraded through the streets in shackles. There this last of the Inka line is walked by one of the Spaniards' holy men onto a scaffold draped in black as the crowds roar and weep. There Túpac holds up his hands and declares, Ccollanan Pachacamac ricuy auccacunac yahuarniy hichascancuta, *Excellent Pachacamac, see how enemies my noble blood have spilled!* and see how the blade falls and how his head thumps and rolls away from the body, over and over and over.

Onwards, too, past an empty plantation where there are shrieks and gunshots in the night, the clanking of chains, a maddening grinding of teeth and a tortured voice moaning and intermittently crying out ¡*Miércoles!* A figure drags itself around those fields in the dark. His skin, sallow and ashen, hangs from his bones – there is no meat on him. At the ends of his legs and the tips of his arms are only stumps, cut off before ankle and wrist, blunt and crusted: on these stumps-for-feet he teeters, wincing, hobbling like a newborn goat. He is hunchbacked, but backwards, his spine curving like a wonky spoon: it bends forward from the pelvis so that his ribcage thrusts out far beyond the knees, his shoulders are pinned back unnaturally far and, at last, his neck and head crane painfully, tilting his face towards the sky, forcing his jaw open in permanent horror. To fix his gaze on the unwary traveller that crosses his path, he has to roll his eyes so far down that they strain in their sockets, revealing the yellow-white of his eyeballs, veined with black.

¡Oye! he hisses, from a gaping mouth that does not move, with a voice rasping from deep in the gullet. *¡Óyeme, carajo!*

He wants food. He is always hungry, but he has not eaten in some considerable time.

Bring me bread and wine, at least. Meat is better: rare, the blood still in it.

It is a horror to watch him eat: his jaws snap without agility, clacking like the mouth of a ventriloquist's dummy, the teeth chattering in their sockets, the elongated tongue, inhumanly loose, lashing and circling maniacally, trying to catch the masticated victuals before they fall from the lipless corners. But worst of all, the stuff of nightmares, is the scream of abject torment, the shriek of a steam train from across the mountains, which he gives when he realises that his hunger is not sated because – though he eats the entire loaf, the whole cake, wolfs all the meat and knocks back all the wine – all of it, every last morsel, just mashes to pulp and, glistening with saliva, falls straight through him and lands in a festering pile on the earth.

I starve! I starve! It is always this way!

He shrieks at Julia as she passes tonight, but she has no food to offer. She leaves him behind her and he is swallowed by the darkness, screaming *Feed me, carajo!* and then *¡Miércoles! ¡Miércoles! ¡Miércoles!*

Siblingsmine, shall we help the girl?

    Arí, siblingkuna.

    Yanapasun. Let us help her.

        Let us warn the selvaruna she approaches.

In the jungle there are many dangers, as many (perhaps more than) in the mountains. Many times Julia heard the voices of her loved ones – her younger brothers and sisters calling out to her for help with homework, her mother saying *My darling Julita, you are home!* and her father laughing – but she knew not to follow those voices because it was the vengeful Chullachaki, protector of the forest, who leads explorers astray into the bowels of the jungle by mimicking their most beloved until, sanity uprooted by the noise and the chaos and the hauntings of the selva, the poor men turn savage and end their lives as primitive as beasts, smearing themselves with their own faeces and braying at the moon.

She walked along the river so she would not lose her way because those who become disoriented deep in the jungle find that they walk in circles and never emerge. Julia was careful not to walk too close to the water where the wolves of the river, giant otters, were watching with wary eyes and the pink dolphins were swimming, clicking at her and rotating flirtatiously on the surface of the current. A little way along she saw a pair of foreign men approaching from another direction and at first Julia was wary of them and had the instinct to hide; she was afraid, on account of the pinkness of their skin, that they might be bufeo-men, those who live in the rivers of the rainforest as beautiful pink dolphins. She had heard how, when the villages that sit near the water's edge have parties, when the musicians start to beat their drums, play their flutes and sing, the sounds reach the depths of the river and the bufeo-men come to the surface and sneakily, so sneakily, swim towards the celebrations. No one sees how the dolphin sends forth two catfish onto the shore and how they turn, down there among the rushes, into a pair of black brogues. Nor does anyone see the eel slither out of the water and become a belt, or the flatfish that turns to a panama hat. As the party continues, a gringo emerges clandestinely from the river; his clothes (ivory linen suit, white shirt) are miraculously dry. He slips on the shoes, the belt, the hat (worn jauntily, jovially, and never removed), and moves towards the celebrations. He is a handsome man, this gringo – angular jawline, vivid laughing eyes, strong sculpted legs from so much swimming. Why has he come? What business has he here with the villagers of the forest?

Of course, he has come to choose a woman, and he charms the young girls, dancing with them, making them laugh with his jokes. He has a winning manner. The villagers like him, trust him, share their alcohol with him. He, in turn, encourages the villagers to drink, to dance, enjoy the evening, let go of worldly cares, but all the time he is dissembling because before dawn, once the adults of the village are too drunk and merry to notice, he will lead a girl from the village out to the water's edge. There, he will discard his shoes, his belt and his hat, under which the girl will see, at last, the blowhole that sits like a pink cervix on the top of his head, the only part of the dolphin-man that cannot transform. By then it is too late. He is leading her into the river, and she cannot resist his powers. He leads her deeper and deeper: the water reaches her knees, her waist, rises up to her shoulders, her neck, until at last her face is submerged and she disappears beneath the surface.

When Julia saw these two gringos walking towards her along the banks of the river, her first instinct was to escape and hide. But these men were not dolphins. Their clothes were soiled and powdery from too much digging in the dust and one of them, the taller, removed his hat, stooped to retie a shoelace, and there was no pink cervix on the top of his head. They were not bufeo-men but explorers. Dr Leonard Gest had come from the other side of the ocean to play out his childhood fantasies of *Coral Island*, *The Lost World*, *Around the World in Eighty Days*, of Hernán Cortés and

Francisco Pizarro and being a conquistador, leaping from armchairs to slay resistant armies with his wooden sword, of crossing seas or traipsing through jungles to discover great treasures. A Hiram Bingham discovery, this was his dream, and now, alongside the burly but incompetent American, Chad Walker Stone, who had a similar dream and, more usefully, a fortune to squander, Leonard Gest believed he was close.

Gest and Stone had ignored the warnings of the locals that, unless they were capable of crossing over from the visible realm to the invisible, they would never find Paititi. The Peruvians told him that the lost city of gold was situated across a sea which could only be traversed on a horse that rides on the backs of two tigers, and when you reach the other shore, señores, there are two towns full of fierce inhabitants who, if they do not sense in you traces of the Inka, will turn you back and drive you out. Even if these denizens see in you the ancestry of the Inka, señores, you must still get past the two giant jaguars that guard the gates of the city and, what is more, amigos, once inside, if the Inkarrí does not want you there, He will throw you out Himself, because He cannot be found until it is His time to return.

Nonsense and distraction – this is how Gest had interpreted the stories of the locals. These were legends concocted to keep the outsider from finding the wealth and glory of the city of gold. So they kept digging and traipsing, hacking and foraging, and not without some modest success. They found trinkets here and there: ancient pottery, coins from the Virreinato, human bones and such. By publishing these minor findings, Gest was able to maintain some legitimacy among the learned circles back in his world, but all the time what he wanted was to find the lost city that would make Machu Picchu seem a mere hamlet in comparison, a city that would make him a legend.

Julia knows, as Gest and Stone pass by her and continue on their way, that this quest for Paititi will be fruitless. Gest will die dissatisfied and Stone will succumb to the venom of a bite from a spider in his sleeping bag, but Julia cannot help them and her own journey is almost at an end. She has reached the rupa, the selva alta, where the rainforest clings densely to the mountains and the air is hot and thick with humidity from the steam that rises from the canopy below. Here, the lungs grow weary and the skin seems to liquefy as if to run viscously off the body. Climbing the mountain, Julia feels her bones are gelatinous, no longer able to support her. In the trees, the fluorescent frogs croak mockery at her, the spiders hiss, mosquitoes drone endless discouragement (*you cannot make it, you will be lost here*), and the squirrel monkeys simply watch with wide black eyes, judgemental but not enough to intervene. This is their world. They do not care.

She pauses to rest (yes, saints grow weary too) and when she sits there is a peal of primal laughter from somewhere in the forest below – El Tunche, perhaps, or the ghost of an explorer led astray, finally driven mad by walking in endless circles.

Night begins to fall, and still Julia cannot go on. She must wait for intervention from outside herself. She, the answerer of prayers, must pray, and now she does. She prays to the Lord in heaven and to Mother Mary, to Viracocha and Pacha Mama, to the sun and the moon, San Martín and Santa Rosa and Sarita Colonia too. She calls upon the ápus of the mountains, whose names she does not know, and to her ancestors. Just when she has exhausted every prayer she can think of and utter darkness has descended, she hears a song.

It was a fervent and mournful song, melismatic and yearning, in a voice that echoed through the valleys, the melody reverberating from mountain to mountain. It was a song that he, as a child back in Mālaqa, had learned in secret from the muezzin and which now Hamet Alfarraz would proclaim to the mountains, to the rivers and jungles, before he performed the rakats he had learned in his youth from his mother. He believed he was alone. He did not know that when he crept away from the camp in the darkness, he was followed by a young girl with keen dark eyes who would sit a little distance away, hugging her legs, her lliclla stretched around her against the cold, watching.

He sang at dawn and at dusk and sometimes, when he could, also in-between, particularly when the sun was highest in the sky. For this reason, the ñusta believed that the man's song was for the sun, for the stars and the moon, and she assumed that he, like her own people, worshipped Inti and Killa, and this made her trust him.

Chimpu did not know that she owed her life to this singing man. When Chimpu and the other ñustas had been herded into that Cajamarca ransom room, Pizarro's men had been disappointed. So fervently had Atahualpa praised his sisters that he had led the Castilians to expect a superior beauty in them. But the sisters of the Inka were, in the invaders' eyes, nothing special. Beneath the adornments of finely woven cloth and gold jewellery, they were women like any others. There were some far more beautiful – priestesses in the temples all across the Tawantinsuyu – so why bother with these sisters with no particular charms? Why not execute them along with their brothers and send the whole native lineage into oblivion?

While the Spaniards had barked at one another, Chimpu Yupanqui had watched them with scorn. They were not the monstrous warriors she had expected. In fact, she thought them small and gaunt, far less impressive than the auca camayoc. They had the sallow complexions of the unembalmed dead and, with their small, pinched noses and their wide eyes, their heads reminded her of skulls onto which rodent hair had been pasted, for they seemed to wear the pelts of cuys on their chins, the tails of a couple of viscachas coiled ostentatiously below their nostrils. They had strange customs, these yapping boys, and Chimpu Yupanqui scorned them.

Meanwhile, Hamet Alfarraz, leaning against the wall in the

corner of the room, hand clenched around the hilt of his sword, helmet tilted low, had watched the ñusta and witnessed the disgust rise in her countenance, the expressiveness in her sharp black eyes, and felt he had seen, for the first time in his life, a kindred spirit. Here was a woman who felt as much condescension for Pizarro's men as he but whose life and fate were, as his, tied to their choices. Her life or death was in their hands.

So he stepped forward and whispered in his master's ear. It was true, the sisters were not the beauties that the captive king had promised, but consider this: these women were royals. Had he not, the son of a washerwoman, travelled across the seas to find his fortune? To begin again as a noble? And here he had stumbled upon a kingdom that could shower him with riches and place a princess at his feet! This was the very fate he had risked his life to find and here it was being laid before him! Surely he was not so blind as to throw away his destiny when it was being served to him on a platter?

In this way, Hamet Alfarraz convinced the man who called himself Hernando Echeverría y de Vargas to spare the lives of the ñustas. And Hernando Echeverría y de Vargas, in turn, convinced the others.

Ever since, Hamet Alfarraz had watched this ñusta and he had seen how she scorned Hernando. She had scorned him as he cast lots on the women and she had scorned him when he won her, had scorned him as he led her to the river and when he handed her over to the fat one cloaked in black with the pair of wooden sticks in his hand. As she was dunked, once, twice, three times, in the water, she scorned him. When they made the sign of the cross on her brow, she scorned him, and she scorned him every time thereafter that Echeverría called her by a foreign name, a Christian name that was not hers.

So now, Hamet had his suspicions. Meek. Subservient. The girl played the role of conquered wife too well, lowering her eyelashes when her husband spoke to her, avoiding his gaze, muttering *Sí,*

señor, Sí, señor in the little Castilian she had learned. Echeverría
was convinced by her act of servility, but Hamet saw the way her
nostrils flared at the sound of her husband's voice, how a small,
white tooth would nibble at her lower lip. This was not a nervous
nibbling – there was something ferocious in how it gnawed, insistent, sometimes drawing blood. Once, after a long day of traipsing
through thick greenery, Echeverría's men hacking through the vines
with their swords, they had found themselves at nightfall back at the
same tambo from which they had set out at dawn, and Hernando
scolded his wife's servants for the misadventure – flogged them a
little, too. Hamet's eyes had been on the ñusta, on her tooth, specifically, and how it champed, champed, champed at her lip. He had
watched until tooth pierced skin and a drop of blood formed at the
wound and then trickled in a red rivulet down her chin. She had
not wiped it away. When her husband finished his flogging, his shirt
spattered with crimson, he turned to his wife, wiped the blood from
her chin with his thumb, and kissed her violently. Hamet watched
and noted how the ñusta did not return the kiss, just stood there
rigid, not pushing her husband away, not submitting either, like a
woman of stone. This girl had found her methods of resistance,
Hamet believed, like a small but jagged pebble in a soldier's boot.

Yes, Hamet suspected that the ñusta was leading them in a merry
procession to nowhere and, as he observed her silent machinations,
he was confronted with a dilemma. It was the same dilemma he had
been turning over in his mind since his arrival in the New World.
With whom did his loyalties lie? The Empire of the Tawantinsuyu
had, to his mind, done nothing to call upon it such ignominy and
violence. In particular, the peasants they had encountered on
their journeys, those living in small towns and villages, working
the land – what had these people done to deserve to be handed
from one kingdom to another? And in the ñusta's situation he
saw the reflection of his own: she, like Hamet himself, was yoked
to Echeverría, her fate tethered to his, and yet she had found her

surreptitious rebellion – to lead him fruitlessly around and around until Allah only knew when. Whatever her plan, Hamet was amused by the audacity with which she humiliated her husband, and in his heart, he wanted her to win, despite the promise Echeverría had made him: in exchange for helping the Spaniard establish his place in the New World, Hamet would earn his freedom. So Hamet was two people: Echeverría's scribe and henchman on the one hand, and Chimpu Yupanqui's observer and devotee on the other.

Meanwhile, Chimpu also observed Hamet. She had discovered that this man knew how to interpret the stars for navigation; one night, when she sneaked out to watch him pay homage to the dying sun, she found him crouching over a large parchment, alternately looking up at the night sky, measuring distances with his fingers and making annotations on the page across which a meandering line had been scrawled. He was charting their course and he had noticed that their passage doubled back and crossed over itself many times, tracing and retracing the same terrain. One word from him and he could betray her to her husband, and yet, she realised, this man had chosen not to uncover her secret. He had, from the looks of his drawings, known for some time that she had been deliberately leading them astray. The ñusta asked herself why this man, khipumayuq to her husband, would protect her with his silence. What loyalty did he owe to her, strangers as they were to each other, above the man with whom he had travelled across oceans? It was suspicious. She ought, she told herself, to beware.

In this way, for three years, as Hernando Echeverría's troops wandered through the mountains and forests, sleeping under the stars, searching for the promised land of free-flowing gold, Hamet and Chimpu observed each other with wariness and admiration. Hernando, for his part, watched them both, for he had faith in neither. He suspected that the ñusta was mocking him, but he understood, too, that the compliance of the natives who parted before them like the Red Sea before Moses must be down to the influence of the Inka princess who travelled by his side. He did not dare to lay a hand on her, for there had been Indian uprisings already which had cost many Castilian lives, whereas his passage, though long and winding, had been thus far without battle. As pertained to the Morisco slave, Alfarraz was intelligent and capable and, what was more, knew the secret that Hernando's claims of nobility were fabrications; there were several men, upstarts among Hernando's troops, who might be tempted to mutiny if they discovered that the illustrious Hernando Echeverría y de Vargas was nothing more than a common interloper. No, he must keep them close, both the Morisco and the Indian. He must pretend to trust them while not trusting them at all, and he must treat them just well enough that they not be driven to open insurrection. His time would come – a time when he would be sufficiently powerful not to have to pander to inferiors. Until then, he would be wily, patiently bearing the indignity of his situation until the Lord in heaven should see fit to elevate him to his proper state.

It was five years after setting foot in the Americas that Hernando Echeverría sank his sword into the earth near Pisco and called it home. Chimpu Yupanqui had lost her energy to lead the endless march to nowhere: she was pregnant and unable to keep her insides from spewing out. Her mamacona said that the child inside her (spawn of the bearded dogman) was poisoning her and this was the reason for her inexorable fits of vomiting from sunrise to sunset. Chimpu did not have the strength to tell the mamacona that the child inside her was not the Spaniard's but rather the child of the man who sang to the stars.

The father is not who we thought it was.
Atatay!
This family is more knotted than a khipu.
Or woven like a tapestry.
So many busy fingers weaving, hermanukunay!

In the morning, after Hamet had prayed in secret, the caravan of travellers packed their things onto their horses and moved away, leaving Julia alone. Despite having rested through the night, she could not find the energy to pick herself up and carry on her journey; she worried that perhaps she would have to remain in this exact spot forever, the monotony of eternity broken only by the occasional passing spectre.

This did not happen. Julia's prayers had not gone unheard, for the mountains had watched her trajectory and conspired among themselves to help her on her way. All through the night, as Julia dozed in and out of dreams alongside the members of Hernando Echeverría's camp, the apus conferred, whispering from mighty ear to mighty ear. And they agreed to help the girl. Sachamama had heard Julia's cry for help, and she, mother of the jungle, rose now from her hiding place. Thick-limbed trees began to lift their dreadful feet out of the earth and, uprooted, slid this way, that way. Branches and trunks began to bend upon themselves, curving and undulating. Greenery was swelling, fragmenting, billowing somehow, leaves were stretching, exploding to five times their original size while the flowers were closing, tucking themselves away, receding into their buds. In the thick undergrowth, a dark green circle appeared, flickered, and opened to reveal an orange eye as large as a truck tyre with, at first, the thinnest blade of a pupil, which dilated, contracted, and dilated again.

It had all been an illusion – the trees, the fronds, the tangled vines were simply the markings on the scales of Sachamama who had lain there, hidden, watching, listening. It was on her very back that the campers had slept and into her ears Julia's prayers had sunk the night before. Now she stirred, roused herself to help the maid-saint complete her journey and carried Julia on her back all the way to the summit where the sky stretches infinitely, vast and clear and blue, in that place where, on all sides, verdant mountains yawn, ancient titans, megaliths of stone and loam, inside them colossal hearts of ore pulsing slow, each thump interrupted by centuries in which generations of brief lives are spent and then swept on before the next beat of the mountain's heart. Up there, time passes slowly. The apu lives on and on. Epochs are born and slain in the space of his breath. Eras elapse between the heaves of his mighty lungs, each one a puff of air, a speck, an insignificance. But the apus endure and endure.

She is getting sispapuni.

Arí, very near now.

We are almost there.

Up here, there was a clearing. Trees had been felled to make way for excavations under the management of the selfsame Professor Leonard Gest who had discovered strange patterns of stone, unnatural patterns that suggested there was an edifice buried beneath the loam. Upon digging deeper, it became clear that there was a tambo, a lodge or inn of some sort, and he became excited that it might be Paititi. But this tambo, sunk so deep into the earth, tangled up with the centuries-old tree roots, thick as boas, had to be extremely ancient – far more ancient than the legendary lost golden city of the Inkas.

Here, on the archaeological site managed by Professor Gest, Sachamama deposited Julia and slithered away. This was the place Julia had set out to reach and it was also the moment she had hoped to find because, down on the ground, rolling and writhing in the soil, are two bodies – one male, one female. The blanket the couple laid down has scrunched up and been pushed away by their restless limbs and now they are coated in silt and clay, bodies painted with stripes of reddish brown, flecks of dust, tiny stones pressed into their thighs and backs, leaves and dirt in their hair. All around, the sounds of the forest continue – chirping and croaking, the incessant hum of mosquitoes and cicadas, and the chainsaws of illegal logging. There are the graa-graa calls of macaws and the dinosauric growls of the toucan, the snarling of jaguars lying in wait, quien

quien birds that laugh with a jajaja and click their tongues like jesting men while monkeys screech, endlessly amused, appalled, incensed by one another. In the distance, a rain shower rumbles with thunder. Close by, there is the munching of insectan pincers on leaf, the grunt of a beetle as it heaves itself onto a fallen log.

And then, above it all, there is a voice.

Suyarqayki, it says, and the voice stirs the magma.

He has been waiting.

He knew she would come.

'How did you know?' Julia asks, and he replies,

The apus have guarded your journey, Julicha. Whispers from ear to ear came to me. The grains of Lima, ari, the dust under your feet, guarded your steps. And the dust told the sand and the sand told the pebbles. The pebbles told the stones told the hillocks told the hills until the tayta mountains conversed from peak to peak about you. But it started with the dust. Uchuypuni uchuypuni – even the smallest particles can be great.

'Imam sutiyki, taytay?' Julia asks. 'Father, what is your name?'

Yes, what was his name, this being whose knees were mountain summits and whose shoulders shadowed the clouds? Who was this king in whose palms rivers of lava flowed and around whose neck a chain of gold shone like suns?

Ayar Cachi kani.

Yes, this was Ayar Cachi, released from his mountain prison by the excavations of a foreign man scrabbling in the dust who even now was conceiving (and had already conceived and would conceive again many times to come) a child who already had been (and would again be) born with wide black eyes and a gift for seeing into kaylla pacha. She was the child whom Julia had come all this way to assist, the child whose spirit was trapped inside the hill under the yellow house, imprisoned there by a minor but disgruntled wamani with a grudge against the Echeverrías and all people like them.

*

On the shoulders of Ayar Cachi, Julia returned to Lima, but by the time they arrived at the yellow house on the hill, much time had passed in the realm of the living. Mamabue had died and Anaïs had long since left, gone to a place far across the sea, to the land of her father, a place beyond their reach.

Then Ayar Cachi was furious and he railed at the wamani, scattering the skeletal dancers with a swipe of his arm and tearing great chunks from the walls of the hill. But the wamani would not yield: this was *his* mountain (*Mountain? This is barely even a hill!*) and this girl was *his* ward, for she had been born on *his* land. Ayar Cachi replied with a roar that made the shutters of the yellow house tremble and opened a crack in the Avenida del Guanero large enough for bicycle tyres to become wedged in the cleft.

And so, compelled by the authority of Ayar Cachi, the wamani was forced for the first time in centuries to step out from the hill under the yellow house, stretch his muscles (cramped from crouching for so many years inside the Mound of Defeat) and set out across the ocean in search of the child whose soul he had stolen.

Will he return the animu to the girl, hermanukunay?

He will, but not as he was instructed.

Atatay! What will Ayar Cachi do?

Takanakunqaku.

They will battle?

They will. And their confrontation will overturn the earth.

So a pachacuti comes…

SIXTEEN

The metronome tick-ticks by my head. I set it going. I needed an anchor to this world because I felt myself slipping again. My mind was going away, lifting above my body to the brightly lit place of watery voices. The barren place, I call it, full of people. I feel their presence. Voices. Echoic. I cannot see them because my eyes stay below, seeing what is down here but my mind lifts to another plane and yields to the slowness and numbness of apathy.

But no: focus on the metronome, on its reassuring clicks, reliable, constant. Each one is like a prod back into reality, a clack of knuckles on my skull saying, *Don't slip away. Don't go towards the light. Stay here. Plic. Plic.*

It could click into eternity, this metronome. I could stay here and let it run ad infinitum through night and day and another night, so on and so on, until the oceans evaporate, the sky turns amber and the house is eroded to dust, granule by granule, and still I would be here, lying with my cheek against the cool floor, and the metronome going tick tick tick.

The body breathes. Now and then the eyes blink. But I have receded – shrunk back, peeled away from my skin and bones, extracted myself from the hollow tubes of fingers, arms, legs, and left the body as a brittle shell. I am sunk into a deeper sphere, and all external stimuli are foghorns heard from a great distance, moving pictures watched through a succession of panes of glass,

323

distorting, refracting. In here, there is light and thrumming stillness and I could stay here until the end of all endings.

Then the metronome clacks again and I am back. This is precarious. A plank in me is broken. A string was twanged too hard and snapped. Something is lost – I cannot get it back. My brain feels off somehow, curdled. Everything is tilted and my head wants to go with it. Lopsided, slanting. If I let my neck go, my mind will slide right off and splat onto the floor.

The intervals are too long. The blanks between each click are stretching too indefinitely and the intervening air has swollen. I am abandoned, utterly desolate. The tick will never come. The gadget has duped me – it wanted me to fall. My sanity scrambles for purchase but everything is slippery and I am going away to where indifference soothes me.

Come away, says the Tiffany lamp.

You cannot talk.

Everything talks when it has things to say.

And the ceramic doe watches me benevolently, intoning condescension to the alabaster owl.

> *It has happened.*
> *She has finally lost her mind.*

>> *Ay, pobre, pobre.*
> *It was the box.*
>> *The box?*
> *The box of papers.*

>> *The ones that Gustave tore.*

She came downstairs in her
mother's nightgown and found the box was
open, empty, shreds of paper strewn about the floor.
What is to be done about such things, I ask you? She got to her knees (a
scene full of pathos), sweeping up the fragments with trembling fingers,
crying streams, trying to piece them together to decipher the message from
her dead mother. ¡Ay! Can you imagine? Lost. Lost. And now, of course,

she is berating herself for the stupidity of leaving the box in the library when she knew.

How could she not have known?

Of course she knew what would happen. Some might say she wished for it, but what kind of a daughter would that be, I ask you? What species of daughter wants to erase her mother from the earth?

Look at her now, crumpled on the floor. What can she do? There is nothing left. And the metronome keeps plic-plicking but can she even hear it any more? She has curled herself up inside a protective shell like an armadillo and rolled away under the sofa.

So close to reconciliation, to atonement and redemption. But it is over now. All gone. Nothing left. She has fallen inside herself, as they always said would happen. The inner world has won. There is no reason in fighting it any more.

And the metronome clicks on. It will click into eternity.

The house is dense with people. They line the walls and, as I drift from room to room, they cheer and shower me with rice, rose petals, shredded bits of paper. They wish me well – *a lifetime of happiness* – and tell me how beautiful I look, mouthing words like 'radiant' and 'blooming'. Thank you. Thank you. Thank you for coming. As I walk, my veil floats behind me, lifted by tiny, compliant bluebirds. I am a fairy-tale princess, the muse of a Pre-Raphaelite scene. *¡Qué bella estás!* Thank you. Thank you.

All these people, here, just for me. Some have come from very far away. I can tell by their clothing: hobble skirts, cloche hats, coats of ermine fur, long strings of pearls and velvet stoles. Many have brought gifts and want to know where to put them. I don't know, I tell them. Ask my mother: she will know. Where is she? Oh, I don't know, somewhere around. I wave my hand vaguely. She'll be here presently. I don't want to speak about my mother. This is my day. *My* day. Inexplicably, some try to thrust wooden spoons towards me. I bat them away. This is no time for cooking! This is my day.

There are flowers everywhere. Their smell perfumes the air. I don't like it. Cloying – a *cloying* stench. Oh, that word! Onomatopoeic, almost. I have to stop myself from saying it out loud. *Cloying*. *Cloying*. It sounds like clawing. Like how the flowers' odours are *clawing* their way up the inside of my nose like tiny mountaineers armed with pickaxes. I have to keep covering my face with a handkerchief to block them out. I try to make it seem flirtatious and coy, but it's hard to look coquettish with a white napkin pressed desperately against your face. The flowers seem to keep multiplying – festoons growing upwards, snaking around the banisters and door frames, coiling around the cornices, dropping on vines from balconies. Flowers with enormous heads and long limbs explode from pedestals placed in every corner and somehow the arrangements remind me of lions' mouths, gaping mid-roar, wanting to swallow me up. Who brought all these flowers? Where did they come from?

Music is playing – two guitars, Spanish-style, one of them playing bordones, the other strumming out a waltz, and a deep, contralto voice singing about a memory of jasmines and roses in the hair of a beautiful woman. No more flowers, please. And a river – laughing under a whispering bridge. Something like that. But then the music changes. From room to room, it switches. Now a psychedelic chicha with pan pipes and synthesisers, wah-wahs on the electric guitar, bongos and a crybaby pedal. And there are hippies: daisies in long hair, baggy clothes, staggering in a ring, brincando to the huayno beat. In the next room: opera. A soprano, haunting, wailing like an attention-seeking ghost. I know the song. Oh, yes, I know that shrieking well. Delibes's *Lakmé*. A song about bells. Or flowers. Or bells and flowers. Something like that, anyway. Jasmines and roses again. Why is it always jasmines and roses?

Oú va la jeune Hindoue, fille des parias?
Here she comes! Here comes la novia!
Qué bella está.

They contemplate me, all these people (most of them I don't even recognise) with drooping, tender eyes. Melting eyes. No, not melting – crying. I know what they're all thinking. They're thinking *She's done it.* They're thinking how I've proved them all wrong. How I was going to be left on the shelf (on the shelf? Like an old tin of anchovies?) but then, when everyone had given up on me, I pulled it out of the bag. A rabbit from a top hat. Now here I am getting married, having a baby, and it's all going to be fine. They used to ask me all the time, *Do you have a boyfriend? Do you have a boyfriend? ¿Ya? ¿Por fin?* And now I do, and I'm walking down the aisle in a long white gown (lace, sweetheart neckline) smiling and waving to all the guests and the choir are singing,

Arroz con leche,
me quiero casar
con una señorita
de la capital.

I will admit it is not the entrance music I would have chosen, but here we are, all these people in out-of-date fashions, all these ghosts, and me walking down the aisle to nasal voices singing: *Rice pudding, rice pudding, I want to marry a girl from the capital. Que sepa coser, que sepa bordar, que sepa abrir la puerta para ir a bailar.* But isn't it tragic that marriage should have to be the happy ending, that the story always ends with a marriage and a kiss and then… then nothing more. We will live happily ever after until death do us part, forever and ever, amen. Except that death does not make people part. If anything, death makes them linger. I've never found the living to be very reliable, but the dead are always there when I need them and more often when I don't.

At least she found a man who will marry her, they say. She can't be as loca as we thought. Not so loca loca loca.

And he's an Englishman!

They're gentlemen, you know. Englishmen.

Sí, pues. Not like Peruvians. All machistas.

Yes, with a Latino, you can be sure he will cheat.

Oh, but not the English!

They have Anglo-Saxon blood.

Cold. As a stone.

What luck, to marry a Westerner!

But no, this isn't what they say to me. This is what they said to my mother. I remember them saying it, all those years ago, as we packed our things, ready to move to England, to go and find my father and make him marry us. Well, not us. My mother. Make him marry my mother and take responsibility for his children – Leandro and me. How lucky, to have found an Englishman. Not a machista Peruvian. Oh, but my father proved them wrong, because this is the age of equal opportunities. No one has a monopoly on machismo any more. Shame on you, Tías! Shame on you!

My father is not here, of course (he never was), so I walk myself down the aisle. Right foot. Left foot. Right foot. Left foot. And they are feet, not paintbrushes or egg whisks or anything mad like that. Above me the mural of Noah's ark bursts into applause, all the animals whooping and cheering, the turtle-skunks and lion-toads weeping into their tissues. So proud. So proud of me. From the chandelier, the little pink fish dangles. She is a lobster now. Giant. As large as a mastiff. Bigger, maybe. Her swimmerets shiver, legs waving in celebration, antennae writhing above the heads of the guests.

Elle court sur la mousse
et ne se souvient pas
que partout on repousse
l'enfant des parias...

At the altar, Rupert – morning suit and waistcoat, a white rose for the buttonhole – is looking at me and smiling such a wide smile. He loves me. So, so much he loves me. As I glide towards him, I pass Mimita with her flick-flick-flickering butterfly lashes and she is weeping. Yes, you see, Mimita, with your ya-ya and your ven-ven, that I can be beautiful too! I toss my hair and it is bouncy and long. It knocks Mimita off her feet and sends her rolling around the ballroom floor like a skittle, which I like at first until the sound of her rolling against the parquet crescendoes and now it is a rising wind or the roar of nearby thunder and it is drowning out the string quartet playing Pachelbel's Canon in D. Just like Mimita to take my limelight. Just like her to have to be better. It's not fair. It's not fair it's not fair it's not fair until the Doña comes over, enormous and loping, with a dustpan and brush. She sweeps Mimita away – throws her out of the window.

De las Casas is here too, as are the other doctors, all in white coats waving stethoscopes and thermometers at me. I imagine one of them will leap up during the vows, try to stick a tongue depressor into my mouth.

Say aaaaaahhhhhh.

Aaaaaahhhhhh.

Aaaaaahhhhhh.

No, this will not happen. They have no right to intrude upon my big day. It is *my* day. I just hope they cannot see the little pink fish, now a giant, swollen lobster, scuttling across the walls, her sharp, crustacean feet scratching and scrabbling at the plaster. With her enormous pincers she clacks, like a flamenco dancer with a pair of castanets, her claws pattering out a zapateo against the ceiling, against the floor. Loca loca loca.

I should fix my eyes on Rupert. Any moment I will be up there with him at the altar making vows, promising things, committing to forever. To forever and forever, por los siglos de los siglos, until the mountains crumble and the sky falls into the sea. It is meant to be comforting, I think, to find your forever person. How do you know you are in love? It is like coming home. That's what they say, isn't it? Coming to Rupert should feel like coming home.

I try to focus on him through my veil, but I can't see well. The lace makes my sight blurry, so I rip a little hole in it with my finger-nails and now things are clearer, but the room has changed. The guests have all got up and are milling around. What happened to the vows? Did we say them already? I want to ask someone nearby but that will make me look crazy – to have forgotten something I did just a few minutes ago. Instead, I wander around trying to look comfortable, the way everyone else looks: champagne flutes in their hands, clicking their fingers at waiters in white jackets carrying silver trays of tiny food. The room is filled with tables now, laid with white cloths, piled high with pyramids of round fruits – oranges, lemons, avocados (strange choice), platters of marzipan sweets, French patisserie decorated with berries and chantilly cream. I don't remember ordering any of this, but it all looks enchanting. Thank you. Thank you.

No one is paying attention to me. Their backs are all turned as they gather in tight circles and make pointed shapes with their lips. Their mouths are triangles and they arch their eyebrows and open their eyes wide. They are all angles – sharp elbows and jut-ting shoulders, bobbed haircuts, silk gloves up to here and dropped waistlines. I'm in the wrong era, clearly. The carousel has turned, again, and taken me with it, away (far away) from Rupert. I need to get out, but the bodies press towards me, closing me in. I have to squeeze myself around them, contorting myself into strange, impossible shapes, moulding myself around their shoulder blades and spines and through the tiny gaps between their forefingers and thumbs as they lift their cigarette holders aloft.

There would be more space in the kitchen, I thought, but I was wrong. In here the floral stench is worse: the room is filled with lilies and wailing. On the worktable there is a rectangular wooden box over which many people are bending and weeping. As I move closer, I can see there is a child inside, pale and still like a doll, but not a doll, and I am offended, because it is not good manners to bring a corpse in an open casket on a day such as this, but then I look again and see that the child is the bebe Vittoria and again I know I am in the wrong decade. I should leave the mourners to their mourning. I carry on.

In the hallway, he comes towards me with open arms, crying epithets of affection: *My Darling! My Sweet!* But this man, though he is dressed in tails and has a white rose in his buttonhole, is not Rupert. I do not know who he is. Still, he lunges towards me with inconsistent faces, now moustached, now clean-shaven, now an old man, now far too young, just a boy. For a second he is Uriel, then my brother, then he is the men (all the men) from the carpenter's yard on Calle Manuel Tovar – leathery skin, grinning, baring sharp shark teeth at me.

I duck out of his embrace and, as I fold myself in two, I catch sight of my own body and see that I am naked. There is no white gown. No veil of lace. Only a pair of greying knickers over which my bulging belly looms – and two enormous breasts glowing in the darkness. It is night. The house is empty. At my feet, a bed sheet in which I seem to have ripped two holes for eyes.

Well, that was odd.

What time is it?

In this place? Who can say!

I am, by now, very, very pregnant. The little pink fish is a lobster. That much is certain. I can hear her chitinous feet clicking across the floor. There is a real possibility that she will eat me or snip me to ribbons with her pincers. I ought to keep an eye on her at all times – not turn my back to her. That's what they say, isn't it, about predators? That's why the animals lower down the food chain have eyes in the side of their heads – so they can see behind them as well as in front. Now that the little pink fish is an oversized crustacean scuttling in my blind spot, I wish my eyes were in the side of my head – or that I could turn my head all the way around, like an owl – so that I could look back at the same time as looking forward. I live in fear that my daughter is going to creep up behind me and swallow me when I'm not looking. She will, of course, eventually. This is what children do. Daughters especially. My mother is dead. What exists of her now is what Leandro and I have imbibed. I have tried so hard to expel her. Leaving Lima was the emetic I tried to purge her with.

But she's still with me, inside me, I have swallowed her (I swallowed her so long ago, in my childhood) and she is the reason for the horror I have of motherhood, I think, because surely I won't be any good at it. I have no model for it – no decent model, anyway. We need models to construct ourselves, the way a sculptor needs a muse or a painter needs someone to sit for them and pose. Our inspiration comes from the outside world. Existence precedes essence. I look inside myself and find nothing, so I start to fill the void by swallowing antecedents – the jumbled members and body parts of my mother and Mamabue and Tía Consuelo and all the ghosts, all thrown together. Even that idea, I didn't come up with it myself. I stole it from experience – from the memory of hiding in Consuelo's closet, lying among the broken body parts, the plastic limbs, porcelain torsos, wooden heads and clumps of synthetic hair. All my thoughts, everything I am, is only bricolage. Even my daughter with her fuchsia, crustacean form flashing through my peripheral vision is a recycled hallucination, probably – a play on Jean-Paul Sartre and his cohort of mescaline-induced crabs that followed him around. There is nothing original about me. I am nothing more than offcuts of other people, masticated and stuck back together, just disparate pieces squashed onto each other like plasticine. I hate plasticine. I hate its starchy smell. Hate how malleable it is. It can become anything. Lying on the table in lumps, plasticine is thing-in-waiting. There is no way of knowing what form it will take, and that terrifies me. De las Casas used to give me plasticine. It was his version of the inkblot test, I think. He would ask me questions and tell me to make my response out of plasticine. People think children are uninhibited in play, but that isn't true. It wasn't true for me, certainly, as I sat moulding shapes out of the plasticine. There were always eyes, the watchful eyes of family at first, dead and alive, but then I became wary of doctors. I absorbed their glare. All those eyes became part of my skin. Imagine that! A girl with dozens – maybe hundreds – of eyes all over her body, all of them swivelling and blinking. Their eyes were inside me too: in my belly and brain, watching me, all the time, watching me. They watch me now, standing in plaintive rows, dabbing their faces with squares of cloth, throwing single red roses at me, throwing handfuls of dirt. Why dirt? What have I done to deserve wet sod to be thrown in my face?

How sad!

How sad!

Rest in peace, querida niña!

What has happened to me? Have I gone the way of all Echeverrías and slipped unwittingly into death? Vaya, the curse got me at last! It gets us all in the end. How did it happen? How was my passing? Painful or tender?

Was the baby born, I wonder. She must have been, because my belly is empty: I run my hands over it, up and down. It slides smoothly over the silvery satin dress I am wearing. Apparently I am elegant in death. But not too much – barefoot. A nymph in silver satin. I should sing, I suppose. I feel I am that sort of ghost. But what is my song?

Todos me dicen la loca, Llorona...

The body hangs, swinging from the ceiling light, and I wonder at first if this is how I died. The face is a livid colour, like a person very angry, and the feet are grey and bloated. The hair hangs, black and knotted, like the hair of la llorona from the legends. She could be me. I will not know until I see the face. I try to stand beneath the body, but the room is full of guests in evening wear drinking and laughing, which is strange because this is a bedroom. But here they are, and they celebrate and live in spite of the death swinging above them.

¡Ayyyy! ¡Ayyyy! ¡Ayyyy!

¡No llores!

Life is for living. Live it now! Before it all ends. Before it is over! Perhaps this is my song now I am dead. I stole my song from my mother, it seems.

The body was not mine. I saw her face: it was Paloma's. She was also lying limp in the red bathwater in my en suite, and splattered against the dining-room wall with a revolver lying nearby. I saw her in the garden, trampled under the feet of the revellers, and also in the study, yellow-skinned, mouth filled with froth, poisoned in some fashion.

¡Paloma! ¡Paloma! How did you die, Paloma?

Palomita, tell me, how did you die?

The answer, I think, was in that box – the leather box file. I must find my way back to it. In the library. I must go there. But the wind blows me back, pugnacious gusts of wind that knock the air out of my lungs (if the dead have lungs) and shove me back – back – back. *Ferrocarril – carril – carril, tres pasos pa'tras – pa'tras – pa'tras.* Every step forward blows me three steps back until I am lifted off my feet and swirled about like Francesca and Paolo in the inferno, whirling eternally.

Dime, what did I do, to deserve such castigation!

Rupert is here too, blowing in the whirlwind. He reaches out his hand, I take it, and the instant we touch we are set down. We are running, slightly crouching, under a tunnel of arms. There are no bodies attached to the arms – only arms. It reminds me of that game they play in England – the game children play – about the axeman coming to chop off heads. *Oranges and lemons, say the bells of St Clement's.* But no one wants to decapitate me today, only to celebrate my nuptials to this wonderful Englishman whose name is—

Consummation. Isn't that a funny word? 'Tis a consummation devoutly to be wished. From the Latin 'consummare', the dictionary tells me (the dictionary in the library, because I checked), which means to complete or perfect – to bring everything together. Not to be confused with to consume. This is not a consume-ation. I am not being eaten. In a way, anatomically speaking, it would be more accurate to say that I am eating him – but do not speak of that. Some children eat plasticine, I believe. I never ate plasticine. For me, that would have been like eating my traumas, which I moulded into tangible shapes from the coloured dough. I have never eaten my traumas. Más bien, when I am traumatised, I forget to eat.

We are on a bed of white sheets and downy pillows and Rupert is feeding me flakes of plaster like tortilla chips. He pops them into my mouth, one after the other. It is not good. No bueno. Not good for the baby. What baby? There is no baby any more. Or yet. I think we might be about to make her, probably. Yes. Correct. I have gone backwards. We are in the apartment. Our/his apartment. No, go back, we are entering the apartment. I am fumbling with the electronic key card (it never liked me, that coso) and he is slippery-lipped on my neck. I do not like wet things near my ears, but I have never told him this. It is late, I am tired, I want to open the door, so I let him hang off my neck like a barnacle. In the commercials (for coffee, jewellery, perfume) it is sensual, neck-kissing. The woman tilts back her head and gives breathy sighs. It is, I suppose, a vampiric thing? But I like my neck dry. If it gets wet, it might wilt, and then I will have to drag my head around like a bowling ball on a rope.

Inside the apartment, I offer him other body parts – a shoulder, a wrist – and dry my neck with my sleeve. He clings to me, pressing against my back, his arms clamped around my diaphragm. We waddle along like this, a two-headed quadruped, him licking my nape just below my hair. The blinds are open, looking over the river. A party boat, strung with coloured electric bulbs, slides past below, its music thumping up to us. The sky is the colour of trout scales, squares of light from the windows of skyscrapers scraping through the twilight.

His hands are under my skirt, kneading at my thighs as if I were dough – unformed, in need of shaping, making tauter, like the girls he grew up with, the ones with horse-riders' thighs and long feet. He will massage me, soften me, make me malleable so that he can craft me. Will he bake me then? Turn me into bread-woman, easily consumable. Will he break me in the end? Share me across the table? *Take, eat, this is my girlfriend's body, given up for—* His fingers, like urgent worms, scrabble under the elastic hems of my knickers and I flinch, take them away, move them up to my breasts where, again, he kneads.

Speak Spanish to me, he says. When I stay silent, he insists again. *Speak Spanish. I like it.*

What does he like exactly? The alveolar trills and velar fricatives? The turbulence of air thrust from the tonsils? Perhaps the vibrations of tongue on palate or the vowels that open wide the lips between each consonant? *Speak to me in the pretérito imperfecto del indicativo.* Is it the verb tenses that excite him? The moods and conjugations that do not exist in English?

Speak Spanish to me, he says as he slurps on my ear, and I do not think it is the language at all but his idea of the qualities that the language inspires in its speaker. Because the Latina is what? Hot-blooded? Uninhibited and carnal? Scratch at my skin with a scalpel: it will flake away like old paint and, oh! of course – she is red underneath. A glossy red devil-woman, scalding and unbridled, screaming into the night. Is that what he wants from me? Scream at me in the throes of ecstasy in your devil Spanish, wide-open woman. Yes, wide open – legs apart, buttocks spread, labia unfurled, and her cavernous mouth agape, everything gaping, belly splitting open like a ripe peach, ribcage cracking open (crustaceous) and still she opens and opens, out of the wound breasts overflowing, hands and feet spilling out, palpitating hearts (she has several – passionate, of course) spilling out, a tangle of arteries, veins, all manner of sinews spilling out, leaves and vines, too, are emerging, tropical birds flying out, lime-green snakes slithering, little monkeys gambolling, ripe fruits dropping down her legs, a lush (don't say it) fertile Eden on the frontier between pre- and postlapsarian and he tearing away with his hands saying *Speak Spanish to me* but what else are you looking for in there, among the papaya seeds and chirimoyas, ah? what else *tu buscas ahí adentro?* tiny denim shorts and wedge sandalias, gold hoop earrings and bouncing waves of mahogany hair, red finger-nails, but what *tú buscas, gringo?* in my pelvis (like a cornucopia) a bottle of tequila, a couple of chilled Argentinian steaks, jalapeños, a handful of sand, pale blue housekeeping uniform and, underneath, a tiny tanga? and me lying splayed on the bed, Aztecan sacrifice to my gringo's predilections.

As he dug around inside me my eyes were on the window, or rather on what had appeared outside the window. Where there ought to have been cuboids of glass and steel, squares of light from the city skyline, there was instead the black bulk of a mountain, hulking and rugged, its colossal broadness blocking the sky. Where had it come from, this mountain? Was it perhaps that we had transported? That our apartment had dislodged itself from the building and flown, a floating cube, elsewhere? Or had the cerro come to me?

The mountain watched us through the window – me lying, spilling open, Rupert searching for whatever it was he thought he could mine from me. I could sense the mountain's disapproval. It derided me for capitulating. *This little man?* it seemed to say. *THIS little man?* It was breathing, and its exhalations were deep and reso-nant, rumbling like thunder, quaking the earth, juddering the bed, rattling the windows in their frames. The spotlights in the ceiling flickered on and off, on and off, and down in the street a car alarm wailed. (The next day I would wake to news that there had been a storm that felled trees, inundated train tracks: out in the street, wheelie bins crashed into car windows and roof tiles sliced through the air, leaving notches in the power cables.)

The mountain came so close that I could see its face, the ledges of its brows, the proud high arch of its nose, its broad angular jaw, the buzzards' nests in the crags of its skin, the long black hair flowing down its back, towns built on its shoulders, huts in bright colours creeping down its arms and thighs. Up the cliff faces of its abdomen, green creepers. On its chest, lush fields of amancaes, and around its waist, a belt of hanging, jangling skeletons. Powerful shins and calves of rock, up and down which sea creatures scuttled and slid, shoals of anchoveta circling its kneecaps, limpets and mussels clinging to the ankles, its feet wet as if just dredged from the sea.

The mountain climbed in through the window and lumbered above us, rising monolithic behind Rupert, dwarfing him in its shadow. Rupert did not notice. The room was filled with the earthiness of its loam, rising petrol, the salty rottenness of sea and the warm, baking scent of hot sand. I reached up my hands and it pulled me up, dangling me like a rag doll from its fingertips, sliding me out from under Rupert's thrusting, away from the creaking bed, from the apartment and its flickering lights, lifting me through the ceiling up into the night, high above the city, which crumbled away beneath its titan feet, cathedrals crushed to dust, bridges snapping like twigs. As it lifted me, I transformed, became enormous, unscalable. The dawn broke out of my mouth, my uvula a sun, rays of citrus light bursting from the gaps between my teeth – teeth of stone, colossal boulders. Stars nestled in my hair, falcons perched on the tips of my lashes. From every pore and follicle, a tree sprang; in every line of my skin was a valley where a river meandered, each a salamander beating its watery tail. Curling where my breasts should be were pumas the size of hillocks, gently growling as they slept. The mountain woke them, made them bare their teeth and roar.

The wamani took me out into the ocean, where we waded together, deeper and deeper. From its own hands, it fed me creatures of the deep – giant squid and sperm whales, which I popped with my tongue – and it smeared my lips with crystals of salt. As we lay back in the water, our bodies rising above the waves like new land masses, the wamani interlinked its fingers with mine, showed me my own hands, how the veins on my palms flowed with copper, with silver and gold, streams that flowed through my wrists and arms, along my torso, down my legs, lacing through my body in glittering threads. My heart was a knot of molten metals pumping. Out of the ocean, forgotten creatures were clambering out of the deep and onto my shores. I fell asleep with the waves beating against me, caressing, lapping, and the sea monsters clicking and moaning in my ear.

Now the little pink fish is a lobster curled against me, purring, nipping at me affectionately with its pincers. I stroke its crust, tickle its playful swimmerets, speak to it in baby language. *Agoo, agoogoo. You are my sunshine. My only sunshine. Aroo. Aroorooroo.*

The guests have returned. It is time to cut the cake, they say, and they drum the table with the butts of their forks. They sing – jovial, robust – to the tune of 'The Death and Burial of the Invincible Marlborough':

> *¡Queremos que partan la torta!*
> *¡Queremos que partan la torta!*
> *¡Queremos que partan la torta!*
> *Si no, nos vamos de aquí.*

It is a protest chant, defiant. They will not leave until their demands are met. The forks are enormous now – pitchforks, torches, blazing links. They have come to slay the beast. Or the cake. They want to kill the cakebeast, feast on its flesh. I am confused. The cake is not a cake, I want to tell them. It is the lobster, *my* lobster, held by force onto the table by many hands while it screams and Rupert stands above it with a carving knife ready to pierce and crack. A chorus of voices sings a lament, about a man who went to war and never came back, not for Easter or Christmas or Trinity Feast, qué dolor, qué dolor, qué pena, until he came home in a coffin and was buried with much pomp and wailing, mironton, mironton, mirontaine! Yes, Mambrú se fue a la guerra and we want a piece of cake. Above his tomb a little bird sings, chibirín, chibirín, chibirín, chin chin, pío pí pío pí pío pa.

Then let them eat cake, I say, but not my child, chibirín, chibirín, chibirín, chin chin, and I rise like a monster of old (do re mi, do re fa), scoop up the little pink fish in my arms and release the ants, yes, enormous ants I call up from the earth and they arrive with their armour, trampling the place underfoot as they march. The guests all scatter, their tiny feet pitter-pattering away.

She should not have done that.

They will return.

Force for force.

And they are right. The birds sense it first and flap away in a panic. From Los Polvos, there is frantic barking, the squall of car alarms piercing and shrill. A vibration commences that sets the conchas to rattling in the kitchen sink, makes an alabaster statuette bounce along the shelf and then fall, shattering into pieces that go skittering against the majolica. From the ceiling, the chandelier begins to swing of its own volition.

Something, someone, is coming. I must hide but I cannot remember where. I should stand in the doorway – no, wrong. It's too late. My arms extend involuntarily to steady myself but the ground jerks away and I am upended, landing heavily on my side. The earth has creaked and shifted, the house is aslant. Furniture jumps across the parquet like crickets. Walls undulate, billowing sails. Through a window, a tree crashes, roots first, showering me with glass shards. I try to crawl away but the earth tips and I slide towards the open window. A pianoforte skids past me, playing the 'Moonlight Sonata', then, with a riot of twanging and reverberation, smashes through a set of oak doors and tumbles into an abyss. Is the house turning? It seems to be revolving very fast on one of its corners, like a spinning top. Meanwhile, inside, I am here being spun, and around me the artefacts of Echeverría history – floral china plates, vials of perfume, Spanish lace mantillas, vinyl records, pictures of the dead in frames, wooden crucifixes, jars of strawberry conserve and bottles of pisco, playing cards, denuded book covers, crystal rosaries, statuettes of saints – fall and explode or are swept away by centrifugal forces.

Suddenly, amidst the chaos, there is a blossoming of pain in my belly. It makes me cry out and reach for something. My hand closes around a fish knife and I cling to it for purchase, though it cannot anchor me to anything. In my bowel, magma stirs. Tectonic plates are shifting, parting, viscous things gurgle, breaching their borders, rearranging. Continents are colliding, possibly, and opening great gashes in the underworld with their friction. My entrails reposition themselves while around me the world is torn apart.

The lobster is terrified, backing into a corner, its black eyes fixed on me, and I sense its betrayal. It thinks I did this – that I brought on the earthquake. All around us, the ground is bubbling, tiles buckling, geysers of soil and sand bursting up through the holes. Armoires fling open like exploded ribcages and pour out their contents (crockery, tins of paint, beaded evening gowns); the debris of life keeps on spilling and spilling over. From the dining room, I hear the smashing of plates, teacups, soup tureens; in the library, the thudding of what remains of the encyclopaedias hitting the ground. From all around, I hear the tortured scraping of furniture cutting gouges into the parquet floor as the house rocks. And we, the lobster and I, here inside, reach for each other across the gulf of the room. She is coming to me. She is arriving.

I breathe through the screaming. When did it begin? Who is screaming? I am not sure, but there are desperate cries. Plucked by a sudden racking, I double over, thrust out a hand and the wall of the room buckles like cardboard, then I am exposed – I can see the Sevillian courtyard, the fountain shaking uncontrollably and then erupting, all twelve heads exploding into a mushroom cloud of dust then raining slowly down in pinkish puffs. A chunk of the external wall on the first floor has fallen away and several bedrooms, side by side (Tía Consuelo's, Tío Ignacio's), hang open like bedrooms in a doll's house, but looted and turned over. I run my eyes across them, ticking them off in my mind until one is gone, just a hole through which I can see the sky, like a missing tooth. I can see bathrooms, too, and hear the tiles crackling as they break, the crunch of the wooden spindles of the balustrade as they snap one after another. Iron bars splinter and crack, steel bars give a hee-haw of agony as they bend into unnatural shapes, marble columns buckle, broken femurs stick out at angles, wishbones snap through ruptures in crumpled plaster. Shutters swing precariously then surrender and fall, saluting, mournful, as they go. Terracotta tiles slide from the roof like raindrops and splash onto the majolica. Mamabue's bedroom is exposed to the street, flesh through a laceration.

I fling back my head and bray. Enormous chunks of ceiling are falling around me. I should find cover, but the rumbling of my womb will not let me move and my haunches are slick with insides flowing out. I am going to die here, deep in this house where room after room is succumbing to an ancient violence, where the world within is trying to erupt into the world without, where what is underneath is reaching up and the world above is collapsing onto the world below – all is turning over, my womb is stirring, inverting, but what is the use, little one? You will come out only to suffocate: the air is granular, thick with dust and ash floating heavily in clouds. The house is ejecting me, miscarrying me, or perhaps it is trying to keep me in, I am not sure. Either way, rejected or stifled, I will die here.

The room above, my mother's old room, falls through the ceiling, but I am preserved, miraculously, under an unsnapped floorboard. Her bed, like a boat run aground, leans, wretchedly askew, its headboard wedged into the rubble, its spine extending at an angle, feet in the air. In the interval between the contractions, I am able to shuffle myself over to it and take shelter under its base, where the mattress, disembowelled, is miraculously still balanced on the slats. Nearby are the remains of the baúl that, during its descent, flipped over, discarded its lid and emptied its contents in a shower. Paloma's face flutters down a dozen times, her bottle of perfume smashed nearby.

As I wait for the next wave of pain, I look up: above me, naked rafters, great holes in the ceiling through which I can see a dash of blue, the dart of a seagull. Somewhere outside, the world continues. At this hour, Rupert is at the apartment, waking up or showering or perhaps packing up my things into boxes, dividing our DVDs, separating out my books, cutting me from photographs – unless the end of the world is happening there, too. But I know it isn't. This is my apocalypse. What will they tell him when they excavate me, ashen and cold, from the rubble? Perhaps I will remain here for centuries, buried into the foundations of some new apartment block, encased in cement, stepped upon, pressed down upon, while above me the living eat and mourn and fornicate, feed their children, watch television, excrete, do all the things that constitute a life. Below I will lie – baby half in, half out – waiting to be discovered, perfectly preserved in some cadaveric spasm like the crusted bodies of Pompeii, displayed in a glass case in a museum of the distant future. *Mother interred in childbirth*. They will give me a cute name – Juanita or María – but the teenagers will come to gawp, thrilled by the double voyeurism, a simultaneous death and birth mummified for posterity.

343

Mon Dieu! Even now, she thinks too much.

Rupert, though, will be buried, peaceful, many decades from now under a mound of green English grass. *Here lies Rupert Napier, who had a very elegant wallet—*

Vaya, pobre niña, she thinks she is dying.

She is not dying.

She might be dying.

Pour l'amour de Dieu!

Of course not, but it is her first labour:
it is natural to think she is dying.

A hand reaches into my abdomen and twists. I cannot do anything but cry out. My feet dig into the rubble and I wrap my toes around something firm. I heave my strength into the earth – so much strength it could, perhaps, move a mountain, but it seems to have no impact on you, little one. You are clinging to me. You are going to break me in two.

Tranquila, Nanita
Tranquiiiiiila, tranquiiiiiila

There are women in the room with me. They are working, peeling me out of my clothes, wiping me down with hot cloths, inspecting between my legs, sticking fingers inside, saying there is still time. They are unaffected by the fragments of house that fall around us. They do not cough or wheeze in the clouds of silt that swirl in the air. One of them (I do not recognise her) sits nearby straddling a washtub, her skirts pulled back to reveal muscular thighs. She is the one who takes the cloths, soiled with my fluids, and plunges them into the steaming water. With algal-green eyes (kind eyes, eyes I feel I should know) she smiles at me. She tells me I should thank God for a daughter. A daughter will never leave me. Standing above her, two women – one in an ermine coat, glossy black hair pressed into finger waves and an eight-legged tamarin reclining on her shoulders; the other, statuesque, long-necked, birthmark of a bird in flight on her cheek – are ripping sheets and dropping the shreds into the tub. They argue back and forth with the sturdy, white-haired woman who barks orders in French about hot towels and bloodletting.

Titi Consuelo is here too, pacing, fretting, wringing her hands, muttering to a blue-eyed, flaxen-haired woman that I look too pale, too weak – that I need donkey milk. But where are we to get donkey milk at a time like this? They kneel together and pray to Santa Margarita of Antioch declaring that just as she was spat from the mouth of the dragon unharmed, so too will my baby be delivered safely. They petition the Virgin Mary, *Dios te salve, María*, and Santa Rosa de Lima, in whose jurisdiction we find ourselves in desperate need. Their frenzied muttering weaves in and out of the cacophony of destruction, the creaking and groaning of the very bones of the earth. There are teaspoons being pressed against my lips. Teaspoons of mazamorra morada and nettle tea, manjar blanco and agua de azahar. The woman who feeds me has sharp, expressive eyes. Black eyes like mine, perhaps. She tells me, *Eat, you need your strength*. By my side, stroking my knee, instructing me on breathing, is Tía Paloma. She tells me I am doing well, that I will not die today. I remind her, between gasps, that the house is falling. *Forget about the house*, she says. *Forget that.*

'I cannot do it,' I tell her. 'I cannot get my daughter out of me.'

The sturdy Frenchwoman overhears. She scolds me, tells me this is no time for wallowing; I must get the child out of me one way or another and if I do not extract her in this world, I will spend eternity extracting her in the world to come, so what will it be? Now, once and for all? Or later, eternally, incessantly, cracking open again and again until the end of time? How would I rather have it? I should make my choice.

'She will break me to pieces.'

She will not break you.

Hail Mary, full of grace, the Lord is with thee.
Tranquiiiiiila, tranquiiiiiila

This is Mama's voice, but I cannot see her. Sweat is dripping soot and ash into my eyes. Someone tips water into my mouth. I swallow it, grateful, and then tip back to rest for a moment. Under my back I feel not the jagged edges of rubble or the wooden skeleton of a bed but the softness of a body. She who is behind me – certainly a she – lets me lean against her, lets me thrust my elbows into her when I arch my spine in response to each contraction, lets me crush her arm, digging my fingers into her skin when the pain is at its worst. Her fingers stroke my cheeks, grazing only gently. She speaks soothing words, tells me she knows me. Even if I come in disguise, she knows me. From the beginning, she knew me. And at the end, too, she will know me.

Blessed art thou amongst women.

She is coming out now.

And blessed is the fruit of thy womb.

Somewhere far off there are voices shouting, calling for auxilio, the yowl of an emergency siren, then a voice telling me to push, and I do.

DIECISIETE

The people of Lima called it a miracle. To rescue a mother and a newborn child from the rubble and find them both alive and without serious injury, with nothing more than a few scratches and a little bruising – it had to have been an act of God. The other remarkable fact (though a sad one, something more like the inverse of a miracle) was that la Casa Echeverría had succumbed to the earthquake. The yellow house on the hill, which had survived for so long, which had not fallen in the earthquakes of 1940 or 1974, had yielded to this, which by all accounts had not been a major seismic event. It was particularly surprising since none of the houses of Los Polvos had fallen, and most of those were still unfinished.

Thanks be to God that Los Polvos had been left untouched because, without their own tragedies to attend to, it was the Polvorinos who had been the first to arrive at the destroyed casona to rescue the woman interred within it. They had sprinted up the hill, clambered over the part-fallen walls on the perimeter of the Echeverría land (walls that had, for decades, divided the mansion from the shanty town), torn through the orange groves and immediately begun sifting the rubble piece by piece, working cautiously lest they unbalance the mound of wreckage and cause it to crush the survivors inside. They laboured quietly, guided by the faint cries of an infant rising from the dust and debris.

By the time the bomberos arrived, the Polvorinos had already been able to identify the precise location of the mother and child trapped under the collapsed roof of the house, and to open up a hole through which they could communicate and lower a bottle of formula for the little one and a flask of water for the woman.

The day's newspapers lamented the loss of the yellow house on the hill in obituaries that remembered its life fondly, as if it had been a living person. The articles quoted from the memories of some of the oldest surviving limeños who had visited the casona in its heyday for dinners, dances and operatic performances. They resurrected, too, the folk stories about a young maid who had taken her life by leaping from a second-floor window (no, this was not correct, the rescued mother told them – the maid had fallen while trying to lure one of the cats off a window ledge and back to safety). Whatever the cause of her fall, certainly the maid had fallen and was swiftly venerated as a saint for the unremarkable – an advocate for the ordinary folk – until, almost as swiftly, she had been forgotten. Although now, what with the miraculous disinterment of mother and child, people were beginning to remember again and wonder whether Santa Julia, saintess of the everyday, had been behind this rescue.

For her part, the young mother who had been plucked from the rubble had never forgotten Santa Julia and she donated a sum of money to the Organising Council of Los Polvos with which they were to construct a medical facility (with an emphasis on antenatal care), and it was to be called the Julia Álvarez Yupanqui Maternity Clinic.

The Polvorinos could hardly believe the mansion was gone. The yellow house on the hill had long pre-dated the pueblo jóven of Los Polvos and nobody now living had ever known this hill without its lúcuma-gold crown. For weeks after the earthquake, the Polvorinos would stand, hands shielding their eyes from the sun, and stare up in disbelief at the emptiness that now sat on the summit. Who would have thought, the elder ones said to one another, that when they first arrived on this empty plot, which had been earmarked as a cemetery for the Echeverría dead, that the casona would fall and the Polvorinos would remain. Who would have thought it?

Where the house had been, they could now watch the sunset blazing across the sky. Instead of skirting around the hill to reach the main road, they could now cut across it, picking oranges and pears from the trees in the orchard as they went, the children playing football on the grass of the Echeverría gardens instead of in the dust of Los Polvos. Some of the more adventurous ones scavenged among the wreckage for treasures – gold picture frames, silver cutlery, solitary pearls from shattered necklaces. A few of the adults discussed the possibility of another land grab.

But soon the land was sold and the construction company, Edificios Pacífico, erected a boundary along the perimeter with large notices in red and yellow that declared in thick imposing fonts, PELIGRO, NO TRESPASAR and PROHIBIDO ENTRAR on pain of various penalties. The day the machinery arrived (diggers, cranes, caterpillars) and crawled arduously up the hill like enormous insects, the children of Los Polvos watched, their little fingers hooked through the gaps in the chain-link fence.

Augusto García Navarro, a Peruvian architect who had acquired an illustrious reputation in Europe, was contracted to design and oversee the construction of the apartment block that would replace la Casa Echeverría. Pacífico Tower was to be a marvel of white-washed concrete, steel and tinted glass, south-facing, overlooking the ocean and built into the hill itself, each storey stepping up in a series of terraces that were, according to the press release, reminiscent of the master architecture of the Inkas. The elevator for the building would rise and fall within a shaft in the very heart of the hill, terminating at the top in the penthouse suite, which sat on the peak and would have 360° views of the city with vast glass windows on all sides, charting the course of the sun in their reflections.

Construction did not advance for long. It was halted by the mischief of the dead. During the first excavations into the hillside, as the digger pulled out its claw, a human arm thrust itself out of the dirt and tried to throttle the foreman. With a spade, one of his colleagues hacked at the arm until it released its grip, but half the labourers did not return to the site the next morning.

A few days later, one of the younger boys on the team had the temerity to lean against the hill's face while he drank his coffee and, according to the reports of several of the other builders, an enormous skull appeared in the dirt and swallowed the boy, sucking him into the hillside where, presumably, he suffocated (though his body was never found).

Before long, as the diggers cut deeper into the dirt and rock, they discovered that this was not an entirely natural land elevation but rather a sort of pyramid scaffolded by human bones. Inside the earth there was an intricate latticework of femurs, skulls and pelvises holding up the edifice. Work had to cease, the police were summoned, and then, once a few of the skeletons had been meticulously extracted and carbon-dated, historians and archaeologists replaced the demolition crew and builders. There was a flurry of excitement, nationally and internationally. Upon examination, it was discovered that all those there interred had suffered violent injuries – shattered ribs, smashed vertebrae, cracks and jagged holes in their crania. The exhumed had not died of natural causes: they had been attacked, bludgeoned with a variety of weapons (of steel and stone) and then dumped here almost five hundred years ago, without ceremony or attentions.

Overseeing the investigations on the construction site (which took many years, much to the consternation of Edificios Pacífico) was a young archaeologist from the University of San Marcos, one Dr José Antonio Ribeiro, who published his findings in several lauded articles, both in Spanish and in English, and ultimately in a book entitled *The Siege of Lima and the Lost Soldiers of Manco Inka*. The dissemination of Dr Ribeiro's work led to the intervention of the Ministry of Culture, which declared (but only after much legal wrangling with Pacífico) that until the archaeological investigations were complete, the land was a protected site of national cultural heritage and no construction of any sort could take place there. By the time Ribeiro's investigations were complete and the protected status had been lifted from the site, the construction company had ascertained through its market research that no one in Lima would buy Pacífico Tower apartments off-plan. It had always been known that the land was cursed, that the Echeverría family had lived on that site with death rattling around them, but now the pitucos knew why and there was no one in the city who would even consider living there and risking the fury of the lingering pre-Hispanic spirits. Edificios Pacífico turned its attentions elsewhere and deprioritised the Pacífico Tower site.

Gradually, almost imperceptibly at first, the Polvorinos arrived.

Just off the Avenida del Guanero, there is a hill. On that hill there stands a yellow house with white shutters and Moorish balconies carved with scenes of the martyrdom of saints. It is a house that glows in the night like a beacon but by the morning it is gone, replaced by another house of avocado green, its shutters painted the orange-red of rocoto salsa. Or you might see there an apartment building, completed but abandoned: inside, the quartz kitchen worktops are still veiled with plastic protective film and the yucca plants in the lobby are dead and dry. The only movement within is that of the ants – enormous ants that march out of every crack, every crevice, so many of them that they have even pushed up the laminate floorboards. Nothing will kill them. Or perhaps there is no building at all, only a mound of bones, piled up after battle, or maybe a mother and her daughter standing cara a cara, reflected in each other's faces forever.

But blink your eyes, wipe away the Limenian dust, and see now Villa Milagros. See the houses, part-constructed, with bricks only up to here, roofs of corrugated metal, rush matting for doors, perhaps glass in the windows, perhaps not. See the children sitting on a row of plastic crates, swinging their legs, drinking cartons of milk through straws. Hear the macaw in the pichkari tree and the playing of a psychedelic cumbia from a transistor radio propped on a rickety stool. Watch the old woman who emerges from her front door and lays down a plate of fish guts for a two-headed cat that croaks like a frog.

Pay close attention to the sky-blue building on the corner. It has glass in the windows and, on the facade, a mural of smiling women framed by flowers. Outside, lined along the wall, are half a dozen red plastic chairs on which expectant mothers sit conversing together, laughing, hands cradling their bellies. Any moment the maternity nurses will arrive, unlock the front door, and invite the mothers in.

APPENDICES

ECHEVERRÍA

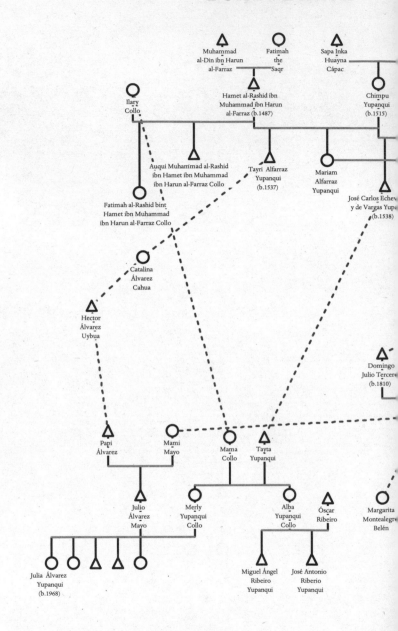

Muhammad al-Din ibn Harun al-Farraz

Fatimah the Saqr

Sapa Inka Huayna Cápac

Hamet al-Rashid ibn Muhammad ibn Harun al-Farraz (b.1487)

Chimpu Yupanqui (b.1515)

Ilary Collo

Auqui Muhammad al-Rashid ibn Hamet ibn Muhammad ibn Harun al-Farraz Collo

Tayri Alfarraz Yupanqui (b.1537)

Mariam Alfarraz Yupanqui

Fatimah al-Rashid bint Hamet ibn Muhammad ibn Harun al-Farraz Collo

José Carlos Echev y de Vargas Yup (b.1538)

Catalina Álvarez Cahua

Hector Álvarez Uybua

Domingo Julio Tercer (b.1810)

Papi Álvarez

Mami Mayo

Mama Collo

Tayta Yupanqui

Julio Álvarez Mayo

Merly Yupanqui Collo

Alba Yupanqui Collo

Óscar Ribeiro

Margarita Montealegr Belén

Julia Álvarez Yupanqui (b.1968)

Miguel Ángel Ribeiro Yupanqui

José Antonio Riberio Yupanqui

FAMILY TREE

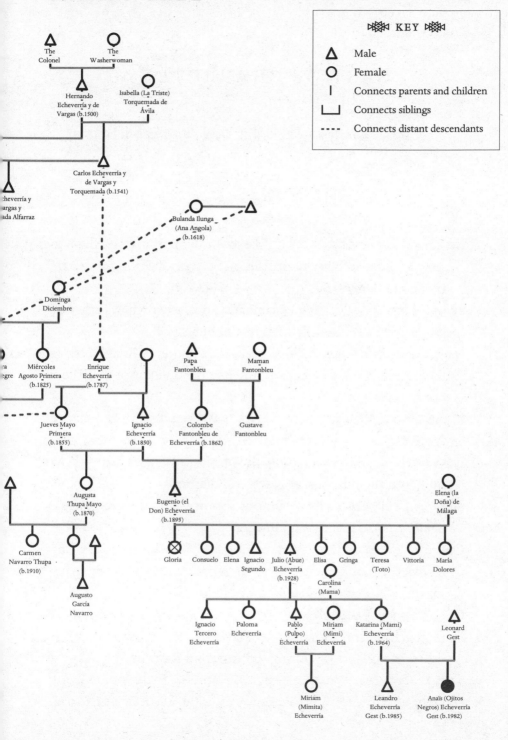

KEY

△ Male
○ Female
| Connects parents and children
⌐⌐ Connects siblings
---- Connects distant descendants

The Colonel

The Washerwoman

Hernando Echeverría y de Vargas (b.1500)

Isabella (La Triste) Torquemada de Ávila

...cheverría y ...argos y ...ada Alfarraz

Carlos Echeverría y de Vargas y Torquemada (b.1541)

Bulanda Ilunga (Ana Angola) (b.1618)

Dominga Diciembre

Miércoles Agosto Primera (b.1825)

Enrique Echeverría (b.1787)

Ignacio Echeverría (b.1850)

Papa Fantonbleu

Maman Fantonbleu

Colombe Fantonbleu de Echeverría (b.1862)

Gustave Fantonbleu

Jueves Mayo Primera (b.1855)

Augusta Thupa Mayo (b.1870)

Eugenio (el Don) Echeverría (b.1895)

Elena (la Doña) de Málaga

Carmen Navarro Thupa (b.1910)

Augusto García Navarro

Gloria

Consuelo

Elena

Ignacio Segundo

Julio (Abue) Echeverría (b.1928)

Elisa

Gringa

Teresa (Toto)

Vittoria

María Dolores

Carolina (Mama)

Ignacio Tercero Echeverría

Paloma Echeverría

Pablo (Pulpo) Echeverría

Miriam (Mimi) Echeverría

Katarina (Mami) Echeverría (b.1964)

Leonard Gest

Miriam (Mimita) Echeverría

Leandro Echeverría Gest (b.1985)

Anaïs (Ojitos Negros) Echeverría Gest (b.1982)

CAST OF CHARACTERS

Some of these characters are historical. Others are inspired by history.

Hernando Echeverría y de Vargas (b.1500): The patriarch of the line and the first Echeverría in the New World. Founder of the Hacienda Echeverría.

Enrique Echeverría (b.1787): Hacendado and slave owner. Father of Jueves Mayo Primera and Ignacio Echeverría.

Ignacio Echeverría (b.1850): Great-great-grandfather to Anaïs. Inherits the Hacienda Echeverría. Commissions the building of the yellow house on the hill.

Colombe Fantonbleu de Echeverría (b.1862): French wife of Ignacio. Anaïs's great-great-grandmother.

Eugenio (el Don) Echeverría (b.1895): Socialite and heir to the yellow house on the hill. Anaïs's great-grandfather.

Elena (la Doña) Echeverría: A famous soprano singer from Málaga, Spain. Anaïs's great-grandmother.

Consuelo Echeverría: The eldest of Eugenio and Elena's nine living children. Anaïs's valetudinarian great-aunt who has been dying for decades and is now unaccounted for.

Ignacio Segundo Echeverría: Eugenio and Elena's eldest and most pugnacious son. Inherits the Hacienda Echeverría, which is expropriated in 1970 during the Agrarian Reform.

Teresa (Toto) Echeverría: One of Eugenio and Elena's nine living children. Commissions a balcony after the earthquake of 1974.

356

Tío Lucho: One of many uncles. Fell from Huayna Picchu and died.

La bebe Vittoria Echeverría: Daughter of Eugenio and Elena, who died of encephalitis in childhood.

María Dolores Echeverría: The youngest and most religious of Eugenio and Elena's nine living children.

Tío Raúl: María Dolores's son. A doctor. Outraged by Medieval Thinking.

Julio (Abue) Echeverría (b.1928): One of Eugenio and Elena's nine living children, and heir to the yellow house on the hill. Anaïs's grandfather.

Carolina (Mama) Echeverría: Anaïs's grandmother.

Ignacio Tercero Echeverría: Anaïs's dead uncle, who emigrated to Miami.

Paloma Echeverría: Anaïs's dead aunt.

Pablo (Tío Pulpo) Echeverría: Anaïs's uncle.

Miriam (Tía Mimi) Echeverría: Tío Pulpo's wife.

Miriam (Mimita) Echeverría: Tío Pulpo and Tía Mimi's daughter. Anaïs's cousin.

Katarina (Mami) Echeverría (b.1964): Anaïs's mother.

Anaïs Rose (Ojitos Negros) Echeverría Gest (b.1982)

Leandro Echeverría Gest (b.1985): Anaïs's brother.

THE LIVING AND THE DEAD

Alba Yupanqui Collo: Member of Sendero Luminoso. Aunt of Julia Álvarez Yupanqui, mother of archaeologist José Antonio Ribeiro.

Alessandra (La Bocona) Flores: Gossipy resident of Los Polvos. Devotee of Santa Julia.

Almendra la Amarga: Cousin of Tía Consuelo and Abuelo Julio. Died from an ayawasca overdose.

Alonso de Sandoval: A Jesuit priest who ministered to slaves in Cartagena in the seventeenth century.

Ana Angola: The imposed Christian name of Bulanda Ilunga.

Antonia Palacios Pérez: Birth name of Juana Jimenez Loayza.

Antonio Bastidas Puyucahua: Brother-in-law of Túpac Amaru II.

Alan García: President of Perú from 1985 to 1990 (at the time of the El Frontón prison massacre), and again from 2006 to 2011.

Andrés Hurtado de Mendoza: Viceroy of Perú from 1556 to 1561.

Anny-Lu Higa Ito: Nurse to La Vieja. Resident of Los Polvos. Granddaughter of Haruto Higa.

Arturo Palacios Pérez: Brother of Antonia Palacios Pérez. Murdered during the El Frontón prison massacre.

Atahualpa: The last Sapa Inka of the Inka Empire, son of Huayna Cápac. He gave his sister to Francisco Pizarro and paid the conquistadors a roomful of gold and two roomfuls of silver as a ransom for his freedom. The conquistadors killed him anyway.

Augusta Thupa Mayo (b.1870): A laundress. Mother of Carmen the cook. Daughter of Ignacio Echeverría and Jueves Mayo Primera.

Augusto García Navarro: Architect. Nephew of Carmen the cook.

Aurora Montealegre: Chosen name of Miércoles Agosto Segunda. An entrepreneur, freed from Enrique Echeverría by the court.

The Ayar brothers and sisters: four brothers and four sisters, children of the Sun, including:

Ayar Manco: The founder of the Inka civilisation. Also known as Manco Cápac.

Ayar Cachi: The strongest of the Ayar brothers.

Mama Ocllo: Sister wife of Ayar Manco. Founded the city of Cusco with Ayar Manco in the place where their golden staffs, at last, sank into the ground.

Bartimeo Cabana Puyucahua: A beggar from outside the Iglesia Santa María Reina. Devotee of Santa Julia. Descendant of Josefa Puyucahua.

Bulanda Ilunga (b.1618): A member of the Luba Bambudye, trafficked and enslaved. Distant ancestor of Carmen Navarro Thupa and Augusto García Navarro.

Carmen Navarro Thupa: Cook to the Echeverría family. Granddaughter of Jueves Mayo Primera and Ignacio Echeverría.

Catalina Álvarez Cahua: Ancestor of Julia Álvarez Yupanqui, who witnessed the execution of Túpac Amaru II.

César Falcón: A Peruvian writer who attended the dance of Norka Rouskaya.

Chad Walker Stone: A wealthy American who financed Leonard Gest's explorations.

Chen (El Quemado) Tan: A Chinese restaurateur and escaped indentured worker who survived the *María Ugarteburu* blaze.

Chimpu Yupanqui: An Inka princess. Daughter of the Inka Huayna Cápac. Mother to some of Hernando Echeverría's children.

Dr de las Casas: Anaïs's psychotherapist.

Delibes: Tía Consuelo's macaw.

Domingo Julio Tercero (1810–1857): Overseer of Enrique Echeverría's indentured guano miners. Husband of Miércoles Agosto Primera.

Eugenia Sánchez: A house-proud resident of Los Polvos. Devotee of Santa Julia.

Fatimah (The Saqr) Alfarraz: Erudite merchant, enslaved by Juan (The Forehead) Calvo. Mother of Hamet Alfarraz.

Felipillo: An Indigenous man who translated for the conquistadors. It is said he deliberately mistranslated between Atahualpa and Pizarro.

Fernandito Condorcanqui Bastidas: Son of Indigenous leader Túpac Amaru II. He was twelve when he witnessed both of his parents being executed.

San Fiacre: Patron saint of taxi drivers and gardeners.

Francisco Pizarro: A conquistador who led the colonisation of Perú.

Guayasamin Quispe: Fellow mitayo with Sayani Cahua. Murdered by kuraka Juan Uybua for exhaustion.

Gustave Fantonbleu: Colombe's brother.

Haruto Higa: Japanese indentured worker who escaped the Hacienda Echeverría. Grandfather of Anny-Lu Higa Ito.

Héctor Álvarez Uybua: Ancestor of Julia Álvarez Yupanqui and foreman to Enrique Echeverría.

Henry Meiggs: A North American entrepreneur who built railroads in South America.

Hernán Cortés: A conquistador who led the colonisation of Mexico.

Hilario García García: A schoolteacher at Los Polvos primary school, Escuela 5086 Santíssima Madre. Devotee of Santa Julia.

Hiram Bingham: A North American explorer credited with discovering Machu Picchu.

Huayna Cápac: The Sapa Inka who significantly expanded the Inka empire. He died of one of the diseases brought to South America by the conquistadors.

Inés Huaylas Yupanqui: The Christian name of Quispe Sisa.

Dr José Antonio Ribeiro Yupanqui: The archaeologist who works on the excavation of the Mound of Defeat, the site of the demolished Echeverría mansion. Cousin of Julia Álvarez Yupanqui.

Inti-Killa: Anaïs's two-headed cat.

José Antonio de Areche: A visitador or representative of the Spanish Crown in Perú during the late eighteenth century. Oversaw the execution of Túpac Amaru II.

Josefa Puyucahua: Mother-in-law to Túpac Amaru II.

José-Maria Villanueva: A resident of Los Polvos. Devotee of Santa Julia.

Juan (The Forehead) Calvo: A torpid Castilian soldier. Gifted Fatimah Alfarraz as a reward for fighting in the Siege of Málaga (then Mālaqa).

Juan Uybua: One-time magistrate to Sapa Inka Atahualpa. Became overseer for Hernando Echeverría.

Juana Jimenez Loayza: Devotee of Santa Julia. Owner of the miraculous cancha. Sister of a victim of the El Frontón prison massacre. Survivor of the Accomarca massacre.

Jueves Mayo Primera (b. 1855): Storyteller. Daughter of Miércoles Agosto Primera and Enrique Echeverría. Lover of Ignacio Echeverría. Grandmother of Carmen the cook.

Santa Julia Álvarez Yupanqui (1968–1986): A girl from Los Polvos. Maid to the Echeverría family. Resurrected saint.

Julio Álvarez Mayo: Julia's father and a descendant of Jueves Mayo Primera.

Professor Leonard Gest: Anaïs's father, an archaeologist and explorer.

Leung Huang: A Chinese indentured guano miner on the Chincha Islands.

Luis Cáceres: A violinist who attended the dance of Norka Rouskaya.

Manco Inka: Son of Huayna Cápac. Installed as a puppet ruler by the Spanish until he founded a Neo-Inka state and engaged his troops in battles against the conquistadors.

Margarita Montealegre Belén: Activist and community organiser from Los Polvos. Descendant of Miércoles Agosto Segunda.

Mariátegui (José Carlos): Marxist writer in Perú, founder of the Peruvian Socialist Party.

Merly Álvarez née *Yupanqui Collo*: Julia Álvarez Yupanqui's mother. Distant descendant of Hamet Alfarraz, Chimpu Yupanqui and Hernando Echeverría.

Miércoles Agosto Primera (b.1825): Wife of Domingo Julio Tercero. Mother of Jueves Mayo Primera.

Miércoles Agosto Segunda (b. 1825): Twin sister of Miércoles Primera. Once freed she became Augusta Montealegre, entrepreneur.

Miguel Ángel Ribeiro Yupanqui: Cousin of Julia Álvarez Yupanqui. Wants a dog.

Norka Rouskaya: A Swiss dancer who visited Perú and, in 1917, scandalised Limenian society with her controversial dance among the graves in the General Cemetery of Lima.

Óscar Ribeiro: Member of Sendero Luminoso. Uncle of Julia Álvarez Yupanqui. Murdered during the El Frontón prison massacre.

Pachacuti: The Sapa Inka credited with turning the Inka state into an empire.

Pacha Mama: Mother Space-Time. Fertility goddess. Wife of the Sun.

Qhawa Pachari: A healer, touched by lightning, consulted by Anaïs's aunts.

Quispe Sisa: Daughter of Huayna Cápac. Given to Francisco Pizarro by the Sapa Inka Atahualpa.

Q'orianka: Works for the Echeverría family as a live-in maid.

Rupert Napier: Anaïs's fiancé.

Sachamama: A serpent goddess, mother of the jungle.

Santa Rosa: Patron saint of Lima.

San Martín (de Porres): Peruvian saint of mixed-race people and public health workers.

Sarita Colonia: The uncanonised folk saint of Lima.

Salvador Dalí: Elena Echeverría's eight-limbed tamarin monkey.

Sayani Cahua (b.1536): An Indigenous Peruvian man. Took his nephew's place in the mita, labour tribute to the Spanish Crown.

Taciturno Huaman (d.1878): A worker on the Ferrocarril Central Andino.

Telmo Hurtado: Commander of the units that executed the Accomarca massacre.

Thunupa: A volcano in Bolivia often personified as a creator god; sometimes an alternative name for the creator god Viracocha.

Túpac Amaru: The last leader of the Neo-Inka State founded by Manco Inca. Executed by the Spanish in 1572.

Túpac Amaru II: Leader of an Indigenous rebellion against the Spanish. Executed by the Spanish in 1782.

Uriel Uybua: Works for the Echeverría family as a gardener.

General Velasco: A military general who became president after a coup in 1968 and initiated an agrarian reform under which millions of hectares of land were expropriated.

La Vieja: An elderly neighbour of the Echeverría family.

Viracocha: The creator god in pre-Hispanic, Andean cosmologies.

The washerwoman: Mother of Hernando Echeverría.

GLOSSARY

abuelo/a – grandfather/grandmother

agua de azahar – orange-flower water

agua de kananga – a kind of holy water

ají – chilli

ajo – garlic

alcatraz – an Afro-Peruvian dance style where one dancer attempts to use a candle flame to light a handkerchief stuck into their partner's waistline

algarrobina – a sweet carob syrup

amancaes – a species of daffodil native to Perú's coastal hills

amor de mi vida – love of my life

anchoveta – a small anchovy found in abundance off the Pacific coast of South America

angustiada – anguished

animu – soul, animating spirit

apagón – blackout

apu – mountain spirit

arí – yes

ari-ari-mamie – from *arrière-arrière-grand-mère*, great-great-grandmother

atatay! – an expression of distaste

auca camayoc – Inka fighters

azahar – orange blossom

barriadas – squatter settlement

basta – that's enough

baúl – storage chest

besos a todos – sending kisses to everyone

bienaventurados los que lloran, porque ellos recibirán consolación – blessed are those who weep, for they shall be comforted

bisabuelo/a – great-grandparent

bodega – corner shop

bolsa – bag

bomberos – firefighters

borrachera – drunken party

brujita – a little witch

bufeo – dolphin

cachivaches – bric-a-brac

cajón – an Afro-Peruvian box-shaped percussion instrument

cambista – money changers, found in busy shopping areas around Lima

campesino/a – a subsistence farmer, a person from the rural provinces who lives off the land

cancha – a Peruvian toasted corn snack

cara a cara – face to face

carajo – damn it!

caramba – damn it!

caramelitos – sweets

carta de horría – letter of freedom from slavery

casona – mansion

castaño – chestnut brown

cerro – a small mountain

cevichería – an eaterie serving ceviche

chasqui – messengers during the Inka Empire, capable of running swiftly at high altitudes

chifa – Chinese-Peruvian cuisine. The word 'chifa' is believed to have come from the Mandarin for 'to eat'.

chillando – shrieking

chiquilina bella – a term of endearment meaning 'beautiful little girl' *chiquilla* – a term of endearment meaning 'little girl'

chismeando – gossiping

cholo – a derogatory racial slur

Chullachaki – shape-shifting protector of the jungle

chupacabra – a monster that attacks livestock and drinks their blood, literally 'goat-sucker'

cocinera/o – cook

combi – in Lima, crammed minivans that run on unofficial routes for a small fare

combista – combi driver

compañero/a – companion

condenado – a damned soul

coya – Inka queen

cupo – an illegal tax charged by organised crime gangs to those living, working or travelling in their territory

cuntur – condor

curandera/o – healer

cuy – guinea pig

de la nada – out of nowhere

de tal palo, tal astilla – from such a stick, such a splinter (an idiom similar to 'the apple doesn't fall far from the tree')

detente milagroso – devotional scapular

diablos – devils; an expletive

dice que – it is said that

Dios te bendiga/cuide – God bless/protect you

ekeko – a small figurine laden with money and sweets, representing a god of prosperity

El Tunche – a demon that protects nature and lures astray those who travel through its territory

empalagoso – sickly sweet

empleada – employee, colloquially used to mean maid

espantoso – dreadful, horrific

extranjero/a – foreigner

festejo – a fast-paced, celebratory Afro-Peruvian dance style
flauta – flute
fracaso – major failure
galletita – little biscuit
guaman – falcon
hapiñuñu – an anthropophagous monster with claw-tipped breasts
hap'iqasqa – an Andean soul sickness caused by the earth grabbing
    one's soul
hermana – sister
hermanukunay – my brothers
hija – daughter
hijo – son
huaca – a sacred site
huaco – a pre-Hispanic pottery artefact often found at sacred sites
huerequeque – a Peruvian bird with a shrill cry
Inkarrí – from 'Inca-rey' or 'Inca-king'. In legend, the resurrected
    Atahualpa, returning to take vengeance on the Spanish colonisers.
izquierdista – leftist
ja – ha
jirón – street
justiprecio – literally 'fair price', the remuneration for expropriated
    property
karamandukas – Peruvian sweet bread-biscuits flavoured with cloves
khipu – a traditional Andean counting system using knotted ropes
khipumayuq – Inka accountant, literally 'keeper of the khipu'
kuna – a Quechua suffix that creates a plural
kuraka – an official serving in the Inka empire, akin to a magistrate
llamadores – people who hang out of the doors of combis and
    microbuses calling out the route
llanto – sobbing
lliclla – Andean shawl
loco/a – mad
lo juro – I swear

locura – madness

lomo saltado – stir-fried beef with vegetables, a Peruvian dish with influences from Chinese cuisine

lúcuma – the sweet, yellow fruit of the Andean lúcuma tree. Lúcuma is a popular ice cream flavour in Perú.

lundu – an Afro-Brazilian dance style believed by some to be a parent dance of Afro-Peruvian dances

machista – chauvinist, chauvinistic

machu wayra – an Andean soul sickness caused by an ancestral wind blown from the realm of the dead

mal de ojo – evil eye

maletero – porter

mamacona – an Inka noblewoman, sometimes serving as a lady-in-waiting

mancharisqa – an Andean soul sickness caused by extreme fright from witnessing a traumatic event

manjar blanco – a sweet made from condensed milk, also known as *dulce de leche*

marinera – a Peruvian dance style originating from the coastal regions, which blends Spanish and Andean influences

mazamorra morada – a Peruvian pudding made with purple corn, fruit, and spices

mendigo/a – beggar

metiche – a busybody

mi amor – my love

mierda – shit

migas – crumbs

mink'a – an act of reciprocal community labour, traditional in Andean communities

mita – mandatory public service during the Inka Empire which was adapted by the Spanish colonisers to require the Indigenous people to undertake forced labour

mitayo – an indentured worker drafted into the mita

moneditas – coins in small denominations

muertita – a little dead girl

muñeca – doll

nalgas – buttocks

naranjo – orange tree

neblina – fog

niñachay – my girl

ñañay – my sister

ñusta – Inka princess

oye – hey, listen up

pacha – the Andean concept of space-time

> *kay pacha* – Here and Now, the realm of the living, literally Being-Time

> *kaylla pacha* – the non-visible realm, comprising uju pacha and urin pacha

>> *uju pacha* – the interior of the Earth

>> *urin pacha* – space-time that comprises belowness and ancientness

> *ñawpa ñawpa pacha* – ancient space-time

> *tiqsi pacha* – the visible realm, comprising janaj pacha and janan pacha

>> *janaj pacha* – the skies, realm of stars and birds

>> *janan pacha* – space-time that comprises aboveness and recentness

pachacuti – a cataclysmic overturning of space and time that brings a new era into being

país – country

Paqariq Tampu – the legendary origin of the Ayar brothers and sisters

pastelería – patisserie

pinche – bloody, fucking

pishtaco – an anthropophagous monster-man

Pitaq chay warmicha – Who is that young woman?

pituco/a – toff

pobre – poor, pitiful

pobrecito/a – poor thing

por fin – at last

porquería – refuse, filth

primo – cousin

pueblo jóven – informal settlement

qarqacha – a monster with the appearance of a llama that attacks livestock and drinks their blood. Those who commit incest are often damned to become qarqachas.

qhapaq – noble

querida/o – darling

quinti – hummingbird

quizás – perhaps

reina de mi corazón – queen of my heart

resentidos – resentful people

requerimiento – a declaration that was read by the conquistadors to the Indigenous people to inform them of the Spanish Crown's divine right to invade

rojos – Reds, communists

runa – people

rupa – high jungle

sahumerio – incense

salsodromo – salsa club

selva – jungle

selvaruna – people of the jungle

Sendero – an abbreviation of Sendero Luminoso, or the Shining Path. Sendero was an offshoot of the Peruvian Communist Party that used guerrilla warfare and extreme violence to try to initiate a revolution in the 1980s and 1990s.

serenazgo – an officer of the municipal police force

shoqma con cuy – a traditional Andean diagnostic procedure using guinea pig entrails

sin duda alguna – without any doubt

sombra – shadow, soul

sombrilla – umbrella

soroche – altitude sickness

suave-suave – gentle-gentle

subida – in Lima, a staircase from the beach up the cliff face to the city

suyarqayki – I waited for you

takanakunqaku – they will have a confrontation

tambo – pre-Hispanic Andean inns

tatarabuelo/a – great-great-grandfather or great-great-grandmother

Tawantinsuyu – The Four Realms, the original name of the Inka Empire

tayta – father

tequeños – fried cheese sticks served with guacamole

temblor – tremor

terruco – terrorist, a term used to refer to members of the Sendero Luminoso

tía/o – aunt/uncle

tía/o abuela/o – great-aunt or great-uncle

titi – auntie

traidora – traitor

tranquila – calm down

trapitos de limpieza – cleaning cloths

travesura – mischief

trueno – thunderclap

t'uqu – opening, hole

uchuypuni – the very smallest

uraña – an Andean soul sickness caused by being blown by the wind of a passing spirit

vals criollo – a genre of Peruvian creole music

vaya – well

ven – come

viejita – little old woman

vista al mar – sea view

volta do mar – literally meaning 'turn of the sea', this is also the name of a technique used by Portuguese seafarers in the late fifteenth century to navigate using sea winds

wamani – mountain spirit

wayqo – landslide

yūrei – Japanese word, a kind of ghost

zamacueca – a Peruvian dance style with African and Andean influences

zampoña – Andean pan pipe

zonza – idiot

zorro – fox

ACKNOWLEDGEMENTS

In the seven years it has taken to birth this book, so many have supported me. Thank you to Patrick Flanery for taking me and this book under his wing. Without your dedication, your belief, your patience, your tireless encouragement, your excellent mentorship and your friendship, this book would not exist. Thank you to Rachael Gilmour and Nisha Ramayya for their unfailing kindness accompanying thoughtful critique. Thank you to my Leeds family, especially Kimberly Campanello, Rachel Bower, David Wylot and Clare Fisher for friendship and faith. Thank you to Andrew van der Vlies for encouragement and cheer. Thank you to my PhD examiners Margaret Reynolds and María del Pilar Blanco for your attentions over the doctoral version of this manuscript. And thank you to José Navarro for checking my Quechua. I must also acknowledge the work of Eusebio Manga Quispe, whose writings have helped me better understand pacha.

So many dear friends and loved ones have watched my writing journey but I must thank, above all, my husband Tom who has believed unconditionally, supported without measure, been my first reader and my best friend. Special thanks are due to Alex Gibson for his belief and for making me laugh when it all felt hopeless. Thank you to my Warrior Queens for empowerment and succour. Thank you to the British Latinx fam, especially Nathalie Teitler for all she does championing our work. Thank you to my parents, Alicia and

Duncan, for nurturing my first stories, my sister Natalie, for listening to them, and to my in-laws, Jan and Des, for dreaming bigger than I dare. Gracias a mi querida familia en Perú: los amo. Y gracias a mis abuelos, Alicia y Julio – los extraño cada día.

I must acknowledge with immense gratitude the British Library, where I have spent many enchanted hours, and the librarians and archivists at the Biblioteca Nacional del Perú who, with patience and good humour, brought me endless manuscripts during my research visit. Thank you also to Queen Mary University of London for funding my research trip to Lima and to my colleagues and doctoral peers there for their companionship when things got exhausting.

I also wish to shower with thanks my agent, Seren Adams, for her belief in my work, for her intelligent, critical eye, her attention to detail, and her friendship. Huge thanks also to Juliet Mabey and Polly Hatfield, my thoughtful and talented editors who understood the soul of this work; to Sarah Terry for her meticulous but sensitive copy-editing and for puzzling out the trickier multilingual and experimental portions; to Alex Billington at Tetragon for making my words look so magical on these pages; to Charlotte Norman for her eagle-eyed proofreading; to Kate Bland, Lucy Cooper and Mark Rusher for working tirelessly to spread the word about this book; to Paul Nash and Laura McFarlane for so attentively and carefully producing these beautiful physical volumes that will accompany readers on their journey and to the whole team at Oneworld.

And, finally, thank you to the mountains, thank you to the dust, thank you to the ghosts, and thank you Lima, you beautiful, fraught city.

© Lara Downie

Karina Lickorish Quinn is a bilingual, Peruvian-British writer raised in the English Midlands, Lima and New York. She has a BA from Oxford University, an MA from University College London and a PhD from Queen Mary University of London. Karina is a lecturer in Creative Writing at the University of Leeds.

Her short fiction features in *Un Nuevo Sol*, the first major anthology of British Latinx writers, published by Flipped Eye. Her work has also appeared in *The Offing, Asymptote, Wasafiri*, the *Journal of Latina Critical Feminism* and *Palabritas*. In 2016 she was shortlisted for the *White Review*'s short-story prize. *The Dust Never Settles* is her first novel.